NINETEEN EIGHTY-FOUR

GEORGE ORWELL

PEACOCK BOOKS

Published by
PEACOCK BOOKS
7/22, Ansari Road, Darya Ganj, New Delhi-110002
Phones : +91-11-40775252, 40775214, 23273880, 23275880
Fax : +91-11-23285873
Web : www.atlanticbooks.com
E-mail : orders@atlanticbooks.com

Peacock Books is an imprint of
Atlantic Publishers and Distributors (P) Ltd

First published 1949

Printed & bound in India by Atlantic Print Services

INTRODUCTION

George Orwell, the great essayist, novelist and journalist, was the pen-name of Eric Arthur Blair. He was born in Bengal, India, in 1903. His father Richard Walmesley Blair was a civil servant for the British Government. Orwell was brought to England at an early age and received his early education at St. Cyprian's and then Eton. He had a passion for writing since an early age. His first patriotic poem appeared in a local *Henley Paper* in 1914.

His first book *Down and Out in Paris and London* (1933) describes his early experiences of suffering rejection. While he was teaching in a public school, he published his second major work, *Burmese Days.* It was followed by *A Clergyman's Daughter* (1935), which describes the adventures of Dorothy, a middle-class woman, who briefly escapes from her narrow spinster's life to join the tramps and hop-pickers through loss of memory. In *Keep the Aspidistra Flying,* Orwell recounts the literary aspirations, financial constraints and shotgun wedding of Gordon Comstock, a young bookseller's assistant, whose aspirations and humiliations closely paralleled his own experiences.

In 1936, Orwell was commissioned by Victor Gollanez to produce a documentary account of unemployment in the north of England for the Left Book Club. It resulted in *The Road to Wigan Pier,* a milestone in the field of literary journalism, which became a classic of its kind and also established him as one of Britain's leading writers. It also marked Orwell's political outlook as an unaligned democratic socialist, a position which he underlined in *Homage to Catalonia* (1938). In this book, Orwell discusses his experiences as a volunteer with the Republican army during the Spanish Civil War. His novel *Coming Up for Air* (1939) reflects the threat of World War II. It deals with the suburban frustration and political concern in the person of George Bowling, an insurance clerk. Orwell remained preoccupied with these thoughts throughout his life.

George Orwell was a socialist, a keen critic of imperialism, fascism, Stalinism, and capitalism. His works are concerned with the socio-political conditions of his time, chiefly with the problem of human freedom. His plain colloquial style made him highly effective as pamphleteer and journalist. Orwell received far and wide reputation and recognition not only for his political shrewdness and sharp satires but also for his marvelously clear style and his essays, which rank with the best ever written.

Nineteen Eighty-Four is a dystopian fiction portraying a society ruled by an oligarchical dictatorship. The Oceanian province of Airstrip One is a world of perpetual war, thorough government surveillance and continuous public mind control. Oceania is ruled by a political party, simply called the Party. The individual is always subordinated to the state, and this philosophy allows the Party to manipulate and control humanity. In the Ministry of Truth, protagonist Winston Smith is a civil servant responsible for perpetuating the Party's propaganda by revising historical records to render the Party omniscient and always correct. Notwithstanding, his meager existence disillusions him to the point of seeking rebellion against Big Brother.

It can be regarded as a literary political fiction. Many of its terms and concepts, such as 'doublethink', 'thoughtcrime', 'newspeak', and 'memory hole' have become contemporary vernacular. The novel has been translated into more than 70 languages. In 1998, the Modern Library ranked *Nineteen Eighty-Four* 13th on its List of Best 20th Century Novels in English.

PART I

CHAPTER ONE

It was a bright cold day in April, and the clocks were striking thirteen. Winston Smith, his chin nuzzled into his breast in an effort to escape the vile wind, slipped quickly through the glass doors of Victory Mansions, though not quickly enough to prevent a swirl of gritty dust from entering along with him.

The hallway smelt of boiled cabbage and old rag mats. At one end of it a coloured poster, too large for indoor display, had been tacked to the wall. It depicted simply an enormous face, more than a metre wide: the face of a man of about forty-five, with a heavy black moustache and ruggedly handsome features. Winston made for the stairs. It was no use trying the lift. Even at the best of times it was seldom working, and at present the electric current was cut off during daylight hours. It was part of the economy drive in preparation for Hate Week. The flat was seven flights up, and Winston, who was thirty-nine and had a varicose ulcer above his right ankle, went slowly, resting several times on the way. On each landing, opposite the lift-shaft, the poster with the enormous face gazed from the wall. It was one of those pictures which are so contrived that the eyes follow you about when you move. BIG BROTHER IS WATCHING YOU, the caption beneath it ran.

Inside the flat a fruity voice was reading out a list of figures which had something to do with the production of pig-iron. The voice came from an oblong metal plaque like a dulled mirror which formed part of the surface of the right-hand wall. Winston turned a switch and the voice sank somewhat, though the words were still distinguishable. The instrument (the telescreen, it was called) could be dimmed, but there was no way of shutting it off completely. He moved over to the window: a smallish, frail figure, the meagreness of his body merely emphasized by the blue overalls which were the uniform of the Party. His hair was very fair, his face naturally sanguine, his skin roughened by coarse soap and blunt razor blades and the cold of the winter that had just ended.

Outside, even through the shut window-pane, the world looked cold. Down in the street little eddies of wind were whirling dust and torn paper into spirals, and though the sun was shining and the sky a harsh blue, there seemed to be no colour in anything, except the posters that were plastered everywhere. The black-moustachio'd face gazed down from every commanding corner. There was one on the house-front immediately opposite. BIG BROTHER IS WATCHING YOU, the caption said, while the dark eyes looked deep into Winston's own. Down at street level another poster, torn at one corner, flapped fitfully in the wind, alternately covering and uncovering the single word INGSOC. In the far distance a helicopter skimmed down between the roofs, hovered for an instant like a bluebottle, and darted away again with a curving flight. It was the police patrol, snooping into people's windows. The patrols did not matter, however. Only the Thought Police mattered.

Behind Winston's back the voice from the telescreen was still babbling away about pig-iron and the overfulfilment of the Ninth Three-Year Plan. The telescreen received and transmitted simultaneously. Any sound that Winston made, above the level of a very low whisper, would be picked up by it; moreover, so long as he remained within the field of vision which the metal plaque commanded, he could be seen as well as heard. There was of course no way of knowing whether you were being watched at any given moment. How often, or on what system, the Thought Police plugged in on any individual wire was guesswork. It was even conceivable that they watched everybody all the time. But at any rate they could plug in your wire whenever they wanted to. You had to live—did live, from habit that became instinct—in the assumption that every sound you made was overheard, and, except in darkness, every movement scrutinized.

Winston kept his back turned to the telescreen. It was safer; though, as he well knew, even a back can be revealing. A kilometre away the Ministry of Truth, his place of work, towered vast and white above the grimy landscape. This, he thought with a sort of vague distaste—this was London, chief city of Airstrip One, itself the third most populous of the provinces of Oceania. He tried to squeeze out some childhood memory that should tell him whether London had always been quite like this. Were there always these vistas of rotting nineteenth-century houses, their sides shored up with baulks of timber, their windows patched with cardboard and their roofs with corrugated iron, their crazy garden walls sagging in all directions? And the bombed sites where the plaster dust swirled in the air and the willow-herb straggled over the heaps of rubble; and the places where the bombs had cleared a larger patch and there had sprung up sordid colonies of wooden dwellings like chicken-houses? But it was no use, he could not remember: nothing remained of his childhood except a series of bright-lit tableaux occurring against no background and mostly unintelligible.

The Ministry of Truth—Minitrue, in Newspeak [Newspeak was the official language of Oceania. For an account of its structure and etymology see Appendix.]—was startlingly different from any other object in sight. It was an enormous pyramidal structure of glittering white concrete, soaring up, terrace after terrace, 300 metres into the air. From where Winston stood it was just possible to read, picked out on its white face in elegant lettering, the three slogans of the Party:

WAR IS PEACE
FREEDOM IS SLAVERY
IGNORANCE IS STRENGTH

The Ministry of Truth contained, it was said, three thousand rooms above ground level, and corresponding ramifications below. Scattered about London there were just three other buildings of similar appearance and size. So completely did they dwarf the surrounding architecture that from the roof of Victory Mansions you could see all four of them simultaneously. They were the homes of the four Ministries between which the entire apparatus of government was divided. The Ministry of Truth, which concerned itself with news, entertainment, education, and the fine arts. The Ministry of Peace, which concerned itself with war. The Ministry of Love, which maintained law and order. And the Ministry of Plenty, which was responsible for economic affairs. Their names, in Newspeak: Minitrue, Minipax, Miniluv, and Miniplenty.

The Ministry of Love was the really frightening one. There were no windows in it at all. Winston had never been inside the Ministry of Love, nor within half a kilometre of it. It was a place impossible to enter except on official business, and then only by penetrating through a maze of barbed-wire entanglements, steel doors, and hidden machine-gun nests. Even the streets leading up to its outer barriers were roamed by gorilla-faced guards in black uniforms, armed with jointed truncheons.

Winston turned round abruptly. He had set his features into the expression of quiet optimism which it was advisable to wear when facing the telescreen. He crossed the room into the tiny kitchen. By leaving the Ministry at this time of day he had sacrificed his lunch in the canteen, and he was aware that there was no food in the kitchen except a hunk of dark-coloured bread which had got to be saved for tomorrow's breakfast. He took down from the shelf a bottle of colourless liquid with a plain white label marked VICTORY GIN. It gave off a sickly, oily smell, as of Chinese rice-spirit. Winston poured out nearly a teacupful, nerved himself for a shock, and gulped it down like a dose of medicine.

Instantly his face turned scarlet and the water ran out of his eyes. The stuff was like nitric acid, and moreover, in swallowing it one had the sensation of being hit on the back of the head with a rubber club. The next moment, however, the burning in his belly died down and the world began to look more cheerful. He took a cigarette from a crumpled packet marked VICTORY CIGARETTES and incautiously held it upright, whereupon the tobacco fell out on to the floor. With the next he was more successful. He went back to the living-room and sat down at a small table that stood to the left of the telescreen. From the table drawer he took out a penholder, a bottle of ink, and a thick, quarto-sized blank book with a red back and a marbled cover.

For some reason the telescreen in the living-room was in an unusual position. Instead of being placed, as was normal, in the end wall, where it could command the whole room, it was in the longer wall, opposite the window. To one side of it there was a shallow alcove in which Winston was now sitting, and which, when the flats were built, had probably been intended to hold bookshelves. By sitting in the alcove, and keeping well back, Winston was able to remain outside the range of the telescreen, so far as sight went. He could be heard, of course, but so long as he stayed in his present position he could not be seen. It was partly the unusual geography of the room that had suggested to him the thing that he was now about to do.

But it had also been suggested by the book that he had just taken out of the drawer. It was a peculiarly beautiful book. Its smooth creamy paper, a little yellowed by age, was of a kind that had not been manufactured for at least forty years past. He could guess, however, that the book was much older than that. He had seen it lying in the window of a frowsy little junk-shop in a slummy quarter of the town (just what quarter he did not now remember) and had been stricken immediately by an overwhelming desire to possess it. Party members were supposed not to go into ordinary shops ('dealing on the free market', it was called), but the rule was not strictly kept, because there were various things, such as shoelaces and razor blades, which it was impossible to get hold of in any other way. He had given a quick glance up and down the street and then had slipped inside and bought the book for two dollars fifty. At the time he was not conscious of wanting it for any particular purpose. He had carried it guiltily home in his briefcase. Even with nothing written in it, it was a compromising possession.

The thing that he was about to do was to open a diary. This was not illegal (nothing was illegal, since there were no longer any laws), but if detected it was reasonably certain that it would be punished by death, or at least by twenty-five years in a forced-labour camp. Winston fitted a nib into the penholder and sucked it to get the grease off. The pen was an archaic instrument, seldom used even for signatures, and he had procured one, furtively and with some difficulty, simply because of a feeling that the beautiful creamy paper deserved to be written on with a real nib instead of being scratched with an ink-pencil. Actually he was not used to writing by hand. Apart from very short notes, it was usual to dictate everything into the speak-write which was of course impossible for his present purpose. He dipped the pen into the ink and then faltered for just a second. A tremor had gone through his bowels. To mark the paper was the decisive act. In small clumsy letters he wrote:

April 4th, 1984.

He sat back. A sense of complete helplessness had descended upon him. To begin with, he did not know with any certainty that this was 1984. It must be round about that date, since he was fairly sure that his age was thirty-nine, and he believed that he had been born in 1944 or 1945; but it was never possible nowadays to pin down any date within a year or two.

For whom, it suddenly occurred to him to wonder, was he writing this diary? For the future, for the unborn. His mind hovered for a moment round the doubtful date on the page, and then fetched up with a bump against the Newspeak word *doublethink*. For the first time the magnitude of what he had undertaken came home to him. How could you communicate with the future? It was of its nature impossible. Either the future would resemble the present, in which case it would not listen to him: or it would be different from it, and his predicament would be meaningless.

For some time he sat gazing stupidly at the paper. The telescreen had changed over to strident military music. It was curious that he seemed not merely to have lost the power of expressing himself, but even to have forgotten what it was that he had originally intended to say. For weeks past he had been making ready for this moment, and it had never crossed his mind that anything would be needed except courage. The actual writing would be easy. All he had to do was to transfer to paper the interminable restless monologue that had been running inside his head, literally for years. At this moment, however, even the monologue had dried up. Moreover his varicose ulcer had begun itching unbearably. He dared not scratch it, because if he did so it always became inflamed. The seconds were ticking by. He was conscious of nothing except the blankness of the page in front of him, the itching of the skin above his ankle, the blaring of the music, and a slight booziness caused by the gin.

Suddenly he began writing in sheer panic, only imperfectly aware of what he was setting down. His small but childish handwriting straggled up and down the page, shedding first its capital letters and finally even its full stops:

April 4th, 1984.

Last night to the flicks. All war films. One very good one of a ship full of refugees being bombed somewhere in the Mediterranean. Audience much amused by shots of a great huge fat man trying to swim away with a helicopter after him, first you saw him wallowing along in the water like a porpoise, then you saw him through the helicopters gunsights, then he was full of holes and the sea round him turned pink and he sank as suddenly as though the holes had let in the water. audience shouting with laughter when he sank. then you saw a lifeboat full of children with a helicopter hovering over it. There was a middle-aged woman might have been a jewess sitting up in the bow with a little boy about three years old in her arms. little boy screaming with fright and hiding his head between her breasts as if he was trying to burrow right into her and the woman putting her arms round him and comforting him although she was blue with fright herself, all the time covering him up as much as possible as if she thought her arms could keep the bullets off him. then the helicopter planted a 20 kilo bomb in among them terrific flash and the boat went all to matchwood. then there was a wonderful shot of a child's arm going up up up right up into the air a helicopter with a camera in its nose must have followed it up and there was a lot of applause from the party seats but a woman down in the prole part of the house suddenly started kicking up a fuss and shouting they didnt oughter of showed it not in front of kids they didnt it aint right not in front of kids it aint until the police turned her turned her out i dont suppose anything happened to her nobody cares what the proles say typical prole reaction they never—

Winston stopped writing, partly because he was suffering from cramp. He did not know what had made him pour out this stream of rubbish. But the curious thing was that while he was doing so a totally different memory had clarified itself in his mind, to the point where he almost felt equal to writing it down. It was, he now realized, because of this other incident that he had suddenly decided to come home and begin the diary today.

It had happened that morning at the Ministry, if anything so nebulous could be said to happen.

It was nearly eleven hundred, and in the Records Department, where Winston worked, they were dragging the chairs out of the cubicles and grouping them in the centre of the hall, opposite the big telescreen, in preparation for the Two Minutes Hate. Winston was just taking his place in one of the middle rows when two people whom he knew by sight, but had never spoken to, came unexpectedly into the room. One of them was a girl whom he often passed in the corridors. He did not know her name, but he knew that she worked in the Fiction Department. Presumably—since he had sometimes seen her with oily hands and carrying a spanner—she had some mechanical job on one of the novel-writing machines. She was a bold-looking girl, of about twenty-seven, with thick dark hair, a freckled face, and swift, athletic movements. A narrow scarlet sash, emblem of the Junior Anti-Sex League, was wound several times round the waist of her overalls, just tightly enough to bring out the shapeliness of her hips. Winston had disliked her from the very first moment of seeing her. He knew the reason. It was because of the atmosphere of hockey-fields and cold baths and community hikes and general clean-mindedness which she managed to carry about with her. He disliked nearly all women, and especially the young and pretty ones. It was always the women, and above all the young ones, who were the most bigoted adherents of the Party, the swallowers of slogans, the amateur spies and nosers-out of unorthodoxy. But this particular girl gave him the impression of being more dangerous than most. Once when they passed in the corridor she gave him a quick sidelong glance which seemed to pierce right into him and for a moment had filled him with black terror. The idea had even crossed his mind that she might be an agent of the Thought Police. That, it was true, was very unlikely. Still, he continued to feel a peculiar uneasiness, which had fear mixed up in it as well as hostility, whenever she was anywhere near him.

The other person was a man named O'Brien, a member of the Inner Party and holder of some post so important and remote that Winston had only a dim idea of its nature. A momentary hush passed over the group of people round the chairs as they saw the black overalls of an Inner Party member approaching. O'Brien was a large, burly man with a thick neck and a coarse, humorous, brutal face. In spite of his formidable appearance he had a certain charm of manner. He had a trick of resettling his spectacles on his nose which was curiously disarming—in some indefinable way, curiously civilized. It was a gesture which, if anyone had still thought in such terms, might have recalled an eighteenth-century nobleman offering his snuffbox. Winston had seen O'Brien perhaps a dozen times in almost as many years. He felt deeply drawn to him, and not solely because he was intrigued by the contrast between O'Brien's urbane manner and his prize-fighter's physique. Much more it was because of a secretly held belief—or perhaps not even a belief, merely a hope—that O'Brien's political orthodoxy was not perfect. Something in his face suggested it irresistibly. And again, perhaps it was not even unorthodoxy that was written in his face, but simply intelligence. But at any rate he had the appearance of being a person that you could talk to if somehow you could cheat the telescreen and get him alone. Winston had never made the smallest effort to verify this guess: indeed, there was no way of doing so. At this moment O'Brien glanced at his wrist-watch, saw that it was nearly eleven hundred, and evidently decided to stay in the Records Department until the Two Minutes Hate was over. He took a chair in the same row as Winston, a couple of places away. A small, sandy-haired woman who worked in the next cubicle to Winston was between them. The girl with dark hair was sitting immediately behind.

The next moment a hideous, grinding speech, as of some monstrous machine running without oil, burst from the big telescreen at the end of the room. It was a noise that set one's teeth on edge and bristled the hair at the back of one's neck. The Hate had started.

As usual, the face of Emmanuel Goldstein, the Enemy of the People, had flashed on to the screen. There were hisses here and there among the audience. The little sandy-haired woman gave a squeak of mingled fear and disgust. Goldstein was the renegade and backslider who once, long ago (how long ago, nobody quite remembered), had been one of the leading figures of the Party, almost on a level with Big Brother himself, and then had engaged in counter-revolutionary activities, had been condemned to death, and had mysteriously escaped and disappeared. The programmes of the Two Minutes Hate varied from day to day, but there was none in which Goldstein was not the principal figure. He was the primal traitor, the earliest defiler of the Party's purity. All subsequent crimes against the Party, all treacheries, acts of sabotage, heresies, deviations, sprang directly out of his teaching. Somewhere or other he was still alive and hatching his conspiracies: perhaps somewhere beyond the sea, under the protection of his foreign paymasters, perhaps even—so it was occasionally rumoured—in some hiding-place in Oceania itself.

Winston's diaphragm was constricted. He could never see the face of Goldstein without a painful mixture of emotions. It was a lean Jewish face, with a great fuzzy aureole of white hair and a small goatee beard—a clever face, and yet somehow inherently despicable, with a kind of senile silliness in the long thin nose, near the end of which a pair of spectacles was perched. It resembled the face of a sheep, and the voice, too, had a sheep-like quality. Goldstein was delivering his usual venomous attack upon the doctrines of the Party—an attack so exaggerated and perverse that a child should have been able to see through it, and yet just plausible enough to fill one with an alarmed feeling that other people, less level-headed than oneself, might be taken in by it. He was abusing Big Brother, he was denouncing the dictatorship of the Party, he was demanding the immediate conclusion of peace with Eurasia, he was advocating freedom of speech, freedom of the Press, freedom of assembly, freedom of thought, he was crying hysterically that the revolution had been betrayed—and all this in rapid polysyllabic speech which was a sort of parody of the habitual style of the orators of the Party, and even contained Newspeak words: more Newspeak words, indeed, than any Party member would normally use in real life. And all the while, lest one should be in any doubt as to the reality which Goldstein's specious claptrap covered, behind his head on the telescreen there marched the endless columns of the Eurasian army—row after row of solid-looking men with expressionless Asiatic faces, who swam up to the surface of the screen and vanished, to be replaced by others exactly similar. The dull rhythmic tramp of the soldiers' boots formed the background to Goldstein's bleating voice.

Before the Hate had proceeded for thirty seconds, uncontrollable exclamations of rage were breaking out from half the people in the room. The self-satisfied sheep-like face on the screen, and the terrifying power of the Eurasian army behind it, were too much to be borne: besides, the sight or even the thought of Goldstein produced fear and anger automatically. He was an object of hatred more constant than either Eurasia or Eastasia, since when Oceania was at war with one of these Powers it was generally at peace with the other. But what was strange was that although Goldstein was hated and despised by everybody, although every day and a thousand times a day, on platforms, on the telescreen, in newspapers, in books, his theories were refuted, smashed, ridiculed, held up to the general gaze for the pitiful rubbish that they were—in spite of all this, his influence never seemed to grow less. Always there were fresh dupes waiting to be seduced by him. A day never passed when spies and saboteurs acting under his directions were not unmasked by the Thought Police. He was the commander of a vast shadowy army, an underground network of conspirators dedicated to the overthrow of the State. The Brotherhood, its name was supposed to be. There were also whispered stories of a terrible book, a compendium of all the heresies, of which Goldstein was the author and which circulated clandestinely here and there. It was a book without a title. People referred to it, if at all, simply as *the book*. But one knew of such things only through vague rumours. Neither the Brotherhood nor *the book* was a subject that any ordinary Party member would mention if there was a way of avoiding it.

In its second minute the Hate rose to a frenzy. People were leaping up and down in their places and shouting at the tops of their voices in an effort to drown the maddening bleating voice that came from the screen. The little sandy-haired woman had turned bright pink, and her mouth was opening and shutting like that of a landed fish. Even O'Brien's heavy face was flushed. He was sitting very straight in his chair, his powerful chest swelling and quivering as though he were standing up to the assault of a wave. The dark-haired girl behind Winston had begun crying out 'Swine! Swine! Swine!' and suddenly she picked up a heavy Newspeak dictionary and flung it at the screen. It struck Goldstein's nose and bounced off; the voice continued inexorably. In a lucid moment Winston found that he was shouting with the others and kicking his heel violently against the rung of his chair. The horrible thing about the Two Minutes Hate was not that one was obliged to act a part, but, on the contrary, that it was impossible to avoid joining in. Within thirty seconds any pretence was always unnecessary. A hideous ecstasy of fear and vindictiveness, a desire to kill, to torture, to smash faces in with a sledge-hammer, seemed to flow through the whole group of people like an electric current, turning one even against one's will into a grimacing, screaming lunatic. And yet the rage that one felt was an abstract, undirected emotion which could be switched from one object to another like the flame of a blowlamp. Thus, at one moment Winston's hatred was not turned against Goldstein at all, but, on the contrary, against Big Brother, the Party, and the Thought Police; and at such moments his heart went out to the lonely, derided heretic on the screen, sole guardian of truth and sanity in a world of lies. And yet the very next instant he was at one with the people about him, and all that was said of Goldstein seemed to him to be true. At those moments his secret loathing of Big Brother changed into adoration, and Big Brother seemed to tower up, an invincible, fearless protector, standing like a rock against the hordes of Asia, and Goldstein, in spite of his isolation, his helplessness, and the doubt that hung about his very existence, seemed like some sinister enchanter, capable by the mere power of his voice of wrecking the structure of civilization.

It was even possible, at moments, to switch one's hatred this way or that by a voluntary act. Suddenly, by the sort of violent effort with which one wrenches one's head away from the pillow in a nightmare, Winston succeeded in transferring his hatred from the face on the screen to the dark-haired girl behind him. Vivid, beautiful hallucinations flashed through his mind. He would flog her to death with a rubber truncheon. He would tie her naked to a stake and shoot her full of arrows like Saint Sebastian. He would ravish her and cut her throat at the moment of climax. Better than before, moreover, he realized WHY it was that he hated her. He hated her because she was young and pretty and sexless, because he wanted to go to bed with her and would never do so, because round her sweet supple waist, which seemed to ask you to encircle it with your arm, there was only the odious scarlet sash, aggressive symbol of chastity.

The Hate rose to its climax. The voice of Goldstein had become an actual sheep's bleat, and for an instant the face changed into that of a sheep. Then the sheep-face melted into the figure of a Eurasian soldier who seemed to be advancing, huge and terrible, his sub-machine gun roaring, and seeming to spring out of the surface of the screen, so that some of the people in the front row actually flinched backwards in their seats. But in the same moment, drawing a deep sigh of relief from everybody, the hostile figure melted into the face of Big Brother, black-haired, black-moustachio'd, full of power and mysterious calm, and so vast that it almost filled up the screen. Nobody heard what Big Brother was saying. It was merely a few words of encouragement, the sort of words that are uttered in the din of battle, not distinguishable individually but restoring confidence by the fact of being spoken. Then the face of Big Brother faded away again, and instead the three slogans of the Party stood out in bold capitals:

WAR IS PEACE
FREEDOM IS SLAVERY
IGNORANCE IS STRENGTH

But the face of Big Brother seemed to persist for several seconds on the screen, as though the impact that it had made on everyone's eyeballs was too vivid to wear off immediately. The little sandy-haired woman had flung herself forward over the back of the chair in front of her. With a tremulous murmur that sounded like 'My Saviour!' she extended her arms towards the screen. Then she buried her face in her hands. It was apparent that she was uttering a prayer.

At this moment the entire group of people broke into a deep, slow, rhythmical chant of 'B-B!...B-B!'—over and over again, very slowly, with a long pause between the first 'B' and the second—a heavy, murmurous sound, somehow curiously savage, in the background of which one seemed to hear the stamp of naked feet and the throbbing of tom-toms. For perhaps as much as thirty seconds they kept it up. It was a refrain that was often heard in moments of overwhelming emotion. Partly it was a sort of hymn to the wisdom and majesty of Big Brother, but still more it was an act of self-hypnosis, a deliberate drowning of consciousness by means of rhythmic noise. Winston's entrails seemed to grow cold. In the Two Minutes Hate he could not help sharing in the general delirium, but this sub-human chanting of 'B-B!...B-B!' always filled him with horror. Of course he chanted with the rest: it was impossible to do otherwise. To dissemble your feelings, to control your face, to do what everyone else was doing, was an instinctive reaction. But there was a space of a couple of seconds during which the expression of his eyes might conceivably have betrayed him. And it was exactly at this moment that the significant thing happened—if, indeed, it did happen.

Momentarily he caught O'Brien's eye. O'Brien had stood up. He had taken off his spectacles and was in the act of resettling them on his nose with his characteristic gesture. But there was a fraction of a second when their eyes met, and for as long as it took to happen Winston knew—yes, he KNEW!—that O'Brien was thinking the same thing as himself. An unmistakable message had passed. It was as though their two minds had opened and the thoughts were flowing from one into the other through their eyes. 'I am with you,' O'Brien seemed to be saying to him. 'I know precisely what you are feeling. I know all about your contempt, your hatred, your disgust. But don't worry, I am on your side!' And then the flash of intelligence was gone, and O'Brien's face was as inscrutable as everybody else's.

That was all, and he was already uncertain whether it had happened. Such incidents never had any sequel. All that they did was to keep alive in him the belief, or hope, that others besides himself were the enemies of the Party. Perhaps the rumours of vast underground conspiracies were true after all—perhaps the Brotherhood really existed! It was impossible, in spite of the endless arrests and confessions and executions, to be sure that the Brotherhood was not simply a myth. Some days he believed in it, some days not. There was no evidence, only fleeting glimpses that might mean anything or nothing: snatches of overheard conversation, faint scribbles on lavatory walls—once, even, when two strangers met, a small movement of the hand which had looked as though it might be a signal of recognition. It was all guesswork: very likely he had imagined everything. He had gone back to his cubicle without looking at O'Brien again. The idea of following up their momentary contact hardly crossed his mind. It would have been inconceivably dangerous even if he had known how to set about doing it. For a second, two seconds, they had exchanged an equivocal glance, and that was the end of the story. But even that was a memorable event, in the locked loneliness in which one had to live.

Winston roused himself and sat up straighter. He let out a belch. The gin was rising from his stomach.

His eyes re-focused on the page. He discovered that while he sat helplessly musing he had also been writing, as though by automatic action. And it was no longer the same cramped, awkward handwriting as before. His pen had slid voluptuously over the smooth paper, printing in large neat capitals—

DOWN WITH BIG BROTHER
DOWN WITH BIG BROTHER
DOWN WITH BIG BROTHER
DOWN WITH BIG BROTHER
DOWN WITH BIG BROTHER

over and over again, filling half a page.

He could not help feeling a twinge of panic. It was absurd, since the writing of those particular words was not more dangerous than the initial act of opening the diary, but for a moment he was tempted to tear out the spoiled pages and abandon the enterprise altogether.

He did not do so, however, because he knew that it was useless. Whether he wrote DOWN WITH BIG BROTHER, or whether he refrained from writing it, made no difference. Whether he went on with the diary, or whether he did not go on with it, made no difference. The Thought Police would get him just the same. He had committed—would still have committed, even if he had never set pen to paper—the essential crime that contained all others in itself. Thoughtcrime, they called it. Thoughtcrime was not a thing that could be concealed for ever. You might dodge successfully for a while, even for years, but sooner or later they were bound to get you.

It was always at night—the arrests invariably happened at night. The sudden jerk out of sleep, the rough hand shaking your shoulder, the lights glaring in your eyes, the ring of hard faces round the bed. In the vast majority of cases there was no trial, no report of the arrest. People simply disappeared, always during the night. Your name was removed from the registers, every record of everything you had ever done was wiped out, your one-time existence was denied and then forgotten. You were abolished, annihilated: VAPORIZED was the usual word.

For a moment he was seized by a kind of hysteria. He began writing in a hurried untidy scrawl:

they'll shoot me i don't care theyll shoot me in the back of the neck i dont care down with big brother they always shoot you in the back of the neck i dont care down with big brother—

He sat back in his chair, slightly ashamed of himself, and laid down the pen. The next moment he started violently. There was a knocking at the door.

Already! He sat as still as a mouse, in the futile hope that whoever it was might go away after a single attempt. But no, the knocking was repeated. The worst thing of all would be to delay. His heart was thumping like a drum, but his face, from long habit, was probably expressionless. He got up and moved heavily towards the door.

CHAPTER TWO

As he put his hand to the door-knob Winston saw that he had left the diary open on the table. DOWN WITH BIG BROTHER was written all over it, in letters almost big enough to be legible across the room. It was an inconceivably stupid thing to have done. But, he realized, even in his panic he had not wanted to smudge the creamy paper by shutting the book while the ink was wet.

He drew in his breath and opened the door. Instantly a warm wave of relief flowed through him. A colourless, crushed-looking woman, with wispy hair and a lined face, was standing outside.

'Oh, comrade,' she began in a dreary, whining sort of voice, 'I thought I heard you come in. Do you think you could come across and have a look at our kitchen sink? It's got blocked up and....'

It was Mrs Parsons, the wife of a neighbour on the same floor. ('Mrs' was a word somewhat discountenanced by the Party—you were supposed to call everyone 'comrade'—but with some women one used it instinctively.) She was a woman of about thirty, but looking much older. One had the impression that there was dust in the creases of her face. Winston followed her down the passage. These amateur repair jobs were an almost daily irritation. Victory Mansions were old flats, built in 1930 or thereabouts, and were falling to pieces. The plaster flaked constantly from ceilings and walls, the pipes burst in every hard frost, the roof leaked whenever there was snow, the heating system was usually running at half steam when it was not closed down altogether from motives of economy. Repairs, except what you could do for yourself, had to be sanctioned by remote committees which were liable to hold up even the mending of a window-pane for two years.

'Of course it's only because Tom isn't home,' said Mrs Parsons vaguely.

The Parsons' flat was bigger than Winston's, and dingy in a different way. Everything had a battered, trampled-on look, as though the place had just been visited by some large violent animal. Games impedimenta—hockey-sticks, boxing-gloves, a burst football, a pair of sweaty shorts turned inside out—lay all over the floor, and on the table there was a litter of dirty dishes and dog-eared exercise-books. On the walls were scarlet banners of the Youth League and the Spies, and a full-sized poster of Big Brother. There was the usual boiled-cabbage smell, common to the whole building, but it was shot through by a sharper reek of sweat, which—one knew this at the first sniff, though it was hard to say how—was the sweat of some person not present at the moment. In another room someone with a comb and a piece of toilet paper was trying to keep tune with the military music which was still issuing from the telescreen.

'It's the children,' said Mrs Parsons, casting a half-apprehensive glance at the door. 'They haven't been out today. And of course....'

She had a habit of breaking off her sentences in the middle. The kitchen sink was full nearly to the brim with filthy greenish water which smelt worse than ever of cabbage. Winston knelt down and examined the angle-joint of the pipe. He hated using his hands, and he hated bending down, which was always liable to start him coughing. Mrs Parsons looked on helplessly.

'Of course if Tom was home he'd put it right in a moment,' she said. 'He loves anything like that. He's ever so good with his hands, Tom is.'

Parsons was Winston's fellow-employee at the Ministry of Truth. He was a fattish but active man of paralysing stupidity, a mass of imbecile enthusiasms—one of those completely unquestioning, devoted drudges on whom, more even than on the Thought Police, the stability of the Party depended. At thirty-five he had just been unwillingly evicted from the Youth League, and before graduating into the Youth League he had managed to stay on in the Spies for a year beyond the statutory age. At the Ministry he was employed in some subordinate post for which intelligence was not required, but on the other hand he was a leading figure on the Sports Committee and all the other committees engaged in organizing community hikes, spontaneous demonstrations, savings campaigns, and voluntary activities generally. He would inform you with quiet pride, between whiffs of his pipe, that he had put in an appearance at the Community Centre every evening for the past four years. An overpowering smell of sweat, a sort of unconscious testimony to the strenuousness of his life, followed him about wherever he went, and even remained behind him after he had gone.

'Have you got a spanner?' said Winston, fiddling with the nut on the angle-joint.

'A spanner,' said Mrs Parsons, immediately becoming invertebrate. 'I don't know, I'm sure. Perhaps the children....'

There was a trampling of boots and another blast on the comb as the children charged into the living-room. Mrs Parsons brought the spanner. Winston let out the water and disgustedly removed the clot of human hair that had blocked up the pipe. He cleaned his fingers as best he could in the cold water from the tap and went back into the other room.

'Up with your hands!' yelled a savage voice.

A handsome, tough-looking boy of nine had popped up from behind the table and was menacing him with a toy automatic pistol, while his small sister, about two years younger, made the same gesture with a fragment of wood. Both of them were dressed in the blue shorts, grey shirts, and red neckerchiefs which were the uniform of the Spies. Winston raised his hands above his head, but with an uneasy feeling, so vicious was the boy's demeanour, that it was not altogether a game.

'You're a traitor!' yelled the boy. 'You're a thought-criminal! You're a Eurasian spy! I'll shoot you, I'll vaporize you, I'll send you to the salt mines!'

Suddenly they were both leaping round him, shouting 'Traitor!' and 'Thought-criminal!' the little girl imitating her brother in every movement. It was somehow slightly frightening, like the gambolling of tiger cubs which will soon grow up into man-eaters. There was a sort of calculating ferocity in the boy's eye, a quite evident desire to hit or kick Winston and a consciousness of being very nearly big enough to do so. It was a good job it was not a real pistol he was holding, Winston thought.

Mrs Parsons' eyes flitted nervously from Winston to the children, and back again. In the better light of the living-room he noticed with interest that there actually was dust in the creases of her face.

'They do get so noisy,' she said. 'They're disappointed because they couldn't go to see the hanging, that's what it is. I'm too busy to take them and Tom won't be back from work in time.'

'Why can't we go and see the hanging?' roared the boy in his huge voice.

'Want to see the hanging! Want to see the hanging!' chanted the little girl, still capering round.

Some Eurasian prisoners, guilty of war crimes, were to be hanged in the Park that evening, Winston remembered. This happened about once a month, and was a popular spectacle. Children always clamoured to be taken to see it. He took his leave of Mrs Parsons and made for the door. But he had not gone six steps down the passage when something hit the back of his neck an agonizingly painful blow. It was as though a red-hot wire had been jabbed into him. He spun round just in time to see Mrs Parsons dragging her son back into the doorway while the boy pocketed a catapult.

'Goldstein!' bellowed the boy as the door closed on him. But what most struck Winston was the look of helpless fright on the woman's greyish face.

Back in the flat he stepped quickly past the telescreen and sat down at the table again, still rubbing his neck. The music from the telescreen had stopped. Instead, a clipped military voice was reading out, with a sort of brutal relish, a description of the armaments of the new Floating Fortress which had just been anchored between Iceland and the Faroe Islands.

With those children, he thought, that wretched woman must lead a life of terror. Another year, two years, and they would be watching her night and day for symptoms of unorthodoxy. Nearly all children nowadays were horrible. What was worst of all was that by means of such organizations as the Spies they were systematically turned into ungovernable little savages, and yet this produced in them no tendency whatever to rebel against the discipline of the Party. On the contrary, they adored the Party and everything connected with it. The songs, the processions, the banners, the hiking, the drilling with dummy rifles, the yelling of slogans, the worship of Big Brother—it was all a sort of glorious game to them. All their ferocity was turned outwards, against the enemies of the State, against foreigners, traitors, saboteurs, thought-criminals. It was almost normal for people over thirty to be frightened of their own children. And with good reason, for hardly a week passed in which the *Times* did not carry a paragraph describing how some eavesdropping little sneak—'child hero' was the phrase generally used—had overheard some compromising remark and denounced its parents to the Thought Police.

The sting of the catapult bullet had worn off. He picked up his pen half-heartedly, wondering whether he could find something more to write in the diary. Suddenly he began thinking of O'Brien again.

Years ago—how long was it? Seven years it must be—he had dreamed that he was walking through a pitch-dark room. And someone sitting to one side of him had said as he passed: 'We shall meet in the place where there is no darkness.' It was said very quietly, almost casually—a statement, not a command. He had walked on without pausing. What was curious was that at the time, in the dream, the words had not made much impression on him. It was only later and by degrees that they had seemed to take on significance. He could not now remember whether it was before or after having the dream that he had seen O'Brien for the first time, nor could he remember when he had first identified the voice as O'Brien's. But at any rate the identification existed. It was O'Brien who had spoken to him out of the dark.

Winston had never been able to feel sure—even after this morning's flash of the eyes it was still impossible to be sure whether O'Brien was a friend or an enemy. Nor did it even seem to matter greatly. There was a link of understanding between them, more important than affection or partisanship. 'We shall meet in the place where there is no darkness,' he had said. Winston did not know what it meant, only that in some way or another it would come true.

The voice from the telescreen paused. A trumpet call, clear and beautiful, floated into the stagnant air. The voice continued raspingly:

'Attention! Your attention, please! A newsflash has this moment arrived from the Malabar front. Our forces in South India have won a glorious victory. I am authorized to say that the action we are now reporting may well bring the war within measurable distance of its end. Here is the newsflash—'

Bad news coming, thought Winston. And sure enough, following on a gory description of the annihilation of a Eurasian army, with stupendous figures of killed and prisoners, came the announcement that, as from next week, the chocolate ration would be reduced from thirty grammes to twenty.

Winston belched again. The gin was wearing off, leaving a deflated feeling. The telescreen—perhaps to celebrate the victory, perhaps to drown the memory of the lost chocolate—crashed into 'Oceania, 'tis for thee'. You were supposed to stand to attention. However, in his present position he was invisible.

'Oceania, 'tis for thee' gave way to lighter music. Winston walked over to the window, keeping his back to the telescreen. The day was still cold and clear. Somewhere far away a rocket bomb exploded with a dull, reverberating roar. About twenty or thirty of them a week were falling on London at present.

Down in the street the wind flapped the torn poster to and fro, and the word INGSOC fitfully appeared and vanished. Ingsoc. The sacred principles of Ingsoc. Newspeak, doublethink, the mutability of the past. He felt as though he were wandering in the forests of the sea bottom, lost in a monstrous world where he himself was the monster. He was alone. The past was dead, the future was unimaginable. What certainty had he that a single human creature now living was on his side? And what way of knowing that the dominion of the Party would not endure *for ever*? Like an answer, the three slogans on the white face of the Ministry of Truth came back to him:

WAR IS PEACE
FREEDOM IS SLAVERY
IGNORANCE IS STRENGTH

He took a twenty-five cent piece out of his pocket. There, too, in tiny clear lettering, the same slogans were inscribed, and on the other face of the coin the head of Big Brother. Even from the coin the eyes pursued you. On coins, on stamps, on the covers of books, on banners, on posters, and on the wrappings of a cigarette packet—everywhere. Always the eyes watching you and the voice enveloping you. Asleep or awake, working or eating, indoors or out of doors, in the bath or in bed—no escape. Nothing was your own except the few cubic centimetres inside your skull.

The sun had shifted round, and the myriad windows of the Ministry of Truth, with the light no longer shining on them, looked grim as the loopholes of a fortress. His heart quailed before the enormous pyramidal shape. It was too strong, it could not be stormed. A thousand rocket bombs would not batter it down. He wondered again for whom he was writing the diary. For the future, for the past—for an age that might be imaginary. And in front of him there lay not death but annihilation. The diary would be reduced to ashes and himself to vapour. Only the Thought Police would read what he had written, before they wiped it out of existence and out of memory. How could you make appeal to the future when not a trace of you, not even an anonymous word scribbled on a piece of paper, could physically survive?

The telescreen struck fourteen. He must leave in ten minutes. He had to be back at work by fourteen-thirty.

Curiously, the chiming of the hour seemed to have put new heart into him. He was a lonely ghost uttering a truth that nobody would ever hear. But so long as he uttered it, in some obscure way the continuity was not broken. It was not by making yourself heard but by staying sane that you carried on the human heritage. He went back to the table, dipped his pen, and wrote:

To the future or to the past, to a time when thought is free, when men are different from one another and do not live alone — to a time when truth exists and what is done cannot be undone:

From the age of uniformity, from the age of solitude, from the age of Big Brother, from the age of doublethink — greetings!

He was already dead, he reflected. It seemed to him that it was only now, when he had begun to be able to formulate his thoughts, that he had taken the decisive step. The consequences of every act are included in the act itself. He wrote:

Thoughtcrime does not entail death: thoughtcrime IS death.

Now he had recognized himself as a dead man it became important to stay alive as long as possible. Two fingers of his right hand were inkstained. It was exactly the kind of detail that might betray you. Some nosing zealot in the Ministry (a woman, probably: someone like the little sandy-haired woman or the dark-haired girl from the Fiction Department) might start wondering why he had been writing during the lunch interval, why he had used an old-fashioned pen, *what* he had been writing — and then drop a hint in the appropriate quarter. He went to the bathroom and carefully scrubbed the ink away with the gritty dark-brown soap which rasped your skin like sandpaper and was therefore well adapted for this purpose.

He put the diary away in the drawer. It was quite useless to think of hiding it, but he could at least make sure whether or not its existence had been discovered. A hair laid across the page-ends was too obvious. With the tip of his finger he picked up an identifiable grain of whitish dust and deposited it on the corner of the cover, where it was bound to be shaken off if the book was moved.

CHAPTER THREE

Winston was dreaming of his mother.

He must, he thought, have been ten or eleven years old when his mother had disappeared. She was a tall, statuesque, rather silent woman with slow movements and magnificent fair hair. His father he remembered more vaguely as dark and thin, dressed always in neat dark clothes (Winston remembered especially the very thin soles of his father's shoes) and wearing spectacles. The two of them must evidently have been swallowed up in one of the first great purges of the fifties.

At this moment his mother was sitting in some place deep down beneath him, with his young sister in her arms. He did not remember his sister at all, except as a tiny, feeble baby, always silent, with large, watchful eyes. Both of them were looking up at him. They were down in some subterranean place—the bottom of a well, for instance, or a very deep grave—but it was a place which, already far below him, was itself moving downwards. They were in the saloon of a sinking ship, looking up at him through the darkening water. There was still air in the saloon, they could still see him and he them, but all the while they were sinking down, down into the green waters which in another moment must hide them from sight for ever. He was out in the light and air while they were being sucked down to death, and they were down there *because* he was up here. He knew it and they knew it, and he could see the knowledge in their faces. There was no reproach either in their faces or in their hearts, only the knowledge that they must die in order that he might remain alive, and that this was part of the unavoidable order of things.

He could not remember what had happened, but he knew in his dream that in some way the lives of his mother and his sister had been sacrificed to his own. It was one of those dreams which, while retaining the characteristic dream scenery, are a continuation of one's intellectual life, and in which one becomes aware of facts and ideas which still seem new and valuable after one is awake. The thing that now suddenly struck Winston was that his mother's death, nearly thirty years ago, had been tragic and sorrowful in a way that was no longer possible. Tragedy, he perceived, belonged to the ancient time, to a time when there was still privacy, love, and friendship, and when the members of a family stood by one another without needing to know the reason. His mother's memory tore at his heart because she had died loving him, when he was too young and selfish to love her in return, and because somehow, he did not remember how, she had sacrificed herself to a conception of loyalty that was private and unalterable. Such things, he saw, could not happen today. Today there were fear, hatred, and pain, but no dignity of emotion, no deep or complex sorrows. All this he seemed to see in the large eyes of his mother and his sister, looking up at him through the green water, hundreds of fathoms down and still sinking.

Suddenly he was standing on short springy turf, on a summer evening when the slanting rays of the sun gilded the ground. The landscape that he was looking at recurred so often in his dreams that he was never fully certain whether or not he had seen it in the real world. In his waking thoughts he called it the Golden Country. It was an old, rabbit-bitten pasture, with a foot-track wandering across it and a molehill here and there. In the ragged hedge on the opposite side of the field the boughs of the elm trees were swaying very faintly in the breeze, their leaves just stirring in dense masses like women's hair. Somewhere near at hand, though out of sight, there was a clear, slow-moving stream where dace were swimming in the pools under the willow trees.

The girl with dark hair was coming towards them across the field. With what seemed a single movement she tore off her clothes and flung them disdainfully aside. Her body was white and smooth, but it aroused no desire in him, indeed he barely looked at it. What overwhelmed him in that instant was admiration for the gesture with which she had thrown her clothes aside. With its grace and carelessness it seemed to annihilate a whole culture, a whole system of thought, as though Big Brother and the Party and the Thought Police could all be swept into nothingness by a single splendid movement of the arm. That too was a gesture belonging to the ancient time. Winston woke up with the word 'Shakespeare' on his lips.

The telescreen was giving forth an ear-splitting whistle which continued on the same note for thirty seconds. It was nought seven fifteen, getting-up time for office workers. Winston wrenched his body out of bed—naked, for a member of the Outer Party received only 3,000 clothing coupons annually, and a suit of pyjamas was 600—and seized a dingy singlet and a pair of shorts that were lying across a chair. The Physical Jerks would begin in three minutes. The next moment he was doubled up by a violent coughing fit which nearly always attacked him soon after waking up. It emptied his lungs so completely that he could only begin breathing again by lying on his back and taking a series of deep gasps. His veins had swelled with the effort of the cough, and the varicose ulcer had started itching.

'Thirty to forty group!' yapped a piercing female voice. 'Thirty to forty group! Take your places, please. Thirties to forties!'

Winston sprang to attention in front of the telescreen, upon which the image of a youngish woman, scrawny but muscular, dressed in tunic and gym-shoes, had already appeared.

'Arms bending and stretching!' she rapped out. 'Take your time by me. *one*, two, three, four! *one*, two, three, four! Come on, comrades, put a bit of life into it! *one*, two, three four! *one* two, three, four!...'

The pain of the coughing fit had not quite driven out of Winston's mind the impression made by his dream, and the rhythmic movements of the exercise restored it somewhat. As he mechanically shot his arms back and forth, wearing on his face the look of grim enjoyment which was considered proper during the Physical Jerks, he was struggling to think his way backward into the dim period of his early childhood. It was extraordinarily difficult. Beyond the late fifties everything faded. When there were no external records that you could refer to, even the outline of your own life lost its sharpness. You remembered huge events which had quite probably not happened, you remembered the detail of incidents without being able to recapture their atmosphere, and there were long blank periods to which you could assign nothing. Everything had been different then. Even the names of countries, and their shapes on the map, had been different. Airstrip One, for instance, had not been so called in those days: it had been called England or Britain, though London, he felt fairly certain, had always been called London.

Winston could not definitely remember a time when his country had not been at war, but it was evident that there had been a fairly long interval of peace during his childhood, because one of his early memories was of an air raid which appeared to take everyone by surprise. Perhaps it was the time when the atomic bomb had fallen on Colchester. He did not remember the raid itself, but he did remember his father's hand clutching his own as they hurried down, down, down into some place deep in the earth, round and round a spiral staircase which rang under his feet and which finally so wearied his legs that he began whimpering and they had to stop and rest. His mother, in her slow, dreamy way, was following a long way behind them. She was carrying his baby sister—or perhaps it was only a bundle of blankets that she was carrying: he was not certain whether his sister had been born then. Finally they had emerged into a noisy, crowded place which he had realized to be a Tube station.

There were people sitting all over the stone-flagged floor, and other people, packed tightly together, were sitting on metal bunks, one above the other. Winston and his mother and father found themselves a place on the floor, and near them an old man and an old woman were sitting side by side on a bunk. The old man had on a decent dark suit and a black cloth cap pushed back from very white hair: his face was scarlet and his eyes were blue and full of tears. He reeked of gin. It seemed to breathe out of his skin in place of sweat, and one could have fancied that the tears welling from his eyes were pure gin. But though slightly drunk he was also suffering under some grief that was genuine and unbearable. In his childish way Winston grasped that some terrible thing, something that was beyond forgiveness and could never be remedied, had just happened. It also seemed to him that he knew what it was. Someone whom the old man loved—a little granddaughter, perhaps—had been killed. Every few minutes the old man kept repeating:

'We didn't ought to 'ave trusted 'em. I said so, Ma, didn't I? That's what comes of trusting 'em. I said so all along. We didn't ought to 'ave trusted the buggers.'

But which buggers they didn't ought to have trusted Winston could not now remember.

Since about that time, war had been literally continuous, though strictly speaking it had not always been the same war. For several months during his childhood there had been confused street fighting in London itself, some of which he remembered vividly. But to trace out the history of the whole period, to say who was fighting whom at any given moment, would have been utterly impossible, since no written record, and no spoken word, ever made mention of any other alignment than the existing one. At this moment, for example, in 1984 (if it was 1984), Oceania was at war with Eurasia and in alliance with Eastasia. In no public or private utterance was it ever admitted that the three powers had at any time been grouped along different lines. Actually, as Winston well knew, it was only four years since Oceania had been at war with Eastasia and in alliance with Eurasia. But that was merely a piece of furtive knowledge which he happened to possess because his memory was not satisfactorily under control. Officially the change of partners had never happened. Oceania was at war with Eurasia: therefore Oceania had always been at war with Eurasia. The enemy of the moment always represented absolute evil, and it followed that any past or future agreement with him was impossible.

The frightening thing, he reflected for the ten thousandth time as he forced his shoulders painfully backward (with hands on hips, they were gyrating their bodies from the waist, an exercise that was supposed to be good for the back muscles)—

the frightening thing was that it might all be true. If the Party could thrust its hand into the past and say of this or that event, *it never happened*—that, surely, was more terrifying than mere torture and death?

The Party said that Oceania had never been in alliance with Eurasia. He, Winston Smith, knew that Oceania had been in alliance with Eurasia as short a time as four years ago. But where did that knowledge exist? Only in his own consciousness, which in any case must soon be annihilated. And if all others accepted the lie which the Party imposed—if all records told the same tale—then the lie passed into history and became truth. 'Who controls the past,' ran the Party slogan, 'controls the future: who controls the present controls the past.' And yet the past, though of its nature alterable, never had been altered. Whatever was true now was true from everlasting to everlasting. It was quite simple. All that was needed was an unending series of victories over your own memory. 'Reality control', they called it: in Newspeak, 'doublethink'.

'Stand easy!' barked the instructress, a little more genially.

Winston sank his arms to his sides and slowly refilled his lungs with air. His mind slid away into the labyrinthine world of doublethink. To know and not to know, to be conscious of complete truthfulness while telling carefully constructed lies, to hold simultaneously two opinions which cancelled out, knowing them to be contradictory and believing in both of them, to use logic against logic, to repudiate morality while laying claim to it, to believe that democracy was impossible and that the Party was the guardian of democracy, to forget whatever it was necessary to forget, then to draw it back into memory again at the moment when it was needed, and then promptly to forget it again: and above all, to apply the same process to the process itself. That was the ultimate subtlety: consciously to induce unconsciousness, and then, once again, to become unconscious of the act of hypnosis you had just performed. Even to understand the word 'doublethink' involved the use of doublethink.

The instructress had called them to attention again. 'And now let's see which of us can touch our toes!' she said enthusiastically. 'Right over from the hips, please, comrades. *one*-two! *one*-two!...'

Winston loathed this exercise, which sent shooting pains all the way from his heels to his buttocks and often ended by bringing on another coughing fit. The half-pleasant quality went out of his meditations. The past, he reflected, had not merely been altered, it had been actually destroyed. For how could you establish even the most obvious fact when there existed no record outside your own memory? He tried to remember in what year he had first heard mention of Big Brother. He thought it must have been at some time in the sixties, but it was impossible to be certain. In the Party histories, of course, Big Brother figured as the leader and guardian of the Revolution since its very earliest days. His exploits had been gradually pushed backwards in time until already they extended into the fabulous world of the forties and the thirties, when the capitalists in their strange cylindrical hats still rode through the streets of London in great gleaming motor-cars or horse carriages with glass sides. There was no knowing how much of this legend was true and how much invented. Winston could not even remember at what date the Party itself had come into existence. He did not believe he had ever heard the word Ingsoc before 1960, but it was possible that in its Oldspeak form—'English Socialism', that is to say—it had been current earlier. Everything melted into mist. Sometimes, indeed, you could put your finger on a definite lie. It was not true, for example, as was claimed in the Party history books, that the Party had invented aeroplanes. He remembered aeroplanes since his earliest childhood. But you could prove nothing. There was never any evidence. Just once in his whole life he had held in his hands unmistakable documentary proof of the falsification of a historical fact. And on that occasion—

'Smith!' screamed the shrewish voice from the telescreen. '6079 Smith W.! Yes, *you*! Bend lower, please! You can do better than that. You're not trying. Lower, please! *That's* better, comrade. Now stand at ease, the whole squad, and watch me.'

A sudden hot sweat had broken out all over Winston's body. His face remained completely inscrutable. Never show dismay! Never show resentment! A single flicker of the eyes could give you away. He stood watching while the instructress raised her arms above her head and—one could not say gracefully, but with remarkable neatness and efficiency—bent over and tucked the first joint of her fingers under her toes.

'*There*, comrades! *That's* how I want to see you doing it. Watch me again. I'm thirty-nine and I've had four children. Now look.' She bent over again. 'You see *my* knees aren't bent. You can all do it if you want to,' she added as she straightened herself up. 'Anyone under forty-five is perfectly capable of touching his toes. We don't all have the privilege of fighting in the front line, but at least we can all keep fit. Remember our boys on the Malabar front! And the sailors in the Floating Fortresses! Just think what *they* have to put up with. Now try again. That's better, comrade, that's *much* better,' she added encouragingly as Winston, with a violent lunge, succeeded in touching his toes with knees unbent, for the first time in several years.

CHAPTER FOUR

With the deep, unconscious sigh which not even the nearness of the telescreen could prevent him from uttering when his day's work started, Winston pulled the speakwrite towards him, blew the dust from its mouthpiece, and put on his spectacles. Then he unrolled and clipped together four small cylinders of paper which had already flopped out of the pneumatic tube on the right-hand side of his desk.

In the walls of the cubicle there were three orifices. To the right of the speakwrite, a small pneumatic tube for written messages, to the left, a larger one for newspapers; and in the side wall, within easy reach of Winston's arm, a large oblong slit protected by a wire grating. This last was for the disposal of waste paper. Similar slits existed in thousands or tens of thousands throughout the building, not only in every room but at short intervals in every corridor. For some reason they were nicknamed memory holes. When one knew that any document was due for destruction, or even when one saw a scrap of waste paper lying about, it was an automatic action to lift the flap of the nearest memory hole and drop it in, whereupon it would be whirled away on a current of warm air to the enormous furnaces which were hidden somewhere in the recesses of the building.

Winston examined the four slips of paper which he had unrolled. Each contained a message of only one or two lines, in the abbreviated jargon—not actually Newspeak, but consisting largely of Newspeak words—which was used in the Ministry for internal purposes. They ran:

times 17.3.84 bb speech malreported africa rectify,

times 19.12.83 forecasts 3 yp 4th quarter 83 misprints verify current issue

times 14.2.84 miniplenty malquoted chocolate rectify

times 3.12.83 reporting bb dayorder double-plusungood refs unpersons rewrite fullwise upsub antefiling.

With a faint feeling of satisfaction Winston laid the fourth message aside. It was an intricate and responsible job and had better be dealt with last. The other three were routine matters, though the second one would probably mean some tedious wading through lists of figures.

Winston dialled 'back numbers' on the telescreen and called for the appropriate issues of the *Times*, which slid out of the pneumatic tube after only a few minutes' delay. The messages he had received referred to articles or news items which for one reason or another it was thought necessary to alter, or, as the official phrase had it, to rectify. For example, it appeared from the *Times* of the seventeenth of March that Big Brother, in his speech of the previous day, had predicted that the South Indian front would remain quiet but that a Eurasian offensive would shortly be launched in North Africa. As it happened, the Eurasian Higher Command had launched its offensive in South India and left North Africa alone. It was therefore necessary to rewrite a paragraph of Big Brother's speech, in such a way as to make him predict the thing that had actually happened. Or again, the *Times* of the nineteenth of December had published the official forecasts of the output of various classes of consumption goods in the fourth quarter of 1983, which was also the sixth quarter of the Ninth Three-Year Plan. Today's issue contained a statement of the actual output, from which it appeared that the forecasts were in every instance grossly wrong. Winston's job was to rectify the original figures by making them agree with the later ones. As for the third message, it referred to a very simple error which could be set right in a couple of minutes. As short a time ago as February, the Ministry of Plenty had issued a promise (a 'categorical pledge' were the official words) that there would be no reduction of the chocolate ration during 1984. Actually, as Winston was aware, the chocolate ration was to be reduced from thirty grammes to twenty at the end of the present week. All that was needed was to substitute for the original promise a warning that it would probably be necessary to reduce the ration at some time in April.

As soon as Winston had dealt with each of the messages, he clipped his speakwritten corrections to the appropriate copy of the *Times* and pushed them into the pneumatic tube. Then, with a movement which was as nearly as possible unconscious, he crumpled up the original message and any notes that he himself had made, and dropped them into the memory hole to be devoured by the flames.

What happened in the unseen labyrinth to which the pneumatic tubes led, he did not know in detail, but he did know in general terms. As soon as all the corrections which happened to be necessary in any particular number of the *Times* had been assembled and collated, that number would be reprinted, the original copy destroyed, and the corrected copy placed on the files in its stead. This process of continuous alteration was applied not only to newspapers, but to books, periodicals, pamphlets, posters, leaflets, films, sound-tracks, cartoons, photographs—to every kind of literature or documentation which might conceivably hold any political or ideological significance. Day by day and almost minute by minute the past was brought up to date. In this way every prediction made by the Party could be shown by documentary evidence to have been correct, nor was any item of news, or any expression of opinion, which conflicted with the needs of the moment, ever allowed to remain on record. All history was a palimpsest, scraped clean and reinscribed exactly as often as was necessary. In no case would it have been possible, once the deed was done, to prove that any falsification had taken place. The largest section of the Records Department, far larger than the one on which Winston worked, consisted simply of persons whose duty it was to track down and collect all copies of books, newspapers, and other documents which had been superseded and were due for destruction. A number of the *Times* which might, because of changes in political alignment, or mistaken prophecies uttered by Big Brother, have been rewritten a dozen times still stood on the files bearing its original date, and no other copy existed to contradict it. Books, also, were recalled and rewritten again and again, and were invariably reissued without any admission that any alteration had been made. Even the written instructions which Winston received, and which he invariably got rid of as soon as he had dealt with them, never stated or implied that an act of forgery was to be committed: always the reference was to slips, errors, misprints, or misquotations which it was necessary to put right in the interests of accuracy.

But actually, he thought as he re-adjusted the Ministry of Plenty's figures, it was not even forgery. It was merely the substitution of one piece of nonsense for another. Most of the material that you were dealing with had no connection with anything in the real world, not even the kind of connection that is contained in a direct lie. Statistics were just as much a fantasy in their original version as in their rectified version. A great deal of the time you were expected to make them up out of your head. For example, the Ministry of Plenty's forecast had estimated the output of boots for the quarter at 145 million pairs. The actual output was given as sixty-two millions. Winston, however, in rewriting the forecast, marked the figure down to fifty-seven millions, so as to allow for the usual claim that the quota had been overfulfilled. In any case, sixty-two millions was no nearer the truth than fifty-seven millions, or than 145 millions. Very likely no boots had been produced at all. Likelier still, nobody knew how many had been produced, much less cared. All one knew was that every quarter astronomical numbers of boots were produced on paper, while perhaps half the population of Oceania went barefoot. And so it was with every class of recorded fact, great or small. Everything faded away into a shadow-world in which, finally, even the date of the year had become uncertain.

Winston glanced across the hall. In the corresponding cubicle on the other side a small, precise-looking, dark-chinned man named Tillotson was working steadily away, with a folded newspaper on his knee and his mouth very close to the mouthpiece of the speakwrite. He had the air of trying to keep what he was saying a secret between himself and the telescreen. He looked up, and his spectacles darted a hostile flash in Winston's direction.

Winston hardly knew Tillotson, and had no idea what work he was employed on. People in the Records Department did not readily talk about their jobs. In the long, windowless hall, with its double row of cubicles and its endless rustle of papers and hum of voices murmuring into speakwrites, there were quite a dozen people whom Winston did not even know by name, though he daily saw them hurrying to and fro in the corridors or gesticulating in the Two Minutes Hate. He knew that in the cubicle next to him the little woman with sandy hair toiled day in day out, simply at tracking down and deleting from the Press the names of people who had been vaporized and were therefore considered never to have existed. There was a certain fitness in this, since her own husband had been vaporized a couple of years earlier. And a few cubicles away a mild, ineffectual, dreamy creature named Ampleforth, with very hairy ears and a surprising talent for juggling with rhymes and metres, was engaged in producing garbled versions—definitive texts, they were called—of poems which had become ideologically offensive, but which for one reason or another were to be retained in the anthologies. And this hall, with its fifty workers or thereabouts, was only one subsection, a single cell, as it were, in the huge complexity of the Records Department. Beyond, above, below, were other swarms of workers engaged in an unimaginable multitude of jobs. There were the huge printing-shops with their subeditors, their typography experts, and their elaborately equipped studios for the faking of photographs. There was the tele-programmes section with its engineers, its producers, and its teams of actors specially chosen for their skill in imitating voices. There were the armies of reference clerks whose job was simply to draw up lists of books and periodicals which were due for recall. There were the vast repositories where the corrected documents were stored, and the hidden furnaces where the original copies were destroyed. And somewhere or other, quite anonymous, there were the directing brains who co-ordinated the whole effort and laid down the lines of policy which made it necessary that this fragment of the past should be preserved, that one falsified, and the other rubbed out of existence.

And the Records Department, after all, was itself only a single branch of the Ministry of Truth, whose primary job was not to reconstruct the past but to supply the citizens of

Oceania with newspapers, films, textbooks, telescreen-programmes, plays, novels—with every conceivable kind of information, instruction, or entertainment, from a statue to a slogan, from a lyric poem to a biological treatise, and from a child's spelling-book to a Newspeak dictionary. And the Ministry had not only to supply the multifarious needs of the Party, but also to repeat the whole operation at a lower level for the benefit of the proletariat. There was a whole chain of separate departments dealing with proletarian literature, music, drama, and entertainment generally. Here were produced rubbishy newspapers containing almost nothing except sport, crime and astrology, sensational five-cent novelettes, films oozing with sex, and sentimental songs which were composed entirely by mechanical means on a special kind of kaleidoscope known as a versificator. There was even a whole sub-section—*Pornosec*, it was called in Newspeak—engaged in producing the lowest kind of pornography, which was sent out in sealed packets and which no Party member, other than those who worked on it, was permitted to look at.

Three messages had slid out of the pneumatic tube while Winston was working, but they were simple matters, and he had disposed of them before the Two Minutes Hate interrupted him. When the Hate was over he returned to his cubicle, took the Newspeak dictionary from the shelf, pushed the speakwrite to one side, cleaned his spectacles, and settled down to his main job of the morning.

Winston's greatest pleasure in life was in his work. Most of it was a tedious routine, but included in it there were also jobs so difficult and intricate that you could lose yourself in them as in the depths of a mathematical problem—delicate pieces of forgery in which you had nothing to guide you except your knowledge of the principles of Ingsoc and your estimate of what the Party wanted you to say. Winston was good at this kind of thing. On occasion he had even been entrusted with the rectification of the *Times* leading articles, which were written entirely in Newspeak. He unrolled the message that he had set aside earlier. It ran:

times 3.12.83 reporting bb dayorder doubleplusungood refs unpersons rewrite fullwiseupsubantefiling

In Oldspeak (or Standard English) this might be rendered:

> The reporting of Big Brother's Order for the Day in the *Times* of December 3rd 1983 is extremely unsatisfactory and makes references to non-existent persons. Rewrite it in full and submit your draft to higher authority before filing.

Winston read through the offending article. Big Brother's Order for the Day, it seemed, had been chiefly devoted to praising the work of an organization known as FFCC, which supplied cigarettes and other comforts to the sailors in the Floating Fortresses. A certain Comrade Withers, a prominent member of the Inner Party, had been singled out for special mention and awarded a decoration, the Order of Conspicuous Merit, Second Class.

Three months later FFCC had suddenly been dissolved with no reasons given. One could assume that Withers and his associates were now in disgrace, but there had been no report of the matter in the Press or on the telescreen. That was to be expected, since it was unusual for political offenders to be put on trial or even publicly denounced. The great purges involving thousands of people, with public trials of traitors and thought-criminals who made abject confession of their crimes and were afterwards executed, were special show-pieces not occurring oftener than once in a couple of years. More commonly, people who had incurred the displeasure of the Party simply disappeared and were never heard of again. One never had the smallest clue as to what had happened to them. In some cases they might not even be dead. Perhaps thirty people personally known to Winston, not counting his parents, had disappeared at one time or another.

Winston stroked his nose gently with a paper-clip. In the cubicle across the way Comrade Tillotson was still crouching secretively over his speakwrite. He raised his head for a moment: again the hostile spectacle-flash. Winston wondered whether Comrade Tillotson was engaged on the same job as himself. It was perfectly possible. So tricky a piece of work would never be entrusted to a single person: on the other hand, to turn it over to a committee would be to admit openly that an act of fabrication was taking place. Very likely as many as a dozen people were now working away on rival versions of what Big Brother had actually said. And presently some master brain in the Inner Party would select this version or that, would re-edit it and set in motion the complex processes of cross-referencing that would be required, and then the chosen lie would pass into the permanent records and become truth.

Winston did not know why Withers had been disgraced. Perhaps it was for corruption or incompetence. Perhaps Big Brother was merely getting rid of a too-popular subordinate. Perhaps Withers or someone close to him had been suspected of heretical tendencies. Or perhaps—what was likeliest of all—the thing had simply happened because purges and vaporizations were a necessary part of the mechanics of government. The only real clue lay in the words 'refs unpersons', which indicated that Withers was already dead. You could not invariably assume this to be the case when people were arrested. Sometimes they were released and allowed to remain at liberty for as much as a year or two years before being executed. Very occasionally some person whom you had believed dead long since would make a ghostly reappearance at some public trial where he would implicate hundreds of others by his testimony before vanishing, this time for ever. Withers, however, was already an UNPERSON. He did not exist: he had never existed. Winston decided that it would not be enough simply to reverse the tendency of Big Brother's speech. It was better to make it deal with something totally unconnected with its original subject.

He might turn the speech into the usual denunciation of traitors and thought-criminals, but that was a little too obvious, while to invent a victory at the front, or some triumph of over-production in the Ninth Three-Year Plan, might complicate the records too much. What was needed was a piece of pure fantasy. Suddenly there sprang into his mind, ready made as it were, the image of a certain Comrade Ogilvy, who had recently died in battle, in heroic circumstances. There were occasions when Big Brother devoted his Order for the Day to commemorating some humble, rank-and-file Party member whose life and death he held up as an example worthy to be followed. Today he should commemorate Comrade Ogilvy. It was true that there was no such person as Comrade

Ogilvy, but a few lines of print and a couple of faked photographs would soon bring him into existence.

Winston thought for a moment, then pulled the speakwrite towards him and began dictating in Big Brother's familiar style: a style at once military and pedantic, and, because of a trick of asking questions and then promptly answering them ('What lessons do we learn from this fact, comrades? The lesson—which is also one of the fundamental principles of Ingsoc—that,' etc., etc.), easy to imitate.

At the age of three Comrade Ogilvy had refused all toys except a drum, a sub-machine gun, and a model helicopter. At six—a year early, by a special relaxation of the rules—he had joined the Spies, at nine he had been a troop leader. At eleven he had denounced his uncle to the Thought Police after overhearing a conversation which appeared to him to have criminal tendencies. At seventeen he had been a district organizer of the Junior Anti-Sex League. At nineteen he had designed a hand-grenade which had been adopted by the Ministry of Peace and which, at its first trial, had killed thirty-one Eurasian prisoners in one burst. At twenty-three he had perished in action. Pursued by enemy jet planes while flying over the Indian Ocean with important despatches, he had weighted his body with his machine gun and leapt out of the helicopter into deep water, despatches and all—an end, said Big Brother, which it was impossible to contemplate without feelings of envy. Big Brother added a few remarks on the purity and single-mindedness of Comrade Ogilvy's life. He was a total abstainer and a non-smoker, had no recreations except a daily hour in the gymnasium, and had taken a vow of celibacy, believing marriage and the care of a family to be incompatible with a twenty-four-hour-a-day devotion to duty. He had no subjects of conversation except the principles of Ingsoc, and no aim in life except the defeat of the Eurasian enemy and the hunting-down of spies, saboteurs, thought-criminals, and traitors generally.

Winston debated with himself whether to award Comrade Ogilvy the Order of Conspicuous Merit: in the end he decided against it because of the unnecessary cross-referencing that it would entail.

Once again he glanced at his rival in the opposite cubicle. Something seemed to tell him with certainty that Tillotson was busy on the same job as himself. There was no way of knowing whose job would finally be adopted, but he felt a profound conviction that it would be his own. Comrade Ogilvy, unimagined an hour ago, was now a fact. It struck him as curious that you could create dead men but not living ones. Comrade Ogilvy, who had never existed in the present, now existed in the past, and when once the act of forgery was forgotten, he would exist just as authentically, and upon the same evidence, as Charlemagne or Julius Caesar.

CHAPTER FIVE

In the low-ceilinged canteen, deep under ground, the lunch queue jerked slowly forward. The room was already very full and deafeningly noisy. From the grille at the counter the steam of stew came pouring forth, with a sour metallic smell which did not quite overcome the fumes of Victory Gin. On the far side of the room there was a small bar, a mere hole in the wall, where gin could be bought at ten cents the large nip.

'Just the man I was looking for,' said a voice at Winston's back.

He turned round. It was his friend Syme, who worked in the Research Department. Perhaps 'friend' was not exactly the right word. You did not have friends nowadays, you had comrades: but there were some comrades whose society was pleasanter than that of others. Syme was a philologist, a specialist in Newspeak. Indeed, he was one of the enormous team of experts now engaged in compiling the Eleventh Edition of the Newspeak Dictionary. He was a tiny creature, smaller than Winston, with dark hair and large, protuberant eyes, at once mournful and derisive, which seemed to search your face closely while he was speaking to you.

'I wanted to ask you whether you'd got any razor blades,' he said.

'Not one!' said Winston with a sort of guilty haste. 'I've tried all over the place. They don't exist any longer.'

Everyone kept asking you for razor blades. Actually he had two unused ones which he was hoarding up. There had been a famine of them for months past. At any given moment there was some necessary article which the Party shops were unable to supply. Sometimes it was buttons, sometimes it was darning wool, sometimes it was shoelaces; at present it was razor blades. You could only get hold of them, if at all, by scrounging more or less furtively on the 'free' market.

'I've been using the same blade for six weeks,' he added untruthfully.

The queue gave another jerk forward. As they halted he turned and faced Syme again. Each of them took a greasy metal tray from a pile at the end of the counter.

'Did you go and see the prisoners hanged yesterday?' said Syme.

'I was working,' said Winston indifferently. 'I shall see it on the flicks, I suppose.'

'A very inadequate substitute,' said Syme.

His mocking eyes roved over Winston's face. 'I know you,' the eyes seemed to say, 'I see through you. I know very well why you didn't go to see those prisoners hanged.' In an intellectual way, Syme was venomously orthodox. He would talk with a disagreeable gloating satisfaction of helicopter raids on enemy villages, and trials and confessions of thought-criminals, the executions in the cellars of the Ministry of Love. Talking to him was largely a matter of getting him away from such subjects and entangling him, if possible, in the technicalities of Newspeak, on which he was authoritative and interesting. Winston turned his head a little aside to avoid the scrutiny of the large dark eyes.

'It was a good hanging,' said Syme reminiscently. 'I think it spoils it when they tie their feet together. I like to see them kicking. And above all, at the end, the tongue sticking right out, and blue—a quite bright blue. That's the detail that appeals to me.'

'Nex', please!' yelled the white-aproned prole with the ladle.

Winston and Syme pushed their trays beneath the grille. On to each was dumped swiftly the regulation lunch—a metal pannikin of pinkish-grey stew, a hunk of bread, a cube of cheese, a mug of milkless Victory Coffee, and one saccharine tablet.

'There's a table over there, under that telescreen,' said Syme. 'Let's pick up a gin on the way.'

The gin was served out to them in handleless china mugs. They threaded their way across the crowded room and unpacked their trays on to the metal-topped table, on one corner of which someone had left a pool of stew, a filthy liquid mess that had the appearance of vomit. Winston took up his mug of gin, paused for an instant to collect his nerve, and gulped the oily-tasting stuff down. When he had winked the tears out of his eyes he suddenly discovered that he was hungry. He began swallowing spoonfuls of the stew, which, in among its general sloppiness, had cubes of spongy pinkish stuff which was probably a preparation of meat. Neither of them spoke again till they had emptied their pannikins. From the table at Winston's left, a little behind his back, someone was talking rapidly and continuously, a harsh gabble almost like the quacking of a duck, which pierced the general uproar of the room.

'How is the Dictionary getting on?' said Winston, raising his voice to overcome the noise.

'Slowly,' said Syme. 'I'm on the adjectives. It's fascinating.'

He had brightened up immediately at the mention of Newspeak. He pushed his pannikin aside, took up his hunk of bread in one delicate hand and his cheese in the other, and leaned across the table so as to be able to speak without shouting.

'The Eleventh Edition is the definitive edition,' he said. 'We're getting the language into its final shape—the shape it's going to have when nobody speaks anything else. When we've finished with it, people like you will have to learn it all over again. You think, I dare say, that our chief job is inventing new words. But not a bit of it! We're destroying words—scores of them, hundreds of them, every day. We're cutting the language down to the bone. The Eleventh Edition won't contain a single word that will become obsolete before the year 2050.'

He bit hungrily into his bread and swallowed a couple of mouthfuls, then continued speaking, with a sort of pedant's passion. His thin dark face had become animated, his eyes had lost their mocking expression and grown almost dreamy.

'It's a beautiful thing, the destruction of words. Of course the great wastage is in the verbs and adjectives, but there are hundreds of nouns that can be got rid of as well. It isn't only the synonyms; there are also the antonyms. After all, what justification is there for a word which is simply the opposite of some other word? A word contains its opposite in itself. Take "good", for instance. If you have a word like "good", what need is there for a word like "bad"? "Ungood" will do just as well—better, because it's an exact opposite, which the other is not. Or again, if you want a stronger version of "good", what sense is there in having a whole string of vague useless words like "excellent" and "splendid" and all the rest of them? "Plusgood" covers the meaning, or "doubleplusgood" if you want something stronger still. Of course we use those forms already, but in the final version of Newspeak there'll be nothing else. In the end the whole notion of goodness and badness will be covered by only six words—in reality, only one word. Don't you see the beauty of that, Winston? It was B.B.'s idea originally, of course,' he added as an afterthought.

A sort of vapid eagerness flitted across Winston's face at the mention of Big Brother. Nevertheless Syme immediately detected a certain lack of enthusiasm.

'You haven't a real appreciation of Newspeak, Winston,' he said almost sadly. 'Even when you write it you're still thinking in Oldspeak. I've read some of those pieces that you write in the *Times* occasionally. They're good enough, but they're translations. In your heart you'd prefer to stick to Oldspeak, with all its vagueness and its useless shades of meaning. You don't grasp the beauty of the destruction of words. Do you know that Newspeak is the only language in the world whose vocabulary gets smaller every year?'

Winston did know that, of course. He smiled, sympathetically he hoped, not trusting himself to speak. Syme bit off another fragment of the dark-coloured bread, chewed it briefly, and went on:

'Don't you see that the whole aim of Newspeak is to narrow the range of thought? In the end we shall make thoughtcrime literally impossible, because there will be no words in which to express it. Every concept that can ever be needed, will be expressed by exactly one word, with its meaning rigidly defined and all its subsidiary meanings rubbed out and forgotten. Already, in the Eleventh Edition, we're not far from that point. But the process will still be continuing long after you and I are dead. Every year fewer and fewer words, and the range of consciousness always a little smaller. Even now, of course, there's no reason or excuse for committing thoughtcrime. It's merely a question of self-discipline, reality-control. But in the end there won't be any need even for that. The Revolution will be complete when the language is perfect. Newspeak is Ingsoc and Ingsoc is Newspeak,' he added with a sort of mystical satisfaction. 'Has it ever occurred to you, Winston, that by the year 2050, at the very latest, not a single human being will be alive who could understand such a conversation as we are having now?'

'Except—' began Winston doubtfully, and he stopped.

It had been on the tip of his tongue to say 'Except the proles,' but he checked himself, not feeling fully certain that this remark was not in some way unorthodox. Syme, however, had divined what he was about to say.

'The proles are not human beings,' he said carelessly. 'By 2050—earlier, probably—all real knowledge of Oldspeak will have disappeared. The whole literature of the past will have been destroyed. Chaucer, Shakespeare, Milton, Byron—they'll exist only in Newspeak versions, not merely changed into something different, but actually changed into something contradictory of what they used to be. Even the literature of the Party will change. Even the slogans will change. How could you have a slogan like "freedom is slavery" when the concept of freedom has been abolished? The whole climate of thought will be different. In fact there will *be* no thought, as we understand it now. Orthodoxy means not thinking—not needing to think. Orthodoxy is unconsciousness.'

One of these days, thought Winston with sudden deep conviction, Syme will be vaporized. He is too intelligent. He sees too clearly and speaks too plainly. The Party does not like such people. One day he will disappear. It is written in his face.

Winston had finished his bread and cheese. He turned a little sideways in his chair to drink his mug of coffee. At the table on his left the man with the strident voice was still talking remorselessly away. A young woman who was perhaps his secretary, and who was sitting with her back to Winston, was listening to him and seemed to be eagerly agreeing with everything that he said. From time to time Winston caught some such remark as 'I think you're so right, I do *so* agree with you', uttered in a youthful and rather silly feminine voice. But the other voice never stopped for an instant, even when the girl was speaking. Winston knew the man by sight, though he knew no more about him than that he held some important post in the Fiction Department. He was a man of about thirty, with a muscular throat and a large, mobile mouth. His head was thrown back a little, and because of the angle at which he was sitting, his spectacles caught the light and presented to Winston two blank discs instead of eyes. What was slightly horrible, was that from the stream of sound that poured out of his mouth it was almost impossible to distinguish a single word. Just once Winston caught a phrase—'complete and final elimination of Goldsteinism'—jerked out very rapidly and, as it seemed, all in one piece, like a line of type cast solid. For the rest it was just a noise, a quack-quack-quacking. And yet, though you could not actually hear what the man was saying, you could not be in any doubt about its general nature. He might be denouncing Goldstein and demanding sterner measures against thought-criminals and saboteurs, he might be fulminating against the atrocities of the Eurasian army, he might be praising Big Brother or the heroes on the Malabar front—it made no difference. Whatever it was, you could be certain that every word of it was pure orthodoxy, pure Ingsoc. As he watched the eyeless face with the jaw moving rapidly up and down, Winston had a curious feeling that this was not a real human being but some kind of dummy. It was not the man's brain that was speaking, it was his larynx. The stuff that was coming out of him consisted of words, but it was not speech in the true sense: it was a noise uttered in unconsciousness, like the quacking of a duck.

Syme had fallen silent for a moment, and with the handle of his spoon was tracing patterns in the puddle of stew. The voice from the other table quacked rapidly on, easily audible in spite of the surrounding din.

'There is a word in Newspeak,' said Syme, 'I don't know whether you know it: *duckspeak*, to quack like a duck. It is one of those interesting words that have two contradictory meanings. Applied to an opponent, it is abuse, applied to someone you agree with, it is praise.'

Unquestionably Syme will be vaporized, Winston thought again. He thought it with a kind of sadness, although well knowing that Syme despised him and slightly disliked him, and was fully capable of denouncing him as a thought-criminal if he saw any reason for doing so. There was something subtly wrong with Syme. There was something that he lacked: discretion, aloofness, a sort of saving stupidity. You could not say that he was unorthodox. He believed in the principles of Ingsoc, he venerated Big Brother, he rejoiced over victories, he hated heretics, not merely with sincerity but with a sort of restless zeal, an up-to-dateness of information, which the ordinary Party member did not approach. Yet a faint air of disreputability always clung to him. He said things that would have been better unsaid, he had read too many books, he frequented the Chestnut Tree Cafe, haunt of painters and musicians. There was no law, not even an unwritten law, against frequenting the Chestnut Tree Cafe, yet the place was somehow ill-omened. The old, discredited leaders of the Party had been used to gather there before they were finally purged. Goldstein himself, it was said, had sometimes been seen there, years and decades ago. Syme's fate was not difficult to foresee. And yet it was a fact that if Syme grasped, even for three seconds, the nature of his, Winston's, secret opinions, he would betray him instantly to the Thought Police. So would anybody else, for that matter: but Syme more than most. Zeal was not enough. Orthodoxy was unconsciousness.

Syme looked up. 'Here comes Parsons,' he said.

Something in the tone of his voice seemed to add, 'that bloody fool'. Parsons, Winston's fellow-tenant at Victory Mansions, was in fact threading his way across the room—a tubby, middle-sized man with fair hair and a froglike face. At thirty-five he was already putting on rolls of fat at neck and waistline, but his movements were brisk and boyish. His whole appearance was that of a little boy grown large, so much so that although he was wearing the regulation overalls, it was almost impossible not to think of him as being dressed in the blue shorts, grey shirt, and red neckerchief of the Spies. In visualizing him one saw always a picture of dimpled knees and sleeves rolled back from pudgy forearms. Parsons did, indeed, invariably revert to shorts when a community hike or any other physical activity gave him an excuse for doing so. He greeted them both with a cheery 'Hullo, hullo!' and sat down at the table, giving off an intense smell of sweat. Beads of moisture stood out all over his pink face. His powers of sweating were extraordinary. At the Community Centre you could always tell when he had been playing table-tennis by the dampness of the bat handle. Syme had produced a strip of paper on which there was a long column of words, and was studying it with an ink-pencil between his fingers.

'Look at him working away in the lunch hour,' said Parsons, nudging Winston. 'Keenness, eh? What's that you've got there, old boy? Something a bit too brainy for me, I expect. Smith, old boy, I'll tell you why I'm chasing you. It's that sub you forgot to give me.'

'Which sub is that?' said Winston, automatically feeling for money. About a quarter of one's salary had to be earmarked for voluntary subscriptions, which were so numerous that it was difficult to keep track of them.

'For Hate Week. You know—the house-by-house fund. I'm treasurer for our block. We're making an all-out effort—going to put on a tremendous show. I tell you, it won't be my fault if old Victory Mansions doesn't have the biggest outfit of flags in the whole street. Two dollars you promised me.'

Winston found and handed over two creased and filthy notes, which Parsons entered in a small notebook, in the neat handwriting of the illiterate.

'By the way, old boy,' he said. 'I hear that little beggar of mine let fly at you with his catapult yesterday. I gave him a good dressing-down for it. In fact I told him I'd take the catapult away if he does it again.'

'I think he was a little upset at not going to the execution,' said Winston.

'Ah, well—what I mean to say, shows the right spirit, doesn't it? Mischievous little beggars they are, both of them, but talk about keenness! All they think about is the Spies, and the war, of course. D'you know what that little girl of mine did last Saturday, when her troop was on a hike out Berkhamsted way? She got two other girls to go with her, slipped off from the hike, and spent the whole afternoon following a strange man. They kept on his tail for two hours, right through the woods, and then, when they got into Amersham, handed him over to the patrols.'

'What did they do that for?' said Winston, somewhat taken aback. Parsons went on triumphantly:

My kid made sure he was some kind of enemy agent—might have been dropped by parachute, for instance. But here's the point, old boy. What do you think put her on to him in the first place? She spotted he was wearing a funny kind of shoes—said she'd never seen anyone wearing shoes like that before. So the chances were he was a foreigner. Pretty smart for a nipper of seven, eh?

'What happened to the man?' said Winston.

'Ah, that I couldn't say, of course. But I wouldn't be altogether surprised if——' Parsons made the motion of aiming a rifle, and clicked his tongue for the explosion.

'Good,' said Syme abstractedly, without looking up from his strip of paper.

'Of course we can't afford to take chances,' agreed Winston dutifully.

'What I mean to say, there is a war on,' said Parsons.

As though in confirmation of this, a trumpet call floated from the telescreen just above their heads. However, it was not the proclamation of a military victory this time, but merely an announcement from the Ministry of Plenty.

'Comrades!' cried an eager youthful voice. 'Attention, comrades! We have glorious news for you. We have won the battle for production! Returns now completed of the output of all classes of consumption goods show that the standard of living has risen by no less than 20 per cent over the past year. All over Oceania this morning there were irrepressible spontaneous demonstrations when workers marched out of factories and offices and paraded through the streets with banners voicing their gratitude to Big Brother for the new, happy life which his wise leadership has bestowed upon us. Here are some of the completed figures. Foodstuffs—'

The phrase 'our new, happy life' recurred several times. It had been a favourite of late with the Ministry of Plenty. Parsons, his attention caught by the trumpet call, sat listening with a sort of gaping solemnity, a sort of edified boredom. He could not follow the figures, but he was aware that they were in some way a cause for satisfaction. He had lugged out a huge and filthy pipe which was already half full of charred tobacco. With the tobacco ration at 100 grammes a week it was seldom possible to fill a pipe to the top. Winston was smoking a Victory Cigarette which he held carefully horizontal. The new ration did not start till tomorrow and he had only four cigarettes left. For the moment he had shut his ears to the remoter noises and was listening to the stuff that streamed out of the telescreen. It appeared that there had even been demonstrations to thank Big Brother for raising the chocolate ration to twenty grammes a week. And only yesterday, he reflected, it had been announced that the ration was to be *reduced* to twenty grammes a week. Was it possible that they could swallow that, after only twenty-four hours? Yes, they swallowed it. Parsons swallowed it easily, with the stupidity of an animal. The eyeless creature at the other table swallowed it fanatically, passionately, with a furious desire to track down, denounce, and vaporize anyone who should suggest that last week the ration had been thirty grammes. Syme, too—in some more complex way, involving doublethink, Syme swallowed it. Was he, then, *alone* in the possession of a memory?

The fabulous statistics continued to pour out of the telescreen. As compared with last year there was more food, more clothes, more houses, more furniture, more cooking-pots, more fuel, more ships, more helicopters, more books, more babies—more of everything except disease, crime, and insanity. Year by year and minute by minute, everybody and everything was whizzing rapidly upwards. As Syme had done earlier Winston had taken up his spoon and was dabbling in the pale-coloured gravy that dribbled across the table, drawing a long streak of it out into a pattern. He meditated resentfully on the physical texture of life. Had it always been like this? Had food always tasted like this? He looked round the canteen. A low-ceilinged, crowded room, its walls grimy from the contact of innumerable bodies; battered metal tables and chairs, placed so close together that you sat with elbows touching; bent spoons, dented trays, coarse white mugs; all surfaces greasy, grime in every crack; and a sourish, composite smell of bad gin and bad coffee and metallic stew and dirty clothes. Always in your stomach and in your skin there was a sort of protest, a feeling that you had been cheated of something that you had a right to. It was true that he had no memories of anything greatly different. In any time that he could accurately remember, there had never been quite enough to eat, one had never had socks or underclothes that were not full of holes, furniture had always been battered and rickety, rooms underheated, tube trains crowded, houses falling to pieces, bread dark-coloured, tea a rarity, coffee filthy-tasting, cigarettes insufficient—nothing cheap and plentiful except synthetic gin. And though, of course, it grew worse as one's body aged, was it not a sign that this was *not* the natural order of things, if one's heart sickened at the discomfort and dirt and scarcity, the interminable winters, the stickiness of one's socks, the lifts that never worked, the cold water, the gritty soap, the cigarettes that came to pieces, the food with its strange evil tastes? Why should one feel it to be intolerable unless one had some kind of ancestral memory that things had once been different?

He looked round the canteen again. Nearly everyone was ugly, and would still have been ugly even if dressed otherwise than in the uniform blue overalls. On the far side of the room, sitting at a table alone, a small, curiously beetle-like man was drinking a cup of coffee, his little eyes darting suspicious glances from side to side. How easy it was, thought Winston, if you did not look about you, to believe that the physical type set up by the Party as an ideal—tall muscular youths and deep-bosomed maidens, blond-haired, vital, sunburnt, carefree—existed and even predominated. Actually, so far as he could judge, the majority of people in Airstrip One were small, dark, and ill-favoured. It was curious how that beetle-like type proliferated in the Ministries: little dumpy men, growing stout very early in life, with short legs, swift scuttling movements, and fat inscrutable faces with very small eyes. It was the type that seemed to flourish best under the dominion of the Party.

The announcement from the Ministry of Plenty ended on another trumpet call and gave way to tinny music. Parsons, stirred to vague enthusiasm by the bombardment of figures, took his pipe out of his mouth.

'The Ministry of Plenty's certainly done a good job this year,' he said with a knowing shake of his head. 'By the way, Smith old boy, I suppose you haven't got any razor blades you can let me have?'

'Not one,' said Winston. 'I've been using the same blade for six weeks myself.'

'Ah, well—just thought I'd ask you, old boy.'

'Sorry,' said Winston.

The quacking voice from the next table, temporarily silenced during the Ministry's announcement, had started up again, as loud as ever. For some reason Winston suddenly found himself thinking of Mrs Parsons, with her wispy hair and the dust in the creases of her face. Within two years those children would be denouncing her to the Thought Police. Mrs Parsons would be vaporized. Syme would be vaporized. Winston would be vaporized. O'Brien would be vaporized. Parsons, on the other hand, would never be vaporized. The eyeless creature with the quacking voice would never be vaporized. The little beetle-like men who scuttle so nimbly through the labyrinthine corridors of Ministries they, too, would never be vaporized. And the girl with dark hair, the girl from the Fiction Department—she would never be vaporized either. It seemed to him that he knew instinctively who would survive and who would perish: though just what it was that made for survival, it was not easy to say.

At this moment he was dragged out of his reverie with a violent jerk. The girl at the next table had turned partly round and was looking at him. It was the girl with dark hair. She was looking at him in a sidelong way, but with curious intensity. The instant she caught his eye she looked away again.

The sweat started out on Winston's backbone. A horrible pang of terror went through him. It was gone almost at once, but it left a sort of nagging uneasiness behind. Why was she watching him? Why did she keep following him about? Unfortunately he could not remember whether she had already been at the table when he arrived, or had come there afterwards. But yesterday, at any rate, during the Two Minutes Hate, she had sat immediately behind him when there was no apparent need to do so. Quite likely her real object had been to listen to him and make sure whether he was shouting loudly enough.

His earlier thought returned to him: probably she was not actually a member of the Thought Police, but then it was precisely the amateur spy who was the greatest danger of all. He did not know how long she had been looking at him, but perhaps for as much as five minutes, and it was possible that his features had not been perfectly under control. It was terribly dangerous to let your thoughts wander when you were in any public place or within range of a telescreen. The smallest thing could give you away. A nervous tic, an unconscious look of anxiety, a habit of muttering to yourself—anything that carried with it the suggestion of abnormality, of having something to hide. In any case, to wear an improper expression on your face (to look incredulous when a victory was announced, for example) was itself a punishable offence. There was even a word for it in Newspeak: *facecrime*, it was called.

The girl had turned her back on him again. Perhaps after all she was not really following him about; perhaps it was coincidence that she had sat so close to him two days running. His cigarette had gone out, and he laid it carefully on the edge of the table. He would finish smoking it after work, if he could keep the tobacco in it. Quite likely the person at the next table was a spy of the Thought Police, and quite likely he would be in the cellars of the Ministry of Love within three days, but a cigarette end must not be wasted. Syme had folded up his strip of paper and stowed it away in his pocket. Parsons had begun talking again.

'Did I ever tell you, old boy,' he said, chuckling round the stem of his pipe, 'about the time when those two nippers of mine set fire to the old market-woman's skirt because they saw her wrapping up sausages in a poster of B.B.? Sneaked up behind her and set fire to it with a box of matches. Burned her quite badly, I believe. Little beggars, eh? But keen as mustard! That's a first-rate training they give them in the Spies nowadays—better than in my day, even. What d'you think's the latest thing they've served them out with? Ear trumpets for listening through keyholes! My little girl brought one home the other night—tried it out on our sitting-room door, and reckoned she could hear twice as much as with her ear to the hole. Of course it's only a toy, mind you. Still, gives 'em the right idea, eh?'

At this moment the telescreen let out a piercing whistle. It was the signal to return to work. All three men sprang to their feet to join in the struggle round the lifts, and the remaining tobacco fell out of Winston's cigarette.

CHAPTER SIX

Winston was writing in his diary:

It was three years ago. It was on a dark evening, in a narrow side-street near one of the big railway stations. She was standing near a doorway in the wall, under a street lamp that hardly gave any light. She had a young face, painted very thick. It was really the paint that appealed to me, the whiteness of it, like a mask, and the bright red lips. Party women never paint their faces. There was nobody else in the street, and no telescreens. She said two dollars. I....

For the moment it was too difficult to go on. He shut his eyes and pressed his fingers against them, trying to squeeze out the vision that kept recurring. He had an almost overwhelming temptation to shout a string of filthy words at the top of his voice. Or to bang his head against the wall, to kick over the table, and hurl the inkpot through the window—to do any violent or noisy or painful thing that might black out the memory that was tormenting him.

Your worst enemy, he reflected, was your own nervous system. At any moment the tension inside you was liable to translate itself into some visible symptom. He thought of a man whom he had passed in the street a few weeks back; a quite ordinary-looking man, a Party member, aged thirty-five to forty, tallish and thin, carrying a brief-case. They were a few metres apart when the left side of the man's face was suddenly contorted by a sort of spasm. It happened again just as they were passing one another: it was only a twitch, a quiver, rapid as the clicking of a camera shutter, but obviously habitual. He remembered thinking at the time: That poor devil is done for. And what was frightening was that the action was quite possibly unconscious. The most deadly danger of all was talking in your sleep. There was no way of guarding against that, so far as he could see.

He drew his breath and went on writing:

I went with her through the doorway and across a backyard into a basement kitchen. There was a bed against the wall, and a lamp on the table, turned down very low. She...

His teeth were set on edge. He would have liked to spit. Simultaneously with the woman in the basement kitchen he thought of Katharine, his wife. Winston was married—had been married, at any rate: probably he still was married, so far as he knew his wife was not dead. He seemed to breathe again the warm stuffy odour of the basement kitchen, an odour compounded of bugs and dirty clothes and villainous cheap scent, but nevertheless alluring, because no woman of the Party ever used scent, or could be imagined as doing so. Only the proles used scent. In his mind the smell of it was inextricably mixed up with fornication.

When he had gone with that woman it had been his first lapse in two years or thereabouts. Consorting with prostitutes was forbidden, of course, but it was one of those rules that you could occasionally nerve yourself to break. It was dangerous, but it was not a life-and-death matter. To be caught with a prostitute might mean five years in a forced-labour camp: not more, if you had committed no other offence. And it was easy enough, provided that you could avoid being caught in the act. The poorer quarters swarmed with women who were ready to sell themselves. Some could even be purchased for a bottle of gin, which the proles were not supposed to drink. Tacitly the Party was even inclined to encourage prostitution, as an outlet for instincts which could not be altogether suppressed. Mere debauchery did not matter very much, so long as it was furtive and joyless and only involved the women of a submerged and despised class. The unforgivable crime was promiscuity between Party members. But—though this was one of the crimes that the accused in the great purges invariably confessed to—it was difficult to imagine any such thing actually happening.

The aim of the Party was not merely to prevent men and women from forming loyalties which it might not be able to control. Its real, undeclared purpose was to remove all pleasure from the sexual act. Not love so much as eroticism was the enemy, inside marriage as well as outside it. All marriages between Party members had to be approved by a committee appointed for the purpose, and—though the principle was never clearly stated—permission was always refused if the couple concerned gave the impression of being physically attracted to one another. The only recognized purpose of marriage was to beget children for the service of the Party. Sexual intercourse was to be looked on as a slightly disgusting minor operation, like having an enema. This again was never put into plain words, but in an indirect way it was rubbed into every Party member from childhood onwards. There were even organizations such as the Junior Anti-Sex League, which advocated complete celibacy for both sexes. All children were to be begotten by artificial insemination (*artsem*, it was called in Newspeak) and brought up in public institutions. This, Winston was aware, was not meant altogether seriously, but somehow it fitted in with the general ideology of the Party. The Party was trying to kill the sex instinct, or, if it could not be killed, then to distort it and dirty it. He did not know why this was so, but it seemed natural that it should be so. And as far as the women were concerned, the Party's efforts were largely successful.

He thought again of Katharine. It must be nine, ten—nearly eleven years since they had parted. It was curious how seldom he thought of her. For days at a time he was capable of forgetting that he had ever been married. They had only been together for about fifteen months. The Party did not permit divorce, but it rather encouraged separation in cases where there were no children.

Katharine was a tall, fair-haired girl, very straight, with splendid movements. She had a bold, aquiline face, a face that one might have called noble until one discovered that there was as nearly as possible nothing behind it. Very early in her married life he had decided—though perhaps it was only that he knew her more intimately than he knew most people—that she had without exception the most stupid, vulgar, empty mind that he had ever encountered. She had not a thought in her head that was not a slogan, and there was no imbecility, absolutely none that she was not capable of swallowing if the Party handed it out to her. 'The human sound-track' he nicknamed her in his own mind. Yet he could have endured living with her if it had not been for just one thing—sex.

As soon as he touched her she seemed to wince and stiffen. To embrace her was like embracing a jointed wooden image. And what was strange was that even when she was clasping him against her he had the feeling that she was simultaneously pushing him away with all her strength. The rigidity of her muscles managed to convey that impression. She would lie there with shut eyes, neither resisting nor co-operating but *submitting*. It was extraordinarily embarrassing, and, after a while, horrible. But even then he could have borne living with her if it had been agreed that they should remain celibate. But curiously enough it was Katharine who refused this. They must, she said, produce a child if they could. So the performance continued to happen, once a week quite regularly, whenever it was not impossible. She even used to remind him of it in the morning, as something which had to be done that evening and which must not be forgotten. She had two names for it. One was 'making a baby', and the other was 'our duty to the Party' (yes, she had actually used that phrase). Quite soon he grew to have a feeling of positive dread when the appointed day came round. But luckily no child appeared, and in the end she agreed to give up trying, and soon afterwards they parted.

Winston sighed inaudibly. He picked up his pen again and wrote:

She threw herself down on the bed, and at once, without any kind of preliminary in the most coarse, horrible way you can imagine, pulled up her skirt. I....

He saw himself standing there in the dim lamplight, with the smell of bugs and cheap scent in his nostrils, and in his heart a feeling of defeat and resentment which even at that moment was mixed up with the thought of Katharine's white body, frozen for ever by the hypnotic power of the Party. Why did it always have to be like this? Why could he not have a woman of his own instead of these filthy scuffles at intervals of years? But a real love affair was an almost unthinkable event. The women of the Party were all alike. Chastity was as deep ingrained in them as Party loyalty. By careful early conditioning, by games and cold water, by the rubbish that was dinned into them at school and in the Spies and the Youth League, by lectures, parades, songs, slogans, and martial music, the natural feeling had been driven out of them. His reason told him that there must be exceptions, but his heart did not believe it. They were all impregnable, as the Party intended that they should be. And what he wanted, more even than to be loved, was to break down that wall of virtue, even if it were only once in his whole life. The sexual act, successfully performed, was rebellion. Desire was thoughtcrime. Even to have awakened Katharine, if he could have achieved it, would have been like a seduction, although she was his wife.

But the rest of the story had got to be written down. He wrote:

I turned up the lamp. When I saw her in the light....

After the darkness the feeble light of the paraffin lamp had seemed very bright. For the first time he could see the woman properly. He had taken a step towards her and then halted, full of lust and terror. He was painfully conscious of the risk he had taken in coming here. It was perfectly possible that the patrols would catch him on the way out: for that matter they might be waiting outside the door at this moment. If he went away without even doing what he had come here to do—!

It had got to be written down, it had got to be confessed. What he had suddenly seen in the lamplight was that the woman was OLD. The paint was plastered so thick on her face that it looked as though it might crack like a cardboard mask. There were streaks of white in her hair; but the truly dreadful detail was that her mouth had fallen a little open, revealing nothing except a cavernous blackness. She had no teeth at all.

He wrote hurriedly, in scrabbling handwriting:

When I saw her in the light she was quite an old woman, fifty years old at least. But I went ahead and did it just the same.

He pressed his fingers against his eyelids again. He had written it down at last, but it made no difference. The therapy had not worked. The urge to shout filthy words at the top of his voice was as strong as ever.

CHAPTER SEVEN

If there is hope, wrote Winston, *it lies in the proles.*

If there was hope, it *must* lie in the proles, because only there in those swarming disregarded masses, 85 per cent of the population of Oceania, could the force to destroy the Party ever be generated. The Party could not be overthrown from within. Its enemies, if it had any enemies, had no way of coming together or even of identifying one another. Even if the legendary Brotherhood existed, as just possibly it might, it was inconceivable that its members could ever assemble in larger numbers than twos and threes. Rebellion meant a look in the eyes, an inflexion of the voice, at the most, an occasional whispered word. But the proles, if only they could somehow become conscious of their own strength would have no need to conspire. They needed only to rise up and shake themselves like a horse shaking off flies. If they chose they could blow the Party to pieces tomorrow morning. Surely sooner or later it must occur to them to do it? And yet...!

He remembered how once he had been walking down a crowded street when a tremendous shout of hundreds of voices—women's voices—had burst from a side-street a little way ahead. It was a great formidable cry of anger and despair, a deep, loud 'Oh-o-o-o-oh!' that went humming on like the reverberation of a bell. His heart had leapt. It's started! he had thought. A riot! The proles are breaking loose at last! When he had reached the spot it was to see a mob of two or three hundred women crowding round the stalls of a street market, with faces as tragic as though they had been the doomed passengers on a sinking ship. But at this moment the general despair broke down into a multitude of individual quarrels. It appeared that one of the stalls had been selling tin saucepans. They were wretched, flimsy things, but cooking-pots of any kind were always difficult to get. Now the supply had unexpectedly given out. The successful women, bumped and jostled by the rest, were trying to make off with their saucepans while dozens of others clamoured round the stall, accusing the stall-keeper of favouritism and of having more saucepans somewhere in reserve. There was a fresh outburst of yells. Two bloated women, one of them with her hair coming down, had got hold of the same saucepan and were trying to tear it out of one another's hands. For a moment they were both tugging, and then the handle came off. Winston watched them disgustedly. And yet, just for a moment, what almost frightening power had sounded in that cry from only a few hundred throats! Why was it that they could never shout like that about anything that mattered?

He wrote:

Until they become conscious they will never rebel, and until after they have rebelled they cannot become conscious.

That, he reflected, might almost have been a transcription from one of the Party textbooks. The Party claimed, of course, to have liberated the proles from bondage. Before the Revolution they had been hideously oppressed by the capitalists, they had been starved and flogged, women had been forced to work in the coal mines (women still did work in the coal mines, as a matter of fact), children had been sold into the factories at the age of six. But simultaneously, true to the principles of doublethink, the Party taught that the proles were natural inferiors who must be kept in subjection, like animals, by the application of a few simple rules. In reality very little was known about the proles. It was not necessary to know much. So long as they continued to work and breed, their other activities were without importance. Left to themselves, like cattle turned loose upon the plains of Argentina, they had reverted to a style of life that appeared to be natural to them, a sort of ancestral pattern. They were born, they grew up in the gutters, they went to work at twelve, they passed through a brief blossoming-period of beauty and sexual desire, they married at twenty, they were middle-aged at thirty, they died, for the most part, at sixty. Heavy physical work, the care of home and children, petty quarrels with neighbours, films, football, beer, and above all, gambling, filled up the horizon of their minds. To keep them in control was not difficult. A few agents of the Thought Police moved always among them, spreading false rumours and marking down and eliminating the few individuals who were judged capable of becoming dangerous; but no attempt was made to indoctrinate them with the ideology of the Party. It was not desirable that the proles should have strong political feelings. All that was required of them was a primitive patriotism which could be appealed to whenever it was necessary to make them accept longer working-hours or shorter rations. And even when they became discontented, as they sometimes did, their discontent led nowhere, because, being without general ideas, they could only focus it on petty specific grievances. The larger evils invariably escaped their notice. The great majority of proles did not even have telescreens in their homes. Even the civil police interfered with them very little. There was a vast amount of criminality in London, a whole world-within-a-world of thieves, bandits, prostitutes, drug-peddlers, and racketeers of every description; but since it all happened among the proles themselves, it was of no importance. In all questions of morals they were allowed to follow their ancestral code. The sexual puritanism of the Party was not imposed upon them. Promiscuity went unpunished, divorce was permitted. For that matter, even religious worship would have been permitted if the proles had shown any sign of needing or wanting it. They were beneath suspicion. As the Party slogan put it: 'Proles and animals are free.'

Winston reached down and cautiously scratched his varicose ulcer. It had begun itching again. The thing you invariably came back to was the impossibility of knowing what life before the Revolution had really been like. He took out of the drawer a copy of a children's history textbook which he had borrowed from Mrs Parsons, and began copying a passage into the diary:

In the old days (it ran), *before the glorious Revolution, London was not the beautiful city that we know today. It was a dark, dirty, miserable place where hardly anybody had enough to eat and where hundreds and thousands of poor people had no boots on their feet and not even a roof to sleep under. Children no older than you had to work twelve hours a day for cruel masters who flogged them with whips if they worked too slowly and fed them on nothing but stale breadcrusts and water. But in among all this terrible poverty there were just a few great big beautiful houses that were lived in by rich men who had as many as thirty servants to look after them. These rich men were called capitalists. They were fat, ugly men with wicked faces, like the one in the picture on the opposite page. You can see that he is dressed in a long black coat which was called a frock coat, and a queer, shiny hat shaped like a stovepipe, which was called a top hat. This was the uniform of the capitalists, and no one else was allowed to wear it. The capitalists owned everything in the world, and everyone else was their slave. They owned all the land, all the houses, all the factories, and all the money. If anyone disobeyed them they could throw them into prison, or they could take his job away and starve him to death. When any ordinary person spoke to a capitalist he had to cringe and bow to him, and take off his cap and address him as 'Sir'. The chief of all the capitalists was called the King, and....*

But he knew the rest of the catalogue. There would be mention of the bishops in their lawn sleeves, the judges in their ermine robes, the pillory, the stocks, the treadmill, the cat-o'-nine tails, the Lord Mayor's Banquet, and the practice of kissing the Pope's toe. There was also something called the *jus primae noctis*, which would probably not be mentioned in a textbook for children. It was the law by which every capitalist had the right to sleep with any woman working in one of his factories.

How could you tell how much of it was lies? It *might* be true that the average human being was better off now than he had been before the Revolution. The only evidence to the contrary was the mute protest in your own bones, the instinctive feeling that the conditions you lived in were intolerable and that at some other time they must have been different. It struck him that the truly characteristic thing about modern life was not its cruelty and insecurity, but simply its bareness, its dinginess, its listlessness. Life, if you looked about you, bore no resemblance not only to the lies that streamed out of the telescreens, but even to the ideals that the Party was trying to achieve. Great areas of it, even for a Party member, were neutral and non-political, a matter of slogging through dreary jobs, fighting for a place on the Tube, darning a worn-out sock, cadging a saccharine tablet, saving a cigarette end. The ideal set up by the Party was something huge, terrible, and glittering—a world of steel and concrete, of monstrous machines and terrifying weapons—a nation of warriors and fanatics, marching forward in perfect unity, all thinking the same thoughts and shouting the same slogans, perpetually working, fighting, triumphing, persecuting—three hundred million people all with the same face. The reality was decaying, dingy cities where underfed people shuffled to and fro in leaky shoes, in patched-up nineteenth-century houses that smelt always of cabbage and bad lavatories. He seemed to see a vision of London, vast and ruinous, city of a million dustbins, and mixed up with it was a picture of Mrs Parsons, a woman with lined face and wispy hair, fiddling helplessly with a blocked waste-pipe.

He reached down and scratched his ankle again. Day and night the telescreens bruised your ears with statistics proving that people today had more food, more clothes, better houses, better recreations—that they lived longer, worked shorter hours, were bigger, healthier, stronger, happier, more intelligent, better educated, than the people of fifty years ago. Not a word of it could ever be proved or disproved. The Party claimed for example, that today 40 per cent of adult proles were literate: before the Revolution, it was said, the number had only been 15 per cent. The Party claimed that the infant mortality rate was now only 160 per thousand, whereas before the Revolution it had been 300—and so it went on. It was like a single equation with two unknowns. It might very well be that literally every word in the history books, even the things that one accepted without question, was pure fantasy. For all he knew there might never have been any such law as the *jus primae noctis*, or any such creature as a capitalist, or any such garment as a top hat.

Everything faded into mist. The past was erased, the erasure was forgotten, the lie became truth. Just once in his life he had possessed—*after* the event: that was what counted—concrete, unmistakable evidence of an act of falsification. He had held it between his fingers for as long as thirty seconds. In 1973, it must have been—at any rate, it was at about the time when he and Katharine had parted. But the really relevant date was seven or eight years earlier.

The story really began in the middle sixties, the period of the great purges in which the original leaders of the Revolution were wiped out once and for all. By 1970 none of them was left, except Big Brother himself. All the rest had by that time been exposed as traitors and counter-revolutionaries. Goldstein had fled and was hiding no one knew where, and of the others, a few had simply disappeared, while the majority had been executed after spectacular public trials at which they made confession of their crimes. Among the last survivors were three men named Jones, Aaronson, and Rutherford. It must have been in 1965 that these three had been arrested. As often happened, they had vanished for a year or more, so that one did not know whether they were alive or dead, and then had suddenly been brought forth to incriminate themselves in the usual way. They had confessed to intelligence with the enemy (at that date, too, the enemy was Eurasia), embezzlement of public funds, the murder of various trusted Party members, intrigues against the leadership of Big Brother which had started long before the Revolution happened, and acts of sabotage causing the death of hundreds of thousands of people. After confessing to these things they had been pardoned, reinstated in the Party, and given posts which were in fact sinecures but which sounded important. All three had written long, abject articles in the *Times*, analysing the reasons for their defection and promising to make amends.

Some time after their release Winston had actually seen all three of them in the Chestnut Tree Café. He remembered the sort of terrified fascination with which he had watched them out of the corner of his eye. They were men far older than himself, relics of the ancient world, almost the last great figures left over from the heroic days of the Party. The glamour of the underground struggle and the civil war still faintly clung to them. He had the feeling, though already at that time facts and dates were growing blurry, that he had known their names years earlier than he had known that of Big Brother. But also they were outlaws, enemies, untouchables, doomed with absolute certainty to extinction within a year or two. No one who had once fallen into the hands of the Thought Police ever escaped in the end. They were corpses waiting to be sent back to the grave.

There was no one at any of the tables nearest to them. It was not wise even to be seen in the neighbourhood of such people. They were sitting in silence before glasses of the gin flavoured with cloves which was the speciality of the café. Of the three, it was Rutherford whose appearance had most impressed Winston. Rutherford had once been a famous caricaturist, whose brutal cartoons had helped to inflame popular opinion before and during the Revolution. Even now, at long intervals, his cartoons were appearing in the *Times.* They were simply an imitation of his earlier manner, and curiously lifeless and unconvincing. Always they were a rehashing of the ancient themes—slum tenements, starving children, street battles, capitalists in top hats—even on the barricades the capitalists still seemed to cling to their top hats an endless, hopeless effort to get back into the past. He was a monstrous man, with a mane of greasy grey hair, his face pouched and seamed, with thick negroid lips. At one time he must have been immensely strong; now his great body was sagging, sloping, bulging, falling away in every direction. He seemed to be breaking up before one's eyes, like a mountain crumbling.

It was the lonely hour of fifteen. Winston could not now remember how he had come to be in the cafe at such a time. The place was almost empty. A tinny music was trickling from the telescreens. The three men sat in their corner almost motionless, never speaking. Uncommanded, the waiter brought fresh glasses of gin. There was a chessboard on the table beside them, with the pieces set out but no game started. And then, for perhaps half a minute in all, something happened to the telescreens. The tune that they were playing changed, and the tone of the music changed too. There came into it—but it was something hard to describe. It was a peculiar, cracked, braying, jeering note: in his mind Winston called it a yellow note. And then a voice from the telescreen was singing:

Under the spreading chestnut tree
I sold you and you sold me:
There lie they, and here lie we
Under the spreading chestnut tree.

The three men never stirred. But when Winston glanced again at Rutherford's ruinous face, he saw that his eyes were full of tears. And for the first time he noticed, with a kind of inward shudder, and yet not knowing *at what* he shuddered, that both Aaronson and Rutherford had broken noses.

A little later all three were re-arrested. It appeared that they had engaged in fresh conspiracies from the very moment of their release. At their second trial they confessed to all their old crimes over again, with a whole string of new ones. They were executed, and their fate was recorded in the Party histories, a warning to posterity. About five years after this, in 1973, Winston was unrolling a wad of documents which had just flopped out of the pneumatic tube on to his desk when he came on a fragment of paper which had evidently been slipped in among the others and then forgotten. The instant he had flattened it out he saw its significance. It was a half-page torn out of the *Times* of about ten years earlier—the top half of the page, so that it included the date—and it contained a photograph of the delegates at some Party function in New York. Prominent in the middle of the group were Jones, Aaronson, and Rutherford. There was no mistaking them, in any case their names were in the caption at the bottom.

The point was that at both trials all three men had confessed that on that date they had been on Eurasian soil. They had flown from a secret airfield in Canada to a rendezvous somewhere in Siberia, and had conferred with members of the Eurasian General Staff, to whom they had betrayed important military secrets. The date had stuck in Winston's memory because it chanced to be midsummer day; but the whole story must be on record in countless other places as well. There was only one possible conclusion: the confessions were lies.

Of course, this was not in itself a discovery. Even at that time Winston had not imagined that the people who were wiped out in the purges had actually committed the crimes that they were accused of. But this was concrete evidence; it was a fragment of the abolished past, like a fossil bone which turns up in the wrong stratum and destroys a geological theory. It was enough to blow the Party to atoms, if in some way it could have been published to the world and its significance made known.

He had gone straight on working. As soon as he saw what the photograph was, and what it meant, he had covered it up with another sheet of paper. Luckily, when he unrolled it, it had been upside-down from the point of view of the telescreen.

He took his scribbling pad on his knee and pushed back his chair so as to get as far away from the telescreen as possible. To keep your face expressionless was not difficult, and even your breathing could be controlled, with an effort: but you could not control the beating of your heart, and the telescreen was quite delicate enough to pick it up. He let what he judged to be ten minutes go by, tormented all the while by the fear that some accident—a sudden draught blowing across his desk, for instance—would betray him. Then, without uncovering it again, he dropped the photograph into the memory hole, along with some other waste papers. Within another minute, perhaps, it would have crumbled into ashes.

That was ten-eleven years ago. Today, probably, he would have kept that photograph. It was curious that the fact of having held it in his fingers seemed to him to make a difference even now, when the photograph itself, as well as the event it recorded, was only memory. Was the Party's hold upon the past less strong, he wondered, because a piece of evidence which existed no longer *had once* existed?

But today, supposing that it could be somehow resurrected from its ashes, the photograph might not even be evidence. Already, at the time when he made his discovery, Oceania was no longer at war with Eurasia, and it must have been to the agents of Eastasia that the three dead men had betrayed their country. Since then there had been other changes—two, three, he could not remember how many. Very likely the confessions had been rewritten and rewritten until the original facts and dates no longer had the smallest significance. The past not only changed, but changed continuously. What most afflicted him with the sense of nightmare was that he had never clearly understood why the huge imposture was undertaken. The immediate advantages of falsifying the past were obvious, but the ultimate motive was mysterious. He took up his pen again and wrote:

I understand HOW: I do not understand WHY.

He wondered, as he had many times wondered before, whether he himself was a lunatic. Perhaps a lunatic was simply a minority of one. At one time it had been a sign of madness to believe that the earth goes round the sun; today, to believe that the past is unalterable. He might be ALONE in holding that belief, and if alone, then a lunatic. But the thought of being a lunatic did not greatly trouble him: the horror was that he might also be wrong.

He picked up the children's history book and looked at the portrait of Big Brother which formed its frontispiece. The hypnotic eyes gazed into his own. It was as though some huge force were pressing down upon you—something that penetrated inside your skull, battering against your brain, frightening you out of your beliefs, persuading you, almost, to deny the evidence of your senses. In the end the Party would announce that two and two made five, and you would have to believe it. It was inevitable that they should make that claim sooner or later: the logic of their position demanded it. Not merely the validity of experience, but the very existence of external reality, was tacitly denied by their philosophy. The heresy of heresies was common sense. And what was terrifying was not that they would kill you for thinking otherwise, but that they might be right. For, after all, how do we know that two and two make four? Or that the force of gravity works? Or that the past is unchangeable? If both the past and the external world exist only in the mind, and if the mind itself is controllable what then?

But no! His courage seemed suddenly to stiffen of its own accord. The face of O'Brien, not called up by any obvious association, had floated into his mind. He knew, with more certainty than before, that O'Brien was on his side. He was writing the diary for O'Brien—TO O'Brien: it was like an interminable letter which no one would ever read, but which was addressed to a particular person and took its colour from that fact.

The Party told you to reject the evidence of your eyes and ears. It was their final, most essential command. His heart sank as he thought of the enormous power arrayed against him, the ease with which any Party intellectual would overthrow him in debate, the subtle arguments which he would not be able to understand, much less answer. And yet he was in the right! They were wrong and he was right. The obvious, the silly, and the true had got to be defended. Truisms are true, hold on to that! The solid world exists, its laws do not change. Stones are hard, water is wet, objects unsupported fall towards the earth's centre. With the feeling that he was speaking to O'Brien, and also that he was setting forth an important axiom, he wrote:

Freedom is the freedom to say that two plus two make four. If that is granted, all else follows.

CHAPTER EIGHT

From somewhere at the bottom of a passage the smell of roasting coffee—real coffee, not Victory Coffee—came floating out into the street. Winston paused involuntarily. For perhaps two seconds he was back in the half-forgotten world of his childhood. Then a door banged, seeming to cut off the smell as abruptly as though it had been a sound.

He had walked several kilometres over pavements, and his varicose ulcer was throbbing. This was the second time in three weeks that he had missed an evening at the Community Centre: a rash act, since you could be certain that the number of your attendances at the Centre was carefully checked. In principle a Party member had no spare time, and was never alone except in bed. It was assumed that when he was not working, eating, or sleeping he would be taking part in some kind of communal recreation: to do anything that suggested a taste for solitude, even to go for a walk by yourself, was always slightly dangerous. There was a word for it in Newspeak: OWNLIFE, it was called, meaning individualism and eccentricity. But this evening as he came out of the Ministry the balminess of the April air had tempted him. The sky was a warmer blue than he had seen it that year, and suddenly the long, noisy evening at the Centre, the boring, exhausting games, the lectures, the creaking camaraderie oiled by gin, had seemed intolerable. On impulse he had turned away from the bus-stop and wandered off into the labyrinth of London, first south, then east, then north again, losing himself among unknown streets and hardly bothering in which direction he was going.

'If there is hope,' he had written in the diary, 'it lies in the proles.' The words kept coming back to him, statement of a mystical truth and a palpable absurdity. He was somewhere in the vague, brown-coloured slums to the north and east of what had once been Saint Pancras Station. He was walking up a cobbled street of little two-storey houses with battered doorways which gave straight on the pavement and which were somehow curiously suggestive of ratholes. There were puddles of filthy water here and there among the cobbles. In and out of the dark doorways, and down narrow alley-ways that branched off on either side, people swarmed in astonishing numbers—girls in full bloom, with crudely lipsticked mouths, and youths who chased the girls, and swollen waddling women who showed you what the girls would be like in ten years' time, and old bent creatures shuffling along on splayed feet, and ragged barefooted children who played in the puddles and then scattered at angry yells from their mothers. Perhaps a quarter of the windows in the street were broken and boarded up. Most of the people paid no attention to Winston; a few eyed him with a sort of guarded curiosity. Two monstrous women with brick-red forearms folded across their aprons were talking outside a doorway. Winston caught scraps of conversation as he approached.

'"Yes," I says to 'er, "that's all very well," I says. "But if you'd of been in my place you'd of done the same as what I done. It's easy to criticize," I says, "but you ain't got the same problems as what I got."'

'Ah,' said the other, 'that's jest it. That's jest where it is.'

The strident voices stopped abruptly. The women studied him in hostile silence as he went past. But it was not hostility, exactly; merely a kind of wariness, a momentary stiffening, as at the passing of some unfamiliar animal. The blue overalls of the Party could not be a common sight in a street like this. Indeed, it was unwise to be seen in such places, unless you had definite business there. The patrols might stop you if you happened to run into them. 'May I see your papers, comrade? What are you doing here? What time did you leave work? Is this your usual way home?'—and so on and so forth. Not that there was any rule against walking home by an unusual route: but it was enough to draw attention to you if the Thought Police heard about it.

Suddenly the whole street was in commotion. There were yells of warning from all sides. People were shooting into the doorways like rabbits. A young woman leapt out of a doorway a little ahead of Winston, grabbed up a tiny child playing in a puddle, whipped her apron round it, and leapt back again, all in one movement. At the same instant a man in a concertina-like black suit, who had emerged from a side alley, ran towards Winston, pointing excitedly to the sky.

'Steamer!' he yelled. 'Look out, guv'nor! Bang over'ead! Lay down quick!'

'Steamer' was a nickname which, for some reason, the proles applied to rocket bombs. Winston promptly flung himself on his face. The proles were nearly always right when they gave you a warning of this kind. They seemed to possess some kind of instinct which told them several seconds in advance when a rocket was coming, although the rockets supposedly travelled faster than sound. Winston clasped his forearms above his head. There was a roar that seemed to make the pavement heave; a shower of light objects pattered on to his back. When he stood up he found that he was covered with fragments of glass from the nearest window.

He walked on. The bomb had demolished a group of houses 200 metres up the street. A black plume of smoke hung in the sky, and below it a cloud of plaster dust in which a crowd was already forming around the ruins. There was a little pile of plaster lying on the pavement ahead of him, and in the middle of it he could see a bright red streak. When he got up to it he saw that it was a human hand severed at the wrist. Apart from the bloody stump, the hand was so completely whitened as to resemble a plaster cast.

He kicked the thing into the gutter, and then, to avoid the crowd, turned down a side-street to the right. Within three or four minutes he was out of the area which the bomb had affected, and the sordid swarming life of the streets was going on as though nothing had happened. It was nearly twenty hours, and the drinking-shops which the proles frequented ('pubs', they called them) were choked with customers. From their grimy swing doors, endlessly opening and shutting, there came forth a smell of urine, sawdust, and sour beer. In an angle formed by a projecting house-front three men were standing very close together, the middle one of them holding a folded-up newspaper which the other two were studying over his shoulder. Even before he was near enough to make out the expression on their faces, Winston could see absorption in every line of their bodies. It was obviously some serious piece of news that they were reading. He was a few paces away from them when suddenly the group broke up and two of the men were in violent altercation. For a moment they seemed almost on the point of blows.

'Can't you bleeding well listen to what I say? I tell you no number ending in seven ain't won for over fourteen months!'

'Yes, it 'as, then!'

'No, it 'as not! Back 'ome I got the 'ole lot of 'em for over two years wrote down on a piece of paper. I takes 'em down reg'lar as the clock. An' I tell you, no number ending in seven—'

'Yes, a seven 'AS won! I could pretty near tell you the bleeding number. Four oh seven, it ended in. It were in February—second week in February.'

'February your grandmother! I got it all down in black and white. An' I tell you, no number—'

'Oh, pack it in!' said the third man.

They were talking about the Lottery. Winston looked back when he had gone thirty metres. They were still arguing, with vivid, passionate faces. The Lottery, with its weekly pay-out of enormous prizes, was the one public event to which the proles paid serious attention. It was probable that there were some millions of proles for whom the Lottery was the principal if not the only reason for remaining alive. It was their delight, their folly, their anodyne, their intellectual stimulant. Where the Lottery was concerned, even people who could barely read and write seemed capable of intricate calculations and staggering feats of memory. There was a whole tribe of men who made a living simply by selling systems, forecasts, and lucky amulets. Winston had nothing to do with the running of the Lottery, which was managed by the Ministry of Plenty, but he was aware (indeed everyone in the party was aware) that the prizes were largely imaginary. Only small sums were actually paid out, the winners of the big prizes being non-existent persons. In the absence of any real intercommunication between one part of Oceania and another, this was not difficult to arrange.

But if there was hope, it lay in the proles. You had to cling on to that. When you put it in words it sounded reasonable: it was when you looked at the human beings passing you on the pavement that it became an act of faith. The street into which he had turned ran downhill. He had a feeling that he had been in this neighbourhood before, and that there was a main thoroughfare not far away. From somewhere ahead there came a din of shouting voices. The street took a sharp turn and then ended in a flight of steps which led down into a sunken alley where a few stall-keepers were selling tired-looking vegetables. At this moment Winston remembered where he was. The alley led out into the main street, and down the next turning, not five minutes away, was the junk-shop where he had bought the blank book which was now his diary. And in a small stationer's shop not far away he had bought his penholder and his bottle of ink.

He paused for a moment at the top of the steps. On the opposite side of the alley there was a dingy little pub whose windows appeared to be frosted over but in reality were merely coated with dust. A very old man, bent but active, with white moustaches that bristled forward like those of a prawn, pushed open the swing door and went in. As Winston stood watching, it occurred to him that the old man, who must be eighty at the least, had already been middle-aged when the Revolution happened. He and a few others like him were the last links that now existed with the vanished world of capitalism. In the Party itself there were not many people left whose ideas had been formed before the Revolution. The older generation had mostly been wiped out in the great purges of the fifties and sixties, and the few who survived had long ago been terrified into complete intellectual surrender. If there was any one still alive who could give you a truthful account of conditions in the early part of the century, it could only be a prole. Suddenly the passage from the history book that he had copied into his diary came back into Winston's mind, and a lunatic impulse took hold of him. He would go into the pub, he would scrape acquaintance with that old man and question him. He would say to him: 'Tell me about your life when you were a boy. What was it like in those days? Were things better than they are now, or were they worse?'

Hurriedly, lest he should have time to become frightened, he descended the steps and crossed the narrow street. It was madness of course. As usual, there was no definite rule against talking to proles and frequenting their pubs, but it was far too unusual an action to pass unnoticed. If the patrols appeared he might plead an attack of faintness, but it was not likely that they would believe him. He pushed open the door, and a hideous cheesy smell of sour beer hit him in the face. As he entered the din of voices dropped to about half its volume. Behind his back he could feel everyone eyeing his blue overalls. A game of darts which was going on at the other end of the room interrupted itself for perhaps as much as thirty seconds. The old man whom he had followed was standing at the bar, having some kind of altercation with the barman, a large, stout, hook-nosed young man with enormous forearms. A knot of others, standing round with glasses in their hands, were watching the scene.

'I arst you civil enough, didn't I?' said the old man, straightening his shoulders pugnaciously. 'You telling me you ain't got a pint mug in the 'ole bleeding boozer?'

'And what in hell's name IS a pint?' said the barman, leaning forward with the tips of his fingers on the counter.

Ark at 'im! Calls 'isself a barman and don't know what a pint is! Why, a pint's the 'alf of a quart, and there's four quarts to the gallon. 'Ave to teach you the A, B, C next.'

'Never heard of 'em,' said the barman shortly. 'Litre and half litre—that's all we serve. There's the glasses on the shelf in front of you.'

'I likes a pint,' persisted the old man. 'You could 'a drawed me off a pint easy enough. We didn't 'ave these bleeding litres when I was a young man.'

'When you were a young man we were all living in the treetops,' said the barman, with a glance at the other customers.

There was a shout of laughter, and the uneasiness caused by Winston's entry seemed to disappear. The old man's white-stubbled face had flushed pink. He turned away, muttering to himself, and bumped into Winston. Winston caught him gently by the arm.

'May I offer you a drink?' he said.

'You're a gent,' said the other, straightening his shoulders again. He appeared not to have noticed Winston's blue overalls. 'Pint!' he added aggressively to the barman. 'Pint of wallop.'

The barman swished two half-litres of dark-brown beer into thick glasses which he had rinsed in a bucket under the counter. Beer was the only drink you could get in prole pubs. The proles were supposed not to drink gin, though in practice they could get hold of it easily enough. The game of darts was in full swing again, and the knot of men at the bar had begun talking about lottery tickets. Winston's presence was forgotten for a moment. There was a deal table under the window where he and the old man could talk without fear of being overheard. It was horribly dangerous, but at any rate there was no telescreen in the room, a point he had made sure of as soon as he came in.

E could 'a drawed me off a pint,' grumbled the old man as he settled down behind a glass. 'A 'alf litre ain't enough. It don't satisfy. And a 'ole litre's too much. It starts my bladder running. Let alone the price.'

'You must have seen great changes since you were a young man,' said Winston tentatively.

The old man's pale blue eyes moved from the darts board to the bar, and from the bar to the door of the Gents, as though it were in the bar-room that he expected the changes to have occurred.

'The beer was better,' he said finally. 'And cheaper! When I was a young man, mild beer—wallop we used to call it—was fourpence a pint. That was before the war, of course.'

'Which war was that?' said Winston.

'It's all wars,' said the old man vaguely. He took up his glass, and his shoulders straightened again. 'Ere's wishing you the very best of 'ealth!'

In his lean throat the sharp-pointed Adam's apple made a surprisingly rapid up-and-down movement, and the beer vanished. Winston went to the bar and came back with two more half-litres. The old man appeared to have forgotten his prejudice against drinking a full litre.

'You are very much older than I am,' said Winston. 'You must have been a grown man before I was born. You can remember what it was like in the old days, before the Revolution. People of my age don't really know anything about those times. We can only read about them in books, and what it says in the books may not be true. I should like your opinion on that. The history books say that life before the Revolution was completely different from what it is now. There was the most terrible oppression, injustice, poverty worse than anything we can imagine. Here in London, the great mass of the people never had enough to eat from birth to death. Half of them hadn't even boots on their feet. They worked twelve hours a day, they left school at nine, they slept ten in a room. And at the same time there were a very few people, only a few thousands—the capitalists, they were called—who were rich and powerful. They owned everything that there was to own. They lived in great gorgeous houses with thirty servants, they rode about in motor-cars and four-horse carriages, they drank champagne, they wore top hats—'

The old man brightened suddenly.

'Top 'ats!' he said. 'Funny you should mention 'em. The same thing come into my 'ead only yesterday, I dono why. I was jest thinking, I ain't seen a top 'at in years. Gorn right out, they 'ave. The last time I wore one was at my sister-in-law's funeral. And that was—well, I couldn't give you the date, but it must 'a been fifty years ago. Of course it was only 'ired for the occasion, you understand.'

'It isn't very important about the top hats,' said Winston patiently. 'The point is, these capitalists—they and a few lawyers and priests and so forth who lived on them—were the lords of the earth. Everything existed for their benefit. You—the ordinary people, the workers—were their slaves. They could do what they liked with you. They could ship you off to Canada like cattle. They could sleep with your daughters if they chose. They could order you to be flogged with something called a cat-o'-nine tails. You had to take your cap off when you passed them. Every capitalist went about with a gang of lackeys who—'

The old man brightened again.

'Lackeys!' he said. 'Now there's a word I ain't 'eard since ever so long. Lackeys! That reg'lar takes me back, that does. I recollect—oh, donkey's years ago—I used to sometimes go to 'Yde Park of a Sunday afternoon to 'ear the blokes making speeches. Salvation Army, Roman Catholics, Jews, Indians—all sorts there was. And there was one bloke—well, I couldn't give you 'is name, but a real powerful speaker 'e was. 'E didn't 'alf give it 'em! "Lackeys!" 'e says, "lackeys of the bourgeoisie! Flunkies of the ruling class!" Parasites—that was another of them. And 'yenas—'e definitely called 'em 'yenas. Of course 'e was referring to the Labour Party, you understand.'

Winston had the feeling that they were talking at cross-purposes.

'What I really wanted to know was this,' he said. 'Do you feel that you have more freedom now than you had in those days? Are you treated more like a human being? In the old days, the rich people, the people at the top—'

'The 'Ouse of Lords,' put in the old man reminiscently.

'The House of Lords, if you like. What I am asking is, were these people able to treat you as an inferior, simply because they were rich and you were poor? Is it a fact, for instance, that you had to call them "Sir" and take off your cap when you passed them?'

The old man appeared to think deeply. He drank off about a quarter of his beer before answering.

'Yes,' he said. 'They liked you to touch your cap to 'em. It showed respect, like. I didn't agree with it, myself, but I done it often enough. Had to, as you might say.'

'And was it usual—I'm only quoting what I've read in history books—was it usual for these people and their servants to push you off the pavement into the gutter?'

'One of 'em pushed me once,' said the old man. 'I recollect it as if it was yesterday. It was Boat Race night—terribly rowdy they used to get on Boat Race night—and I bumps into a young bloke on Shaftesbury Avenue. Quite a gent, 'e was—dress shirt, top 'at, black overcoat. 'E was kind of zig-zagging across the pavement, and I bumps into 'im accidental-like. 'E says, "Why can't you look where you're going?" 'e says. I say, "Ju think you've bought the bleeding pavement?" 'E says, "I'll twist your bloody 'ead off if you get fresh with me." I says, "You're drunk. I'll give you in charge in 'alf a minute," I says. An' if you'll believe me, 'e puts 'is 'and on my chest and gives me a shove as pretty near sent me under the wheels of a bus. Well, I was young in them days, and I was going to 'ave fetched 'im one, only—'

A sense of helplessness took hold of Winston. The old man's memory was nothing but a rubbish-heap of details. One could question him all day without getting any real information. The party histories might still be true, after a fashion: they might even be completely true. He made a last attempt.

'Perhaps I have not made myself clear,' he said. 'What I'm trying to say is this. You have been alive a very long time; you lived half your life before the Revolution. In 1925, for instance, you were already grown up. Would you say from what you can remember, that life in 1925 was better than it is now, or worse? If you could choose, would you prefer to live then or now?'

The old man looked meditatively at the darts board. He finished up his beer, more slowly than before. When he spoke it was with a tolerant philosophical air, as though the beer had mellowed him.

'I know what you expect me to say,' he said. 'You expect me to say as I'd sooner be young again. Most people'd say they'd sooner be young, if you arst 'em. You got your 'ealth and strength when you're young. When you get to my time of life you ain't never well. I suffer something wicked from my feet, and my bladder's jest terrible. Six and seven times a night it 'as me out of bed. On the other 'and, there's great advantages in being a old man. You ain't got the same worries. No truck with women, and that's a great thing. I ain't 'ad a woman for near on thirty year, if you'd credit it. Nor wanted to, what's more.'

Winston sat back against the window-sill. It was no use going on. He was about to buy some more beer when the old man suddenly got up and shuffled rapidly into the stinking urinal at the side of the room. The extra half-litre was already working on him. Winston sat for a minute or two gazing at his empty glass, and hardly noticed when his feet carried him out into the street again. Within twenty years at the most, he reflected, the huge and simple question, 'Was life better before the Revolution than it is now?' would have ceased once and for all to be answerable. But in effect it was unanswerable even now, since the few scattered survivors from the ancient world were incapable of comparing one age with another. They remembered a million useless things, a quarrel with a workmate, a hunt for a lost bicycle pump, the expression on a long-dead sister's face, the swirls of dust on a windy morning seventy years ago: but all the relevant facts were outside the range of their vision. They were like the ant, which can see small objects but not large ones. And when memory failed and written records were falsified—when that happened, the claim of the Party to have improved the conditions of human life had got to be accepted, because there did not exist, and never again could exist, any standard against which it could be tested.

At this moment his train of thought stopped abruptly. He halted and looked up. He was in a narrow street, with a few dark little shops, interspersed among dwelling-houses. Immediately above his head there hung three discoloured metal balls which looked as if they had once been gilded. He seemed to know the place. Of course! He was standing outside the junk-shop where he had bought the diary.

A twinge of fear went through him. It had been a sufficiently rash act to buy the book in the beginning, and he had sworn never to come near the place again. And yet the instant that he allowed his thoughts to wander, his feet had brought him back here of their own accord. It was precisely against suicidal impulses of this kind that he had hoped to guard himself by opening the diary. At the same time he noticed that although it was nearly twenty-one hours the shop was still open. With the feeling that he would be less conspicuous inside than hanging about on the pavement, he stepped through the doorway. If questioned, he could plausibly say that he was trying to buy razor blades.

The proprietor had just lighted a hanging oil lamp which gave off an unclean but friendly smell. He was a man of perhaps sixty, frail and bowed, with a long, benevolent nose, and mild eyes distorted by thick spectacles. His hair was almost white, but his eyebrows were bushy and still black. His spectacles, his gentle, fussy movements, and the fact that he was wearing an aged jacket of black velvet, gave him a vague air of intellectuality, as though he had been some kind of literary man, or perhaps a musician. His voice was soft, as though faded, and his accent less debased than that of the majority of proles.

'I recognized you on the pavement,' he said immediately. 'You're the gentleman that bought the young lady's keepsake album. That was a beautiful bit of paper, that was. Cream-laid, it used to be called. There's been no paper like that made for—oh, I dare say fifty years.' He peered at Winston over the top of his spectacles. 'Is there anything special I can do for you? Or did you just want to look round?'

'I was passing,' said Winston vaguely. 'I just looked in. I don't want anything in particular.'

'It's just as well,' said the other, 'because I don't suppose I could have satisfied you.' He made an apologetic gesture with his softpalmed hand. 'You see how it is; an empty shop, you might say. Between you and me, the antique trade's just about finished. No demand any longer, and no stock either. Furniture, china, glass it's all been broken up by degrees. And of course the metal stuff's mostly been melted down. I haven't seen a brass candlestick in years.'

The tiny interior of the shop was in fact uncomfortably full, but there was almost nothing in it of the slightest value. The floorspace was very restricted, because all round the walls were stacked innumerable dusty picture-frames. In the window there were trays of nuts and bolts, worn-out chisels, penknives with broken blades, tarnished watches that did not even pretend to be in going order, and other miscellaneous rubbish. Only on a small table in the corner was there a litter of odds and ends—lacquered snuffboxes, agate brooches, and the like—which looked as though they might include something interesting. As Winston wandered towards the table his eye was caught by a round, smooth thing that gleamed softly in the lamplight, and he picked it up.

It was a heavy lump of glass, curved on one side, flat on the other, making almost a hemisphere. There was a peculiar softness, as of rainwater, in both the colour and the texture of the glass. At the heart of it, magnified by the curved surface, there was a strange, pink, convoluted object that recalled a rose or a sea anemone.

'What is it?' said Winston, fascinated.

'That's coral, that is,' said the old man. 'It must have come from the Indian Ocean. They used to kind of embed it in the glass. That wasn't made less than a hundred years ago. More, by the look of it.'

'It's a beautiful thing,' said Winston.

'It is a beautiful thing,' said the other appreciatively. 'But there's not many that'd say so nowadays.' He coughed. 'Now, if it so happened that you wanted to buy it, that'd cost you four dollars. I can remember when a thing like that would have fetched eight pounds, and eight pounds was—well, I can't work it out, but it was a lot of money. But who cares about genuine antiques nowadays—even the few that's left?'

Winston immediately paid over the four dollars and slid the coveted thing into his pocket. What appealed to him about it was not so much its beauty as the air it seemed to possess of belonging to an age quite different from the present one. The soft, rainwatery glass was not like any glass that he had ever seen. The thing was doubly attractive because of its apparent uselessness, though he could guess that it must once have been intended as a paperweight. It was very heavy in his pocket, but fortunately it did not make much of a bulge. It was a queer thing, even a compromising thing, for a Party member to have in his possession. Anything old, and for that matter anything beautiful, was always vaguely suspect. The old man had grown noticeably more cheerful after receiving the four dollars. Winston realized that he would have accepted three or even two.

'There's another room upstairs that you might care to take a look at,' he said. 'There's not much in it. Just a few pieces. We'll do with a light if we're going upstairs.'

He lit another lamp, and, with bowed back, led the way slowly up the steep and worn stairs and along a tiny passage, into a room which did not give on the street but looked out on a cobbled yard and a forest of chimney-pots. Winston noticed that the furniture was still arranged as though the room were meant to be lived in. There was a strip of carpet on the floor, a picture or two on the walls, and a deep, slatternly arm-chair drawn up to the fireplace. An old-fashioned glass clock with a twelve-hour face was ticking away on the mantelpiece. Under the window, and occupying nearly a quarter of the room, was an enormous bed with the mattress still on it.

'We lived here till my wife died,' said the old man half apologetically. 'I'm selling the furniture off by little and little. Now that's a beautiful mahogany bed, or at least it would be if you could get the bugs out of it. But I dare say you'd find it a little bit cumbersome.'

He was holding the lamp high up, so as to illuminate the whole room, and in the warm dim light the place looked curiously inviting. The thought flitted through Winston's mind that it would probably be quite easy to rent the room for a few dollars a week, if he dared to take the risk. It was a wild, impossible notion, to be abandoned as soon as thought of; but the room had awakened in him a sort of nostalgia, a sort of ancestral memory. It seemed to him that he knew exactly what it felt like to sit in a room like this, in an arm-chair beside an open fire with your feet in the fender and a kettle on the hob; utterly alone, utterly secure, with nobody watching you, no voice pursuing you, no sound except the singing of the kettle and the friendly ticking of the clock.

'There's no telescreen!' he could not help murmuring.

'Ah,' said the old man, 'I never had one of those things. Too expensive. And I never seemed to feel the need of it, somehow. Now that's a nice gateleg table in the corner there. Though of course you'd have to put new hinges on it if you wanted to use the flaps.'

There was a small bookcase in the other corner, and Winston had already gravitated towards it. It contained nothing but rubbish. The hunting-down and destruction of books had been done with the same thoroughness in the prole quarters as everywhere else. It was very unlikely that there existed anywhere in Oceania a copy of a book printed earlier than 1960. The old man, still carrying the lamp, was standing in front of a picture in a rosewood frame which hung on the other side of the fireplace, opposite the bed.

'Now, if you happen to be interested in old prints at all—' he began delicately.

Winston came across to examine the picture. It was a steel engraving of an oval building with rectangular windows, and a small tower in front. There was a railing running round the building, and at the rear end there was what appeared to be a statue. Winston gazed at it for some moments. It seemed vaguely familiar, though he did not remember the statue.

'The frame's fixed to the wall,' said the old man, 'but I could unscrew it for you, I dare say.'

'I know that building,' said Winston finally. 'It's a ruin now. It's in the middle of the street outside the Palace of Justice.'

'That's right. Outside the Law Courts. It was bombed in—oh, many years ago. It was a church at one time, St Clement Danes, its name was.' He smiled apologetically, as though conscious of saying something slightly ridiculous, and added: 'Oranges and lemons, say the bells of St Clement's!'

'What's that?' said Winston.

'Oh—"Oranges and lemons, say the bells of St Clement's." That was a rhyme we had when I was a little boy. How it goes on I don't remember, but I do know it ended up, "Here comes a candle to light you to bed, Here comes a chopper to chop off your head." It was a kind of a dance. They held out their arms for you to pass under, and when they came to "Here comes a chopper to chop off your head" they brought their arms down and caught you. It was just names of churches. All the London churches were in it—all the principal ones, that is.'

Winston wondered vaguely to what century the church belonged. It was always difficult to determine the age of a

London building. Anything large and impressive, if it was reasonably new in appearance, was automatically claimed as having been built since the Revolution, while anything that was obviously of earlier date was ascribed to some dim period called the Middle Ages. The centuries of capitalism were held to have produced nothing of any value. One could not learn history from architecture any more than one could learn it from books. Statues, inscriptions, memorial stones, the names of streets—anything that might throw light upon the past had been systematically altered.

'I never knew it had been a church,' he said.

'There's a lot of them left, really,' said the old man, 'though they've been put to other uses. Now, how did that rhyme go? Ah! I've got it!

'Oranges and lemons,' say the bells of St Clement's,

'You owe me three farthings,' say the bells of St Martin's...

there, now, that's as far as I can get. A farthing, that was a small copper coin, looked something like a cent.'

'Where was St Martin's?' said Winston.

'St Martin's? That's still standing. It's in Victory Square, alongside the picture gallery. A building with a kind of a triangular porch and pillars in front, and a big flight of steps.'

Winston knew the place well. It was a museum used for propaganda displays of various kinds—scale models of rocket bombs and Floating Fortresses, waxwork tableaux illustrating enemy atrocities, and the like.

'St Martin's-in-the-Fields it used to be called,' supplemented the old man, 'though I don't recollect any fields anywhere in those parts.'

Winston did not buy the picture. It would have been an even more incongruous possession than the glass paperweight, and impossible to carry home, unless it were taken out of its frame. But he lingered for some minutes more, talking to the old man, whose name, he discovered, was not Weeks—as one might have gathered from the inscription over the shop-front—but Charrington. Mr Charrington, it seemed, was a widower aged sixty-three and had inhabited this shop for thirty years. Throughout that time he had been intending to alter the name over the window, but had never quite got to the point of doing it. All the while that they were talking the half-remembered rhyme kept running through Winston's head. Oranges and lemons say the bells of St Clement's, you owe me three farthings, say the bells of St Martin's! It was curious, but when you said it to yourself you had the illusion of actually hearing bells, the bells of a lost London that still existed somewhere or other, disguised and forgotten. From one ghostly steeple after another he seemed to hear them pealing forth. Yet so far as he could remember he had never in real life heard church bells ringing.

He got away from Mr Charrington and went down the stairs alone, so as not to let the old man see him reconnoitring the street before stepping out of the door. He had already made up his mind that after a suitable interval—a month, say—he would take the risk of visiting the shop again. It was perhaps not more dangerous than shirking an evening at the Centre. The serious piece of folly had been to come back here in the first place, after buying the diary and without knowing whether the proprietor of the shop could be trusted. However—!

Yes, he thought again, he would come back. He would buy further scraps of beautiful rubbish. He would buy the engraving of St Clement Danes, take it out of its frame, and carry it home concealed under the jacket of his overalls. He would drag the rest of that poem out of MrCharrington's memory. Even the lunatic project of renting the room upstairs flashed momentarily through his mind again. For perhaps five seconds exaltation made him careless, and he stepped out on to the pavement without so much as a preliminary glance through the window. He had even started humming to an improvised tune

'Oranges and lemons,' say the bells of St Clement's,
'You owe me three farthings,' say the—

Suddenly his heart seemed to turn to ice and his bowels to water. A figure in blue overalls was coming down the pavement, not ten metres away. It was the girl from the Fiction Department, the girl with dark hair. The light was failing, but there was no difficulty in recognizing her. She looked him straight in the face, then walked quickly on as though she had not seen him.

For a few seconds Winston was too paralysed to move. Then he turned to the right and walked heavily away, not noticing for the moment that he was going in the wrong direction. At any rate, one question was settled. There was no doubting any longer that the girl was spying on him. She must have followed him here, because it was not credible that by pure chance she should have happened to be walking on the same evening up the same obscure backstreet, kilometres distant from any quarter where Party members lived. It was too great a coincidence. Whether she was really an agent of the Thought Police, or simply an amateur spy actuated by officiousness, hardly mattered. It was enough that she was watching him. Probably she had seen him go into the pub as well.

It was an effort to walk. The lump of glass in his pocket banged against his thigh at each step, and he was half minded to take it out and throw it away. The worst thing was the pain in his belly. For a couple of minutes he had the feeling that he would die if he did not reach a lavatory soon. But there would be no public lavatories in a quarter like this. Then the spasm passed, leaving a dull ache behind.

The street was a blind alley. Winston halted, stood for several seconds wondering vaguely what to do, then turned round and began to retrace his steps. As he turned it occurred to him that the girl had only passed him three minutes ago and that by running he could probably catch up with her. He could keep on her track till they were in some quiet place, and then smash her skull in with a cobblestone. The piece of glass in his pocket would be heavy enough for the job. But he abandoned the idea immediately, because even the thought of making any physical effort was unbearable. He could not run, he could not strike a blow. Besides, she was young and lusty and would defend herself. He thought also of hurrying to the Community Centre and staying there till the place closed, so as to establish a partial alibi for the evening. But that too was impossible. A deadly lassitude had taken hold of him. All he wanted was to get home quickly and then sit down and be quiet.

It was after twenty-two hours when he got back to the flat. The lights would be switched off at the main at twenty-three thirty. He went into the kitchen and swallowed nearly a teacupful of Victory Gin. Then he went to the table in the alcove, sat down, and took the diary out of the drawer. But he did not open it at once. From the telescreen a brassy female voice was squalling a patriotic song. He sat staring at the marbled cover of the book, trying without success to shut the voice out of his consciousness.

It was at night that they came for you, always at night. The proper thing was to kill yourself before they got you. Undoubtedly some people did so. Many of the disappearances were actually suicides. But it needed desperate courage to kill yourself in a world where firearms, or any quick and certain poison, were completely unprocurable. He thought with a kind of astonishment of the biological uselessness of pain and fear, the treachery of the human body which always freezes into inertia at exactly the moment when a special effort is needed. He might have silenced the dark-haired girl if only he had acted quickly enough: but precisely because of the extremity of his danger he had lost the power to act. It struck him that in moments of crisis one is never fighting against an external enemy, but always against one's own body. Even now, in spite of the gin, the dull ache in his belly made consecutive thought impossible. And it is the same, he perceived, in all seemingly heroic or tragic situations. On the battlefield, in the torture chamber, on a sinking ship, the issues that you are fighting for are always forgotten, because the body swells up until it fills the universe, and even when you are not paralysed by fright or screaming with pain, life is a moment-to-moment struggle against hunger or cold or sleeplessness, against a sour stomach or an aching tooth.

He opened the diary. It was important to write something down. The woman on the telescreen had started a new song. Her voice seemed to stick into his brain like jagged splinters of glass. He tried to think of O'Brien, for whom, or to whom, the diary was written, but instead he began thinking of the things that would happen to him after the Thought Police took him away. It would not matter if they killed you at once. To be killed was what you expected. But before death (nobody spoke of such things, yet everybody knew of them) there was the routine of confession that had to be gone through: the grovelling on the floor and screaming for mercy, the crack of broken bones, the smashed teeth and bloody clots of hair. Why did you have to endure it, since the end was always the same? Why was it not possible to cut a few days or weeks out of your life? Nobody ever escaped detection, and nobody ever failed to confess. When once you had succumbed to thoughtcrime it was certain that by a given date you would be dead. Why then did that horror, which altered nothing, have to lie embedded in future time?

He tried with a little more success than before to summon up the image of O'Brien. 'We shall meet in the place where there is no darkness,' O'Brien had said to him. He knew what it meant, or thought he knew. The place where there is no darkness was the imagined future, which one would never see, but which, by foreknowledge, one could mystically share in. But with the voice from the telescreen nagging at his ears he could not follow the train of thought further. He put a cigarette in his mouth. Half the tobacco promptly fell out on to his tongue, a bitter dust which was difficult to spit out again. The face of Big Brother swam into his mind, displacing that of O'Brien. Just as he had done a few days earlier, he slid a coin out of his pocket and looked at it. The face gazed up at him, heavy, calm, protecting: but what kind of smile was hidden beneath the dark moustache? Like a leaden knell the words came back at him:

WAR IS PEACE
FREEDOM IS SLAVERY
IGNORANCE IS STRENGTH.

PART II

CHAPTER ONE

It was the middle of the morning, and Winston had left the cubicle to go to the lavatory.

A solitary figure was coming towards him from the other end of the long, brightly-lit corridor. It was the girl with dark hair. Four days had gone past since the evening when he had run into her outside the junk-shop. As she came nearer he saw that her right arm was in a sling, not noticeable at a distance because it was of the same colour as her overalls. Probably she had crushed her hand while swinging round one of the big kaleidoscopes on which the plots of novels were 'roughed in'. It was a common accident in the Fiction Department.

They were perhaps four metres apart when the girl stumbled and fell almost flat on her face. A sharp cry of pain was wrung out of her. She must have fallen right on the injured arm. Winston stopped short. The girl had risen to her knees. Her face had turned a milky yellow colour against which her mouth stood out redder than ever. Her eyes were fixed on his, with an appealing expression that looked more like fear than pain.

A curious emotion stirred in Winston's heart. In front of him was an enemy who was trying to kill him: in front of him, also, was a human creature, in pain and perhaps with a broken bone. Already he had instinctively started forward to help her. In the moment when he had seen her fall on the bandaged arm, it had been as though he felt the pain in his own body.

'You're hurt?' he said.

'It's nothing. My arm. It'll be all right in a second.'

She spoke as though her heart were fluttering. She had certainly turned very pale.

'You haven't broken anything?'

'No, I'm all right. It hurt for a moment, that's all.'

She held out her free hand to him, and he helped her up. She had regained some of her colour, and appeared very much better.

'It's nothing,' she repeated shortly. 'I only gave my wrist a bit of a bang. Thanks, comrade!'

And with that she walked on in the direction in which she had been going, as briskly as though it had really been nothing. The whole incident could not have taken as much as half a minute. Not to let one's feelings appear in one's face was a habit that had acquired the status of an instinct, and in any case they had been standing straight in front of a telescreen when the thing happened. Nevertheless it had been very difficult not to betray a momentary surprise, for in the two or three seconds while he was helping her up the girl had slipped something into his hand. There was no question that she had done it intentionally. It was something small and flat. As he passed through the lavatory door he transferred it to his pocket and felt it with the tips of his fingers. It was a scrap of paper folded into a square.

While he stood at the urinal he managed, with a little more fingering, to get it unfolded. Obviously there must be a message of some kind written on it. For a moment he was tempted to take it into one of the water-closets and read it at once. But that would be shocking folly, as he well knew. There was no place where you could be more certain that the telescreens were watched continuously.

He went back to his cubicle, sat down, threw the fragment of paper casually among the other papers on the desk, put on his spectacles and hitched the speakwrite towards him. 'Five minutes,' he told himself, 'five minutes at the very least!' His heart bumped in his breast with frightening loudness. Fortunately the piece of work he was engaged on was mere routine, the rectification of a long list of figures, not needing close attention.

Whatever was written on the paper, it must have some kind of political meaning. So far as he could see there were two possibilities. One, much the more likely, was that the girl was an agent of the Thought Police, just as he had feared. He did not know why the Thought Police should choose to deliver their messages in such a fashion, but perhaps they had their reasons. The thing that was written on the paper might be a threat, a summons, an order to commit suicide, a trap of some description. But there was another, wilder possibility that kept raising its head, though he tried vainly to suppress it. This was, that the message did not come from the Thought Police at all, but from some kind of underground organization. Perhaps the Brotherhood existed after all! Perhaps the girl was part of it! No doubt the idea was absurd, but it had sprung into his mind in the very instant of feeling the scrap of paper in his hand. It was not till a couple of minutes later that the other, more probable explanation had occurred to him. And even now, though his intellect told him that the message probably meant death—still, that was not what he believed, and the unreasonable hope persisted, and his heart banged, and it was with difficulty that he kept his voice from trembling as he murmured his figures into the speakwrite.

He rolled up the completed bundle of work and slid it into the pneumatic tube. Eight minutes had gone by. He re-adjusted his spectacles on his nose, sighed, and drew the next batch of work towards him, with the scrap of paper on top of it. He flattened it out. On it was written, in a large unformed handwriting:

I love you.

For several seconds he was too stunned even to throw the incriminating thing into the memory hole. When he did so, although he knew very well the danger of showing too much interest, he could not resist reading it once again, just to make sure that the words were really there.

For the rest of the morning it was very difficult to work. What was even worse than having to focus his mind on a series of niggling jobs was the need to conceal his agitation from the telescreen. He felt as though a fire were burning in his belly. Lunch in the hot, crowded, noise-filled canteen was torment. He had hoped to be alone for a little while during the lunch hour, but as bad luck would have it the imbecile Parsons flopped down beside him, the tang of his sweat almost defeating the tinny smell of stew, and kept up a stream of talk about the preparations for Hate Week. He was particularly enthusiastic about a papier-mâché model of Big Brother's head, two metres wide, which was being made for the occasion by his daughter's troop of Spies. The irritating thing was that in the racket of voices Winston could hardly hear what Parsons was saying, and was constantly having to ask for some fatuous remark to be repeated. Just once he caught a glimpse of the girl, at a table with two other girls at the far end of the room. She appeared not to have seen him, and he did not look in that direction again.

The afternoon was more bearable. Immediately after lunch there arrived a delicate, difficult piece of work which would take several hours and necessitated putting everything else aside. It consisted in falsifying a series of production reports of two years ago, in such a way as to cast discredit on a prominent member of the Inner Party, who was now under a cloud. This was the kind of thing that Winston was good at, and for more than two hours he succeeded in shutting the girl out of his mind altogether. Then the memory of her face came back, and with it a raging, intolerable desire to be alone. Until he could be alone it was impossible to think this new development out. Tonight was one of his nights at the Community Centre. He wolfed another tasteless meal in the canteen, hurried off to the Centre, took part in the solemn foolery of a 'discussion group', played two games of table tennis, swallowed several glasses of gin, and sat for half an hour through a lecture entitled 'Ingsoc in relation to chess'. His soul writhed with boredom, but for once he had had no impulse to shirk his evening at the Centre. At the sight of the words *I love you* the desire to stay alive had welled up in him, and the taking of minor risks suddenly seemed stupid. It was not till twenty-three hours, when he was home and in bed—in the darkness, where you were safe even from the telescreen so long as you kept silent—that he was able to think continuously.

It was a physical problem that had to be solved: how to get in touch with the girl and arrange a meeting. He did not consider any longer the possibility that she might be laying some kind of trap for him. He knew that it was not so, because of her unmistakable agitation when she handed him the note. Obviously she had been frightened out of her wits, as well she might be. Nor did the idea of refusing her advances even cross his mind. Only five nights ago he had contemplated smashing her skull in with a cobblestone, but that was of no importance. He thought of her naked, youthful body, as he had seen it in his dream. He had imagined her a fool like all the rest of them, her head stuffed with lies and hatred, her belly full of ice. A kind of fever seized him at the thought that he might lose her, the white youthful body might slip away from him! What he feared more than anything else was that she would simply change her mind if he did not get in touch with her quickly. But the physical difficulty of meeting was enormous. It was like trying to make a move at chess when you were already mated. Whichever way you turned, the telescreen faced you. Actually, all the possible ways of communicating with her had occurred to him within five minutes of reading the note; but now, with time to think, he went over them one by one, as though laying out a row of instruments on a table.

Obviously the kind of encounter that had happened this morning could not be repeated. If she had worked in the Records Department it might have been comparatively simple, but he had only a very dim idea whereabouts in the building the Fiction Department lay, and he had no pretext for going there. If he had known where she lived, and at what time she left work, he could have contrived to meet her somewhere on her way home; but to try to follow her home was not safe, because it would mean loitering about outside the Ministry, which was bound to be noticed. As for sending a letter through the mails, it was out of the question. By a routine that was not even secret, all letters were opened in transit. Actually, few people ever wrote letters. For the messages that it was occasionally necessary to send, there were printed postcards with long lists of phrases, and you struck out the ones that were inapplicable. In any case he did not know the girl's name, let alone her address. Finally he decided that the safest place was the canteen. If he could get her at a table by herself, somewhere in the middle of the room, not too near the telescreens, and with a sufficient buzz of conversation all round—if these conditions endured for, say, thirty seconds, it might be possible to exchange a few words.

For a week after this, life was like a restless dream. On the next day she did not appear in the canteen until he was leaving it, the whistle having already blown. Presumably she had been changed on to a later shift. They passed each other without a glance. On the day after that she was in the canteen at the usual time, but with three other girls and immediately under a telescreen. Then for three dreadful days she did not appear at all. His whole mind and body seemed to bc afflicted with an unbearable sensitivity, a sort of transparency, which made every movement, every sound, every contact, every word that he had to speak or listen to, an agony. Even in sleep he could not altogether escape from her image. He did not touch the diary during those days. If there was any relief, it was in his work, in which he could sometimes forget himself for ten minutes at a stretch. He had absolutely no clue as to what had happened to her. There was no enquiry he could make. She might have been vaporized, she might have committed suicide, she might have been transferred to the other end of Oceania: worst and likeliest of all, she might simply have changed her mind and decided to avoid him.

The next day she reappeared. Her arm was out of the sling and she had a band of sticking-plaster round her wrist. The relief of seeing her was so great that he could not resist staring directly at her for several seconds. On the following day he very nearly succeeded in speaking to her. When he came into the canteen she was sitting at a table well out from the wall, and was quite alone. It was early, and the place was not very full. The queue edged forward till Winston was almost at the counter, then was held up for two minutes because someone in front was complaining that he had not received his tablet of saccharine. But the girl was still alone when Winston secured his tray and began to make for her table. He walked casually towards her, his eyes searching for a place at some table beyond her. She was perhaps three metres away from him. Another two seconds would do it. Then a voice behind him called, 'Smith!' He pretended not to hear. 'Smith!' repeated the voice, more loudly. It was no use. He turned round. A blond-headed, silly-faced young man named Wilsher, whom he barely knew, was inviting him with a smile to a vacant place at his table. It was not safe to refuse. After having been recognized, he could not go and sit at a table with an unattended girl. It was too noticeable. He sat down with a friendly smile. The silly blond face beamed into his. Winston had a hallucination of himself smashing a pick-axe right into the middle of it. The girl's table filled up a few minutes later.

But she must have seen him coming towards her, and perhaps she would take the hint. Next day he took care to arrive early. Surely enough, she was at a table in about the same place, and again alone. The person immediately ahead of him in the queue was a small, swiftly-moving, beetle-like man with a flat face and tiny, suspicious eyes. As Winston turned away from the counter with his tray, he saw that the little man was making straight for the girl's table. His hopes sank again. There was a vacant place at a table further away, but something in the little man's appearance suggested that he would be sufficiently attentive to his own comfort to choose the emptiest table. With ice at his heart Winston followed. It was no use unless he could get the girl alone. At this moment there was a tremendous crash. The little man was sprawling on all fours, his tray had gone flying, two streams of soup and coffee were flowing across the floor. He started to his feet with a malignant glance at Winston, whom he evidently suspected of having tripped him up. But it was all right. Five seconds later, with a thundering heart, Winston was sitting at the girl's table.

He did not look at her. He unpacked his tray and promptly began eating. It was all-important to speak at once, before anyone else came, but now a terrible fear had taken possession of him. A week had gone by since she had first approached him. She would have changed her mind, she must have changed her mind! It was impossible that this affair should end successfully; such things did not happen in real life. He might have flinched altogether from speaking if at this moment he had not seen Ampleforth, the hairy-eared poet, wandering limply round the room with a tray, looking for a place to sit down. In his vague way Ampleforth was attached to Winston, and would certainly sit down at his table if he caught sight of him. There was perhaps a minute in which to act. Both Winston and the girl were eating steadily. The stuff they were eating was a thin stew, actually a soup, of haricot beans. In a low murmur Winston began speaking. Neither of them looked up; steadily they spooned the watery stuff into their mouths, and between spoonfuls exchanged the few necessary words in low expressionless voices.

'What time do you leave work?'

'Eighteen-thirty.'

'Where can we meet?'

'Victory Square, near the monument.'

'It's full of telescreens.'

'It doesn't matter if there's a crowd.'

'Any signal?'

'No. Don't come up to me until you see me among a lot of people. And don't look at me. Just keep somewhere near me.'

'What time?'

'Nineteen hours.'

'All right.'

Ampleforth failed to see Winston and sat down at another table. They did not speak again, and, so far as it was possible for two people sitting on opposite sides of the same table, they did not look at one another. The girl finished her lunch quickly and madc off, while Winston stayed to smoke a cigarette.

Winston was in Victory Square before the appointed time. He wandered round the base of the enormous fluted column, at the top of which Big Brother's statue gazed southward towards the skies where he had vanquished the Eurasian aeroplanes (the Eastasian aeroplanes, it had been, a few years ago) in the Battle of Airstrip One. In the street in front of it there was a statue of a man on horseback which was supposed to represent Oliver Cromwell. At five minutes past the hour the girl had still not appeared. Again the terrible fear seized upon Winston. She was not coming, she had changed her mind! He walked slowly up to the north side of the square and got a sort of pale-coloured pleasure from identifying St Martin's Church, whose bells, when it had bells, had chimed 'You owe me three farthings.' Then he saw the girl standing at the base of the monument, reading or pretending to read a poster which ran spirally up the column. It was not safe to go near her until some more people had accumulated. There were telescreens all round the pediment. But at this moment there was a din of shouting and a zoom of heavy vehicles from somewhere to the left. Suddenly everyone seemed to be running across the square. The girl nipped nimbly round the lions at the base of the monument and joined in the rush. Winston followed. As he ran, he gathered from some shouted remarks that a convoy of Eurasian prisoners was passing.

Already a dense mass of people was blocking the south side of the square. Winston, at normal times the kind of person who gravitates to the outer edge of any kind of scrimmage, shoved, butted, squirmed his way forward into the heart of the crowd. Soon he was within arm's length of the girl, but the way was blocked by an enormous prole and an almost equally enormous woman, presumably his wife, who seemed to form an impenetrable wall of flesh. Winston wriggled himself sideways, and with a violent lunge managed to drive his shoulder between them. For a moment it felt as though his entrails were being ground to pulp between the two muscular hips, then he had broken through, sweating a little. He was next to the girl. They were shoulder to shoulder, both staring fixedly in front of them.

A long line of trucks, with wooden-faced guards armed with sub-machine guns standing upright in each corner, was passing slowly down the street. In the trucks little yellow men in shabby greenish uniforms were squatting, jammed close together. Their sad Mongolian faces gazed out over the sides of the trucks utterly incurious. Occasionally when a truck jolted there was a clank-clank of metal: all the prisoners were wearing leg-irons. Truck-load after truck-load of the sad faces passed.

Winston knew they were there but he saw them only intermittently. The girl's shoulder, and her arm right down to the elbow, were pressed against his. Her cheek was almost near enough for him to feel its warmth. She had immediately taken charge of the situation, just as she had done in the canteen. She began speaking in the same expressionless voice as before, with lips barely moving, a mere murmur easily drowned by the din of voices and the rumbling of the trucks.

'Can you hear me?'

'Yes.'

'Can you get Sunday afternoon off?'

'Yes.'

'Then listen carefully. You'll have to remember this. Go to Paddington Station—'

With a sort of military precision that astonished him, she outlined the route that he was to follow. A half-hour railway journey; turn left outside the station; two kilometres along the road; a gate with the top bar missing; a path across a field; a grass-grown lane; a track between bushes; a dead tree with moss on it. It was as though she had a map inside her head. 'Can you remember all that?' she murmured finally.

'Yes.'

'You turn left, then right, then left again. And the gate's got no top bar.'

'Yes. What time?'

'About fifteen. You may have to wait. I'll get there by another way. Are you sure you remember everything?'

'Yes.'

'Then get away from me as quick as you can.'

She need not have told him that. But for the moment they could not extricate themselves from the crowd. The trucks were still filing past, the people still insatiably gaping. At the start there had been a few boos and hisses, but it came only from the Party members among the crowd, and had soon stopped. The prevailing emotion was simply curiosity. Foreigners, whether from Eurasia or from Eastasia, were a kind of strange animal. One literally never saw them except in the guise of prisoners, and even as prisoners one never got more than a momentary glimpse of them. Nor did one know what became of them, apart from the few who were hanged as war-criminals: the others simply vanished, presumably into forced-labour camps. The round Mogol faces had given way to faces of a more European type, dirty, bearded and exhausted. From over scrubby cheekbones eyes looked into Winston's, sometimes with strange intensity, and flashed away again. The convoy was drawing to an end. In the last truck he could see an aged man, his face a mass of grizzled hair, standing upright with wrists crossed in front of him, as though he were used to having them bound together. It was almost time for Winston and the girl to part. But at the last moment, while the crowd still hemmed them in, her hand felt for his and gave it a fleeting squeeze.

It could not have been ten seconds, and yet it seemed a long time that their hands were clasped together. He had time to learn every detail of her hand. He explored the long fingers, the shapely nails, the work-hardened palm with its row of callouses, the smooth flesh under the wrist. Merely from feeling it he would have known it by sight. In the same instant it occurred to him that he did not know what colour the girl's eyes were. They were probably brown, but people with dark hair sometimes had blue eyes. To turn his head and look at her would have been inconceivable folly. With hands locked together, invisible among the press of bodies, they stared steadily in front of them, and instead of the eyes of the girl, the eyes of the aged prisoner gazed mournfully at Winston out of nests of hair.

CHAPTER TWO

Winston picked his way up the lane through dappled light and shade, stepping out into pools of gold wherever the boughs parted. Under the trees to the left of him the ground was misty with bluebells. The air seemed to kiss one's skin. It was the second of May. From somewhere deeper in the heart of the wood came the droning of ring-doves.

He was a bit early. There had been no difficulties about the journey, and the girl was so evidently experienced that he was less frightened than he would normally have been. Presumably she could be trusted to find a safe place. In general you could not assume that you were much safer in the country than in London. There were no telescreens, of course, but there was always the danger of concealed microphones by which your voice might be picked up and recognized; besides, it was not easy to make a journey by yourself without attracting attention. For distances of less than 100 kilometres it was not necessary to get your passport endorsed, but sometimes there were patrols hanging about the railway stations, who examined the papers of any Party member they found there and asked awkward questions. However, no patrols had appeared, and on the walk from the station he had made sure by cautious backward glances that he was not being followed. The train was full of proles, in holiday mood because of the summery weather. The wooden-seated carriage in which he travelled was filled to overflowing by a single enormous family, ranging from a toothless great-grandmother to a month-old baby, going out to spend an afternoon with 'in-laws' in the country, and, as they freely explained to Winston, to get hold of a little black-market butter.

The lane widened, and in a minute he came to the footpath she had told him of, a mere cattle-track which plunged between the bushes. He had no watch, but it could not be fifteen yet. The bluebells were so thick underfoot that it was impossible not to tread on them. He knelt down and began picking some partly to pass the time away, but also from a vague idea that he would like to have a bunch of flowers to offer to the girl when they met. He had got together a big bunch and was smelling their faint sickly scent when a sound at his back froze him, the unmistakable crackle of a foot on twigs. He went on picking bluebells. It was the best thing to do. It might be the girl, or he might have been followed after all. To look round was to show guilt. He picked another and another. A hand fell lightly on his shoulder.

He looked up. It was the girl. She shook her head, evidently as a warning that he must keep silent, then parted the bushes and quickly led the way along the narrow track into the wood. Obviously she had been that way before, for she dodged the boggy bits as though by habit. Winston followed, still clasping his bunch of flowers. His first feeling was relief, but as he watched the strong slender body moving in front of him, with the scarlet sash that was just tight enough to bring out the curve of her hips, the sense of his own inferiority was heavy upon him. Even now it seemed quite likely that when she turned round and looked at him she would draw back after all. The sweetness of the air and the greenness of the leaves daunted him. Already on the walk from the station the May sunshine had made him feel dirty and etiolated, a creature of indoors, with the sooty dust of London in the pores of his skin. It occurred to him that till now she had probably never seen him in broad daylight in the open. They came to the fallen tree that she had spoken of. The girl hopped over and forced apart the bushes, in which there did not seem to be an opening. When Winston followed her, he found that they were in a natural clearing, a tiny grassy knoll surrounded by tall saplings that shut it in completely. The girl stopped and turned.

'Here we are,' she said.

He was facing her at several paces' distance. As yet he did not dare move nearer to her.

'I didn't want to say anything in the lane,' she went on, 'in case there's a mike hidden there. I don't suppose there is, but

there could be. There's always the chance of one of those swine recognizing your voice. We're all right here.'

He still had not the courage to approach her. 'We're all right here?' he repeated stupidly.

'Yes. Look at the trees.' They were small ashes, which at some time had been cut down and had sprouted up again into a forest of poles, none of them thicker than one's wrist. 'There's nothing big enough to hide a mike in. Besides, I've been here before.'

They were only making conversation. He had managed to move closer to her now. She stood before him very upright, with a smile on her face that looked faintly ironical, as though she were wondering why he was so slow to act. The bluebells had cascaded on to the ground. They seemed to have fallen of their own accord. He took her hand.

'Would you believe,' he said, 'that till this moment I didn't know what colour your eyes were?' They were brown, he noted, a rather light shade of brown, with dark lashes. 'Now that you've seen what I'm really like, can you still bear to look at me?'

'Yes, easily.'

'I'm thirty-nine years old. I've got a wife that I can't get rid of. I've got varicose veins. I've got five false teeth.'

'I couldn't care less,' said the girl.

The next moment, it was hard to say by whose act, she was in his his arms. At the beginning he had no feeling except sheer incredulity. The youthful body was strained against his own, the mass of dark hair was against his face, and yes! actually she had turned her face up and he was kissing the wide red mouth. She had clasped her arms about his neck, she was calling him darling, precious one, loved one. He had pulled her down on to the ground, she was utterly unresisting, he could do what he liked with her. But the truth was that he had no physical sensation, except that of mere contact. All he felt was incredulity and pride. He was glad that this was happening, but he had no physical desire. It was too soon, her youth and prettiness had frightened him, he was too much used to living without women—he did not know the reason. The girl picked herself up and pulled a bluebell out of her hair. She sat against him, putting her arm round his waist.

'Never mind, dear. There's no hurry. We've got the whole afternoon. Isn't this a splendid hide-out? I found it when I got lost once on a community hike. If anyone was coming you could hear them a hundred metres away.'

'What is your name?' said Winston.

'Julia. I know yours. It's Winston—Winston Smith.'

'How did you find that out?'

'I expect I'm better at finding things out than you are, dear. Tell me, what did you think of me before that day I gave you the note?'

He did not feel any temptation to tell lies to her. It was even a sort of love-offering to start off by telling the worst.

'I hated the sight of you,' he said. 'I wanted to rape you and then murder you afterwards. Two weeks ago I thought seriously of smashing your head in with a cobblestone. If you really want to know, I imagined that you had something to do with the Thought Police.'

The girl laughed delightedly, evidently taking this as a tribute to the excellence of her disguise.

'Not the Thought Police! You didn't honestly think that?'

'Well, perhaps not exactly that. But from your general appearance—merely because you're young and fresh and healthy, you understand—I thought that probably—'

'You thought I was a good Party member. Pure in word and deed. Banners, processions, slogans, games, community hikes all that stuff. And you thought that if I had a quarter of a chance I'd denounce you as a thought-criminal and get you killed off?'

'Yes, something of that kind. A great many young girls are like that, you know.'

'It's this bloody thing that does it,' she said, ripping off the scarlet sash of the Junior Anti-Sex League and flinging it on to a bough. Then, as though touching her waist had reminded her of something, she felt in the pocket of her overalls and produced a small slab of chocolate. She broke it in half and gave one of the pieces to Winston. Even before he had taken it he knew by the smell that it was very unusual chocolate. It was dark and shiny, and was wrapped in silver paper. Chocolate normally was dull-brown crumbly stuff that tasted, as nearly as one could describe it, like the smoke of a rubbish fire. But at some time or another he had tasted chocolate like the piece she had given him. The first whiff of its scent had stirred up some memory which he could not pin down, but which was powerful and troubling.

'Where did you get this stuff?' he said.

'Black market,' she said indifferently. 'Actually I am that sort of girl, to look at. I'm good at games. I was a troop-leader in the Spies. I do voluntary work three evenings a week for the Junior Anti-Sex League. Hours and hours I've spent pasting their bloody rot all over London. I always carry one end of a banner in the processions. I always look cheerful and I never shirk anything. Always yell with the crowd, that's what I say. It's the only way to be safe.'

The first fragment of chocolate had melted on Winston's tongue. The taste was delightful. But there was still that memory moving round the edges of his consciousness, something strongly felt but not reducible to definite shape, like an object seen out of the corner of one's eye. He pushed it away from him, aware only that it was the memory of some action which he would have liked to undo but could not.

'You are very young,' he said. 'You are ten or fifteen years younger than I am. What could you see to attract you in a man like me?'

'It was something in your face. I thought I'd take a chance. I'm good at spotting people who don't belong. As soon as I saw you I knew you were against *them*.'

Them, it appeared, meant the Party, and above all the Inner Party, about whom she talked with an open jeering hatred which made Winston feel uneasy, although he knew that they were safe here if they could be safe anywhere. A thing that astonished him about her was the coarseness of her language. Party members were supposed not to swear, and Winston himself very seldom did swear, aloud, at any rate. Julia, however, seemed unable to mention the Party, and especially the Inner Party, without using the kind of words that you saw chalked up in dripping alley-ways. He did not dislike it. It was merely one symptom of her revolt against the Party and all its ways, and somehow it seemed natural and healthy, like the sneeze of a horse that smells bad hay. They had left the clearing and were wandering again through the chequered shade, with their arms round each other's waists whenever it was wide enough to walk two abreast. He noticed how much softer her waist seemed to feel now that the sash was gone. They did not speak above a whisper. Outside the clearing, Julia said, it was better to go quietly. Presently they had reached the edge of the little wood. She stopped him.

'Don't go out into the open. There might be someone watching. We're all right if we keep behind the boughs.'

They were standing in the shade of hazel bushes. The sunlight, filtering through innumerable leaves, was still hot on their faces. Winston looked out into the field beyond, and underwent a curious, slow shock of recognition. He knew it by sight. An old, close-bitten pasture, with a footpath wandering across it and a molehill here and there. In the ragged hedge on the opposite side the boughs of the elm trees swayed just perceptibly in the breeze, and their leaves stirred faintly in dense masses like women's hair. Surely somewhere nearby, but out of sight, there must be a stream with green pools where dace were swimming?

'Isn't there a stream somewhere near here?' he whispered.

'That's right, there is a stream. It's at the edge of the next field, actually. There are fish in it, great big ones. You can watch them lying in the pools under the willow trees, waving their tails.'

'It's the Golden Country—almost,' he murmured.

'The Golden Country?'

'It's nothing, really. A landscape I've seen sometimes in a dream.'

'Look!' whispered Julia.

A thrush had alighted on a bough not five metres away, almost at the level of their faces. Perhaps it had not seen them. It was in the sun, they in the shade. It spread out its wings, fitted them carefully into place again, ducked its head for a moment, as though making a sort of obeisance to the sun, and then began to pour forth a torrent of song. In the afternoon hush the volume of sound was startling. Winston and Julia clung together, fascinated. The music went on and on, minute after minute, with astonishing variations, never once repeating itself, almost as though the bird were deliberately showing off its virtuosity. Sometimes it stopped for a few seconds, spread out and resettled its wings, then swelled its speckled breast and again burst into song. Winston watched it with a sort of vague reverence. For whom, for what, was that bird singing? No mate, no rival was watching it. What made it sit at the edge of the lonely wood and pour its music into nothingness? He wondered whether after all there was a microphone hidden somewhere near. He and Julia had spoken only in low whispers, and it would not pick up what they had said, but it would pick up the thrush. Perhaps at the other end of the instrument some small, beetle-like man was listening intently—listening to that. But by degrees the flood of music drove all speculations out of his mind. It was as though it were a kind of liquid stuff that poured all over him and got mixed up with the sunlight that filtered through the leaves. He stopped thinking and merely felt. The girl's waist in the bend of his arm was soft and warm. He pulled her round so that they were breast to breast; her body seemed to melt into his. Wherever his hands moved it was all as yielding as water. Their mouths clung together; it was quite different from the hard kisses they had exchanged earlier. When they moved their faces apart again both of them sighed deeply. The bird took fright and fled with a clatter of wings.

Winston put his lips against her ear. '*now,*' he whispered.

'Not here,' she whispered back. 'Come back to the hide-out. It's safer.'

Quickly, with an occasional crackle of twigs, they threaded their way back to the clearing. When they were once inside the ring of saplings she turned and faced him. They were both breathing fast, but the smile had reappeared round the corners of her mouth. She stood looking at him for an instant, then felt at the zipper of her overalls. And, yes! it was almost as in his dream. Almost as swiftly as he had imagined it, she had torn her clothes off, and when she flung them aside it was with that same magnificent gesture by which a whole civilization seemed to be annihilated. Her body gleamed white in the sun. But for a moment he did not look at her body; his eyes were anchored by the freckled face with its faint, bold smile. He knelt down before her and took her hands in his.

'Have you done this before?'

'Of course. Hundreds of times—well, scores of times, anyway.'

'With Party members?'

'Yes, always with Party members.'

'With members of the Inner Party?'

'Not with those swine, no. But there's plenty that *would* if they got half a chance. They're not so holy as they make out.'

His heart leapt. Scores of times she had done it: he wished it had been hundreds—thousands. Anything that hinted at corruption always filled him with a wild hope. Who knew, perhaps the Party was rotten under the surface, its cult of strenuousness and self-denial simply a sham concealing iniquity. If he could have infected the whole lot of them with leprosy or syphilis, how gladly he would have done so! Anything to rot, to weaken, to undermine! He pulled her down so that they were kneeling face to face.

'Listen. The more men you've had, the more I love you. Do you understand that?'

'Yes, perfectly.'

'I hate purity, I hate goodness! I don't want any virtue to exist anywhere. I want everyone to be corrupt to the bones.'

'Well then, I ought to suit you, dear. I'm corrupt to the bones.'

'You like doing this? I don't mean simply me: I mean the thing in itself?'

'I adore it.'

That was above all what he wanted to hear. Not merely the love of one person but the animal instinct, the simple undifferentiated desire: that was the force that would tear the Party to pieces. He pressed her down upon the grass, among the fallen bluebells. This time there was no difficulty. Presently the rising and falling of their breasts slowed to normal speed, and in a sort of pleasant helplessness they fell apart. The sun seemed to have grown hotter. They were both sleepy. He reached out for the discarded overalls and pulled them partly over her. Almost immediately they fell asleep and slept for about half an hour.

Winston woke first. He sat up and watched the freckled face, still peacefully asleep, pillowed on the palm of her hand. Except for her mouth, you could not call her beautiful. There was a line or two round the eyes, if you looked closely. The short dark hair was extraordinarily thick and soft. It occurred to him that he still did not know her surname or where she lived.

The young, strong body, now helpless in sleep, awoke in him a pitying, protecting feeling. But the mindless tenderness that he had felt under the hazel tree, while the thrush was singing, had not quite come back. He pulled the overalls aside and studied her smooth white flank. In the old days, he thought, a man looked at a girl's body and saw that it was desirable, and that was the end of the story. But you could not have pure love or pure lust nowadays. No emotion was pure, because everything was mixed up with fear and hatred. Their embrace had been a battle, the climax a victory. It was a blow struck against the Party. It was a political act.

CHAPTER THREE

'We can come here once again,' said Julia. 'It's generally safe to use any hide-out twice. But not for another month or two, of course.'

As soon as she woke up her demeanour had changed. She became alert and business-like, put her clothes on, knotted the scarlet sash about her waist, and began arranging the details of the journey home. It seemed natural to leave this to her. She obviously had a practical cunning which Winston lacked, and she seemed also to have an exhaustive knowledge of the countryside round London, stored away from innumerable community hikes. The route she gave him was quite different from the one by which he had come, and brought him out at a different railway station. 'Never go home the same way as you went out,' she said, as though enunciating an important general principle. She would leave first, and Winston was to wait half an hour before following her.

She had named a place where they could meet after work, four evenings hence. It was a street in one of the poorer quarters, where there was an open market which was generally crowded and noisy. She would be hanging about among the stalls, pretending to be in search of shoelaces or sewing-thread. If she judged that the coast was clear she would blow her nose when he approached; otherwise he was to walk past her without recognition. But with luck, in the middle of the crowd, it would be safe to talk for a quarter of an hour and arrange another meeting.

'And now I must go,' she said as soon as he had mastered his instructions. 'I'm due back at nineteen-thirty. I've got to put in two hours for the Junior Anti-Sex League, handing out leaflets, or something. Isn't it bloody? Give me a brush-down, would you? Have I got any twigs in my hair? Are you sure? Then good-bye, my love, good-bye!'

She flung herself into his arms, kissed him almost violently, and a moment later pushed her way through the saplings and disappeared into the wood with very little noise. Even now he had not found out her surname or her address. However, it made no difference, for it was inconceivable that they could ever meet indoors or exchange any kind of written communication.

As it happened they never went back to the clearing in the wood. During the month of May there was only one further occasion on which they actually succeeded in making love. That was in another hiding-place known to Julia, the belfry of a ruinous church in an almost-deserted stretch of country where an atomic bomb had fallen thirty years earlier. It was a good hiding-place when once you got there, but the getting there was very dangerous. For the rest they could meet only in the streets, in a different place every evening and never for more than half an hour at a time. In the street it was usually possible to talk, after a fashion. As they drifted down the crowded pavements, not quite abreast and never looking at one another, they carried on a curious, intermittent conversation which flicked on and off like the beams of a lighthouse, suddenly nipped into silence by the approach of a Party uniform or the proximity of a telescreen, then taken up again minutes later in the middle of a sentence, then abruptly cut short as they parted at the agreed spot, then continued almost without introduction on the following day. Julia appeared to be quite used to this kind of conversation, which she called 'talking by instalments'. She was also surprisingly adept at speaking without moving her lips. Just once in almost a month of nightly meetings they managed to exchange a kiss. They were passing in silence down a side-street (Julia would never speak when they were away from the main streets) when there was a deafening roar, the earth heaved, and the air darkened, and Winston found himself lying on his side, bruised and terrified. A rocket bomb must have dropped quite near at hand. Suddenly he became aware of Julia's face a few centimetres from his own, deathly white, as white as chalk.

Even her lips were white. She was dead! He clasped her against him and found that he was kissing a live warm face. But there was some powdery stuff that got in the way of his lips. Both of their faces were thickly coated with plaster.

There were evenings when they reached their rendezvous and then had to walk past one another without a sign, because a patrol had just come round the corner or a helicopter was hovering overhead. Even if it had been less dangerous, it would still have been difficult to find time to meet. Winston's working week was sixty hours, Julia's was even longer, and their free days varied according to the pressure of work and did not often coincide. Julia, in any case, seldom had an evening completely free. She spent an astonishing amount of time in attending lectures and demonstrations, distributing literature for the Junior Anti-Sex League, preparing banners for Hate Week, making collections for the savings campaign, and such-like activities. It paid, she said, it was camouflage. If you kept the small rules, you could break the big ones. She even induced Winston to mortgage yet another of his evenings by enrolling himself for the part-time munition work which was done voluntarily by zealous Party members. So, one evening every week, Winston spent four hours of paralysing boredom, screwing together small bits of metal which were probably parts of bomb fuses, in a draughty, ill-lit workshop where the knocking of hammers mingled drearily with the music of the telescreens.

When they met in the church tower the gaps in their fragmentary conversation were filled up. It was a blazing afternoon. The air in the little square chamber above the bells was hot and stagnant, and smelt overpoweringly of pigeon dung. They sat talking for hours on the dusty, twig-littered floor, one or other of them getting up from time to time to cast a glance through the arrowslits and make sure that no one was coming.

Julia was twenty-six years old. She lived in a hostel with thirty other girls ('Always in the stink of women! How I hate women!' she said parenthetically), and she worked, as he had guessed, on the novel-writing machines in the Fiction Department. She enjoyed her work, which consisted chiefly in running and servicing a powerful but tricky electric motor. She was 'not clever', but was fond of using her hands and felt at home with machinery. She could describe the whole process of composing a novel, from the general directive issued by the Planning Committee down to the final touching-up by the Rewrite Squad. But she was not interested in the finished product. She 'didn't much care for reading,' she said. Books were just a commodity that had to be produced, like jam or bootlaces.

She had no memories of anything before the early sixties and the only person she had ever known who talked frequently of the days before the Revolution was a grandfather who had disappeared when she was eight. At school she had been captain of the hockey team and had won the gymnastics trophy two years running. She had been a troop-leader in the Spies and a branch secretary in the Youth League before joining the Junior Anti-Sex League. She had always borne an excellent character. She had even (an infallible mark of good reputation) been picked out to work in Pornosec, the sub-section of the Fiction Department which turned out cheap pornography for distribution among the proles. It was nicknamed Muck House by the people who worked in it, she remarked. There she had remained for a year, helping to produce booklets in sealed packets with titles like 'Spanking Stories' or 'One Night in a Girls' School', to be bought furtively by proletarian youths who were under the impression that they were buying something illegal.

'What are these books like?' said Winston curiously.

'Oh, ghastly rubbish. They're boring, really. They only have six plots, but they swap them round a bit. Of course I was only on the kaleidoscopes. I was never in the Rewrite Squad. I'm not literary, dear—not even enough for that.'

He learned with astonishment that all the workers in Pornosec, except the heads of the departments, were girls. The theory was that men, whose sex instincts were less controllable than those of women, were in greater danger of being corrupted by the filth they handled.

'They don't even like having married women there,' she added. Girls are always supposed to be so pure. Here's one who isn't, anyway.

She had had her first love-affair when she was sixteen, with a Party member of sixty who later committed suicide to avoid arrest. 'And a good job too,' said Julia, 'otherwise they'd have had my name out of him when he confessed.' Since then there had been various others. Life as she saw it was quite simple. You wanted a good time; 'they', meaning the Party, wanted to stop you having it; you broke the rules as best you could. She seemed to think it just as natural that 'they' should want to rob you of your pleasures as that you should want to avoid being caught. She hated the Party, and said so in the crudest words, but she made no general criticism of it. Except where it touched upon her own life she had no interest in Party doctrine. He noticed that she never used Newspeak words except the ones that had passed into everyday use. She had never heard of the Brotherhood, and refused to believe in its existence. Any kind of organized revolt against the Party, which was bound to be a failure, struck her as stupid. The clever thing was to break the rules and stay alive all the same. He wondered vaguely how many others like her there might be in the younger generation people who had grown up in the world of the Revolution, knowing nothing else, accepting the Party as something unalterable, like the sky, not rebelling against its authority but simply evading it, as a rabbit dodges a dog.

They did not discuss the possibility of getting married. It was too remote to be worth thinking about. No imaginable committee would ever sanction such a marriage even if Katharine, Winston's wife, could somehow have been got rid of. It was hopeless even as a daydream.

'What was she like, your wife?' said Julia.

'She was—do you know the Newspeak word *goodthinkful*? Meaning naturally orthodox, incapable of thinking a bad thought?'

'No, I didn't know the word, but I know the kind of person, right enough.'

He began telling her the story of his married life, but curiously enough she appeared to know the essential parts of it already. She described to him, almost as though she had seen or felt it, the stiffening of Katharine's body as soon as he touched her, the way in which she still seemed to be pushing him from her with all her strength, even when her arms were clasped tightly round him. With Julia he felt no difficulty in talking about such things: Katharine, in any case, had long ceased to be a painful memory and became merely a distasteful one.

'I could have stood it if it hadn't been for one thing,' he said. He told her about the frigid little ceremony that Katharine had forced him to go through on the same night every week. 'She hated it, but nothing would make her stop doing it. She used to call it—but you'll never guess.'

'Our duty to the Party,' said Julia promptly.

'How did you know that?'

'I've been at school too, dear. Sex talks once a month for the over-sixteens. And in the Youth Movement. They rub it into you for years. I dare say it works in a lot of cases. But of course you can never tell; people are such hypocrites.'

She began to enlarge upon the subject. With Julia, everything came back to her own sexuality. As soon as this was touched upon in any way she was capable of great acuteness. Unlike Winston, she had grasped the inner meaning of the Party's sexual puritanism. It was not merely that the sex instinct created a world of its own which was outside the Party's control and which therefore had to be destroyed if possible. What was more important was that sexual privation induced hysteria, which was desirable because it could be transformed into war-fever and leader-worship. The way she put it was:

'When you make love you're using up energy; and afterwards you feel happy and don't give a damn for anything. They can't bear you to feel like that. They want you to be bursting with energy all the time. All this marching up and down and cheering and waving flags is simply sex gone sour. If you're happy inside yourself, why should you get excited about

Big Brother and the Three-Year Plans and the Two Minutes Hate and all the rest of their bloody rot?'

That was very true, he thought. There was a direct intimate connection between chastity and political orthodoxy. For how could the fear, the hatred, and the lunatic credulity which the Party needed in its members be kept at the right pitch, except by bottling down some powerful instinct and using it as a driving force? The sex impulse was dangerous to the Party, and the Party had turned it to account. They had played a similar trick with the instinct of parenthood. The family could not actually be abolished, and, indeed, people were encouraged to be fond of their children, in almost the old-fashioned way. The children, on the other hand, were systematically turned against their parents and taught to spy on them and report their deviations. The family had become in effect an extension of the Thought Police. It was a device by means of which everyone could be surrounded night and day by informers who knew him intimately.

Abruptly his mind went back to Katharine. Katharine would unquestionably have denounced him to the Thought Police if she had not happened to be too stupid to detect the unorthodoxy of his opinions. But what really recalled her to him at this moment was the stifling heat of the afternoon, which had brought the sweat out on his forehead. He began telling Julia of something that had happened, or rather had failed to happen, on another sweltering summer afternoon, eleven years ago.

It was three or four months after they were married. They had lost their way on a community hike somewhere in Kent. They had only lagged behind the others for a couple of minutes, but they took a wrong turning, and presently found themselves pulled up short by the edge of an old chalk quarry. It was a sheer drop of ten or twenty metres, with boulders at the bottom. There was nobody of whom they could ask the way. As soon as she realized that they were lost Katharine became very uneasy. To be away from the noisy mob of hikers even for a moment gave her a feeling of wrong-doing. She wanted to hurry back by the way they had come and start searching in the other direction. But at this moment Winston noticed some tufts of loosestrife growing in the cracks of the cliff beneath them. One tuft was of two colours, magenta and brick-red, apparently growing on the same root. He had never seen anything of the kind before, and he called to Katharine to come and look at it.

'Look, Katharine! Look at those flowers. That clump down near the bottom. Do you see they're two different colours?'

She had already turned to go, but she did rather fretfully come back for a moment. She even leaned out over the cliff face to see where he was pointing. He was standing a little behind her, and he put his hand on her waist to steady her. At this moment it suddenly occurred to him how completely alone they were. There was not a human creature anywhere, not a leaf stirring, not even a bird awake. In a place like this the danger that there would be a hidden microphone was very small, and even if there was a microphone it would only pick up sounds. It was the hottest sleepiest hour of the afternoon. The sun blazed down upon them, the sweat tickled his face. And the thought struck him....

'Why didn't you give her a good shove?' said Julia. 'I would have.'

'Yes, dear, you would have. I would, if I'd been the same person then as I am now. Or perhaps I would—I'm not certain.'

'Are you sorry you didn't?'

'Yes. On the whole I'm sorry I didn't.'

They were sitting side by side on the dusty floor. He pulled her closer against him. Her head rested on his shoulder, the pleasant smell of her hair conquering the pigeon dung. She was very young, he thought, she still expected something from life, she did not understand that to push an inconvenient person over a cliff solves nothing.

'Actually it would have made no difference,' he said.

'Then why are you sorry you didn't do it?'

'Only because I prefer a positive to a negative. In this game that we're playing, we can't win. Some kinds of failure are better than other kinds, that's all.'

He felt her shoulders give a wriggle of dissent. She always contradicted him when he said anything of this kind. She would not accept it as a law of nature that the individual is always defeated. In a way she realized that she herself was doomed, that sooner or later the Thought Police would catch her and kill her, but with another part of her mind she believed that it was somehow possible to construct a secret world in which you could live as you chose. All you needed was luck and cunning and boldness. She did not understand that there was no such thing as happiness, that the only victory lay in the far future, long after you were dead, that from the moment of declaring war on the Party it was better to think of yourself as a corpse.

'We are the dead,' he said.

'We're not dead yet,' said Julia prosaically.

'Not physically. Six months, a year—five years, conceivably. I am afraid of death. You are young, so presumably you're more afraid of it than I am. Obviously we shall put it off as long as we can. But it makes very little difference. So long as human beings stay human, death and life are the same thing.'

'Oh, rubbish! Which would you sooner sleep with, me or a skeleton? Don't you enjoy being alive? Don't you like feeling: This is me, this is my hand, this is my leg, I'm real, I'm solid, I'm alive! Don't you like THIS?'

She twisted herself round and pressed her bosom against him. He could feel her breasts, ripe yet firm, through her overalls. Her body seemed to be pouring some of its youth and vigour into his.

'Yes, I like that,' he said.

'Then stop talking about dying. And now listen, dear, we've got to fix up about the next time we meet. We may as well go back to the place in the wood. We've given it a good long rest. But you must get there by a different way this time. I've got it all planned out. You take the train—but look, I'll draw it out for you.'

And in her practical way she scraped together a small square of dust, and with a twig from a pigeon's nest began drawing a map on the floor.

CHAPTER FOUR

Winston looked round the shabby little room above Mr Charrington's shop. Beside the window the enormous bed was made up, with ragged blankets and a coverless bolster. The old-fashioned clock with the twelve-hour face was ticking away on the mantelpiece. In the corner, on the gate-leg table, the glass paperweight which he had bought on his last visit gleamed softly out of the half-darkness.

In the fender was a battered tin oilstove, a saucepan and two cups, provided by Mr Charrington. Winston lit the burner and set a pan of water to boil. He had brought an envelope full of Victory Coffee and some saccharine tablets. The clock's hands said seven-twenty: it was nineteen-twenty really. She was coming at nineteen-thirty.

Folly, folly, his heart kept saying: conscious, gratuitous, suicidal folly. Of all the crimes that a Party member could commit, this one was the least possible to conceal. Actually the idea had first floated into his head in the form of a vision of the glass paperweight mirrored by the surface of the gate-leg table. As he had foreseen, Mr Charrington had made no difficulty about letting the room. He was obviously glad of the few dollars that it would bring him. Nor did he seem shocked or become offensively knowing when it was made clear that Winston wanted the room for the purpose of a love-affair. Instead he looked into the middle distance and spoke in generalities, with so delicate an air as to give the impression that he had become partly invisible. Privacy, he said, was a very valuable thing. Everyone wanted a place where they could be alone occasionally. And when they had such a place, it was only common courtesy in anyone else who knew of it to keep his knowledge to himself. He even, seeming almost to fade out of existence as he did so, added that there were two entries to the house, one of them through the back yard, which gave on an alley.

Under the window somebody was singing. Winston peeped out, secure in the protection of the muslin curtain. The June sun was still high in the sky, and in the sun-filled court below, a monstrous woman, solid as a Norman pillar, with brawny red forearms and a sacking apron strapped about her middle, was stumping to and fro between a washtub and a clothes line, pegging out a series of square white things which Winston recognized as babies' diapers. Whenever her mouth was not corked with clothes pegs she was singing in a powerful contralto:

It was only an 'opeless fancy.
It passed like an Ipril dye,
But a look an' a word an' the dreams they stirred!
They 'ave stolen my 'eart awye!

The tune had been haunting London for weeks past. It was one of countless similar songs published for the benefit of the proles by a sub-section of the Music Department. The words of these songs were composed without any human intervention whatever on an instrument known as a versificator. But the woman sang so tunefully as to turn the dreadful rubbish into an almost pleasant sound. He could hear the woman singing and the scrape of her shoes on the flagstones, and the cries of the children in the street, and somewhere in the far distance a faint roar of traffic, and yet the room seemed curiously silent, thanks to the absence of a telescreen.

Folly, folly, folly! he thought again. It was inconceivable that they could frequent this place for more than a few weeks without being caught. But the temptation of having a hiding-place that was truly their own, indoors and near at hand, had been too much for both of them. For some time after their visit to the church belfry it had been impossible to arrange meetings. Working hours had been drastically increased in anticipation of Hate Week. It was more than a month distant, but the enormous, complex preparations that it entailed were throwing extra work on to everybody. Finally both of them managed to secure a free afternoon on the same day. They had agreed to go back to the clearing in the wood. On the evening beforehand they met briefly in the street. As usual, Winston hardly looked at Julia as they drifted towards one another in the crowd, but from the short glance he gave her it seemed to him that she was paler than usual.

'It's all off,' she murmured as soon as she judged it safe to speak. 'Tomorrow, I mean.'

'What?'

'Tomorrow afternoon. I can't come.'

'Why not?'

'Oh, the usual reason. It's started early this time.'

For a moment he was violently angry. During the month that he had known her the nature of his desire for her had changed. At the beginning there had been little true sensuality in it. Their first love-making had been simply an act of the will. But after the second time it was different. The smell of her hair, the taste of her mouth, the feeling of her skin seemed to have got inside him, or into the air all round him. She had become a physical necessity, something that he not only wanted but felt that he had a right to. When she said that she could not come, he had the feeling that she was cheating him. But just at this moment the crowd pressed them together and their hands accidentally met. She gave the tips of his fingers a quick squeeze that seemed to invite not desire but affection. It struck him that when one lived with a woman this particular disappointment must be a normal, recurring event; and a deep tenderness, such as he had not felt for her before, suddenly took hold of him. He wished that they were a married couple of ten years' standing. He wished that he were walking through the streets with her just as they were doing now but openly and without fear, talking of trivialities and buying odds and ends for the household. He wished above all that they had some place where they could be alone together without feeling the obligation to make love every time they met. It was not actually at that moment, but at some time on the following day, that the idea of renting Mr Charrington's room had occurred to him. When he suggested it to Julia she had agreed with unexpected readiness. Both of them knew that it was lunacy. It was as though they were intentionally stepping nearer to their graves. As he sat waiting on the edge of the bed he thought again of the cellars of the Ministry of Love. It was curious how that predestined horror moved in and out of one's consciousness. There it lay, fixed in future times, preceding death as surely as 99 precedes 100. One could not avoid it, but one could perhaps postpone it: and yet instead, every now and again, by a conscious, wilful act, one chose to shorten the interval before it happened.

At this moment there was a quick step on the stairs. Julia burst into the room. She was carrying a tool-bag of coarse brown canvas, such as he had sometimes seen her carrying to and fro at the Ministry. He started forward to take her in his arms, but she disengaged herself rather hurriedly, partly because she was still holding the tool-bag.

'Half a second,' she said. 'Just let me show you what I've brought. Did you bring some of that filthy Victory Coffee? I thought you would. You can chuck it away again, because we shan't be needing it. Look here.'

She fell on her knees, threw open the bag, and tumbled out some spanners and a screwdriver that filled the top part of it. Underneath were a number of neat paper packets. The first packet that she passed to Winston had a strange and yet vaguely familiar feeling. It was filled with some kind of heavy, sand-like stuff which yielded wherever you touched it.

'It isn't sugar?' he said.

'Real sugar. Not saccharine, sugar. And here's a loaf of bread—proper white bread, not our bloody stuff—and a little pot of jam. And here's a tin of milk—but look! This is the one I'm really proud of. I had to wrap a bit of sacking round it, because—'

But she did not need to tell him why she had wrapped it up. The smell was already filling the room, a rich hot smell which seemed like an emanation from his early childhood, but which one did occasionally meet with even now, blowing down a passage-way before a door slammed, or diffusing itself mysteriously in a crowded street, sniffed for an instant and then lost again.

'It's coffee,' he murmured, 'real coffee.'

'It's Inner Party coffee. There's a whole kilo here,' she said.

'How did you manage to get hold of all these things?'

'It's all Inner Party stuff. There's nothing those swine don't have, nothing. But of course waiters and servants and people pinch things, and—look, I got a little packet of tea as well.'

Winston had squatted down beside her. He tore open a corner of the packet.

'It's real tea. Not blackberry leaves.'

'There's been a lot of tea about lately. They've captured India, or something,' she said vaguely. 'But listen, dear. I want you to turn your back on me for three minutes. Go and sit on the other side of the bed. Don't go too near the window. And don't turn round till I tell you.'

Winston gazed abstractedly through the muslin curtain. Down in the yard the red-armed woman was still marching to and fro between the washtub and the line. She took two more pegs out of her mouth and sang with deep feeling:

They sye that time 'eals all things,
They sye you can always forget;
But the smiles an' the tears acrorss the years
They twist my 'eart-strings yet!

She knew the whole drivelling song by heart, it seemed. Her voice floated upward with the sweet summer air, very tuneful, charged with a sort of happy melancholy. One had the feeling that she would have been perfectly content, if the June evening had been endless and the supply of clothes inexhaustible, to remain there for a thousand years, pegging out diapers and singing rubbish. It struck him as a curious fact that he had never heard a member of the Party singing alone and spontaneously. It would even have seemed slightly unorthodox, a dangerous eccentricity, like talking to oneself. Perhaps it was only when people were somewhere near the starvation level that they had anything to sing about.

'You can turn round now,' said Julia.

He turned round, and for a second almost failed to recognize her. What he had actually expected was to see her naked. But she was not naked. The transformation that had happened was much more surprising than that. She had painted her face.

She must have slipped into some shop in the proletarian quarters and bought herself a complete set of make-up materials. Her lips were deeply reddened, her cheeks rouged, her nose powdered; there was even a touch of something under the eyes to make them brighter. It was not very skilfully done, but Winston's standards in such matters were not high. He had never before seen or imagined a woman of the Party with cosmetics on her face. The improvement in her appearance was startling. With just a few dabs of colour in the right places she had become not only very much prettier, but, above all, far more feminine. Her short hair and boyish overalls merely added to the effect. As he took her in his arms a wave of synthetic violets flooded his nostrils. He remembered the half-darkness of a basement kitchen, and a woman's cavernous mouth. It was the very same scent that she had used; but at the moment it did not seem to matter.

'Scent too!' he said.

'Yes, dear, scent too. And do you know what I'm going to do next? I'm going to get hold of a real woman's frock from somewhere and wear it instead of these bloody trousers. I'll wear silk stockings and high-heeled shoes! In this room I'm going to be a woman, not a Party comrade.'

They flung their clothes off and climbed into the huge mahogany bed. It was the first time that he had stripped himself naked in her presence. Until now he had been too much ashamed of his pale and meagre body, with the varicose veins standing out on his calves and the discoloured patch over his ankle. There were no sheets, but the blanket they lay on was threadbare and smooth, and the size and springiness of the bed astonished both of them. 'It's sure to be full of bugs, but who cares?' said Julia. One never saw a double bed nowadays, except in the homes of the proles. Winston had occasionally slept in one in his boyhood: Julia had never been in one before, so far as she could remember.

Presently they fell asleep for a little while. When Winston woke up the hands of the clock had crept round to nearly nine. He did not stir, because Julia was sleeping with her head in the crook of his arm. Most of her make-up had transferred itself to his own face or the bolster, but a light stain of rouge still brought out the beauty of her cheekbone. A yellow ray from the sinking sun fell across the foot of the bed and lighted up the fireplace, where the water in the pan was boiling fast. Down in the yard the woman had stopped singing, but the faint shouts of children floated in from the street. He wondered vaguely whether in the abolished past it had been a normal experience to lie in bed like this, in the cool of a summer evening, a man and a woman with no clothes on, making love when they chose, talking of what they chose, not feeling any compulsion to get up, simply lying there and listening to peaceful sounds outside. Surely there could never have been a time when that seemed ordinary? Julia woke up, rubbed her eyes, and raised herself on her elbow to look at the oilstove.

'Half that water's boiled away,' she said. 'I'll get up and make some coffee in another moment. We've got an hour. What time do they cut the lights off at your flats?'

'Twenty-three thirty.'

'It's twenty-three at the hostel. But you have to get in earlier than that, because—Hi! Get out, you filthy brute!'

She suddenly twisted herself over in the bed, seized a shoe from the floor, and sent it hurtling into the corner with a boyish jerk of her arm, exactly as he had seen her fling the dictionary at Goldstein, that morning during the Two Minutes Hate.

'What was it?' he said in surprise.

'A rat. I saw him stick his beastly nose out of the wainscoting. There's a hole down there. I gave him a good fright, anyway.'

'Rats!' murmured Winston. 'In this room!'

'They're all over the place,' said Julia indifferently as she lay down again. 'We've even got them in the kitchen at the hostel. Some parts of London are swarming with them. Did you know they attack children? Yes, they do. In some of these streets a woman daren't leave a baby alone for two minutes. It's the great huge brown ones that do it. And the nasty thing is that the brutes always—'

'*Don't go on*!' said Winston, with his eyes tightly shut.

'Dearest! You've gone quite pale. What's the matter? Do they make you feel sick?'

'Of all horrors in the world—a rat!'

She pressed herself against him and wound her limbs round him, as though to reassure him with the warmth of her body. He did not reopen his eyes immediately. For several moments he had had the feeling of being back in a nightmare which had recurred from time to time throughout his life. It was always very much the same. He was standing in front of a wall of darkness, and on the other side of it there was something unendurable, something too dreadful to be faced. In the dream his deepest feeling was always one of self-deception, because he did in fact know what was behind the wall of darkness. With a deadly effort, like wrenching a piece out of his own brain, he could even have dragged the thing into the open. He always woke up without discovering what it was: but somehow it was connected with what Julia had been saying when he cut her short.

'I'm sorry,' he said, 'it's nothing. I don't like rats, that's all.'

'Don't worry, dear, we're not going to have the filthy brutes in here. I'll stuff the hole with a bit of sacking before we go. And next time we come here I'll bring some plaster and bung it up properly.'

Already the black instant of panic was half-forgotten. Feeling slightly ashamed of himself, he sat up against the bedhead. Julia got out of bed, pulled on her overalls, and made the coffee. The smell that rose from the saucepan was so powerful and exciting that they shut the window lest anybody outside should notice it and become inquisitive. What was even better than the taste of the coffee was the silky texture given to it by the sugar, a thing Winston had almost forgotten after years of saccharine. With one hand in her pocket and a piece of bread and jam in the other, Julia wandered about the room, glancing indifferently at the bookcase, pointing out the best way of repairing the gate-leg table, plumping herself down in the ragged arm-chair to see if it was comfortable, and examining the absurd twelve-hour clock with a sort of tolerant amusement. She brought the glass paperweight over to the bed to have a look at it in a better light. He took it out of her hand, fascinated, as always, by the soft, rainwatery appearance of the glass.

'What is it, do you think?' said Julia.

'I don't think it's anything—I mean, I don't think it was ever put to any use. That's what I like about it. It's a little chunk of history that they've forgotten to alter. It's a message from a hundred years ago, if one knew how to read it.'

'And that picture over there'—she nodded at the engraving on the opposite wall—'would that be a hundred years old?'

'More. Two hundred, I dare say. One can't tell. It's impossible to discover the age of anything nowadays.'

She went over to look at it. 'Here's where that brute stuck his nose out,' she said, kicking the wainscoting immediately below the picture. 'What is this place? I've seen it before somewhere.'

'It's a church, or at least it used to be. St Clement's Dane its name was.' The fragment of rhyme that Mr Charrington had taught him came back into his head, and he added half-nostalgically: "Oranges and lemons, say the bells of St Clement's!"

To his astonishment she capped the line:

'You owe me three farthings, say the bells of St Martin's,

When will you pay me? say the bells of Old Bailey....'

'I can't remember how it goes on after that. But anyway I remember it ends up, "Here comes a candle to light you to bed, here comes a chopper to chop off your head!"'

It was like the two halves of a countersign. But there must be another line after 'the bells of Old Bailey'. Perhaps it could be dug out of Mr Charrington's memory, if he were suitably prompted.

'Who taught you that?' he said.

'My grandfather. He used to say it to me when I was a little girl. He was vaporized when I was eight—at any rate, he disappeared. I wonder what a lemon was,' she added inconsequently. 'I've seen oranges. They're a kind of round yellow fruit with a thick skin.'

'I can remember lemons,' said Winston. 'They were quite common in the 'fifties. They were so sour that it set your teeth on edge even to smell them.'

'I bet that picture's got bugs behind it,' said Julia. 'I'll take it down and give it a good clean some day. I suppose it's almost time we were leaving. I must start washing this paint off. What a bore! I'll get the lipstick off your face afterwards.'

Winston did not get up for a few minutes more. The room was darkening. He turned over towards the light and lay gazing into the glass paperweight. The inexhaustibly interesting thing was not the fragment of coral but the interior of the glass itself. There was such a depth of it, and yet it was almost as transparent as air. It was as though the surface of the glass had been the arch of the sky, enclosing a tiny world with its atmosphere complete. He had the feeling that he could get inside it, and that in fact he was inside it, along with the mahogany bed and the gate leg table, and the clock and the steel engraving and the paperweight itself. The paperweight was the room he was in, and the coral was Julia's life and his own, fixed in a sort of eternity at the heart of the crystal.

CHAPTER FIVE

Syme had vanished. A morning came, and he was missing from work: a few thoughtless people commented on his absence. On the next day nobody mentioned him. On the third day Winston went into the vestibule of the Records Department to look at the notice-board. One of the notices carried a printed list of the members of the Chess Committee, of whom Syme had been one. It looked almost exactly as it had looked before—nothing had been crossed out—but it was one name shorter. It was enough. Syme had ceased to exist: he had never existed.

The weather was baking hot. In the labyrinthine Ministry the windowless, air-conditioned rooms kept their normal temperature, but outside the pavements scorched one's feet and the stench of the Tubes at the rush hours was a horror. The preparations for Hate Week were in full swing, and the staffs of all the Ministries were working overtime. Processions, meetings, military parades, lectures, waxworks, displays, film shows, telescreen programmes all had to be organized; stands had to be erected, effigies built, slogans coined, songs written, rumours circulated, photographs faked. Julia's unit in the Fiction Department had been taken off the production of novels and was rushing out a series of atrocity pamphlets. Winston, in addition to his regular work, spent long periods every day in going through back files of the *Times* and altering and embellishing news items which were to be quoted in speeches. Late at night, when crowds of rowdy proles roamed the streets, the town had a curiously febrile air. The rocket bombs crashed oftener than ever, and sometimes in the far distance there were enormous explosions which no one could explain and about which there were wild rumours.

The new tune which was to be the theme-song of Hate Week (the Hate Song, it was called) had already been composed and was being endlessly plugged on the telescreens. It had a savage, barking rhythm which could not exactly be called music, but resembled the beating of a drum. Roared out by hundreds of voices to the tramp of marching feet, it was terrifying. The proles had taken a fancy to it, and in the midnight streets it competed with the still-popular 'It was only a hopeless fancy'. The Parsons children played it at all hours of the night and day, unbearably, on a comb and a piece of toilet paper. Winston's evenings were fuller than ever. Squads of volunteers, organized by Parsons, were preparing the street for Hate Week, stitching banners, painting posters, erecting flagstaffs on the roofs, and perilously slinging wires across the street for the reception of streamers. Parsons boasted that Victory Mansions alone would display four hundred metres of bunting. He was in his native element and as happy as a lark. The heat and the manual work had even given him a pretext for reverting to shorts and an open shirt in the evenings. He was everywhere at once, pushing, pulling, sawing, hammering, improvising, jollying everyone along with comradely exhortations and giving out from every fold of his body what seemed an inexhaustible supply of acrid-smelling sweat.

A new poster had suddenly appeared all over London. It had no caption, and represented simply the monstrous figure of a Eurasian soldier, three or four metres high, striding forward with expressionless Mongolian face and enormous boots, a submachine gun pointed from his hip. From whatever angle you looked at the poster, the muzzle of the gun, magnified by the foreshortening, seemed to be pointed straight at you. The thing had been plastered on every blank space on every wall, even outnumbering the portraits of Big Brother. The proles, normally apathetic about the war, were being lashed into one of their periodical frenzies of patriotism. As though to harmonize with the general mood, the rocket bombs had been killing larger numbers of people than usual. One fell on a crowded film theatre in Stepney, burying several hundred victims among the ruins. The whole population of the neighbourhood turned out for a long, trailing funeral which went on for hours and was in effect an indignation meeting. Another bomb fell on a piece of waste ground which was used as a playground and several dozen children were blown to pieces. There were further angry demonstrations, Goldstein was burned in effigy, hundreds of copies of the poster of the Eurasian soldier were torn down and added to the flames, and a number of shops were looted in the turmoil; then a rumour flew round that spies were directing the rocket bombs by means of wireless waves, and an old couple who were suspected of being of foreign extraction had their house set on fire and perished of suffocation.

In the room over Mr Charrington's shop, when they could get there, Julia and Winston lay side by side on a stripped bed under the open window, naked for the sake of coolness. The rat had never come back, but the bugs had multiplied hideously in the heat. It did not seem to matter. Dirty or clean, the room was paradise. As soon as they arrived they would sprinkle everything with pepper bought on the black market, tear off their clothes, and make love with sweating bodies, then fall asleep and wake to find that the bugs had rallied and were massing for the counter-attack.

Four, five, six—seven times they met during the month of June. Winston had dropped his habit of drinking gin at all hours. He seemed to have lost the need for it. He had grown fatter, his varicose ulcer had subsided, leaving only a brown stain on the skin above his ankle, his fits of coughing in the early morning had stopped. The process of life had ceased to be intolerable, he had no longer any impulse to make faces at the telescreen or shout curses at the top of his voice. Now that they had a secure hiding-place, almost a home, it did not even seem a hardship that they could only meet infrequently and for a couple of hours at a time. What mattered was that the room over the junk-shop should exist. To know that it was there, inviolate, was almost the same as being in it. The room was a world, a pocket of the past where extinct animals could walk. Mr Charrington, thought Winston, was another extinct animal. He usually stopped to talk with Mr Charrington for a few minutes on his way upstairs. The old man seemed seldom or never to go out of doors, and on the other hand to have almost no customers. He led a ghostlike existence between the tiny, dark shop, and an even tinier back kitchen where he prepared his meals and which contained, among other things, an unbelievably ancient gramophone with an enormous horn. He seemed glad of the opportunity to talk. Wandering about among his worthless stock, with his long nose and thick spectacles and his bowed shoulders in the velvet jacket, he had always vaguely the air of being a collector rather than a tradesman. With a sort of faded enthusiasm he would finger this scrap of rubbish or that—a china bottle-stopper, the painted lid of a broken snuffbox, a pinchbeck locket containing a strand of some long-dead baby's hair—never asking that Winston should buy it, merely that he should admire it. To talk to him was like listening to the tinkling of a worn-out musical-box. He had dragged out from the corners of his memory some more fragments of forgotten rhymes. There was one about four and twenty blackbirds, and another about a cow with a crumpled horn, and another about the death of poor Cock Robin. 'It just occurred to me you might be interested,' he would say with a deprecating little laugh whenever he produced a new fragment. But he could never recall more than a few lines of any one rhyme.

Both of them knew—in a way, it was never out of their minds that what was now happening could not last long. There were times when the fact of impending death seemed as palpable as the bed they lay on, and they would cling together with a sort of despairing sensuality, like a damned soul grasping at his last morsel of pleasure when the clock is within five minutes of striking. But there were also times when they had the illusion not only of safety but of permanence. So long as they were actually in this room, they both felt, no harm could come to them. Getting there was difficult and dangerous, but the room itself was sanctuary. It was as when Winston had gazed into the heart of the paperweight, with the feeling that it would be possible to get inside that glassy world, and that once inside it time could be arrested. Often they gave themselves up to daydreams of escape. Their luck would hold indefinitely, and they would carry on their intrigue, just like this, for the remainder of their natural lives. Or Katharine would die, and by subtle manoeuvrings Winston and Julia would succeed in getting married. Or they would commit suicide together. Or they would disappear, alter themselves out of recognition, learn to speak with proletarian accents, get jobs in a factory and live out their lives undetected in a back-street. It was all nonsense, as they both knew. In reality there was no escape. Even the one plan that was practicable, suicide, they had no intention of carrying out. To hang on from day to day and from week to week, spinning out a present that had no future, seemed an unconquerable instinct, just as one's lungs will always draw the next breath so long as there is air available.

Sometimes, too, they talked of engaging in active rebellion against the Party, but with no notion of how to take the first step. Even if the fabulous Brotherhood was a reality, there still remained the difficulty of finding one's way into it. He told her of the strange intimacy that existed, or seemed to exist, between himself and O'Brien, and of the impulse he sometimes felt, simply to walk into O'Brien's presence, announce that he was the enemy of the Party, and demand his help. Curiously enough, this did not strike her as an impossibly rash thing to do. She was used to judging people by their faces, and it seemed natural to her that Winston should believe O'Brien to be trustworthy on the strength of a single flash of the eyes. Moreover she took it for granted that everyone, or nearly everyone, secretly hated the Party and would break the rules if he thought it safe to do so. But she refused to believe that widespread, organized opposition existed or could exist. The tales about Goldstein and his underground army, she said, were simply a lot of rubbish which the Party had invented for its own purposes and which you had to pretend to believe in. Times beyond number, at Party rallies and spontaneous demonstrations, she had shouted at the top of her voice for the execution of people whose names she had never heard and in whose supposed crimes she had not the faintest belief. When public trials were happening she had taken her place in the detachments from the Youth League who surrounded the courts from morning to night, chanting at intervals 'Death to the traitors!' During the Two

Minutes Hate she always excelled all others in shouting insults at Goldstein. Yet she had only the dimmest idea of who Goldstein was and what doctrines he was supposed to represent. She had grown up since the Revolution and was too young to remember the ideological battles of the fifties and sixties. Such a thing as an independent political movement was outside her imagination: and in any case the Party was invincible. It would always exist, and it would always be the same. You could only rebel against it by secret disobedience or, at most, by isolated acts of violence such as killing somebody or blowing something up.

In some ways she was far more acute than Winston, and far less susceptible to Party propaganda. Once when he happened in some connexion to mention the war against Eurasia, she startled him by saying casually that in her opinion the war was not happening. The rocket bombs which fell daily on London were probably fired by the Government of Oceania itself, 'just to keep people frightened'. This was an idea that had literally never occurred to him. She also stirred a sort of envy in him by telling him that during the Two Minutes Hate her great difficulty was to avoid bursting out laughing. But she only questioned the teachings of the Party when they in some way touched upon her own life. Often she was ready to accept the official mythology, simply because the difference between truth and falsehood did not seem important to her. She believed, for instance, having learnt it at school, that the Party had invented aeroplanes. (In his own schooldays, Winston remembered, in the late fifties, it was only the helicopter that the Party claimed to have invented; a dozen years later, when Julia was at school, it was already claiming the aeroplane; one generation more, and it would be claiming the steam engine.) And when he told her that aeroplanes had been in existence before he was born and long before the Revolution, the fact struck her as totally uninteresting. After all, what did it matter who had invented aeroplanes? It was rather more of a shock to him when he discovered from some chance remark that she did not remember that Oceania, four years ago, had been at war with Eastasia and at peace with Eurasia. It was true that she regarded the whole war as a sham: but apparently she had not even noticed that the name of the enemy had changed. 'I thought we'd always been at war with Eurasia,' she said vaguely. It frightened him a little. The invention of aeroplanes dated from long before her birth, but the switchover in the war had happened only four years ago, well after she was grown up. He argued with her about it for perhaps a quarter of an hour. In the end he succeeded in forcing her memory back until she did dimly recall that at one time Eastasia and not Eurasia had been the enemy. But the issue still struck her as unimportant. 'Who cares?' she said impatiently. 'It's always one bloody war after another, and one knows the news is all lies anyway.'

Sometimes he talked to her of the Records Department and the impudent forgeries that he committed there. Such things did not appear to horrify her. She did not feel the abyss opening beneath her feet at the thought of lies becoming truths. He told her the story of Jones, Aaronson, and Rutherford and the momentous slip of paper which he had once held between his fingers. It did not make much impression on her. At first, indeed, she failed to grasp the point of the story.

'Were they friends of yours?' she said.

'No, I never knew them. They were Inner Party members. Besides, they were far older men than I was. They belonged to the old days, before the Revolution. I barely knew them by sight.'

'Then what was there to worry about? People are being killed off all the time, aren't they?'

He tried to make her understand. 'This was an exceptional case. It wasn't just a question of somebody being killed. Do you realize that the past, starting from yesterday, has been actually abolished? If it survives anywhere, it's in a few solid objects with no words attached to them, like that lump of glass there. Already we know almost literally nothing about the Revolution and the years before the Revolution. Every record has been destroyed or falsified, every book has been rewritten, every picture has been repainted, every statue and street and building has been renamed, every date has been altered. And that process is continuing day by day and minute by minute. History has stopped. Nothing exists except an endless present in which the Party is always right. I *know*, of course, that the past is falsified, but it would never be possible for me to prove it, even when I did the falsification myself. After the thing is done, no evidence ever remains. The only evidence is inside my own mind, and I don't know with any certainty that any other human being shares my memories. Just in that one instance, in my whole life, I did possess actual concrete evidence *after* the event—years after it.'

'And what good was that?'

'It was no good, because I threw it away a few minutes later. But if the same thing happened today, I should keep it.'

'Well, I wouldn't!' said Julia. 'I'm quite ready to take risks, but only for something worth while, not for bits of old newspaper. What could you have done with it even if you had kept it?'

'Not much, perhaps. But it was evidence. It might have planted a few doubts here and there, supposing that I'd dared to show it to anybody. I don't imagine that we can alter anything in our own lifetime. But one can imagine little knots of resistance springing up here and there—small groups of people banding themselves together, and gradually growing, and even leaving a few records behind, so that the next generations can carry on where we leave off.'

'I'm not interested in the next generation, dear. I'm interested in US.'

'You're only a rebel from the waist downwards,' he told her.

She thought this brilliantly witty and flung her arms round him in delight.

In the ramifications of party doctrine she had not the faintest interest. Whenever he began to talk of the principles of Ingsoc, doublethink, the mutability of the past, and the denial of objective reality, and to use Newspeak words, she became bored and confused and said that she never paid any attention to that kind of thing. One knew that it was all rubbish, so why let oneself be worried by it? She knew when to cheer and when to boo, and that was all one needed. If he persisted in talking of such subjects, she had a disconcerting habit of falling asleep. She was one of those people who can go to sleep at any hour and in any position. Talking to her, he realized how easy it was to present an appearance of orthodoxy while having no grasp whatever of what orthodoxy meant. In a way, the world-view of the Party imposed itself most successfully on people incapable of understanding it. They could be made to accept the most flagrant violations of reality, because they never fully grasped the enormity of what was demanded of them, and were not sufficiently interested in public events to notice what was happening. By lack of understanding they remained sane. They simply swallowed everything, and what they swallowed did them no harm, because it left no residue behind, just as a grain of corn will pass undigested through the body of a bird.

CHAPTER SIX

It had happened at last. The expected message had come. All his life, it seemed to him, he had been waiting for this to happen.

He was walking down the long corridor at the Ministry and he was almost at the spot where Julia had slipped the note into his hand when he became aware that someone larger than himself was walking just behind him. The person, whoever it was, gave a small cough, evidently as a prelude to speaking. Winston stopped abruptly and turned. It was O'Brien.

At last they were face to face, and it seemed that his only impulse was to run away. His heart bounded violently. He would have been incapable of speaking. O'Brien, however, had continued forward in the same movement, laying a friendly hand for a moment on Winston's arm, so that the two of them were walking side by side. He began speaking with the peculiar grave courtesy that differentiated him from the majority of Inner Party members.

'I had been hoping for an opportunity of talking to you,' he said. 'I was reading one of your Newspeak articles in the *Times* the other day. You take a scholarly interest in Newspeak, I believe?'

Winston had recovered part of his self-possession. 'Hardly scholarly,' he said. 'I'm only an amateur. It's not my subject. I have never had anything to do with the actual construction of the language.'

'But you write it very elegantly,' said O'Brien. 'That is not only my own opinion. I was talking recently to a friend of yours who is certainly an expert. His name has slipped my memory for the moment.'

Again Winston's heart stirred painfully. It was inconceivable that this was anything other than a reference to Syme. But Syme was not only dead, he was abolished, an *unperson*. Any identifiable reference to him would have been mortally dangerous. O'Brien's remark must obviously have been intended as a signal, a codeword. By sharing a small act of thoughtcrime he had turned the two of them into accomplices. They had continued to stroll slowly down the corridor, but now O'Brien halted. With the curious, disarming friendliness that he always managed to put in to the gesture he resettled his spectacles on his nose. Then he went on:

'What I had really intended to say was that in your article I noticed you had used two words which have become obsolete. But they have only become so very recently. Have you seen the tenth edition of the Newspeak Dictionary?'

'No,' said Winston. 'I didn't think it had been issued yet. We are still using the ninth in the Records Department.'

'The tenth edition is not due to appear for some months, I believe. But a few advance copies have been circulated. I have one myself. It might interest you to look at it, perhaps?'

'Very much so,' said Winston, immediately seeing where this tended.

'Some of the new developments are most ingenious. The reduction in the number of verbs—that is the point that will appeal to you, I think. Let me see, shall I send a messenger to you with the dictionary? But I am afraid I invariably forget anything of that kind. Perhaps you could pick it up at my flat at some time that suited you? Wait. Let me give you my address.'

They were standing in front of a telescreen. Somewhat absent-mindedly O'Brien felt two of his pockets and then produced a small leather-covered notebook and a gold ink-pencil. Immediately beneath the telescreen, in such a position that anyone who was watching at the other end of the instrument could read what he was writing, he scribbled an address, tore out the page and handed it to Winston.

'I am usually at home in the evenings,' he said. 'If not, my servant will give you the dictionary.'

He was gone, leaving Winston holding the scrap of paper, which this time there was no need to conceal. Nevertheless he carefully memorized what was written on it, and some hours later dropped it into the memory hole along with a mass of other papers.

They had been talking to one another for a couple of minutes at the most. There was only one meaning that the episode could possibly have. It had been contrived as a way of letting Winston know O'Brien's address. This was necessary, because except by direct enquiry it was never possible to discover where anyone lived. There were no directories of any kind. 'If you ever want to see me, this is where I can be found,' was what O'Brien had been saying to him. Perhaps there would even be a message concealed somewhere in the dictionary. But at any rate, one thing was certain. The conspiracy that he had dreamed of did exist, and he had reached the outer edges of it.

He knew that sooner or later he would obey O'Brien's summons. Perhaps tomorrow, perhaps after a long delay—he was not certain. What was happening was only the working-out of a process that had started years ago. The first step had been a secret, involuntary thought, the second had been the opening of the diary. He had moved from thoughts to words, and now from words to actions. The last step was something that would happen in the Ministry of Love. He had accepted it. The end was contained in the beginning. But it was frightening: or, more exactly, it was like a foretaste of death, like being a little less alive. Even while he was speaking to O'Brien, when the meaning of the words had sunk in, a chilly shuddering feeling had taken possession of his body. He had the sensation of stepping into the dampness of a grave, and it was not much better because he had always known that the grave was there and waiting for him.

CHAPTER SEVEN

Winston had woken up with his eyes full of tears. Julia rolled sleepily against him, murmuring something that might have been 'What's the matter?'

'I dreamt—' he began, and stopped short. It was too complex to be put into words. There was the dream itself, and there was a memory connected with it that had swum into his mind in the few seconds after waking.

He lay back with his eyes shut, still sodden in the atmosphere of the dream. It was a vast, luminous dream in which his whole life seemed to stretch out before him like a landscape on a summer evening after rain. It had all occurred inside the glass paperweight, but the surface of the glass was the dome of the sky, and inside the dome everything was flooded with clear soft light in which one could see into interminable distances. The dream had also been comprehended by—indeed, in some sense it had consisted in—a gesture of the arm made by his mother, and made again thirty years later by the Jewish woman he had seen on the news film, trying to shelter the small boy from the bullets, before the helicopter blew them both to pieces.

'Do you know,' he said, 'that until this moment I believed I had murdered my mother?'

'Why did you murder her?' said Julia, almost asleep.

'I didn't murder her. Not physically.'

In the dream he had remembered his last glimpse of his mother, and within a few moments of waking the cluster of small events surrounding it had all come back. It was a memory that he must have deliberately pushed out of his consciousness over many years. He was not certain of the date, but he could not have been less than ten years old, possibly twelve, when it had happened.

His father had disappeared some time earlier, how much earlier he could not remember. He remembered better the rackety, uneasy circumstances of the time: the periodical panics about air-raids and the sheltering in Tube stations, the piles of rubble everywhere, the unintelligible proclamations posted at street corners, the gangs of youths in shirts all the same colour, the enormous queues outside the bakeries, the intermittent machine-gun fire in the distance—above all, the fact that there was never enough to eat. He remembered long afternoons spent with other boys in scrounging round dustbins and rubbish heaps, picking out the ribs of cabbage leaves, potato peelings, sometimes even scraps of stale breadcrust from which they carefully scraped away the cinders; and also in waiting for the passing of trucks which travelled over a certain route and were known to carry cattle feed, and which, when they jolted over the bad patches in the road, sometimes spilt a few fragments of oil-cake.

When his father disappeared, his mother did not show any surprise or any violent grief, but a sudden change came over her. She seemed to have become completely spiritless. It was evident even to Winston that she was waiting for something that she knew must happen. She did everything that was needed—cooked, washed, mended, made the bed, swept the floor, dusted the mantelpiece—always very slowly and with a curious lack of superfluous motion, like an artist's lay-figure moving of its own accord. Her large shapely body seemed to relapse naturally into stillness. For hours at a time she would sit almost immobile on the bed, nursing his young sister, a tiny, ailing, very silent child of two or three, with a face made simian by thinness. Very occasionally she would take Winston in her arms and press him against her for a long time without saying anything. He was aware, in spite of his youthfulness and selfishness, that this was somehow connected with the never-mentioned thing that was about to happen.

He remembered the room where they lived, a dark, close-smelling room that seemed half filled by a bed with a white counterpane. There was a gas ring in the fender, and a shelf where food was kept, and on the landing outside there was a brown earthenware sink, common to several rooms. He remembered his mother's statuesque body bending over the gas ring to stir at something in a saucepan. Above all he remembered his continuous hunger, and the fierce sordid battles at mealtimes. He would ask his mother naggingly, over and over again, why there was not more food, he would shout and storm at her (he even remembered the tones of his voice, which was beginning to break prematurely and sometimes boomed in a peculiar way), or he would attempt a snivelling note of pathos in his efforts to get more than his share. His mother was quite ready to give him more than his share. She took it for granted that he, 'the boy', should have the biggest portion; but however much she gave him he invariably demanded more. At every meal she would beseech him not to be selfish and to remember that his little sister was sick and also needed food, but it was no use. He would cry out with rage when she stopped ladling, he would try to wrench the saucepan and spoon out of her hands, he would grab bits from his sister's plate. He knew that he was starving the other two, but he could not help it; he even felt that he had a right to do it. The clamorous hunger in his belly seemed to justify him. Between meals, if his mother did not stand guard, he was constantly pilfering at the wretched store of food on the shelf.

One day a chocolate ration was issued. There had been no such issue for weeks or months past. He remembered quite clearly that precious little morsel of chocolate. It was a two-ounce slab (they still talked about ounces in those days) between the three of them. It was obvious that it ought to be divided into three equal parts. Suddenly, as though he were listening to somebody else, Winston heard himself demanding in a loud booming voice that he should be given the whole piece. His mother told him not to be greedy. There was a long, nagging argument that went round and round, with shouts, whines, tears, remonstrances, bargainings. His tiny sister, clinging to her mother with both hands, exactly like a baby monkey, sat looking over her shoulder at him with large, mournful eyes. In the end his mother broke off three-quarters of the chocolate and gave it to Winston, giving the other quarter to his sister. The little girl took hold of it and looked at it dully, perhaps not knowing what it was. Winston stood watching her for a moment. Then with a sudden swift spring he had snatched the piece of chocolate out of his sister's hand and was fleeing for the door.

'Winston, Winston!' his mother called after him. 'Come back! Give your sister back her chocolate!'

He stopped, but did not come back. His mother's anxious eyes were fixed on his face. Even now he was thinking about the thing, he did not know what it was that was on the point of happening. His sister, conscious of having been robbed of something, had set up a feeble wail. His mother drew her arm round the child and pressed its face against her breast. Something in the gesture told him that his sister was dying. He turned and fled down the stairs, with the chocolate growing sticky in his hand.

He never saw his mother again. After he had devoured the chocolate he felt somewhat ashamed of himself and hung about in the streets for several hours, until hunger drove him home. When he came back his mother had disappeared. This was already becoming normal at that time. Nothing was gone from the room except his mother and his sister. They had not taken any clothes, not even his mother's overcoat. To this day he did not know with any certainty that his mother was dead. It was perfectly possible that she had merely been sent to a forced-labour camp. As for his sister, she might have been removed, like Winston himself, to one of the colonies for homeless children (Reclamation Centres, they were called) which had grown up as a result of the civil war, or she might have been sent to the labour camp along with his mother, or simply left somewhere or other to die.

The dream was still vivid in his mind, especially the enveloping protecting gesture of the arm in which its whole meaning seemed to be contained. His mind went back to another dream of two months ago. Exactly as his mother had sat on the dingy white-quilted bed, with the child clinging to her, so she had sat in the sunken ship, far underneath him, and drowning deeper every minute, but still looking up at him through the darkening water.

He told Julia the story of his mother's disappearance. Without opening her eyes she rolled over and settled herself into a more comfortable position.

'I expect you were a beastly little swine in those days,' she said indistinctly. 'All children are swine.'

'Yes. But the real point of the story—'

From her breathing it was evident that she was going off to sleep again. He would have liked to continue talking about his mother. He did not suppose, from what he could remember of her, that she had been an unusual woman, still less an intelligent one; and yet she had possessed a kind of nobility, a kind of purity, simply because the standards that she obeyed were private ones. Her feelings were her own, and could not be altered from outside. It would not have occurred to her that an action which is ineffectual thereby becomes meaningless. If you loved someone, you loved him, and when you had nothing else to give, you still gave him love. When the last of the chocolate was gone, his mother had clasped the child in her arms. It was no use, it changed nothing, it did not produce more chocolate, it did not avert the child's death or her own; but it seemed natural to her to do it. The refugee woman in the boat had also covered the little boy with her arm, which was no more use against the bullets than a sheet of paper. The terrible thing that the Party had done was to persuade you that mere impulses, mere feelings, were of no account, while at the same time robbing you of all power over the material world. When once you were in the grip of the Party, what you felt or did not feel, what you did or refrained from doing, made literally no difference. Whatever happened you vanished, and neither you nor your actions were ever heard of again. You were lifted clean out of the stream of history. And yet to the people of only two generations ago this would not have seemed all-important, because they were not attempting to alter history. They were governed by private loyalties which they did not question. What mattered were individual relationships, and a completely helpless gesture, an embrace, a tear, a word spoken to a dying man, could have value in itself. The proles, it suddenly occurred to him, had remained in this condition. They were not loyal to a party or a country or an idea, they were loyal to one another. For the first time in his life he did not despise the proles or think of them merely as an inert force which would one day spring to life and regenerate the world. The proles had stayed human. They had not become hardened inside. They had held on to the primitive emotions which he himself had to re-learn by conscious effort. And in thinking this he remembered, without apparent relevance, how a few weeks ago he had seen a severed hand lying on the pavement and had kicked it into the gutter as though it had been a cabbage-stalk.

'The proles are human beings,' he said aloud. 'We are not human.'

'Why not?' said Julia, who had woken up again.

He thought for a little while. 'Has it ever occurred to you,' he said, 'that the best thing for us to do would be simply to walk out of here before it's too late, and never see each other again?'

'Yes, dear, it has occurred to me, several times. But I'm not going to do it, all the same.'

'We've been lucky,' he said 'but it can't last much longer. You're young. You look normal and innocent. If you keep clear of people like me, you might stay alive for another fifty years.'

'No. I've thought it all out. What you do, I'm going to do. And don't be too downhearted. I'm rather good at staying alive.'

'We may be together for another six months-a year—there's no knowing. At the end we're certain to be apart. Do you realize how utterly alone we shall be? When once they get hold of us there will be nothing, literally nothing, that either of us can do for the other. If I confess, they'll shoot you, and if I refuse to confess, they'll shoot you just the same. Nothing that I can do or say, or stop myself from saying, will put off your death for as much as five minutes. Neither of us will even know whether the other is alive or dead. We shall be utterly without power of any kind. The one thing that matters is that we shouldn't betray one another, although even that can't make the slightest difference.'

'If you mean confessing,' she said, 'we shall do that, right enough. Everybody always confesses. You can't help it. They torture you.'

'I don't mean confessing. Confession is not betrayal. What you say or do doesn't matter: only feelings matter. If they could make me stop loving you—that would be the real betrayal.'

She thought it over. 'They can't do that,' she said finally. 'It's the one thing they can't do. They can make you say anything—*anything*—but they can't make you believe it. They can't get inside you.'

'No,' he said a little more hopefully, 'no; that's quite true. They can't get inside you. If you can *feel* that staying human is worthwhile, even when it can't have any result whatever, you've beaten them.'

He thought of the telescreen with its never-sleeping ear. They could spy upon you night and day, but if you kept your head you could still outwit them. With all their cleverness they had never mastered the secret of finding out what another human being was thinking. Perhaps that was less true when you were actually in their hands. One did not know what happened inside the Ministry of Love, but it was possible to guess: tortures, drugs, delicate instruments that registered your nervous reactions, gradual wearing-down by sleeplessness and solitude and persistent questioning. Facts, at any rate, could not be kept hidden. They could be tracked down by enquiry, they could be squeezed out of you by torture. But if the object was not to stay alive but to stay human, what difference did it ultimately make? They could not alter your feelings: for that matter you could not alter them yourself, even if you wanted to. They could lay bare in the utmost detail everything that you had done or said or thought; but the inner heart, whose workings were mysterious even to yourself, remained impregnable.

CHAPTER EIGHT

They had done it, they had done it at last!

The room they were standing in was long-shaped and softly lit. The telescreen was dimmed to a low murmur; the richness of the dark-blue carpet gave one the impression of treading on velvet. At the far end of the room O'Brien was sitting at a table under a green-shaded lamp, with a mass of papers on either side of him. He had not bothered to look up when the servant showed Julia and Winston in.

Winston's heart was thumping so hard that he doubted whether he would be able to speak. They had done it, they had done it at last, was all he could think. It had been a rash act to come here at all, and sheer folly to arrive together; though it was true that they had come by different routes and only met on O'Brien's doorstep. But merely to walk into such a place needed an effort of the nerve. It was only on very rare occasions that one saw inside the dwelling-places of the Inner Party, or even penetrated into the quarter of the town where they lived. The whole atmosphere of the huge block of flats, the richness and spaciousness of everything, the unfamiliar smells of good food and good tobacco, the silent and incredibly rapid lifts sliding up and down, the white-jacketed servants hurrying to and fro—everything was intimidating. Although he had a good pretext for coming here, he was haunted at every step by the fear that a black-uniformed guard would suddenly appear from round the corner, demand his papers, and order him to get out. O'Brien's servant, however, had admitted the two of them without demur. He was a small, dark-haired man in a white jacket, with a diamond-shaped, completely expressionless face which might have been that of a Chinese. The passage down which he led them was softly carpeted, with cream-papered walls and white wainscoting, all exquisitely clean. That too was intimidating. Winston could not remember ever to have seen a passageway whose walls were not grimy from the contact of human bodies.

O'Brien had a slip of paper between his fingers and seemed to be studying it intently. His heavy face, bent down so that one could see the line of the nose, looked both formidable and intelligent. For perhaps twenty seconds he sat without stirring. Then he pulled the speakwrite towards him and rapped out a message in the hybrid jargon of the Ministries:

> Items one comma five comma seven approved fullwise stop suggestion contained item six doubleplus ridiculous verging crimethink cancel stop unproceed constructionwise antegetting plusfull estimates machinery overheads stop end message.

He rose deliberately from his chair and came towards them across the soundless carpet. A little of the official atmosphere seemed to have fallen away from him with the Newspeak words, but his expression was grimmer than usual, as though he were not pleased at being disturbed. The terror that Winston already felt was suddenly shot through by a streak of ordinary embarrassment. It seemed to him quite possible that he had simply made a stupid mistake. For what evidence had he in reality that O'Brien was any kind of political conspirator? Nothing but a flash of the eyes and a single equivocal remark: beyond that, only his own secret imaginings, founded on a dream. He could not even fall back on the pretence that he had come to borrow the dictionary, because in that case Julia's presence was impossible to explain. As O'Brien passed the telescreen a thought seemed to strike him. He stopped, turned aside and pressed a switch on the wall. There was a sharp snap. The voice had stopped.

Julia uttered a tiny sound, a sort of squeak of surprise. Even in the midst of his panic, Winston was too much taken aback to be able to hold his tongue.

'You can turn it off!' he said.

'Yes,' said O'Brien, 'we can turn it off. We have that privilege.'

He was opposite them now. His solid form towered over the pair of them, and the expression on his face was still indecipherable. He was waiting, somewhat sternly, for Winston to speak, but about what? Even now it was quite conceivable that he was simply a busy man wondering irritably why he had been interrupted. Nobody spoke. After the stopping of the telescreen the room seemed deadly silent. The seconds marched past, enormous. With difficulty Winston continued to keep his eyes fixed on O'Brien's. Then suddenly the grim face broke down into what might have been the beginnings of a smile. With his characteristic gesture O'Brien resettled his spectacles on his nose.

'Shall I say it, or will you?' he said.

'I will say it,' said Winston promptly. 'That thing is really turned off?'

'Yes, everything is turned off. We are alone.'

'We have come here because—'

He paused, realizing for the first time the vagueness of his own motives. Since he did not in fact know what kind of help he expected from O'Brien, it was not easy to say why he had come here. He went on, conscious that what he was saying must sound both feeble and pretentious:

'We believe that there is some kind of conspiracy, some kind of secret organization working against the Party, and that you are involved in it. We want to join it and work for it. We are enemies of the Party. We disbelieve in the principles of Ingsoc. We are thought-criminals. We are also adulterers. I tell you this because we want to put ourselves at your mercy. If you want us to incriminate ourselves in any other way, we are ready.'

He stopped and glanced over his shoulder, with the feeling that the door had opened. Sure enough, the little yellow-faced servant had come in without knocking. Winston saw that he was carrying a tray with a decanter and glasses.

'Martin is one of us,' said O'Brien impassively. 'Bring the drinks over here, Martin. Put them on the round table. Have we enough chairs? Then we may as well sit down and talk in comfort. Bring a chair for yourself, Martin. This is business. You can stop being a servant for the next ten minutes.'

The little man sat down, quite at his ease, and yet still with a servant-like air, the air of a valet enjoying a privilege.

Winston regarded him out of the corner of his eye. It struck him that the man's whole life was playing a part, and that he felt it to be dangerous to drop his assumed personality even for a moment. O'Brien took the decanter by the neck and filled up the glasses with a dark-red liquid. It aroused in Winston dim memories of something seen long ago on a wall or a hoarding—a vast bottle composed of electric lights which seemed to move up and down and pour its contents into a glass. Seen from the top the stuff looked almost black, but in the decanter it gleamed like a ruby. It had a sour-sweet smell. He saw Julia pick up her glass and sniff at it with frank curiosity.

'It is called wine,' said O'Brien with a faint smile. 'You will have read about it in books, no doubt. Not much of it gets to the Outer Party, I am afraid.' His face grew solemn again, and he raised his glass: 'I think it is fitting that we should begin by drinking a health. To our Leader: To Emmanuel Goldstein.'

Winston took up his glass with a certain eagerness. Wine was a thing he had read and dreamed about. Like the glass paperweight or Mr Charrington's half-remembered rhymes, it belonged to the vanished, romantic past, the olden time as he liked to call it in his secret thoughts. For some reason he had always thought of wine as having an intensely sweet taste, like that of blackberry jam and an immediate intoxicating effect. Actually, when he came to swallow it, the stuff was distinctly disappointing. The truth was that after years of gin-drinking he could barely taste it. He set down the empty glass.

'Then there is such a person as Goldstein?' he said.

'Yes, there is such a person, and he is alive. Where, I do not know.'

'And the conspiracy—the organization? Is it real? It is not simply an invention of the Thought Police?'

'No, it is real. The Brotherhood, we call it. You will never learn much more about the Brotherhood than that it exists and that you belong to it. I will come back to that presently.' He looked at his wrist-watch. 'It is unwise even for members of the Inner Party to turn off the telescreen for more than half an hour. You ought not to have come here together, and you will have to leave separately. You, comrade'—he bowed his head to

Julia—'will leave first. We have about twenty minutes at our disposal. You will understand that I must start by asking you certain questions. In general terms, what are you prepared to do?'

'Anything that we are capable of,' said Winston.

O'Brien had turned himself a little in his chair so that he was facing Winston. He almost ignored Julia, seeming to take it for granted that Winston could speak for her. For a moment the lids flitted down over his eyes. He began asking his questions in a low, expressionless voice, as though this were a routine, a sort of catechism, most of whose answers were known to him already.

'You are prepared to give your lives?'

'Yes.'

'You are prepared to commit murder?'

'Yes.'

'To commit acts of sabotage which may cause the death of hundreds of innocent people?'

'Yes.'

'To betray your country to foreign powers?'

'Yes.'

'You are prepared to cheat, to forge, to blackmail, to corrupt the minds of children, to distribute habit-forming drugs, to encourage prostitution, to disseminate venereal diseases—to do anything which is likely to cause demoralization and weaken the power of the Party?'

'Yes.'

'If, for example, it would somehow serve our interests to throw sulphuric acid in a child's face—are you prepared to do that?'

'Yes.'

'You are prepared to lose your identity and live out the rest of your life as a waiter or a dock-worker?'

'Yes.'

'You are prepared to commit suicide, if and when we order you to do so?'

'Yes.'

'You are prepared, the two of you, to separate and never see one another again?'

'No!' broke in Julia.

It appeared to Winston that a long time passed before he answered. For a moment he seemed even to have been deprived of the power of speech. His tongue worked soundlessly, forming the opening syllables first of one word, then of the other, over and over again. Until he had said it, he did not know which word he was going to say. 'No,' he said finally.

'You did well to tell me,' said O'Brien. 'It is necessary for us to know everything.'

He turned himself toward Julia and added in a voice with somewhat more expression in it:

'Do you understand that even if he survives, it may be as a different person? We may be obliged to give him a new identity. His face, his movements, the shape of his hands, the colour of his hair—even his voice would be different. And you yourself might have become a different person. Our surgeons can alter people beyond recognition. Sometimes it is necessary. Sometimes we even amputate a limb.'

Winston could not help snatching another sidelong glance at Martin's Mongolian face. There were no scars that he could see. Julia had turned a shade paler, so that her freckles were showing, but she faced O'Brien boldly. She murmured something that seemed to be assent.

'Good. Then that is settled.'

There was a silver box of cigarettes on the table. With a rather absent-minded air O'Brien pushed them towards the others, took one himself, then stood up and began to pace slowly to and fro, as though he could think better standing. They were very good cigarettes, very thick and well-packed, with an unfamiliar silkiness in the paper. O'Brien looked at his wrist-watch again.

'You had better go back to your Pantry, Martin,' he said. 'I shall switch on in a quarter of an hour. Take a good look at these comrades' faces before you go. You will be seeing them again. I may not.'

Exactly as they had done at the front door, the little man's dark eyes flickered over their faces. There was not a trace of friendliness in his manner. He was memorizing their appearance, but he felt no interest in them, or appeared to feel none. It occurred to Winston that a synthetic face was perhaps incapable of changing its expression. Without speaking or giving any kind of salutation, Martin went out, closing the door silently behind him. O'Brien was strolling up and down, one hand in the pocket of his black overalls, the other holding his cigarette.

'You understand,' he said, 'that you will be fighting in the dark. You will always be in the dark. You will receive orders and you will obey them, without knowing why. Later I shall send you a book from which you will learn the true nature of the society we live in, and the strategy by which we shall destroy it. When you have read the book, you will be full members of the Brotherhood. But between the general aims that we are fighting for and the immediate tasks of the moment, you will never know anything. I tell you that the Brotherhood exists, but I cannot tell you whether it numbers a hundred members, or ten million. From your personal knowledge you will never be able to say that it numbers even as many as a dozen. You will have three or four contacts, who will be renewed from time to time as they disappear. As this was your first contact, it will be preserved. When you receive orders, they will come from me. If we find it necessary to communicate with you, it will be through Martin. When you are finally caught, you will confess. That is unavoidable. But you will have very little to confess, other than your own actions. You will not be able to betray more than a handful of unimportant people. Probably you will not even betray me. By that time I may be dead, or I shall have become a different person, with a different face.'

He continued to move to and fro over the soft carpet. In spite of the bulkiness of his body there was a remarkable grace in his movements. It came out even in the gesture with which he thrust a hand into his pocket, or manipulated a cigarette. More even than of strength, he gave an impression of confidence and of an understanding tinged by irony. However much in earnest he might be, he had nothing of the single-mindedness that belongs to a fanatic. When he spoke of murder, suicide, venereal disease, amputated limbs, and altered faces, it was with a faint air of persiflage. 'This is unavoidable,' his voice seemed to say; 'this is what we have got to do, unflinchingly. But this is not what we shall be doing when life is worth living again.' A wave of admiration, almost of worship, flowed out from Winston towards O'Brien. For the moment he had forgotten the shadowy figure of Goldstein. When you looked at O'Brien's powerful shoulders and his blunt-featured face, so ugly and yet so civilized, it was impossible to believe that he could be defeated. There was no stratagem that he was not equal to, no danger that he could not foresee. Even Julia seemed to be impressed. She had let her cigarette go out and was listening intently. O'Brien went on:

'You will have heard rumours of the existence of the Brotherhood. No doubt you have formed your own picture of it. You have imagined, probably, a huge underworld of conspirators, meeting secretly in cellars, scribbling messages on walls, recognizing one another by codewords or by special movements of the hand. Nothing of the kind exists. The members of the Brotherhood have no way of recognizing one another, and it is impossible for any one member to be aware of the identity of more than a few others. Goldstein himself, if he fell into the hands of the Thought Police, could not give them a complete list of members, or any information that would lead them to a complete list. No such list exists. The Brotherhood cannot be wiped out because it is not an organization in the ordinary sense. Nothing holds it together except an idea which is indestructible. You will never have anything to sustain you, except the idea. You will get no comradeship and no encouragement. When finally you are caught, you will get no help. We never help our members. At most, when it is absolutely necessary that someone should be silenced, we are occasionally able to smuggle a razor blade into a prisoner's cell. You will have to get used to living without results and without hope. You will work for a while, you will be caught, you will confess, and then you will die. Those are the only results that you will ever see. There is no possibility that any perceptible change will happen within our own lifetime. We are the dead. Our only true life is in the future. We shall take part in it as handfuls of dust and splinters of bone. But how far away that future may be, there is no knowing. It might be a thousand years. At present nothing is possible except to extend the area of sanity little by little. We cannot act collectively. We can only spread our knowledge outwards from individual to individual, generation after generation. In the face of the Thought Police there is no other way.'

He halted and looked for the third time at his wrist-watch.

'It is almost time for you to leave, comrade,' he said to Julia. 'Wait. The decanter is still half full.'

He filled the glasses and raised his own glass by the stem.

'What shall it be this time?' he said, still with the same faint suggestion of irony. 'To the confusion of the Thought Police? To the death of Big Brother? To humanity? To the future?'

'To the past,' said Winston.

'The past is more important,' agreed O'Brien gravely.

They emptied their glasses, and a moment later Julia stood up to go. O'Brien took a small box from the top of a cabinet and handed her a flat white tablet which he told her to place on her tongue. It was important, he said, not to go out smelling of wine: the lift attendants were very observant. As soon as the door had shut behind her he appeared to forget her existence. He took another pace or two up and down, then stopped.

'There are details to be settled,' he said. 'I assume that you have a hiding-place of some kind?'

Winston explained about the room over Mr Charrington's shop.

'That will do for the moment. Later we will arrange something else for you. It is important to change one's hiding-place frequently. Meanwhile I shall send you a copy of *the book*'—even O'Brien, Winston noticed, seemed to pronounce the words as though they were in italics—'Goldstein's book, you understand, as soon as possible. It may be some days before I can get hold of one. There are not many in existence, as you can imagine. The Thought Police hunt them down and destroy them almost as fast as we can produce them. It makes very little difference. The book is indestructible. If the last copy were gone, we could reproduce it almost word for word. Do you carry a brief-case to work with you?' he added.

'As a rule, yes.'

'What is it like?'

'Black, very shabby. With two straps.'

'Black, two straps, very shabby—good. One day in the fairly near future—I cannot give a date—one of the messages among your morning's work will contain a misprinted word, and you will have to ask for a repeat. On the following day you will go to work without your brief-case. At some time during the day, in the street, a man will touch you on the arm and say "I think you have dropped your brief-case." The one he gives you will contain a copy of Goldstein's book. You will return it within fourteen days.'

They were silent for a moment.

'There are a couple of minutes before you need go,' said O'Brien. 'We shall meet again—if we do meet again—'

Winston looked up at him. 'In the place where there is no darkness?' he said hesitantly.

O'Brien nodded without appearance of surprise. 'In the place where there is no darkness,' he said, as though he had recognized the allusion. 'And in the meantime, is there anything that you wish to say before you leave? Any message? Any question?'

Winston thought. There did not seem to be any further question that he wanted to ask: still less did he feel any impulse to utter high-sounding generalities. Instead of anything directly connected with O'Brien or the Brotherhood, there came into his mind a sort of composite picture of the dark bedroom where his mother had spent her last days, and the little room over Mr Charrington's shop, and the glass paperweight, and the steel engraving in its rosewood frame. Almost at random he said:

'Did you ever happen to hear an old rhyme that begins "Oranges and lemons, say the bells of St Clement's"?'

Again O'Brien nodded. With a sort of grave courtesy he completed the stanza:

'Oranges and lemons,' say the bells of St Clement's,
'You owe me three farthings,' say the bells of St Martin's,
'When will you pay me?' say the bells of Old Bailey,
'When I grow rich', say the bells of Shoreditch.

'You knew the last line!' said Winston.

'Yes, I knew the last line. And now, I am afraid, it is time for you to go. But wait. You had better let me give you one of these tablets.'

As Winston stood up O'Brien held out a hand. His powerful grip crushed the bones of Winston's palm. At the door Winston looked back, but O'Brien seemed already to be in process of putting him out of mind. He was waiting with his hand on the switch that controlled the telescreen. Beyond him Winston could see the writing-table with its green-shaded lamp and the speakwrite and the wire baskets deep-laden with papers. The incident was closed. Within thirty seconds, it occurred to him, O'Brien would be back at his interrupted and important work on behalf of the Party.

CHAPTER NINE

Winston was gelatinous with fatigue. Gelatinous was the right word. It had come into his head spontaneously. His body seemed to have not only the weakness of a jelly, but its translucency. He felt that if he held up his hand he would be able to see the light through it. All the blood and lymph had been drained out of him by an enormous debauch of work, leaving only a frail structure of nerves, bones, and skin. All sensations seemed to be magnified. His overalls fretted his shoulders, the pavement tickled his feet, even the opening and closing of a hand was an effort that made his joints creak.

He had worked more than ninety hours in five days. So had everyone else in the Ministry. Now it was all over, and he had literally nothing to do, no Party work of any description, until tomorrow morning. He could spend six hours in the hiding-place and another nine in his own bed. Slowly, in mild afternoon sunshine, he walked up a dingy street in the direction of Mr Charrington's shop, keeping one eye open for the patrols, but irrationally convinced that this afternoon there was no danger of anyone interfering with him. The heavy brief-case that he was carrying bumped against his knee at each step, sending a tingling sensation up and down the skin of his leg. Inside it was *the book*, which he had now had in his possession for six days and had not yet opened, nor even looked at.

On the sixth day of Hate Week, after the processions, the speeches, the shouting, the singing, the banners, the posters, the films, the waxworks, the rolling of drums and squealing of trumpets, the tramp of marching feet, the grinding of the caterpillars of tanks, the roar of massed planes, the booming of guns—after six days of this, when the great orgasm was quivering to its climax and the general hatred of Eurasia had boiled up into such delirium that if the crowd could have got their hands on the 2,000 Eurasian war-criminals who were to be publicly hanged on the last day of the proceedings, they would unquestionably have torn them to pieces—at just this moment it had been announced that Oceania was not after all at war with Eurasia. Oceania was at war with Eastasia. Eurasia was an ally.

There was, of course, no admission that any change had taken place. Merely it became known, with extreme suddenness and everywhere at once, that Eastasia and not Eurasia was the enemy. Winston was taking part in a demonstration in one of the central London squares at the moment when it happened. It was night, and the white faces and the scarlet banners were luridly floodlit. The square was packed with several thousand people, including a block of about a thousand schoolchildren in the uniform of the Spies. On a scarlet-draped platform an orator of the Inner Party, a small lean man with disproportionately long arms and a large bald skull over which a few lank locks straggled, was haranguing the crowd. A little Rumpelstiltskin figure, contorted with hatred, he gripped the neck of the microphone with one hand while the other, enormous at the end of a bony arm, clawed the air menacingly above his head. His voice, made metallic by the amplifiers, boomed forth an endless catalogue of atrocities, massacres, deportations, lootings, rapings, torture of prisoners, bombing of civilians, lying propaganda, unjust aggressions, broken treaties. It was almost impossible to listen to him without being first convinced and then maddened. At every few moments the fury of the crowd boiled over and the voice of the speaker was drowned by a wild beast-like roaring that rose uncontrollably from thousands of throats. The most savage yells of all came from the schoolchildren. The speech had been proceeding for perhaps twenty minutes when a messenger hurried on to the platform and a scrap of paper was slipped into the speaker's hand. He unrolled and read it without pausing in his speech. Nothing altered in his voice or manner, or in the content of what he was saying, but suddenly the names were different. Without words said, a wave of understanding rippled through the crowd. Oceania was at war with Eastasia! The next moment there was a tremendous commotion. The banners and posters with which the square was decorated were all wrong! Quite half of them had the wrong faces on them. It was sabotage! The agents of Goldstein had been at work! There was a riotous interlude while posters were ripped from the walls, banners torn to shreds and trampled underfoot. The Spies performed prodigies of activity in clambering over the rooftops and cutting the streamers that fluttered from the chimneys. But within two or three minutes it was all over. The orator, still gripping the neck of the microphone, his shoulders hunched forward, his free hand clawing at the air, had gone straight on with his speech. One minute more, and the feral roars of rage were again bursting from the crowd. The Hate continued exactly as before, except that the target had been changed.

The thing that impressed Winston in looking back was that the speaker had switched from one line to the other actually in midsentence, not only without a pause, but without even breaking the syntax. But at the moment he had other things to preoccupy him. It was during the moment of disorder while the posters were being torn down that a man whose face he did not see had tapped him on the shoulder and said, 'Excuse me, I think you've dropped your brief-case.' He took the brief-case abstractedly, without speaking. He knew that it would be days before he had an opportunity to look inside it. The instant that the demonstration was over he went straight to the Ministry of Truth, though the time was now nearly twenty-three hours. The entire staff of the Ministry had done likewise. The orders already issuing from the telescreen, recalling them to their posts, were hardly necessary.

Oceania was at war with Eastasia: Oceania had always been at war with Eastasia. A large part of the political literature of five years was now completely obsolete. Reports and records of all kinds, newspapers, books, pamphlets, films, sound-tracks, photographs—all had to be rectified at lightning speed. Although no directive was ever issued, it was known that the chiefs of the Department intended that within one week no reference to the war with Eurasia, or the alliance with Eastasia, should remain in existence anywhere. The work was overwhelming, all the more so because the processes that it involved could not be called by their true names. Everyone in the Records Department worked eighteen hours in the twenty-four, with two three-hour snatches of sleep. Mattresses were brought up from the cellars and pitched all over the corridors: meals consisted of sandwiches and Victory Coffee wheeled round on trolleys by attendants from the canteen. Each time that Winston broke off for one of his spells of sleep he tried to leave his desk clear of work, and each time that he crawled back sticky-eyed and aching, it was to find that another shower of paper cylinders had covered the desk like a snowdrift, half-burying the speakwrite and overflowing on to the floor, so that the first job was always to stack them into a neat enough pile to give him room to work. What was worst of all was that the work was by no means purely mechanical. Often it was enough merely to substitute one name for another, but any detailed report of events demanded care and imagination. Even the geographical knowledge that one needed in transferring the war from one part of the world to another was considerable.

By the third day his eyes ached unbearably and his spectacles needed wiping every few minutes. It was like struggling with some crushing physical task, something which one had the right to refuse and which one was nevertheless neurotically anxious to accomplish. In so far as he had time to remember it, he was not troubled by the fact that every word he murmured into the speakwrite, every stroke of his ink-pencil, was a deliberate lie. He was as anxious as anyone else in the Department that the forgery should be perfect. On the morning of the sixth day the dribble of cylinders slowed down. For as much as half an hour nothing came out of the tube; then one more cylinder, then nothing. Everywhere at about the same time the work was easing off. A deep and as it were secret sigh went through the Department. A mighty deed, which could never be mentioned, had been achieved. It was now impossible for any human being to prove by documentary evidence that the war with Eurasia had ever happened. At twelve hundred it was unexpectedly announced that all workers in the Ministry were free till tomorrow morning. Winston, still carrying the brief-case containing the book, which had remained between his feet while he worked and under his body while he slept, went home, shaved himself, and almost fell asleep in his bath, although the water was barely more than tepid.

With a sort of voluptuous creaking in his joints he climbed the stair above Mr Charrington's shop. He was tired, but not sleepy any longer. He opened the window, lit the dirty little oilstove and put on a pan of water for coffee. Julia would arrive presently: meanwhile there was *the book*. He sat down in the sluttish armchair and undid the straps of the brief-case.

A heavy black volume, amateurishly bound, with no name or title on the cover. The print also looked slightly irregular. The pages were worn at the edges, and fell apart, easily, as though the book had passed through many hands. The inscription on the title-page ran:

THE THEORY AND PRACTICE OF
OLIGARCHICAL COLLECTIVISM
by
Emmanuel Goldstein

Winston began reading:

Chapter I.
Ignorance is Strength.

Throughout recorded time, and probably since the end of the Neolithic Age, there have been three kinds of people in the world, the High, the Middle, and the Low. They have been subdivided in many ways, they have borne countless different names, and their relative numbers, as well as their attitude towards one another, have varied from age to age: but the essential structure of society has never altered. Even after enormous upheavals and seemingly irrevocable changes, the same pattern has always reasserted itself, just as a gyroscope will always return to equilibrium, however far it is pushed one way or the other. The aims of these groups are entirely irreconcilable....

Winston stopped reading, chiefly in order to appreciate the fact that he *was* reading, in comfort and safety. He was alone: no telescreen, no ear at the keyhole, no nervous impulse to glance over his shoulder or cover the page with his hand. The sweet summer air played against his cheek. From somewhere far away there floated the faint shouts of children: in the room itself there was no sound except the insect voice of the clock. He settled deeper into the arm-chair and put his feet up on the fender. It was bliss, it was eternity. Suddenly, as one sometimes does with a book of which one knows that one will ultimately read and re-read every word, he opened it at a different place and found himself at Chapter III. He went on reading:

Chapter III.
War is Peace.

The splitting up of the world into three great super-states was an event which could be and indeed was foreseen before the middle of the twentieth century. With the absorption of Europe by Russia and of the British Empire by the United States, two of the three existing powers, Eurasia and Oceania, were already effectively in being. The third, Eastasia, only emerged as a distinct unit after another decade of confused fighting. The frontiers between the three super-states are in some places arbitrary, and in others they fluctuate according to the fortunes of war, but in general they follow geographical lines. Eurasia comprises the whole of the northern part of the European and Asiatic land-mass, from Portugal to the Bering Strait. Oceania comprises the Americas, the Atlantic islands including the British Isles, Australasia, and the southern portion of Africa. Eastasia, smaller than the others and with a less definite western frontier, comprises China and the countries to the south of it, the Japanese islands and a large but fluctuating portion of Manchuria, Mongolia, and Tibet.

In one combination or another, these three super-states are permanently at war, and have been so for the past twenty-five years. War, however, is no longer the desperate, annihilating struggle that it was in the early decades of the twentieth century. It is a warfare of limited aims between combatants who are unable to destroy one another, have no material cause for fighting and are not divided by any genuine ideological difference. This is not to say that either the conduct of war, or the prevailing attitude towards it, has become less bloodthirsty or more chivalrous. On the contrary, war hysteria is continuous and universal in all countries, and such acts as raping, looting, the slaughter of children, the reduction of whole populations to slavery, and reprisals against prisoners which extend even to boiling and burying alive, are looked upon as normal, and, when they are committed by one's own side and not by the enemy, meritorious. But in a physical sense war involves very small numbers of people, mostly highly-trained specialists, and causes comparatively few casualties. The fighting, when there is any, takes place on the vague frontiers whose whereabouts the average man can only guess at, or round the Floating Fortresses which guard strategic spots on the sea lanes. In the centres of civilization war means no more than a continuous shortage of consumption goods, and the occasional crash of a rocket bomb which may cause a few scores of deaths. War has in fact changed its character. More exactly, the reasons for which war is waged have changed in their order of importance. Motives which were already present to some small extent in the great wars of the early twentieth century have now become dominant and are consciously recognized and acted upon.

To understand the nature of the present war—for in spite of the regrouping which occurs every few years, it is always the same war—one must realize in the first place that it is impossible for it to be decisive. None of the three super-states could be definitively conquered even by the other two in combination. They are too evenly matched, and their natural defences are too formidable. Eurasia is protected by its vast land spaces, Oceania by the width of the Atlantic and the Pacific, Eastasia by the fecundity and industriousness of its inhabitants. Secondly, there is no longer, in a material sense, anything to fight about. With the establishment of self-contained economies, in which production and consumption are geared to one another, the scramble for markets which was a main cause of previous wars has come to an end, while the competition for raw materials is no longer a matter of life and death. In any case each of the three super-states is so vast that it can obtain almost all the materials that it needs within its own boundaries. In so far as the war has a direct economic purpose, it is a war for labour power. Between the frontiers of the super-states, and not permanently in the possession of any of them, there lies a rough quadrilateral with its corners at

Tangier, Brazzaville, Darwin, and Hong Kong, containing within it about a fifth of the population of the earth. It is for the possession of these thickly-populated regions, and of the northern ice-cap, that the three powers are constantly struggling. In practice no one power ever controls the whole of the disputed area. Portions of it are constantly changing hands, and it is the chance of seizing this or that fragment by a sudden stroke of treachery that dictates the endless changes of alignment.

All of the disputed territories contain valuable minerals, and some of them yield important vegetable products such as rubber which in colder climates it is necessary to synthesize by comparatively expensive methods. But above all they contain a bottomless reserve of cheap labour. Whichever power controls equatorial Africa, or the countries of the Middle East, or Southern India, or the Indonesian Archipelago, disposes also of the bodies of scores or hundreds of millions of ill-paid and hard-working coolies. The inhabitants of these areas, reduced more or less openly to the status of slaves, pass continually from conqueror to conqueror, and are expended like so much coal or oil in the race to turn out more armaments, to capture more territory, to control more labour power, to turn out more armaments, to capture more territory, and so on indefinitely. It should be noted that the fighting never really moves beyond the edges of the disputed areas. The frontiers of Eurasia flow back and forth between the basin of the Congo and the northern shore of the Mediterranean; the islands of the Indian Ocean and the Pacific are constantly being captured and recaptured by Oceania or by Eastasia; in Mongolia the dividing line between Eurasia and Eastasia is never stable; round the Pole all three powers lay claim to enormous territories which in fact are largely uninhabited and unexplored: but the balance of power always remains roughly even, and the territory which forms the heartland of each super-state always remains inviolate. Moreover, the labour of the exploited peoples round the Equator is not really necessary to the world's economy. They add nothing to the wealth of the world, since whatever they produce is used for purposes of war, and the object of waging a war is always to be in a better position in which to wage another war. By their labour the slave populations allow the tempo of continuous warfare to be speeded up. But if they did not exist, the structure of world society, and the process by which it maintains itself, would not be essentially different.

The primary aim of modern warfare (in accordance with the principles of *doublethink*, this aim is simultaneously recognized and not recognized by the directing brains of the Inner Party) is to use up the products of the machine without raising the general standard of living. Ever since the end of the nineteenth century, the problem of what to do with the surplus of consumption goods has been latent in industrial society. At present, when few human beings even have enough to eat, this problem is obviously not urgent, and it might not have become so, even if no artificial processes of destruction had been at work. The world of today is a bare, hungry, dilapidated place compared with the world that existed before 1914, and still more so if compared with the imaginary future to which the people of that period looked forward. In the early twentieth century, the vision of a future society unbelievably rich, leisured, orderly, and efficient—a glittering antiseptic world of glass and steel and snow-white concrete—was part of the consciousness of nearly every literate person. Science and technology were developing at a prodigious speed, and it seemed natural to assume that they would go on developing. This failed to happen, partly because of the impoverishment caused by a long series of wars and revolutions, partly because scientific and technical progress depended on the empirical habit of thought, which could not survive in a strictly regimented society. As a whole the world is more primitive today than it was fifty years ago. Certain backward areas have advanced, and various devices, always in some way connected with warfare and police espionage, have been developed, but experiment and invention have largely stopped, and the ravages of the atomic war of the nineteen-fifties have never been fully repaired. Nevertheless the dangers inherent in the machine are still there. From the moment when the machine first made its appearance it was clear to all thinking people that the need for human drudgery, and therefore to a great extent for human inequality, had disappeared. If the machine were used deliberately for that end, hunger, overwork, dirt, illiteracy, and disease could be eliminated within a few generations. And in fact, without being used for any such purpose, but by a sort of automatic process—by producing wealth which it was sometimes impossible not to distribute—the machine did raise the living standards of the average human being very greatly over a period of about fifty years at the end of the nineteenth and the beginning of the twentieth centuries.

But it was also clear that an all-round increase in wealth threatened the destruction—indeed, in some sense was the destruction—of a hierarchical society. In a world in which everyone worked short hours, had enough to eat, lived in a house with a bathroom and a refrigerator, and possessed a motor-car or even an aeroplane, the most obvious and perhaps the most important form of inequality would already have disappeared. If it once became general, wealth would confer no distinction. It was possible, no doubt, to imagine a society in which *wealth*, in the sense of personal possessions and luxuries, should be evenly distributed, while *power* remained in the hands of a small privileged caste. But in practice such a society could not long remain stable. For if leisure and security were enjoyed by all alike, the great mass of human beings who are normally stupefied by poverty would become literate and would learn to think for themselves; and when once they had done this, they would sooner or later realize that the privileged minority had no function, and they would sweep it away. In the long run, a hierarchical society was only possible on a basis of poverty and ignorance. To return to the agricultural past, as some thinkers about the beginning of the twentieth century dreamed of doing, was not a practicable solution. It conflicted with the tendency towards mechanization which had become quasi-instinctive throughout almost the whole world, and moreover, any country which remained industrially backward was helpless in a military sense and was bound to be dominated, directly or indirectly, by its more advanced rivals.

Nor was it a satisfactory solution to keep the masses in poverty by restricting the output of goods. This happened to a great extent during the final phase of capitalism, roughly between 1920 and 1940. The economy of many countries was allowed to stagnate, land went out of cultivation, capital equipment was not added to, great blocks of the population were prevented from working and kept half alive by State charity. But this, too, entailed military weakness, and since the privations it inflicted were obviously unnecessary, it made opposition inevitable. The problem was how to keep the wheels of industry turning without increasing the real wealth of the world. Goods must be produced, but they must not be distributed. And in practice the only way of achieving this was by continuous warfare.

The essential act of war is destruction, not necessarily of human lives, but of the products of human labour. War is a way of shattering to pieces, or pouring into the stratosphere, or sinking in the depths of the sea, materials which might otherwise be used to make the masses too comfortable, and hence, in the long run, too intelligent. Even when weapons of war are not actually destroyed, their manufacture is still a convenient way of expending labour power without producing anything that can be consumed. A Floating Fortress, for example, has locked up in it the labour that would build several hundred cargo-ships. Ultimately it is scrapped as obsolete, never having brought any material benefit to anybody, and with further enormous labours another Floating Fortress is built. In principle the war effort is always so planned as to eat up any surplus that might exist after meeting the bare needs of the population. In practice the needs of the population are always under-estimated, with the result that there is a chronic shortage of half the necessities of life; but this is looked on as an advantage. It is deliberate policy to keep even the favoured groups somewhere near the brink of hardship, because a general state of scarcity increases the importance of small privileges and thus magnifies the distinction between one group and another. By the standards of the early twentieth century, even a member of the Inner Party lives an austere, laborious kind of life. Nevertheless, the few luxuries that he does enjoy his large, well-appointed flat, the better texture of his clothes, the better quality of his food and drink and tobacco, his two or three servants, his private motor-car or helicopter—set him in a different world from a member of the Outer Party, and the members of the Outer Party have a similar advantage in comparison with the submerged masses whom we call 'the proles'. The social atmosphere is that of a besieged city, where the possession of a lump of horseflesh makes the difference between wealth and poverty. And at the same time the consciousness of being at war, and therefore in danger, makes the handing-over of all power to a small caste seem the natural, unavoidable condition of survival.

War, it will be seen, accomplishes the necessary destruction, but accomplishes it in a psychologically acceptable way. In principle it would be quite simple to waste the surplus labour of the world by building temples and pyramids, by digging holes and filling them up again, or even by producing vast quantities of goods and then setting fire to them. But this would provide only the economic and not the emotional basis for a hierarchical society. What is concerned here is not the morale of masses, whose attitude is unimportant so long as they are kept steadily at work, but the morale of the Party itself. Even the humblest Party member is expected to be competent, industrious, and even intelligent within narrow limits, but it is also necessary that he should be a credulous and ignorant fanatic whose prevailing moods are fear, hatred, adulation, and orgiastic triumph. In other words it is necessary that he should have the mentality appropriate to a state of war. It does not matter whether the war is actually happening, and, since no decisive victory is possible, it does not matter whether the war is going well or badly. All that is needed is that a state of war should exist. The splitting of the intelligence which the Party requires of its members, and which is more easily achieved in an atmosphere of war, is now almost universal, but the higher up the ranks one goes, the more marked it becomes. It is precisely in the Inner Party that war hysteria and hatred of the enemy are strongest. In his capacity as an administrator, it is often necessary for a member of the Inner Party to know that this or that item of war news is untruthful, and he may often be aware that the entire war is spurious and is either not happening or is being waged for purposes quite other than the declared ones: but such knowledge is easily neutralized by the technique of *doublethink*. Meanwhile no Inner Party member wavers for an instant in his mystical belief that the war is real, and that it is bound to end victoriously, with Oceania the undisputed master of the entire world.

All members of the Inner Party believe in this coming conquest as an article of faith. It is to be achieved either by gradually acquiring more and more territory and so building up an overwhelming preponderance of power, or by the discovery of some new and unanswerable weapon. The search for new weapons continues unceasingly, and is one of the very few remaining activities in which the inventive or speculative type of mind can find any outlet. In Oceania at the present day, Science, in the old sense, has almost ceased to exist. In Newspeak there is no word for 'Science'. The empirical method of thought, on which all the scientific achievements of the past were founded, is opposed to the most fundamental principles of Ingsoc. And even technological progress only happens when its products can in some way be used for the diminution of human liberty. In all the useful arts the world is either standing still or going backwards. The fields are cultivated with horse-ploughs while books are written by machinery. But in matters of vital importance—meaning, in effect, war and police espionage—the empirical approach is still encouraged, or at least tolerated. The two aims of the Party are to conquer the whole surface of the earth and to extinguish once and for all the possibility of independent thought. There are therefore two great problems which the Party is concerned to solve. One is how to discover, against his will, what another human being is thinking, and the other is how to kill several hundred million people in a few seconds without giving warning beforehand. In so far as scientific research still continues, this is its subject matter. The scientist of today is either a mixture of psychologist and inquisitor, studying with real ordinary minuteness the meaning of facial expressions, gestures, and tones of voice, and testing the truth-producing effects of drugs, shock therapy, hypnosis, and physical torture; or he is chemist, physicist, or biologist concerned only with such branches of his special subject as are relevant to the taking of life. In the vast laboratories of the Ministry of Peace, and in the experimental stations hidden in the Brazilian forests, or in the Australian desert, or on lost islands of the Antarctic, the teams of experts are indefatigably at work. Some are concerned simply with planning the logistics of future wars; others devise larger and larger rocket bombs, more and more powerful explosives, and more and more impenetrable armour-plating; others search for new and deadlier gases, or for soluble poisons capable of being produced in such quantities as to destroy the vegetation of whole continents, or for breeds of disease germs immunized against all possible antibodies; others strive to produce a vehicle that shall bore its way under the soil like a submarine under the water, or an aeroplane as independent of its base as a sailing-ship; others explore even remoter possibilities such as focusing the sun's rays through lenses suspended thousands of kilometres away in space, or producing artificial earthquakes and tidal waves by tapping the heat at the earth's centre.

But none of these projects ever comes anywhere near realization, and none of the three super-states ever gains a significant lead on the others. What is more remarkable is that all three powers already possess, in the atomic bomb, a weapon far more powerful than any that their present researches are likely to discover. Although the Party, according to its habit, claims the invention for itself, atomic bombs first appeared as early as the nineteen-forties, and were first used on a large scale about ten years later. At that time some hundreds of bombs were dropped on industrial centres, chiefly in European Russia, Western Europe, and North America. The effect was to convince the ruling groups of all countries that a few more atomic bombs would mean the end of organized society, and hence of their own power. Thereafter, although no formal agreement was ever made or hinted at, no more bombs were dropped. All three powers merely continue to produce atomic bombs and store them up against the decisive opportunity which they all believe will come sooner or later. And meanwhile the art of war has remained almost stationary for thirty or forty years. Helicopters are more used than they were formerly, bombing planes have been largely superseded by self-propelled projectiles, and the fragile movable battleship has given way to the almost unsinkable Floating Fortress; but otherwise there has been little development. The tank, the submarine, the torpedo, the machine gun, even the rifle and the hand grenade are still in use. And in spite of the endless slaughters reported in the Press and on the telescreens, the desperate battles of earlier wars, in which hundreds of thousands or even millions of men were often killed in a few weeks, have never been repeated.

None of the three super-states ever attempts any manoeuvre which involves the risk of serious defeat. When any large operation is undertaken, it is usually a surprise attack against an ally. The strategy that all three powers are following, or pretend to themselves that they are following, is the same. The plan is, by a combination of fighting, bargaining, and well-timed strokes of treachery, to acquire a ring of bases completely encircling one or other of the rival states, and then to sign a pact of friendship with that rival and remain on peaceful terms for so many years as to lull suspicion to sleep. During this time rockets loaded with atomic bombs can be assembled at all the strategic spots; finally they will all be fired simultaneously, with effects so devastating as to make retaliation impossible. It will then be time to sign a pact of friendship with the remaining world-power, in preparation for another attack. This scheme, it is hardly necessary to say, is a mere daydream, impossible of realization. Moreover, no fighting ever occurs except in the disputed areas round the Equator and the Pole: no invasion of enemy territory is ever undertaken. This explains the fact that in some places the frontiers between the super-states are arbitrary. Eurasia, for example, could easily conquer the British Isles, which are geographically part of Europe, or on the other hand it would be possible for Oceania to push its frontiers to the Rhine or even to the Vistula. But this would violate the principle, followed on all sides though never formulated, of cultural integrity. If Oceania were to conquer the areas that used once to be known as France and Germany, it would be necessary either to exterminate the inhabitants, a task of great physical difficulty, or to assimilate a population of about a hundred million people, who, so far as technical development goes, are roughly on the Oceanic level. The problem is the same for all three super-states. It is absolutely necessary to their structure that there should be no contact with foreigners, except, to a limited extent, with war prisoners and coloured slaves. Even the official ally of the moment is always regarded with the darkest suspicion. War prisoners apart, the average citizen of Oceania never sets eyes on a citizen of either Eurasia or Eastasia, and he is forbidden the knowledge of foreign languages. If he were allowed contact with foreigners he would discover that they are creatures similar to himself and that most of what he has been told about them is lies. The sealed world in which he lives would be broken, and the fear, hatred, and self-righteousness on which his morale depends might evaporate. It is therefore realized on all sides that however often Persia, or Egypt, or Java, or Ceylon may change hands, the main frontiers must never be crossed by anything except bombs.

Under this lies a fact never mentioned aloud, but tacitly understood and acted upon: namely, that the conditions of life in all three super-states are very much the same. In Oceania the prevailing philosophy is called Ingsoc, in Eurasia it is called Neo-Bolshevism, and in Eastasia it is called by a Chinese name usually translated as Death-Worship, but perhaps better rendered as Obliteration of the Self. The citizen of Oceania is not allowed to know anything of the tenets of the other two philosophies, but he is taught to execrate them as barbarous outrages upon morality and common sense. Actually the three philosophies are barely distinguishable, and the social systems which they support are not distinguishable at all. Everywhere there is the same pyramidal structure, the same worship of semi-divine leader, the same economy existing by and for continuous warfare. It follows that the three super-states not only cannot conquer one another, but would gain no advantage by doing so. On the contrary, so long as they remain in conflict they prop one another up, like three sheaves of corn. And, as usual, the ruling groups of all three powers are simultaneously aware and unaware of what they are doing.

Their lives are dedicated to world conquest, but they also know that it is necessary that the war should continue everlastingly and without victory. Meanwhile the fact that there *is* no danger of conquest makes possible the denial of reality which is the special feature of Ingsoc and its rival systems of thought. Here it is necessary to repeat what has been said earlier, that by becoming continuous war has fundamentally changed its character.

In past ages, a war, almost by definition, was something that sooner or later came to an end, usually in unmistakable victory or defeat. In the past, also, war was one of the main instruments by which human societies were kept in touch with physical reality. All rulers in all ages have tried to impose a false view of the world upon their followers, but they could not afford to encourage any illusion that tended to impair military efficiency. So long as defeat meant the loss of independence, or some other result generally held to be undesirable, the precautions against defeat had to be serious. Physical facts could not be ignored. In philosophy, or religion, or ethics, or politics, two and two might make five, but when one was designing a gun or an aeroplane they had to make four. Inefficient nations were always conquered sooner or later, and the struggle for efficiency was inimical to illusions. Moreover, to be efficient it was necessary to be able to learn from the past, which meant having a fairly accurate idea of what had happened in the past. Newspapers and history books were, of course, always coloured and biased, but falsification of the kind that is practised today would have been impossiblc. War was a sure safeguard of sanity, and so far as the ruling classes were concerned it was probably the most important of all safeguards. While wars could be won or lost, no ruling class could be completely irresponsible.

But when war becomes literally continuous, it also ceases to be dangerous. When war is continuous there is no such thing as military necessity. Technical progress can cease and the most palpable facts can be denied or disregarded. As we have seen, researches that could be called scientific are still carried out for the purposes of war, but they are essentially a kind of daydreaming, and their failure to show results is not important. Efficiency, even military efficiency, is no longer needed. Nothing is efficient in Oceania except the Thought Police. Since each of the three super-states is unconquerable, each is in effect a separate universe within which almost any perversion of thought can be safely practised. Reality only exerts its pressure through the needs of everyday life—the need to eat and drink, to get shelter and clothing, to avoid swallowing poison or stepping out of top-storey windows, and the like. Between life and death, and between physical pleasure and physical pain, there is still a distinction, but that is all. Cut off from contact with the outer world, and with the past, the citizen of Oceania is like a man in interstellar space, who has no way of knowing which direction is up and which is down. The rulers of such a state are absolute, as the Pharaohs or the Caesars could not be. They are obliged to prevent their followers from starving to death in numbers large enough to be inconvenient, and they are obliged to remain at the same low level of military technique as their rivals; but once that minimum is achieved, they can twist reality into whatever shape they choose.

The war, therefore, if we judge it by the standards of previous wars, is merely an imposture. It is like the battles between certain ruminant animals whose horns are set at such an angle that they are incapable of hurting one another. But though it is unreal it is not meaningless. It eats up the surplus of consumable goods, and it helps to preserve the special mental atmosphere that a hierarchical society needs. War, it will be seen, is now a purely internal affair. In the past, the ruling groups of all countries, although they might recognize their common interest and therefore limit the destructiveness of war, did fight against one another, and the victor always plundered the vanquished. In our own day they are not fighting against one another at all. The war is waged by each ruling group against its own subjects, and the object of the war is not to make or prevent conquests of territory, but to keep the structure of society intact. The very word 'war', therefore, has become misleading. It would probably be accurate to say that by becoming continuous war has ceased to exist. The peculiar pressure that it exerted on human beings between the

Neolithic Age and the early twentieth century has disappeared and been replaced by something quite different. The effect would be much the same if the three super-states, instead of fighting one another, should agree to live in perpetual peace, each inviolate within its own boundaries. For in that case each would still be a self-contained universe, freed for ever from the sobering influence of external danger. A peace that was truly permanent would be the same as a permanent war. This—although the vast majority of Party members understand it only in a shallower sense—is the inner meaning of the Party slogan: *War is Peace.*

Winston stopped reading for a moment. Somewhere in remote distance a rocket bomb thundered. The blissful feeling of being alone with the forbidden book, in a room with no telescreen, had not worn off. Solitude and safety were physical sensations, mixed up somehow with the tiredness of his body, the softness of the chair, the touch of the faint breeze from the window that played upon his cheek. The book fascinated him, or more exactly it reassured him. In a sense it told him nothing that was new, but that was part of the attraction. It said what he would have said, if it had been possible for him to set his scattered thoughts in order. It was the product of a mind similar to his own, but enormously more powerful, more systematic, less fear-ridden. The best books, he perceived, are those that tell you what you know already. He had just turned back to Chapter I when he heard Julia's footstep on the stair and started out of his chair to meet her. She dumped her brown tool-bag on the floor and flung herself into his arms. It was more than a week since they had seen one another.

'I've got *the book*,' he said as they disentangled themselves.

'Oh, you've got it? Good,' she said without much interest, and almost immediately knelt down beside the oil stove to make the coffee.

They did not return to the subject until they had been in bed for half an hour. The evening was just cool enough to make it worth while to pull up the counterpane. From below came the familiar sound of singing and the scrape of boots on the flagstones. The brawny red-armed woman whom Winston had seen there on his first visit was almost a fixture in the yard.

There seemed to be no hour of daylight when she was not marching to and fro between the washtub and the line, alternately gagging herself with clothes pegs and breaking forth into lusty song. Julia had settled down on her side and seemed to be already on the point of falling asleep. He reached out for the book, which was lying on the floor, and sat up against the bed-head.

'We must read it,' he said. 'You too. All members of the Brotherhood have to read it.'

'You read it,' she said with her eyes shut. 'Read it aloud. That's the best way. Then you can explain it to me as you go.'

The clock's hands said six, meaning eighteen. They had three or four hours ahead of them. He propped the book against his knees and began reading:

Chapter I.

Ignorance is Strength.

Throughout recorded time, and probably since the end of the Neolithic Age, there have been three kinds of people in the world, the High, the Middle, and the Low. They have been subdivided in many ways, they have borne countless different names, and their relative numbers, as well as their attitude towards one another, have varied from age to age: but the essential structure of society has never altered. Even after enormous upheavals and seemingly irrevocable changes, the same pattern has always reasserted itself, just as a gyroscope will always return to equilibrium, however far it is pushed one way or the other.

'Julia, are you awake?' said Winston.

'Yes, my love, I'm listening. Go on. It's marvellous.'

He continued reading:

The aims of these three groups are entirely irreconcilable. The aim of the High is to remain where they are. The aim of the Middle is to change places with the High. The aim of the Low, when they have an aim—for it is an abiding characteristic of the Low that they are too much crushed by drudgery to be more than intermittently conscious of anything outside their daily lives—is to abolish all distinctions and create a society in which all men shall be equal. Thus throughout history a struggle which is the same in its main outlines recurs over and over again. For long periods the High seem to be securely in power, but sooner or later there always comes a moment when they lose either their belief in themselves or their capacity to govern efficiently, or both. They are then overthrown by the Middle, who enlist the Low on their side by pretending to them that they are fighting for liberty and justice. As soon as they have reached their objective, the Middle thrust the Low back into their old position of servitude, and themselves become the High. Presently a new Middle group splits off from one of the other groups, or from both of them, and the struggle begins over again. Of the three groups, only the Low are never even temporarily successful in achieving their aims. It would be an exaggeration to say that throughout history there has been no progress of a material kind. Even today, in a period of decline, the average human being is physically better off than he was a few centuries ago. But no advance in wealth, no softening of manners, no reform or revolution has ever brought human equality a millimetre nearer. From the point of view of the Low, no historic change has ever meant much more than a change in the name of their masters.

By the late nineteenth century the recurrence of this pattern had become obvious to many observers. There then rose schools of thinkers who interpreted history as a cyclical process and claimed to show that inequality was the unalterable law of human life. This doctrine, of course, had always had its adherents, but in the manner in which it was now put forward there was a significant change. In the past the need for a hierarchical form of society had been the doctrine specifically of the High. It had been preached by kings and aristocrats and by the priests, lawyers, and the like who were parasitical upon them, and it had generally been softened by promises of compensation in an imaginary world beyond the grave. The Middle, so long as it was struggling for power, had always made use of such terms as freedom, justice, and fraternity. Now, however, the concept of human brotherhood began to be assailed by people who were not yet in positions of command, but merely hoped to be so before long. In the past the Middle had made revolutions under the banner of equality, and then had established a fresh tyranny as soon as the old one was overthrown. The new Middle groups in effect proclaimed their tyranny beforehand. Socialism, a theory which appeared in the early nineteenth century and was the last link in a chain of thought stretching back to the slave rebellions of antiquity, was still deeply infected by the Utopianism of past ages. But in each variant of Socialism that appeared from about 1900 onwards the aim of establishing liberty and equality was more and more openly abandoned. The new movements which appeared in the middle years of the century, Ingsoc in Oceania, Neo-Bolshevism in Eurasia, Death-Worship, as it is commonly called, in Eastasia, had the conscious aim of perpetuating *un*freedom and *in*equality. These new movements, of course, grew out of the old ones and tended to keep their names and pay lip-service to their ideology. But the purpose of all of them was to arrest progress and freeze history at a chosen moment. The familiar pendulum swing was to happen once more, and then stop. As usual, the High were to be turned out by the Middle, who would then become the High; but this time, by conscious strategy, the High would be able to maintain their position permanently.

The new doctrines arose partly because of the accumulation of historical knowledge, and the growth of the historical sense, which had hardly existed before the nineteenth century. The cyclical movement of history was now intelligible, or appeared to be so; and if it was intelligible, then it was alterable. But the principal, underlying cause was that, as early as the beginning of the twentieth century, human equality had become technically possible. It was still true that men were not equal in their native talents and that functions had to be specialized in ways that favoured some individuals against others; but there was no longer any real need for class distinctions or for large differences of wealth. In earlier ages, class distinctions had been not only inevitable but desirable. Inequality was the price of civilization. With the development of machine production, however, the case was altered. Even if it was still necessary for human beings to do different kinds of work, it was no longer necessary for them to live at different social or economic levels. Therefore, from the point of view of the new groups who were on the point of seizing power, human equality was no longer an ideal to be striven after, but a danger to be averted. In more primitive ages, when a just and peaceful society was in fact not possible, it had been fairly easy to believe it. The idea of an earthly paradise in which men should live together in a state of brotherhood, without laws and without brute labour, had haunted the human imagination for thousands of years. And this vision had had a certain hold even on the groups who actually profited by each historical change. The heirs of the French, English, and American revolutions had partly believed in their own phrases about the rights of man, freedom of speech, equality before the law, and the like, and have even allowed their conduct to be influenced by them to some extent. But by the fourth decade of the twentieth century all the main currents of political thought were authoritarian. The earthly paradise had been discredited at exactly the moment when it became realizable. Every new political theory, by whatever name it called itself, led back to hierarchy and regimentation. And in the general hardening of outlook that set in round about 1930, practices which had been long abandoned, in some cases for hundreds of years—imprisonment without trial, the use of war prisoners as slaves, public executions, torture to extract confessions, the use of hostages, and the deportation of whole populations—not only became common again, but were tolerated and even defended by people who considered themselves enlightened and progressive. It was only after a decade of national wars, civil wars, revolutions, and counter-revolutions in all parts of the world that Ingsoc and its rivals emerged as fully worked-out political theories. But they had been foreshadowed by the various systems, generally called totalitarian, which had appeared earlier in the century, and the main outlines of the world which would emerge from the prevailing chaos had long been obvious. What kind of people would control this world had been equally obvious. The new aristocracy was made up for the most part of bureaucrats, scientists, technicians, trade-union organizers, publicity experts, sociologists, teachers, journalists, and professional politicians. These people, whose origins lay in the salaried middle class and the upper grades of the working class, had been shaped and brought together by the barren world of monopoly industry and centralized government. As compared with their opposite numbers in past ages, they were less avaricious, less tempted by luxury, hungrier for pure power, and, above all, more conscious of what they were doing and more intent on crushing opposition. This last difference was cardinal. By comparison with that existing today, all the tyrannies of the past were half-hearted and inefficient. The ruling groups were always infected to some extent by liberal ideas, and were content to leave loose ends everywhere, to regard only the overt act and to be uninterested in what their subjects were thinking. Even the Catholic Church of the Middle Ages was tolerant by modern standards. Part of the reason for this was that in the past no government had the power to keep its citizens under constant surveillance. The invention of print, however, made it easier to manipulate public opinion, and the film and the radio carried the process further. With the development of television, and the technical advance which made it possible to receive and transmit simultaneously on the same instrument, private life came to an end. Every citizen, or at least every citizen important enough to be worth watching, could be kept for twenty-four hours a day under the eyes of the police and in the sound of official propaganda, with all other channels of communication closed. The possibility of enforcing not only complete obedience to the will of the State, but complete uniformity of opinion on all subjects, now existed for the first time.

After the revolutionary period of the 'fifties and 'sixties, society regrouped itself, as always, into High, Middle, and Low. But the new High group, unlike all its forerunners, did not act upon instinct but knew what was needed to safeguard its position. It had long been realized that the only secure basis for oligarchy is collectivism. Wealth and privilege are most easily defended when they are possessed jointly. The so-called 'abolition of private property' which took place in the middle years of the century meant, in effect, the concentration of property in far fewer hands than before: but with this difference, that the new owners were a group instead of a mass of individuals. Individually, no member of the Party owns anything, except petty personal belongings. Collectively, the Party owns everything in Oceania, because it controls everything, and disposes of the products as it thinks fit. In the years following the Revolution it was able to step into this commanding position almost unopposed, because the whole process was represented as an act of collectivization. It had always been assumed that if the capitalist class were expropriated, Socialism must follow: and unquestionably the capitalists had been expropriated. Factories, mines, land, houses, transport—everything had been taken away from them: and since these things were no longer private property, it followed that they must be public property. Ingsoc, which grew out of the earlier Socialist movement and inherited its phraseology, has in fact carried out the main item in the Socialist programme; with the result, foreseen and intended beforehand, that economic inequality has been made permanent.

But the problems of perpetuating a hierarchical society go deeper than this. There are only four ways in which a ruling group can fall from power. Either it is conquered from without, or it governs so inefficiently that the masses are stirred to revolt, or it allows a strong and discontented Middle group to come into being, or it loses its own self-confidence and willingness to govern. These causes do not operate singly, and as a rule all four of them are present in some degree. A ruling class which could guard against all of them would remain in power permanently. Ultimately the determining factor is the mental attitude of the ruling class itself.

After the middle of the present century, the first danger had in reality disappeared. Each of the three powers which now divide the world is in fact unconquerable, and could only become conquerable through slow demographic changes which a government with wide powers can easily avert. The second danger, also, is only a theoretical one. The masses never revolt of their own accord, and they never revolt merely because they are oppressed. Indeed, so long as they are not permitted to have standards of comparison, they never even become aware that they are oppressed. The recurrent economic crises of past times were totally unnecessary and are not now permitted to happen, but other and equally large dislocations can and do happen without having political results, because there is no way in which discontent can become articulate. As for the problem of over-production, which has been latent in our society since the development of machine technique, it is solved by the device of continuous warfare (see Chapter III), which is also useful in keying up public morale to the necessary pitch. From the point of view of our present rulers, therefore, the only genuine dangers are the splitting-off of a new group of able, under-employed, power-hungry people, and the growth of liberalism and scepticism in their own ranks. The problem, that is to say, is educational. It is a problem of continuously moulding the consciousness both of the directing group and of the larger executive group that lies immediately below it. The consciousness of the masses needs only to be influenced in a negative way.

Given this background, one could infer, if one did not know it already, the general structure of Oceanic society. At the apex of the pyramid comes Big Brother. Big Brother is infallible and all-powerful. Every success, every achievement, every victory, every scientific discovery, all knowledge, all wisdom, all happiness, all virtue, are held to issue directly from his leadership and inspiration. Nobody has ever seen Big Brother. He is a face on the hoardings, a voice on the telescreen. We may be reasonably sure that he will never die, and there is already considerable uncertainty as to when he was born. Big Brother is the guise in which the Party chooses to exhibit itself to the world. His function is to act as a focusing point for love, fear, and reverence, emotions which are more easily felt towards an individual than towards an organization. Below Big Brother comes the Inner Party. Its numbers limited to six millions, or something less than 2 per cent of the population of Oceania. Below the Inner Party comes the Outer Party, which, if the Inner Party is described as the brain of the State, may be justly likened to the hands. Below that come the dumb masses whom we habitually refer to as 'the proles', numbering perhaps 85 per cent of the population. In the terms of our earlier classification, the proles are the Low: for the slave population of the equatorial lands who pass constantly from conqueror to conqueror, are not a permanent or necessary part of the structure.

In principle, membership of these three groups is not hereditary. The child of Inner Party parents is in theory not born into the Inner Party. Admission to either branch of the Party is by examination, taken at the age of sixteen. Nor is there any racial discrimination, or any marked domination of one province by another. Jews, Negroes, South Americans of pure Indian blood are to be found in the highest ranks of the Party, and the administrators of any area are always drawn from the inhabitants of that area. In no part of Oceania do the inhabitants have the feeling that they are a colonial population ruled from a distant capital. Oceania has no capital, and its titular head is a person whose whereabouts nobody knows. Except that English is its chief *lingua franca* and Newspeak its official language, it is not centralized in any way. Its rulers are not held together by blood-ties but by adherence to a common doctrine. It is true that our society is stratified, and very rigidly stratified, on what at first sight appear to be hereditary lines. There is far less to-and-fro movement between the different groups than happened under capitalism or even in the pre-industrial age. Between the two branches of the Party there is a certain amount of interchange, but only so much as will ensure that weaklings are excluded from the Inner Party and that ambitious members of the Outer Party are made harmless by allowing them to rise. Proletarians, in practice, are not allowed to graduate into the Party. The most gifted among them, who might possibly become nuclei of discontent, are simply marked down by the Thought Police and eliminated. But this state of affairs is not necessarily permanent, nor is it a matter of principle. The Party is not a class in the old sense of the word. It does not aim at transmitting power to its own children, as such; and if there were no other way of keeping the ablest people at the top, it would be perfectly prepared to recruit an entire new generation from the ranks of the proletariat. In the crucial years, the fact that the Party was not a hereditary body did a great deal to neutralize opposition. The older kind of Socialist, who had been trained to fight against something called 'class privilege' assumed that what is not hereditary cannot be permanent. He did not see that the continuity of an oligarchy need not be physical, nor did he pause to reflect that hereditary aristocracies have always been shortlived, whereas adoptive organizations such as the Catholic Church have sometimes lasted for hundreds or thousands of years. The essence of oligarchical rule is not father-to-son inheritance, but the persistence of a certain world-view and a certain way of life, imposed by the dead upon the living. A ruling group is a ruling group so long as it can nominate its successors. The Party is not concerned with perpetuating its blood but with perpetuating itself. *Who* wields power is not important, provided that the hierarchical structure remains always the same.

All the beliefs, habits, tastes, emotions, mental attitudes that characterize our time are really designed to sustain the mystique of the Party and prevent the true nature of present-day society from being perceived. Physical rebellion, or any preliminary move towards rebellion, is at present not possible. From the proletarians nothing is to be feared. Left to themselves, they will continue from generation to generation and from century to century, working, breeding, and dying, not only without any impulse to rebel, but without the power of grasping that the world could be other than it is. They could only become dangerous if the advance of industrial technique made it necessary to educate them more highly; but, since military and commercial rivalry are no longer important, the level of popular education is actually declining. What opinions the masses hold, or do not hold, is looked on as a matter of indifference. They can be granted intellectual liberty because they have no intellect. In a Party member, on the other hand, not even the smallest deviation of opinion on the most unimportant subject can be tolerated. A Party member lives from birth to death under the eye of the Thought Police. Even when he is alone he can never be sure that he is alone. Wherever he may be, asleep or awake, working or resting, in his bath or in bed, he can be inspected without warning and without knowing that he is being inspected. Nothing that he does is indifferent. His friendships, his relaxations, his behaviour towards his wife and children, the expression of his face when he is alone, the words he mutters in sleep, even the characteristic movements of his body, are all jealously scrutinized. Not only any actual misdemeanour, but any eccentricity, however small, any change of habits, any nervous mannerism that could possibly be the symptom of an inner struggle, is certain to be detected. He has no freedom of choice in any direction whatever. On the other hand his actions are not regulated by law or by any clearly formulated code of behaviour. In Oceania there is no law. Thoughts and actions which, when detected, mean certain death are not formally forbidden, and the endless purges, arrests, tortures, imprisonments, and vaporizations are not inflicted as punishment for crimes which have actually been committed, but are merely the wiping-out of persons who might perhaps commit a crime at some time in the future. A Party member is required to have not only the right opinions, but the right instincts. Many of the beliefs and attitudes demanded of him are never plainly stated, and could not be stated without laying bare the contradictions inherent in Ingsoc. If he is a person naturally orthodox (in Newspeak a *goodthinker*), he will in all circumstances know, without taking thought, what is the true belief or the desirable emotion. But in any case an elaborate mental training, undergone in childhood and grouping itself round the Newspeak words *crimestop*, *blackwhite*, and *doublethink*, makes him unwilling and unable to think too deeply on any subject whatever.

A Party member is expected to have no private emotions and no respites from enthusiasm. He is supposed to live in a continuous frenzy of hatred of foreign enemies and internal traitors, triumph over victories, and self-abasement before the power and wisdom of the Party. The discontents produced by his bare, unsatisfying life are deliberately turned outwards and dissipated by such devices as the Two Minutes Hate, and the speculations which might possibly induce a sceptical or rebellious attitude are killed in advance by his early acquired inner discipline. The first and simplest stage in the discipline, which can be taught even to young children, is called, in Newspeak, *crimestop*. *Crimestop* means the faculty of stopping short, as though by instinct, at the threshold of any dangerous thought. It includes the power of not grasping analogies, of failing to perceive logical errors, of misunderstanding the simplest arguments if they are inimical to Ingsoc, and of being bored or repelled by any train of thought which is capable of leading in a heretical direction. *Crimestop*, in short, means protective stupidity. But stupidity is not enough. On the contrary, orthodoxy in the full sense demands a control over one's own mental processes as complete as that of a contortionist over his body. Oceanic society rests ultimately on the belief that Big Brother is omnipotent and that the Party is infallible. But since in reality Big Brother is not omnipotent and the Party is not infallible, there is need for an unwearying, moment-to-moment flexibility in the treatment of facts. The keyword here is *blackwhite*. Like so many Newspeak words, this word has two mutually contradictory meanings. Applied to an opponent, it means the habit of impudently claiming that black is white, in contradiction of the plain facts. Applied to a Party member, it means a loyal willingness to say that black is white when Party discipline demands this. But it means also the ability to *believe* that black is white, and more, to *know* that black is white, and to forget that one has ever believed the contrary. This demands a continuous alteration of the past, made possible by the system of thought which really embraces all the rest, and which is known in Newspeak as *doublethink*.

The alteration of the past is necessary for two reasons, one of which is subsidiary and, so to speak, precautionary. The subsidiary reason is that the Party member, like the proletarian, tolerates present-day conditions partly because he has no standards of comparison. He must be cut off from the past, just as he must be cut off from foreign countries, because it is necessary for him to believe that he is better off than his ancestors and that the average level of material comfort is constantly rising. But by far the more important reason for the readjustment of the past is the need to safeguard the infallibility of the Party. It is not merely that speeches, statistics, and records of every kind must be constantly brought up to date in order to show that the predictions of the

Party were in all cases right. It is also that no change in doctrine or in political alignment can ever be admitted. For to change one's mind, or even one's policy, is a confession of weakness. If, for example, Eurasia or Eastasia (whichever it may be) is the enemy today, then that country must always have been the enemy. And if the facts say otherwise then the facts must be altered. Thus history is continuously rewritten. This day-to-day falsification of the past, carried out by the Ministry of Truth, is as necessary to the stability of the regime as the work of repression and espionage carried out by the Ministry of Love.

The mutability of the past is the central tenet of Ingsoc. Past events, it is argued, have no objective existence, but survive only in written records and in human memories. The past is whatever the records and the memories agree upon. And since the Party is in full control of all records, and in equally full control of the minds of its members, it follows that the past is whatever the Party chooses to make it. It also follows that though the past is alterable, it never has been altered in any specific instance. For when it has been recreated in whatever shape is needed at the moment, then this new version *is* the past, and no different past can ever have existed. This holds good even when, as often happens, the same event has to be altered out of recognition several times in the course of a year. At all times the Party is in possession of absolute truth, and clearly the absolute can never have been different from what it is now. It will be seen that the control of the past depends above all on the training of memory. To make sure that all written records agree with the orthodoxy of the moment is merely a mechanical act. But it is also necessary to *remember* that events happened in the desired manner. And if it is necessary to rearrange one's memories or to tamper with written records, then it is necessary to *forget* that one has done so. The trick of doing this can be learned like any other mental technique. It is learned by the majority of Party members, and certainly by all who are intelligent as well as orthodox. In Oldspeak it is called, quite frankly, 'reality control'. In Newspeak it is called *doublethink*, though *doublethink* comprises much else as well.

Doublethink means the power of holding two contradictory beliefs in one's mind simultaneously, and accepting both of them. The Party intellectual knows in which direction his memories must be altered; he therefore knows that he is playing tricks with reality; but by the exercise of *doublethink* he also satisfies himself that reality is not violated. The process has to be conscious, or it would not be carried out with sufficient precision, but it also has to be unconscious, or it would bring with it a feeling of falsity and hence of guilt. *doublethink* lies at the very heart of Ingsoc, since the essential act of the Party is to use conscious deception while retaining the firmness of purpose that goes with complete honesty. To tell deliberate lies while genuinely believing in them, to forget any fact that has become inconvenient, and then, when it becomes necessary again, to draw it back from oblivion for just so long as it is needed, to deny the existence of objective reality and all the while to take account of the reality which one denies—all this is indispensably necessary. Even in using the word *doublethink* it is necessary to exercise *doublethink*. For by using the word one admits that onc is tampering with reality; by a fresh act of *doublethink* one erases this knowledge; and so on indefinitely, with the lie always one leap ahead of the truth. Ultimately it is by means of *doublethink* that the Party has been able—and may, for all we know, continue to be able for thousands of years—to arrest the course of history.

All past oligarchies have fallen from power either because they ossified or because they grew soft. Either they became stupid and arrogant, failed to adjust themselves to changing circumstances, and were overthrown; or they became liberal and cowardly, made concessions when they should have used force, and once again were overthrown. They fell, that is to say, either through consciousness or through unconsciousness. It is the achievement of the Party to have produced a system of thought in which both conditions can exist simultaneously. And upon no other intellectual basis could the dominion of the Party be made permanent. If one is to rule, and to continue ruling, one must be able to dislocate the sense of reality. For the secret of rulership is to combine a belief in one's own infallibility with the power to learn from past mistakes.

It need hardly be said that the subtlest practitioners of *doublethink* are those who invented *doublethink* and know that it is a vast system of mental cheating. In our society, those who have the best knowledge of what is happening are also those who are furthest from seeing the world as it is. In general, the greater the understanding, the greater the delusion; the more intelligent, the less sane. One clear illustration of this is the fact that war hysteria increases in intensity as one rises in the social scale. Those whose attitude towards the war is most nearly rational are the subject peoples of the disputed territories. To these people the war is simply a continuous calamity which sweeps to and fro over their bodies like a tidal wave. Which side is winning is a matter of complete indifference to them. They are aware that a change of overlordship means simply that they will be doing the same work as before for new masters who treat them in the same manner as the old ones. The slightly more favoured workers whom we call 'the proles' are only intermittently conscious of the war. When it is necessary they can be prodded into frenzies of fear and hatred, but when left to themselves they are capable of forgetting for long periods that the war is happening. It is in the ranks of the Party, and above all of the Inner Party, that the true war enthusiasm is found. World-conquest is believed in most firmly by those who know it to be impossible. This peculiar linking-together of opposites—knowledge with ignorance, cynicism with fanaticism—is one of the chief distinguishing marks of Oceanic society. The official ideology abounds with contradictions even when there is no practical reason for them. Thus, the Party rejects and vilifies every principle for which the Socialist movement originally stood, and it chooses to do this in the name of Socialism. It preaches a contempt for the working class unexampled for centuries past, and it dresses its members in a uniform which was at one time peculiar to manual workers and was adopted for that reason. It systematically undermines the solidarity of the family, and it calls its leader by a name which is a direct appeal to the sentiment of family loyalty. Even the names of the four Ministries by which we are governed exhibit a sort of impudence in their deliberate reversal of the facts. The

Ministry of Peace concerns itself with war, the Ministry of Truth with lies, the Ministry of Love with torture and the Ministry of Plenty with starvation. These contradictions are not accidental, nor do they result from ordinary hypocrisy; they are deliberate exercises in *doublethink*. For it is only by reconciling contradictions that power can be retained indefinitely. In no other way could the ancient cycle be broken. If human equality is to be for ever averted—if the High, as we have called them, are to keep their places permanently—then the prevailing mental condition must be controlled insanity.

But there is one question which until this moment we have almost ignored. It is; why should human equality be averted? Supposing that the mechanics of the process have been rightly described, what is the motive for this huge, accurately planned effort to freeze history at a particular moment of time?

Here we reach the central secret. As we have seen the mystique of the Party, and above all of the Inner Party, depends upon *doublethink*. But deeper than this lies the original motive, the never-questioned instinct that first led to the seizure of power and brought *doublethink*, the Thought Police, continuous warfare, and all the other necessary paraphernalia into existence afterwards. This motive really consists....

Winston became aware of silence, as one becomes aware of a new sound. It seemed to him that Julia had been very still for some time past. She was lying on her side, naked from the waist upwards, with her cheek pillowed on her hand and one dark lock tumbling across her eyes. Her breast rose and fell slowly and regularly.

'Julia.'

No answer.

'Julia, are you awake?'

No answer. She was asleep. He shut the book, put it carefully on the floor, lay down, and pulled the coverlet over both of them.

He had still, he reflected, not learned the ultimate secret. He understood *how*; he did not understand *why*. Chapter I, like Chapter III, had not actually told him anything that he did not know, it had merely systematized the knowledge that he possessed already. But after reading it he knew better than before that he was not mad. Being in a minority, even a minority of one, did not make you mad. There was truth and there was untruth, and if you clung to the truth even against the whole world, you were not mad. A yellow beam from the sinking sun slanted in through the window and fell across the pillow. He shut his eyes. The sun on his face and the girl's smooth body touching his own gave him a strong, sleepy, confident feeling. He was safe, everything was all right. He fell asleep murmuring 'Sanity is not statistical,' with the feeling that this remark contained in it a profound wisdom.

CHAPTER TEN

When he woke it was with the sensation of having slept for a long time, but a glance at the old-fashioned clock told him that it was only twenty-thirty. He lay dozing for a while; then the usual deep-lunged singing struck up from the yard below:

It was only an 'opeless fancy,
It passed like an Ipril dye,
But a look an' a word an' the dreams they stirred
They 'ave stolen my 'eartawye!

The drivelling song seemed to have kept its popularity. You still heard it all over the place. It had outlived the Hate Song. Julia woke at the sound, stretched herself luxuriously, and got out of bed.

'I'm hungry,' she said. 'Let's make some more coffee. Damn! The stove's gone out and the water's cold.' She picked the stove up and shook it. 'There's no oil in it.'

'We can get some from old Charrington, I expect.'

'The funny thing is I made sure it was full. I'm going to put my clothes on,' she added. 'It seems to have got colder.'

Winston also got up and dressed himself. The indefatigable voice sang on:

They sye that time 'eals all things,
They sye you can always forget;
But the smiles an' the tears across the years
They twist my 'eart-strings yet!

As he fastened the belt of his overalls he strolled across to the window. The sun must have gone down behind the houses; it was not shining into the yard any longer. The flagstones were wet as though they had just been washed, and he had the feeling that the sky had been washed too, so fresh and pale was the blue between the chimney-pots. Tirelessly the woman marched to and fro, corking and uncorking herself, singing and falling silent, and pegging out more diapers, and more and yet more. He wondered whether she took in washing for a living or was merely the slave of twenty or thirty grandchildren. Julia had come across to his side; together they gazed down with a sort of fascination at the sturdy figure below. As he looked at the woman in her characteristic attitude, her thick arms reaching up for the line, her powerful mare-like buttocks protruded, it struck him for the first time that she was beautiful. It had never before occurred to him that the body of a woman of fifty, blown up to monstrous dimensions by childbearing, then hardened, roughened by work till it was coarse in the grain like an over-ripe turnip, could be beautiful. But it was so, and after all, he thought, why not? The solid, contourless body, like a block of granite, and the rasping red skin, bore the same relation to the body of a girl as the rose-hip to the rose. Why should the fruit be held inferior to the flower?

'She's beautiful,' he murmured.

'She's a metre across the hips, easily,' said Julia.

'That is her style of beauty,' said Winston.

He held Julia's supple waist easily encircled by his arm. From the hip to the knee her flank was against his. Out of their bodies no child would ever come. That was the one thing they could never do. Only by word of mouth, from mind to mind, could they pass on the secret. The woman down there had no mind, she had only strong arms, a warm heart, and a fertile belly. He wondered how many children she had given birth to. It might easily be fifteen. She had had her momentary flowering, a year, perhaps, of wild-rose beauty and then she had suddenly swollen like a fertilized fruit and grown hard and red and coarse, and then her life had been laundering, scrubbing, darning, cooking, sweeping, polishing, mending, scrubbing, laundering, first for children, then for grandchildren, over thirty unbroken years. At the end of it she was still singing. The mystical reverence that he felt for her was somehow mixed up with the aspect of the pale, cloudless sky, stretching away behind the chimney-pots into interminable distance. It was curious to think that the sky was the same for everybody, in Eurasia or Eastasia as well as here. And the people under the sky were also very much the same—everywhere, all over the world, hundreds of thousands of millions of people just like this, people ignorant of one another's existence, held apart by walls of hatred and lies, and yet almost exactly the same—people who had never learned to think but who were storing up in their hearts and bellies and muscles the power that would one day overturn the world. If there was hope, it lay in the proles! Without having read to the end of *the book*, he knew that that must be Goldstein's final message. The future belonged to the proles. And could he be sure that when their time came the world they constructed would not be just as alien to him, Winston Smith, as the world of the Party? Yes, because at the least it would be a world of sanity. Where there is equality there can be sanity. Sooner or later it would happen, strength would change into consciousness. The proles were immortal, you could not doubt it when you looked at that valiant figure in the yard. In the end their awakening would come. And until that happened, though it might be a thousand years, they would stay alive against all the odds, like birds, passing on from body to body the vitality which the Party did not share and could not kill.

'Do you remember,' he said, 'the thrush that sang to us, that first day, at the edge of the wood?'

'He wasn't singing to us,' said Julia. 'He was singing to please himself. Not even that. He was just singing.'

The birds sang, the proles sang, the Party did not sing. All round the world, in London and New York, in Africa and Brazil, and in the mysterious, forbidden lands beyond the frontiers, in the streets of Paris and Berlin, in the villages of the endless Russian plain, in the bazaars of China and Japan—everywhere stood the same solid unconquerable figure, made monstrous by work and childbearing, toiling from birth to death and still singing. Out of those mighty loins a race of conscious beings must one day come. You were the dead, theirs was the future. But you could share in that future if you kept alive the mind as they kept alive the body, and passed on the secret doctrine that two plus two make four.

'We are the dead,' he said.

'We are the dead,' echoed Julia dutifully.

'You are the dead,' said an iron voice behind them.

They sprang apart. Winston's entrails seemed to have turned into ice. He could see the white all round the irises of Julia's eyes. Her face had turned a milky yellow. The smear of rouge that was still on each cheekbone stood out sharply, almost as though unconnected with the skin beneath.

'You are the dead,' repeated the iron voice.

'It was behind the picture,' breathed Julia.

'It was behind the picture,' said the voice. 'Remain exactly where you are. Make no movement until you are ordered.'

It was starting, it was starting at last! They could do nothing except stand gazing into one another's eyes. To run for life, to get out of the house before it was too late—no such thought occurred to them. Unthinkable to disobey the iron voice from the wall. There was a snap as though a catch had been turned back, and a crash of breaking glass. The picture had fallen to the floor uncovering the telescreen behind it.

'Now they can see us,' said Julia.

'Now we can see you,' said the voice. 'Stand out in the middle of the room. Stand back to back. Clasp your hands behind your heads. Do not touch one another.'

They were not touching, but it seemed to him that he could feel Julia's body shaking. Or perhaps it was merely the shaking of his own. He could just stop his teeth from chattering, but his knees were beyond his control. There was a sound of trampling boots below, inside the house and outside. The yard seemed to be full of men. Something was being dragged across the stones. The woman's singing had stopped abruptly. There was a long, rolling clang, as though the washtub had been flung across the yard, and then a confusion of angry shouts which ended in a yell of pain.

'The house is surrounded,' said Winston.

'The house is surrounded,' said the voice.

He heard Julia snap her teeth together. 'I suppose we may as well say good-bye,' she said.

'You may as well say good-bye,' said the voice. And then another quite different voice, a thin, cultivated voice which Winston had the impression of having heard before, struck in; 'And by the way, while we are on the subject, "Here comes a candle to light you to bed, here comes a chopper to chop off your head"!'

Something crashed on to the bed behind Winston's back. The head of a ladder had been thrust through the window and had burst in the frame. Someone was climbing through the window. There was a stampede of boots up the stairs. The room was full of solid men in black uniforms, with iron-shod boots on their feet and truncheons in their hands.

Winston was not trembling any longer. Even his eyes he barely moved. One thing alone mattered; to keep still, to keep still and not give them an excuse to hit you! A man with a smooth prize-fighter's jowl in which the mouth was only a slit paused opposite him balancing his truncheon meditatively between thumb and forefinger. Winston met his eyes. The feeling of nakedness, with one's hands behind one's head and one's face and body all exposed, was almost unbearable. The man protruded the tip of a white tongue, licked the place where his lips should have been, and then passed on. There was another crash. Someone had picked up the glass paperweight from the table and smashed it to pieces on the hearth-stone.

The fragment of coral, a tiny crinkle of pink like a sugar rosebud from a cake, rolled across the mat. How small, thought Winston, how small it always was! There was a gasp and a thump behind him, and he received a violent kick on the ankle which nearly flung him off his balance. One of the men had smashed his fist into Julia's solar plexus, doubling her up like a pocket ruler. She was thrashing about on the floor, fighting for breath. Winston dared not turn his head even by a millimetre, but sometimes her livid, gasping face came within the angle of his vision. Even in his terror it was as though he could feel the pain in his own body, the deadly pain which nevertheless was less urgent than the struggle to get back her breath. He knew what it was like; the terrible, agonizing pain which was there all the while but could not be suffered yet, because before all else it was necessary to be able to breathe. Then two of the men hoisted her up by knees and shoulders, and carried her out of the room like a sack. Winston had a glimpse of her face, upside down, yellow and contorted, with the eyes shut, and still with a smear of rouge on either cheek; and that was the last he saw of her.

He stood dead still. No one had hit him yet. Thoughts which came of their own accord but seemed totally uninteresting began to flit through his mind. He wondered whether they had got Mr Charrington. He wondered what they had done to the woman in the yard. He noticed that he badly wanted to urinate, and felt a faint surprise, because he had done so only two or three hours ago. He noticed that the clock on the mantelpiece said nine, meaning twenty-one. But the light seemed too strong. Would not the light be fading at twenty-one hours on an August evening? He wondered whether after all he and Julia had mistaken the time—had slept the clock round and thought it was twenty-thirty when really it was nought eight-thirty on the following morning. But he did not pursue the thought further. It was not interesting.

There was another, lighter step in the passage. Mr Charrington came into the room. The demeanour of the black-uniformed men suddenly became more subdued. Something had also changed in Mr Charrington's appearance. His eye fell on the fragments of the glass paperweight.

'Pick up those pieces,' he said sharply.

A man stooped to obey. The cockney accent had disappeared; Winston suddenly realized whose voice it was that he had heard a few moments ago on the telescreen. Mr Charrington was still wearing his old velvet jacket, but his hair, which had been almost white, had turned black. Also he was not wearing his spectacles. He gave Winston a single sharp glance, as though verifying his identity, and then paid no more attention to him. He was still recognizable, but he was not the same person any longer. His body had straightened, and seemed to have grown bigger. His face had undergone only tiny changes that had nevertheless worked a complete transformation. The black eyebrows were less bushy, the wrinkles were gone, the whole lines of the face seemed to have altered; even the nose seemed shorter. It was the alert, cold face of a man of about five-and-thirty. It occurred to Winston that for the first time in his life he was looking, with knowledge, at a member of the Thought Police.

PART III

CHAPTER ONE

He did not know where he was. Presumably he was in the Ministry of Love, but there was no way of making certain.

He was in a high-ceilinged windowless cell with walls of glittering white porcelain. Concealed lamps flooded it with cold light, and there was a low, steady humming sound which he supposed had something to do with the air supply. A bench, or shelf, just wide enough to sit on ran round the wall, broken only by the door and, at the end opposite the door, a lavatory pan with no wooden seat. There were four telescreens, one in each wall.

There was a dull aching in his belly. It had been there ever since they had bundled him into the closed van and driven him away. But he was also hungry, with a gnawing, unwholesome kind of hunger. It might be twenty-four hours since he had eaten, it might be thirty-six. He still did not know, probably never would know, whether it had been morning or evening when they arrested him. Since he was arrested he had not been fed.

He sat as still as he could on the narrow bench, with his hands crossed on his knee. He had already learned to sit still. If you made unexpected movements they yelled at you from the telescreen. But the craving for food was growing upon him. What he longed for above all was a piece of bread. He had an idea that there were a few breadcrumbs in the pocket of his overalls. It was even possible—he thought this because from time to time something seemed to tickle his leg—that there might be a sizeable bit of crust there. In the end the temptation to find out overcame his fear; he slipped a hand into his pocket.

'Smith!' yelled a voice from the telescreen. '6079 Smith W.! Hands out of pockets in the cells!'

He sat still again, his hands crossed on his knee. Before being brought here he had been taken to another place which must have been an ordinary prison or a temporary lock-up used by the patrols. He did not know how long he had been there; some hours at any rate; with no clocks and no daylight it was hard to gauge the time. It was a noisy, evil-smelling place. They had put him into a cell similar to the one he was now in, but filthily dirty and at all times crowded by ten or fifteen people. The majority of them were common criminals, but there were a few political prisoners among them. He had sat silent against the wall, jostled by dirty bodies, too preoccupied by fear and the pain in his belly to take much interest in his surroundings, but still noticing the astonishing difference in demeanour between the Party prisoners and the others. The Party prisoners were always silent and terrified, but the ordinary criminals seemed to care nothing for anybody. They yelled insults at the guards, fought back fiercely when their belongings were impounded, wrote obscene words on the floor, ate smuggled food which they produced from mysterious hiding-places in their clothes, and even shouted down the telescreen when it tried to restore order. On the other hand some of them seemed to be on good terms with the guards, called them by nicknames, and tried to wheedle cigarettes through the spyhole in the door. The guards, too, treated the common criminals with a certain forbearance, even when they had to handle them roughly. There was much talk about the forced-labour camps to which most of the prisoners expected to be sent. It was 'all right' in the camps, he gathered, so long as you had good contacts and knew the ropes. There was bribery, favouritism, and racketeering of every kind, there was homosexuality and prostitution, there was even illicit alcohol distilled from potatoes. The positions of trust were given only to the common criminals, especially the gangsters and the murderers, who formed a sort of aristocracy. All the dirty jobs were done by the politicals.

There was a constant come-and-go of prisoners of every description: drug-peddlers, thieves, bandits, black-marketeers, drunks, prostitutes. Some of the drunks were so violent that the other prisoners had to combine to suppress them. An enormous wreck of a woman, aged about sixty, with great tumbling breasts and thick coils of white hair which had come down in her struggles, was carried in, kicking and shouting, by four guards, who had hold of her one at each corner. They wrenched off the boots with which she had been trying to kick them, and dumped her down across Winston's lap, almost breaking his thigh-bones. The woman hoisted herself upright and followed them out with a yell of 'F—bastards!' Then, noticing that she was sitting on something uneven, she slid off Winston's knees on to the bench.

'Beg pardon, dearie,' she said. 'I wouldn't 'a sat on you, only the buggers put me there. They dono 'ow to treat a lady, do they?' She paused, patted her breast, and belched. 'Pardon,' she said, 'I ain't meself, quite.'

She leant forward and vomited copiously on the floor.

'Thass better,' she said, leaning back with closed eyes. 'Never keep it down, thass what I say. Get it up while it's fresh on your stomach, like.'

She revived, turned to have another look at Winston and seemed immediately to take a fancy to him. She put a vast arm round his shoulder and drew him towards her, breathing beer and vomit into his face.

'Wass your name, dearie?' she said.

'Smith,' said Winston.

'Smith?' said the woman. 'Thass funny. My name's Smith too. Why,' she added sentimentally, 'I might be your mother!'

She might, thought Winston, be his mother. She was about the right age and physique, and it was probable that people changed somewhat after twenty years in a forced-labour camp.

No one else had spoken to him. To a surprising extent the ordinary criminals ignored the Party prisoners. 'The pol*its*,' they called them, with a sort of uninterested contempt. The

Party prisoners seemed terrified of speaking to anybody, and above all of speaking to one another. Only once, when two Party members, both women, were pressed close together on the bench, he overheard amid the din of voices a few hurriedly-whispered words; and in particular a reference to something called 'room one-oh-one', which he did not understand.

It might be two or three hours ago that they had brought him here. The dull pain in his belly never went away, but sometimes it grew better and sometimes worse, and his thoughts expanded or contracted accordingly. When it grew worse he thought only of the pain itself, and of his desire for food. When it grew better, panic took hold of him. There were moments when he foresaw the things that would happen to him with such actuality that his heart galloped and his breath stopped. He felt the smash of truncheons on his elbows and iron-shod boots on his shins; he saw himself grovelling on the floor, screaming for mercy through broken teeth. He hardly thought of Julia. He could not fix his mind on her. He loved her and would not betray her; but that was only a fact, known as he knew the rules of arithmetic. He felt no love for her, and he hardly even wondered what was happening to her. He thought oftener of O'Brien, with a flickering hope. O'Brien might know that he had been arrested. The Brotherhood, he had said, never tried to save its members. But there was the razor blade; they would send the razor blade if they could. There would be perhaps five seconds before the guard could rush into the cell. The blade would bite into him with a sort of burning coldness, and even the fingers that held it would be cut to the bone. Everything came back to his sick body, which shrank trembling from the smallest pain. He was not certain that he would use the razor blade even if he got the chance. It was more natural to exist from moment to moment, accepting another ten minutes' life even with the certainty that there was torture at the end of it.

Sometimes he tried to calculate the number of porcelain bricks in the walls of the cell. It should have been easy, but he always lost count at some point or another. More often he wondered where he was, and what time of day it was. At one moment he felt certain that it was broad daylight outside, and at the next equally certain that it was pitch darkness. In this place, he knew instinctively, the lights would never be turned out. It was the place with no darkness: he saw now why O'Brien had seemed to recognize the allusion. In the Ministry of Love there were no windows. His cell might be at the heart of the building or against its outer wall; it might be ten floors below ground, or thirty above it. He moved himself mentally from place to place, and tried to determine by the feeling of his body whether he was perched high in the air or buried deep underground.

There was a sound of marching boots outside. The steel door opened with a clang. A young officer, a trim black-uniformed figure who seemed to glitter all over with polished leather, and whose pale, straight-featured face was like a wax mask, stepped smartly through the doorway. He motioned to the guards outside to bring in the prisoner they were leading. The poet Ampleforth shambled into the cell. The door clanged shut again.

Ampleforth made one or two uncertain movements from side to side, as though having some idea that there was another door to go out of, and then began to wander up and down the cell. He had not yet noticed Winston's presence. His troubled eyes were gazing at the wall about a metre above the level of Winston's head. He was shoeless; large, dirty toes were sticking out of the holes in his socks. He was also several days away from a shave. A scrubby beard covered his face to the cheekbones, giving him an air of ruffianism that went oddly with his large weak frame and nervous movements.

Winston roused himself a little from his lethargy. He must speak to Ampleforth, and risk the yell from the telescreen. It was even conceivable that Ampleforth was the bearer of the razor blade.

'Ampleforth,' he said.

There was no yell from the telescreen. Ampleforth paused, mildly startled. His eyes focused themselves slowly on Winston.

'Ah, Smith!' he said. 'You too!'

'What are you in for?'

'To tell you the truth—' He sat down awkwardly on the bench opposite Winston. 'There is only one offence, is there not?' he said.

'And have you committed it?'

'Apparently I have.'

He put a hand to his forehead and pressed his temples for a moment, as though trying to remember something.

'These things happen,' he began vaguely. 'I have been able to recall one instance—a possible instance. It was an indiscretion, undoubtedly. We were producing a definitive edition of the poems of Kipling. I allowed the word "God" to remain at the end of a line. I could not help it!' he added almost indignantly, raising his face to look at Winston. 'It was impossible to change the line. The rhyme was "rod". Do you realize that there are only twelve rhymes to "rod" in the entire language? For days I had racked my brains. There *was* no other rhyme.'

The expression on his face changed. The annoyance passed out of it and for a moment he looked almost pleased. A sort of intellectual warmth, the joy of the pedant who has found out some useless fact, shone through the dirt and scrubby hair.

'Has it ever occurred to you,' he said, 'that the whole history of English poetry has been determined by the fact that the English language lacks rhymes?'

No, that particular thought had never occurred to Winston. Nor, in the circumstances, did it strike him as very important or interesting.

'Do you know what time of day it is?' he said.

Ampleforth looked startled again. 'I had hardly thought about it. They arrested me—it could be two days ago—perhaps three.' His eyes flitted round the walls, as though he half expected to find a window somewhere. 'There is no difference between night and day in this place. I do not see how one can calculate the time.'

They talked desultorily for some minutes, then, without apparent reason, a yell from the telescreen bade them be silent. Winston sat quietly, his hands crossed. Ampleforth, too large to sit in comfort on the narrow bench, fidgeted from side to side, clasping his lank hands first round one knee, then round the other. The telescreen barked at him to keep still. Time passed. Twenty minutes, an hour—it was difficult to judge. Once more there was a sound of boots outside. Winston's entrails contracted. Soon, very soon, perhaps in five minutes, perhaps now, the tramp of boots would mean that his own turn had come.

The door opened. The cold-faced young officer stepped into the cell. With a brief movement of the hand he indicated Ampleforth.

'Room 101,' he said.

Ampleforth marched clumsily out between the guards, his face vaguely perturbed, but uncomprehending.

What seemed like a long time passed. The pain in Winston's belly had revived. His mind sagged round and round on the same trick, like a ball falling again and again into the same series of slots. He had only six thoughts. The pain in his belly; a piece of bread; the blood and the screaming; O'Brien; Julia; the razor blade. There was another spasm in his entrails, the heavy boots were approaching. As the door opened, the wave of air that it created brought in a powerful smell of cold sweat. Parsons walked into the cell. He was wearing khaki shorts and a sports-shirt.

This time Winston was startled into self-forgetfulness.

'*You* here!' he said.

Parsons gave Winston a glance in which there was neither interest nor surprise, but only misery. He began walking jerkily up and down, evidently unable to keep still. Each time he straightened his pudgy knees it was apparent that they were trembling. His eyes had a wide-open, staring look, as though he could not prevent himself from gazing at something in the middle distance.

'What are you in for?' said Winston.

'Thoughtcrime!' said Parsons, almost blubbering. The tone of his voice implied at once a complete admission of his guilt and a sort of incredulous horror that such a word could be applied to himself. He paused opposite Winston and began eagerly appealing to him: 'You don't think they'll shoot me, do you, old chap? They don't shoot you if you haven't actually done anything—only thoughts, which you can't help? I know they give you a fair hearing. Oh, I trust them for that! They'll know my record, won't they? *You* know what kind of chap I was. Not a bad chap in my way. Not brainy, of course, but keen. I tried to do my best for the Party, didn't I? I'll get off with five years, don't you think? Or even ten years? A chap like me could make himself pretty useful in a labour-camp. They wouldn't shoot me for going off the rails just once?'

'Are you guilty?' said Winston.

'Of course I'm guilty!' cried Parsons with a servile glance at the telescreen. 'You don't think the Party would arrest an innocent man, do you?' His frog-like face grew calmer, and even took on a slightly sanctimonious expression. 'Thoughtcrime is a dreadful thing, old man,' he said sententiously. 'It's insidious. It can get hold of you without your even knowing it. Do you know how it got hold of me? In my sleep! Yes, that's a fact. There I was, working away, trying to do my bit—never knew I had any bad stuff in my mind at all. And then I started talking in my sleep. Do you know what they heard me saying?'

He sank his voice, like someone who is obliged for medical reasons to utter an obscenity.

'"Down with Big Brother!" Yes, I said that! Said it over and over again, it seems. Between you and me, old man, I'm glad they got me before it went any further. Do you know what I'm going to say to them when I go up before the tribunal? "Thank you," I'm going to say, "thank you for saving me before it was too late."'

'Who denounced you?' said Winston.

'It was my little daughter,' said Parsons with a sort of doleful pride. 'She listened at the keyhole. Heard what I was saying, and nipped off to the patrols the very next day. Pretty smart for a nipper of seven, eh? I don't bear her any grudge for it. In fact I'm proud of her. It shows I brought her up in the right spirit, anyway.'

He made a few more jerky movements up and down, several times, casting a longing glance at the lavatory pan. Then he suddenly ripped down his shorts.

'Excuse me, old man,' he said. 'I can't help it. It's the waiting.'

He plumped his large posterior into the lavatory pan. Winston covered his face with his hands.

'Smith!' yelled the voice from the telescreen. '6079 Smith W.! Uncover your face. No faces covered in the cells.'

Winston uncovered his face. Parsons used the lavatory, loudly and abundantly. It then turned out that the plug was defective and the cell stank abominably for hours afterwards.

Parsons was removed. More prisoners came and went, mysteriously. One, a woman, was consigned to 'Room 101', and, Winston noticed, seemed to shrivel and turn a different colour when she heard the words. A time came when, if it had been morning when he was brought here, it would be afternoon; or if it had been afternoon, then it would be midnight. There were six prisoners in the cell, men and women. All sat very still. Opposite Winston there sat a man with a chinless, toothy face exactly like that of some large, harmless rodent. His fat, mottled cheeks were so pouched at the bottom that it was difficult not to believe that he had little stores of food tucked away there. His pale-grey eyes flitted timorously from face to face and turned quickly away again when he caught anyone's eye.

The door opened, and another prisoner was brought in whose appearance sent a momentary chill through Winston. He was a commonplace, mean-looking man who might have been an engineer or technician of some kind. But what was startling was the emaciation of his face. It was like a skull. Because of its thinness the mouth and eyes looked disproportionately large, and the eyes seemed filled with a murderous, unappeasable hatred of somebody or something.

The man sat down on the bench at a little distance from Winston. Winston did not look at him again, but the tormented, skull-like face was as vivid in his mind as though it had been straight in front of his eyes. Suddenly he realized what was the matter. The man was dying of starvation. The same thought seemed to occur almost simultaneously to everyone in the cell. There was a very faint stirring all the way round the bench. The eyes of the chinless man kept flitting towards the skull-faced man, then turning guiltily away, then being dragged back by an irresistible attraction. Presently he began to fidget on his seat. At last he stood up, waddled clumsily across the cell, dug down into the pocket of his overalls, and, with an abashed air, held out a grimy piece of bread to the skull-faced man.

There was a furious, deafening roar from the telescreen. The chinless man jumped in his tracks. The skull-faced man had quickly thrust his hands behind his back, as though demonstrating to all the world that he refused the gift.

'Bumstead!' roared the voice. '2713 Bumstead J.! Let fall that piece of bread!'

The chinless man dropped the piece of bread on the floor.

'Remain standing where you are,' said the voice. 'Face the door. Make no movement.'

The chinless man obeyed. His large pouchy cheeks were quivering uncontrollably. The door clanged open. As the young officer entered and stepped aside, there emerged from behind him a short stumpy guard with enormous arms and shoulders. He took his stand opposite the chinless man, and then, at a signal from the officer, let free a frightful blow, with all the weight of his body behind it, full in the chinless man's mouth. The force of it seemed almost to knock him clear of the floor. His body was flung across the cell and fetched up against the base of the lavatory seat. For a moment he lay as though stunned, with dark blood oozing from his mouth and nose. A very faint whimpering or squeaking, which seemed unconscious, came out of him. Then he rolled over and raised himself unsteadily on hands and knees. Amid a stream of blood and saliva, the two halves of a dental plate fell out of his mouth.

The prisoners sat very still, their hands crossed on their knees. The chinless man climbed back into his place. Down one side of his face the flesh was darkening. His mouth had swollen into a shapeless cherry-coloured mass with a black hole in the middle of it.

From time to time a little blood dripped on to the breast of his overalls. His grey eyes still flitted from face to face, more guiltily than ever, as though he were trying to discover how much the others despised him for his humiliation.

The door opened. With a small gesture the officer indicated the skull-faced man.

'Room 101,' he said.

There was a gasp and a flurry at Winston's side. The man had actually flung himself on his knees on the floor, with his hand clasped together.

'Comrade! Officer!' he cried. 'You don't have to take me to that place! Haven't I told you everything already? What else is it you want to know? There's nothing I wouldn't confess, nothing! Just tell me what it is and I'll confess straight off. Write it down and I'll sign it—anything! Not room 101!'

'Room 101,' said the officer.

The man's face, already very pale, turned a colour Winston would not have believed possible. It was definitely, unmistakably, a shade of green.

'Do anything to me!' he yelled. 'You've been starving me for weeks. Finish it off and let me die. Shoot me. Hang me. Sentence me to twenty-five years. Is there somebody else you want me to give away? Just say who it is and I'll tell you anything you want. I don't care who it is or what you do to them. I've got a wife and three children. The biggest of them isn't six years old. You can take the whole lot of them and cut their throats in front of my eyes, and I'll stand by and watch it. But not Room 101!'

'Room 101,' said the officer.

The man looked frantically round at the other prisoners, as though with some idea that he could put another victim in his own place. His eyes settled on the smashed face of the chinless man. He flung out a lean arm.

'That's the one you ought to be taking, not me!' he shouted. 'You didn't hear what he was saying after they bashed his face. Give me a chance and I'll tell you every word of it. *He's* the one that's against the Party, not me.' The guards stepped forward. The man's voice rose to a shriek. 'You didn't hear him!' he repeated. 'Something went wrong with the telescreen. *He's* the one you want. Take him, not me!'

The two sturdy guards had stooped to take him by the arms. But just at this moment he flung himself across the floor of the cell and grabbed one of the iron legs that supported the bench. He had set up a wordless howling, like an animal. The guards took hold of him to wrench him loose, but he clung on with astonishing strength. For perhaps twenty seconds they were hauling at him. The prisoners sat quiet, their hands crossed on their knees, looking straight in front of them. The howling stopped; the man had no breath left for anything except hanging on. Then there was a different kind of cry. A kick from a guard's boot had broken the fingers of one of his hands. They dragged him to his feet.

'Room 101,' said the officer.

The man was led out, walking unsteadily, with head sunken, nursing his crushed hand, all the fight had gone out of him.

A long time passed. If it had been midnight when the skull-faced man was taken away, it was morning: if morning, it was afternoon. Winston was alone, and had been alone for hours. The pain of sitting on the narrow bench was such that often he got up and walked about, unreproved by the telescreen. The piece of bread still lay where the chinless man had dropped it. At the beginning it needed a hard effort not to look at it, but presently hunger gave way to thirst. His mouth was sticky and evil-tasting. The humming sound and the unvarying white light induced a sort of faintness, an empty feeling inside his head. He would get up because the ache in his bones was no longer bearable, and then would sit down again almost at once because he was too dizzy to make sure of staying on his feet. Whenever his physical sensations were a little under control the terror returned. Sometimes with a fading hope he thought of O'Brien and the razor blade. It was thinkable that the razor blade might arrive concealed in his food, if he were ever fed. More dimly he thought of Julia. Somewhere or other she was suffering perhaps far worse than he. She might be screaming with pain at this moment. He thought: 'If I could save Julia by doubling my own pain, would I do it? Yes, I would.' But that was merely an intellectual decision, taken because he knew that he ought to take it. He did not feel it. In this place you could not feel anything, except pain and foreknowledge of pain. Besides, was it possible, when you were actually suffering it, to wish for any reason that your own pain should increase? But that question was not answerable yet.

The boots were approaching again. The door opened. O'Brien came in.

Winston started to his feet. The shock of the sight had driven all caution out of him. For the first time in many years he forgot the presence of the telescreen.

'They've got you too!' he cried.

'They got me a long time ago,' said O'Brien with a mild, almost regretful irony. He stepped aside. From behind him there emerged a broad-chested guard with a long black truncheon in his hand.

'You know this, Winston,' said O'Brien. 'Don't deceive yourself. You did know it—you have always known it.'

Yes, he saw now, he had always known it. But there was no time to think of that. All he had eyes for was the truncheon in the guard's hand. It might fall anywhere; on the crown, on the tip of the ear, on the upper arm, on the elbow....

The elbow! He had slumped to his knees, almost paralysed, clasping the stricken elbow with his other hand. Everything had exploded into yellow light. Inconceivable, inconceivable that one blow could cause such pain! The light cleared and he could see the other two looking down at him. The guard was laughing at his contortions. One question at any rate was answered. Never, for any reason on earth, could you wish for an increase of pain. Of pain you could wish only one thing: that it should stop. Nothing in the world was so bad as physical pain. In the face of pain there are no heroes, no heroes, he thought over and over as he writhed on the floor, clutching uselessly at his disabled left arm.

CHAPTER TWO

He was lying on something that felt like a camp bed, except that it was higher off the ground and that he was fixed down in some way so that he could not move. Light that seemed stronger than usual was falling on his face. O'Brien was standing at his side, looking down at him intently. At the other side of him stood a man in a white coat, holding a hypodermic syringe.

Even after his eyes were open he took in his surroundings only gradually. He had the impression of swimming up into this room from some quite different world, a sort of underwater world far beneath it. How long he had been down there he did not know. Since the moment when they arrested him he had not seen darkness or daylight. Besides, his memories were not continuous. There had been times when consciousness, even the sort of consciousness that one has in sleep, had stopped dead and started again after a blank interval. But whether the intervals were of days or weeks or only seconds, there was no way of knowing.

With that first blow on the elbow the nightmare had started. Later he was to realize that all that then happened was merely a preliminary, a routine interrogation to which nearly all prisoners were subjected. There was a long range of crimes—espionage, sabotage, and the like—to which everyone had to confess as a matter of course. The confession was a formality, though the torture was real. How many times he had been beaten, how long the beatings had continued, he could not remember. Always there were five or six men in black uniforms at him simultaneously. Sometimes it was fists, sometimes it was truncheons, sometimes it was steel rods, sometimes it was boots. There were times when he rolled about the floor, as shameless as an animal, writhing his body this way and that in an endless, hopeless effort to dodge the kicks, and simply inviting more and yet more kicks, in his ribs, in his belly, on his elbows, on his shins, in his groin, in his testicles, on the bone at the base of his spine. There were times when it went on and on until the cruel, wicked, unforgivable thing seemed to him not that the guards continued to beat him but that he could not force himself into losing consciousness. There were times when his nerve so forsook him that he began shouting for mercy even before the beating began, when the mere sight of a fist drawn back for a blow was enough to make him pour forth a confession of real and imaginary crimes. There were other times when he started out with the resolve of confessing nothing, when every word had to be forced out of him between gasps of pain, and there were times when he feebly tried to compromise, when he said to himself: 'I will confess, but not yet. I must hold out till the pain becomes unbearable. Three more kicks, two more kicks, and then I will tell them what they want.' Sometimes he was beaten till he could hardly stand, then flung like a sack of potatoes on to the stone floor of a cell, left to recuperate for a few hours, and then taken out and beaten again. There were also longer periods of recovery. He remembered them dimly, because they were spent chiefly in sleep or stupor. He remembered a cell with a plank bed, a sort of shelf sticking out from the wall, and a tin wash-basin, and meals of hot soup and bread and sometimes coffee. He remembered a surly barber arriving to scrape his chin and crop his hair, and businesslike, unsympathetic men in white coats feeling his pulse, tapping his reflexes, turning up his eyelids, running harsh fingers over him in search for broken bones, and shooting needles into his arm to make him sleep.

The beatings grew less frequent, and became mainly a threat, a horror to which he could be sent back at any moment when his answers were unsatisfactory. His questioners now were not ruffians in black uniforms but Party intellectuals, little rotund men with quick movements and flashing spectacles, who worked on him in relays over periods which lasted—he thought, he could not be sure—ten or twelve hours at a stretch. These other questioners saw to it that he was in constant slight pain, but it was not chiefly pain that they relied on. They slapped his face, wrung his ears, pulled his hair, made him stand on one leg, refused him leave to urinate, shone glaring lights in his face until his eyes ran with water; but the aim of this was simply to humiliate him and destroy his power of arguing and reasoning. Their real weapon was the merciless questioning that went on and on, hour after hour, tripping him up, laying traps for him, twisting everything that he said, convicting him at every step of lies and self-contradiction until he began weeping as much from shame as from nervous fatigue. Sometimes he would weep half a dozen times in a single session. Most of the time they screamed abuse at him and threatened at every hesitation to deliver him over to the guards again; but sometimes they would suddenly change their tune, call him comrade, appeal to him in the name of Ingsoc and Big Brother, and ask him sorrowfully whether even now he had not enough loyalty to the Party left to make him wish to undo the evil he had done. When his nerves were in rags after hours of questioning, even this appeal could reduce him to snivelling tears. In the end the nagging voices broke him down more completely than the boots and fists of the guards. He became simply a mouth that uttered, a hand that signed, whatever was demanded of him. His sole concern was to find out what they wanted him to confess, and then confess it quickly, before the bullying started anew. He confessed to the assassination of eminent Party members, the distribution of seditious pamphlets, embezzlement of public funds, sale of military secrets, sabotage of every kind. He confessed that he had been a spy in the pay of the Eastasian government as far back as 1968. He confessed that he was a religious believer, an admirer of capitalism, and a sexual pervert. He confessed that he had murdered his wife, although he knew, and his questioners must have known, that his wife was still alive. He confessed that for years he had been in personal touch with Goldstein and had been a member of an underground organization which had included almost every human being he had ever known. It was easier to confess everything and implicate everybody. Besides, in a sense it was all true. It was true that he had been the enemy of the Party, and in the eyes of the Party there was no distinction between the thought and the deed.

There were also memories of another kind. They stood out in his mind disconnectedly, like pictures with blackness all round them.

He was in a cell which might have been either dark or light, because he could see nothing except a pair of eyes. Near at hand some kind of instrument was ticking slowly and regularly. The eyes grew larger and more luminous. Suddenly he floated out of his seat, dived into the eyes, and was swallowed up.

He was strapped into a chair surrounded by dials, under dazzling lights. A man in a white coat was reading the dials. There was a tramp of heavy boots outside. The door clanged open. The waxed-faced officer marched in, followed by two guards.

'Room 101,' said the officer.

The man in the white coat did not turn round. He did not look at Winston either; he was looking only at the dials.

He was rolling down a mighty corridor, a kilometre wide, full of glorious, golden light, roaring with laughter and shouting out confessions at the top of his voice. He was confessing everything, even the things he had succeeded in holding back under the torture. He was relating the entire history of his life to an audience who knew it already. With him were the guards, the other questioners, the men in white coats, O'Brien, Julia, Mr Charrington, all rolling down the corridor together and shouting with laughter. Some dreadful thing which had lain embedded in the future had somehow been skipped over and had not happened. Everything was all right, there was no more pain, the last detail of his life was laid bare, understood, forgiven.

He was starting up from the plank bed in the half-certainty that he had heard O'Brien's voice. All through his interrogation, although he had never seen him, he had had the feeling that O'Brien was at his elbow, just out of sight. It was O'Brien who was directing everything. It was he who set the guards on to Winston and who prevented them from killing him. It was he who decided when Winston should scream with pain, when he should have a respite, when he should be fed, when he should sleep, when the drugs should be pumped into his arm. It was he who asked the questions and suggested the answers. He was the tormentor, he was the protector, he was the inquisitor, he was the friend. And once—Winston could not remember whether it was in drugged sleep, or in normal sleep, or even in a moment of wakefulness—a voice murmured in his ear: 'Don't worry, Winston; you are in my keeping. For seven years I have watched over you. Now the turning-point has come. I shall save you, I shall make you perfect.' He was not sure whether it was O'Brien's voice; but it was the same voice that had said to him, 'We shall meet in the place where there is no darkness,' in that other dream, seven years ago.

He did not remember any ending to his interrogation. There was a period of blackness and then the cell, or room, in which he now was had gradually materialized round him. He was almost flat on his back, and unable to move. His body was held down at every essential point. Even the back of his head was gripped in some manner. O'Brien was looking down at him gravely and rather sadly. His face, seen from below, looked coarse and worn, with pouches under the eyes and tired lines from nose to chin. He was older than Winston had thought him; he was perhaps forty-eight or fifty. Under his hand there was a dial with a lever on top and figures running round the face.

'I told you,' said O'Brien, 'that if we met again it would be here.'

'Yes,' said Winston.

Without any warning except a slight movement of O'Brien's hand, a wave of pain flooded his body. It was a frightening pain, because he could not see what was happening, and he had the feeling that some mortal injury was being done to him. He did not know whether the thing was really happening, or whether the effect was electrically produced; but his body was being wrenched out of shape, the joints were being slowly torn apart. Although the pain had brought the sweat out on his forehead, the worst of all was the fear that his backbone was about to snap. He set his teeth and breathed hard through his nose, trying to keep silent as long as possible.

'You are afraid,' said O'Brien, watching his face, 'that in another moment something is going to break. Your especial fear is that it will be your backbone. You have a vivid mental picture of the vertebrae snapping apart and the spinal fluid dripping out of them. That is what you are thinking, is it not, Winston?'

Winston did not answer. O'Brien drew back the lever on the dial. The wave of pain receded almost as quickly as it had come.

'That was forty,' said O'Brien. 'You can see that the numbers on this dial run up to a hundred. Will you please remember, throughout our conversation, that I have it in my power to inflict pain on you at any moment and to whatever degree I choose? If you tell me any lies, or attempt to prevaricate in any way, or even fall below your usual level of intelligence, you will cry out with pain, instantly. Do you understand that?'

'Yes,' said Winston.

O'Brien's manner became less severe. He resettled his spectacles thoughtfully, and took a pace or two up and down. When he spoke his voice was gentle and patient. He had the air of a doctor, a teacher, even a priest, anxious to explain and persuade rather than to punish.

'I am taking trouble with you, Winston,' he said, 'because you are worth trouble. You know perfectly well what is the matter with you. You have known it for years, though you have fought against the knowledge. You are mentally deranged. You suffer from a defective memory. You are unable to remember real events and you persuade yourself that you remember other events which never happened. Fortunately it is curable. You have never cured yourself of it, because you did not choose to. There was a small effort of the will that you were not ready to make. Even now, I am well aware, you are clinging to your disease under the impression that it is a virtue. Now we will take an example. At this moment, which power is Oceania at war with?'

'When I was arrested, Oceania was at war with Eastasia.'

'With Eastasia. Good. And Oceania has always been at war with Eastasia, has it not?'

Winston drew in his breath. He opened his mouth to speak and then did not speak. He could not take his eyes away from the dial.

'The truth, please, Winston. *Your* truth. Tell me what you think you remember.'

'I remember that until only a week before I was arrested, we were not at war with Eastasia at all. We were in alliance with them. The war was against Eurasia. That had lasted for four years. Before that—'

O'Brien stopped him with a movement of the hand.

'Another example,' he said. 'Some years ago you had a very serious delusion indeed. You believed that three men, three one-time Party members named Jones, Aaronson, and Rutherford—men who were executed for treachery and sabotage after making the fullest possible confession—were not guilty of the crimes they were charged with. You believed that you had seen unmistakable documentary evidence proving that their confessions were false. There was a certain photograph about which you had a hallucination. You believed that you had actually held it in your hands. It was a photograph something like this.'

An oblong slip of newspaper had appeared between O'Brien's fingers. For perhaps five seconds it was within the angle of Winston's vision. It was a photograph, and there was no question of its identity. It was *the* photograph. It was another copy of the photograph of Jones, Aaronson, and Rutherford at the party function in New York, which he had chanced upon eleven years ago and promptly destroyed. For only an instant it was before his eyes, then it was out of sight again. But he had seen it, unquestionably he had seen it! He made a desperate, agonizing effort to wrench the top half of his body free. It was impossible to move so much as a centimetre in any direction. For the moment he had even forgotten the dial. All he wanted was to hold the photograph in his fingers again, or at least to see it.

'It exists!' he cried.

'No,' said O'Brien.

He stepped across the room. There was a memory hole in the opposite wall. O'Brien lifted the grating. Unseen, the frail slip of paper was whirling away on the current of warm air; it was vanishing in a flash of flame. O'Brien turned away from the wall.

'Ashes,' he said. 'Not even identifiable ashes. Dust. It does not exist. It never existed.'

'But it did exist! It does exist! It exists in memory. I remember it. You remember it.'

'I do not remember it,' said O'Brien.

Winston's heart sank. That was doublethink. He had a feeling of deadly helplessness. If he could have been certain that O'Brien was lying, it would not have seemed to matter. But it was perfectly possible that O'Brien had really forgotten the photograph. And if so, then already he would have forgotten his denial of remembering it, and forgotten the act of forgetting. How could one be sure that it was simple trickery? Perhaps that lunatic dislocation in the mind could really happen: that was the thought that defeated him.

O'Brien was looking down at him speculatively. More than ever he had the air of a teacher taking pains with a wayward but promising child.

'There is a Party slogan dealing with the control of the past,' he said. 'Repeat it, if you please.'

'"Who controls the past controls the future: who controls the present controls the past,"' repeated Winston obediently.

'"Who controls the present controls the past,"' said O'Brien, nodding his head with slow approval. 'Is it your opinion, Winston, that the past has real existence?'

Again the feeling of helplessness descended upon Winston. His eyes flitted towards the dial. He not only did not know whether 'yes' or 'no' was the answer that would save him from pain; he did not even know which answer he believed to be the true one.

O'Brien smiled faintly. 'You are no metaphysician, Winston,' he said. 'Until this moment you had never considered what is meant by existence. I will put it more precisely. Does the past exist concretely, in space? Is there somewhere or other a place, a world of solid objects, where the past is still happening?'

'No.'

'Then where does the past exist, if at all?'

'In records. It is written down.'

'In records. And——?'

'In the mind. In human memories.'

'In memory. Very well, then. We, the Party, control all records, and we control all memories. Then we control the past, do we not?'

'But how can you stop people remembering things?' cried Winston again momentarily forgetting the dial. 'It is involuntary. It is outside oneself. How can you control memory? You have not controlled mine!'

O'Brien's manner grew stern again. He laid his hand on the dial.

'On the contrary,' he said, '*you* have not controlled it. That is what has brought you here. You are here because you have failed in humility, in self-discipline. You would not make the act of submission which is the price of sanity. You preferred to be a lunatic, a minority of one. Only the disciplined mind can see reality, Winston. You believe that reality is something objective, external, existing in its own right. You also believe that the nature of reality is self-evident. When you delude yourself into thinking that you see something, you assume that everyone else sees the same thing as you. But I tell you, Winston, that reality is not external. Reality exists in the human mind, and nowhere else. Not in the individual mind, which can make mistakes, and in any case soon perishes: only in the mind of the Party, which is collective and immortal. Whatever the Party holds to be the truth, is truth. It is impossible to see reality except by looking through the eyes of the Party. That is the fact that you have got to relearn, Winston. It needs an act of self-destruction, an effort of the will. You must humble yourself before you can become sane.'

He paused for a few moments, as though to allow what he had been saying to sink in.

'Do you remember,' he went on, 'writing in your diary, "Freedom is the freedom to say that two plus two make four"?'

'Yes,' said Winston.

O'Brien held up his left hand, its back towards Winston, with the thumb hidden and the four fingers extended.

'How many fingers am I holding up, Winston?'

'Four.'

'And if the party says that it is not four but five—then how many?'

'Four.'

The word ended in a gasp of pain. The needle of the dial had shot up to fifty-five. The sweat had sprung out all over Winston's body. The air tore into his lungs and issued again in deep groans which even by clenching his teeth he could not stop. O'Brien watched him, the four fingers still extended. He drew back the lever. This time the pain was only slightly eased.

'How many fingers, Winston?'

'Four.'

The needle went up to sixty.

'How many fingers, Winston?'

'Four! Four! What else can I say? Four!'

The needle must have risen again, but he did not look at it. The heavy, stern face and the four fingers filled his vision. The fingers stood up before his eyes like pillars, enormous, blurry, and seeming to vibrate, but unmistakably four.

'How many fingers, Winston?'

'Four! Stop it, stop it! How can you go on? Four! Four!'

'How many fingers, Winston?'

'Five! Five! Five!'

'No, Winston, that is no use. You are lying. You still think there are four. How many fingers, please?'

'Four! five! Four! Anything you like. Only stop it, stop the pain!'

Abruptly he was sitting up with O'Brien's arm round his shoulders. He had perhaps lost consciousness for a few seconds. The bonds that had held his body down were loosened. He felt very cold, he was shaking uncontrollably, his teeth were chattering, the tears were rolling down his cheeks. For a moment he clung to O'Brien like a baby, curiously comforted by the heavy arm round his shoulders. He had the feeling that O'Brien was his protector, that the pain was something that came from outside, from some other source, and that it was O'Brien who would save him from it.

'You are a slow learner, Winston,' said O'Brien gently.

'How can I help it?' he blubbered. 'How can I help seeing what is in front of my eyes? Two and two are four.'

'Sometimes, Winston. Sometimes they are five. Sometimes they are three. Sometimes they are all of them at once. You must try harder. It is not easy to become sane.'

He laid Winston down on the bed. The grip of his limbs tightened again, but the pain had ebbed away and the trembling had stopped, leaving him merely weak and cold. O'Brien motioned with his head to the man in the white coat, who had stood immobile throughout the proceedings. The man in the white coat bent down and looked closely into Winston's eyes, felt his pulse, laid an ear against his chest, tapped here and there, then he nodded to O'Brien.

'Again,' said O'Brien.

The pain flowed into Winston's body. The needle must be at seventy, seventy-five. He had shut his eyes this time. He knew that the fingers were still there, and still four. All that mattered was somehow to stay alive until the spasm was over. He had ceased to notice whether he was crying out or not. The pain lessened again. He opened his eyes. O'Brien had drawn back the lever.

'How many fingers, Winston?'

'Four. I suppose there are four. I would see five if I could. I am trying to see five.'

'Which do you wish: to persuade me that you see five, or really to see them?'

'Really to see them.'

'Again,' said O'Brien.

Perhaps the needle was eighty-ninety. Winston could not intermittently remember why the pain was happening. Behind his screwed-up eyelids a forest of fingers seemed to be moving in a sort of dance, weaving in and out, disappearing behind one another and reappearing again. He was trying to count them, he could not remember why. He knew only that it was impossible to count them, and that this was somehow due to the mysterious identity between five and four. The pain died down again. When he opened his eyes it was to find that he was still seeing the same thing. Innumerable fingers, like moving trees, were still streaming past in either direction, crossing and recrossing. He shut his eyes again.

'How many fingers am I holding up, Winston?'

'I don't know. I don't know. You will kill me if you do that again. Four, five, six—in all honesty I don't know.'

'Better,' said O'Brien.

A needle slid into Winston's arm. Almost in the same instant a blissful, healing warmth spread all through his body. The pain was already half-forgotten. He opened his eyes and looked up gratefully at O'Brien. At sight of the heavy, lined face, so ugly and so intelligent, his heart seemed to turn over. If he could have moved he would have stretched out a hand and laid it on O'Brien's arm. He had never loved him so deeply as at this moment, and not merely because he had stopped the pain. The old feeling, that at bottom it did not matter whether O'Brien was a friend or an enemy, had come back. O'Brien was a person who could be talked to. Perhaps one did not want to be loved so much as to be understood. O'Brien had tortured him to the edge of lunacy, and in a little while, it was certain, he would send him to his death. It made no difference. In some sense that went deeper than friendship, they were intimates: somewhere or other, although the actual words might never be spoken, there was a place where they could meet and talk. O'Brien was looking down at him with an expression which suggested that the same thought might be in his own mind. When he spoke it was in an easy, conversational tone.

'Do you know where you are, Winston?' he said.

'I don't know. I can guess. In the Ministry of Love.'

'Do you know how long you have been here?'

'I don't know. Days, weeks, months—I think it is months.'

'And why do you imagine that we bring people to this place?'

'To make them confess.'

'No, that is not the reason. Try again.'

'To punish them.'

'No!' exclaimed O'Brien. His voice had changed extraordinarily, and his face had suddenly become both stern and animated. 'No! Not merely to extract your confession, not to punish you. Shall I tell you why we have brought you here? To cure you! To make you sane! Will you understand, Winston, that no one whom we bring to this place ever leaves our hands uncured? We are not interested in those stupid crimes that you have committed. The Party is not interested in the overt act: the thought is all we care about. We do not merely destroy our enemies, we change them. Do you understand what I mean by that?'

He was bending over Winston. His face looked enormous because of its nearness, and hideously ugly because it was seen from below. Moreover it was filled with a sort of exaltation, a lunatic intensity. Again Winston's heart shrank. If it had been possible he would have cowered deeper into the bed. He felt certain that O'Brien was about to twist the dial out of sheer wantonness. At this moment, however, O'Brien turned away. He took a pace or two up and down. Then he continued less vehemently:

'The first thing for you to understand is that in this place there are no martyrdoms. You have read of the religious persecutions of the past. In the Middle Ages there was the Inquisition. It was a failure. It set out to eradicate heresy, and ended by perpetuating it. For every heretic it burned at the stake, thousands of others rose up. Why was that? Because the Inquisition killed its enemies in the open, and killed them while they were still unrepentant: in fact, it killed them because they were unrepentant. Men were dying because they would not abandon their true beliefs. Naturally all the glory belonged to the victim and all the shame to the Inquisitor who burned him. Later, in the twentieth century, there were the totalitarians, as they were called. There were the German Nazis and the Russian Communists. The Russians persecuted heresy more cruelly than the Inquisition had done. And they imagined that they had learned from the mistakes of the past; they knew, at any rate, that one must not make martyrs. Before they exposed their victims to public trial, they deliberately set themselves to destroy their dignity. They wore them down by torture and solitude until they were despicable, cringing wretches, confessing whatever was put into their mouths, covering themselves with abuse, accusing and sheltering behind one another, whimpering for mercy. And yet after only a few years the same thing had happened over again. The dead men had become martyrs and their degradation was forgotten. Once again, why was it? In the first place, because the confessions that they had made were obviously extorted and untrue. We do not make mistakes of that kind. All the confessions that are uttered here are true. We make them true. And above all we do not allow the dead to rise up against us. You must stop imagining that posterity will vindicate you, Winston. Posterity will never hear of you. You will be lifted clean out from the stream of history. We shall turn you into gas and pour you into the stratosphere. Nothing will remain of you, not a name in a register, not a memory in a living brain. You will be annihilated in the past as well as in the future. You will never have existed.'

Then why bother to torture me? thought Winston, with a momentary bitterness. O'Brien checked his step as though Winston had uttered the thought aloud. His large ugly face came nearer, with the eyes a little narrowed.

'You are thinking,' he said, 'that since we intend to destroy you utterly, so that nothing that you say or do can make the smallest difference—in that case, why do we go to the trouble of interrogating you first? That is what you were thinking, was it not?'

'Yes,' said Winston.

O'Brien smiled slightly. 'You are a flaw in the pattern, Winston. You are a stain that must be wiped out. Did I not tell you just now that we are different from the persecutors of the past? We are not content with negative obedience, nor even with the most abject submission. When finally you surrender to us, it must be of your own free will. We do not destroy the heretic because he resists us: so long as he resists us we never destroy him. We convert him, we capture his inner mind, we reshape him. We burn all evil and all illusion out of him; we bring him over to our side, not in appearance, but genuinely, heart and soul. We make him one of ourselves before we kill him. It is intolerable to us that an erroneous thought should exist anywhere in the world, however secret and powerless it may be. Even in the instant of death we cannot permit any deviation. In the old days the heretic walked to the stake still a heretic, proclaiming his heresy, exulting in it. Even the victim of the Russian purges could carry rebellion locked up in his skull as he walked down the passage waiting for the bullet. But we make the brain perfect before we blow it out. The command of the old despotisms was "Thou shalt not". The command of the totalitarians was "Thou shalt". Our command is "*Thou art*". No one whom we bring to this place ever stands out against us. Everyone is washed clean. Even those three miserable traitors in whose innocence you once believed—Jones, Aaronson, and Rutherford—in the end we broke them down. I took part in their interrogation myself. I saw them gradually worn down, whimpering, grovelling, weeping—and in the end it was not with pain or fear, only with penitence. By the time we had finished with them they were only the shells of men. There was nothing left in them except sorrow for what they had done, and love of Big Brother. It was touching to see how they loved him. They begged to be shot quickly, so that they could die while their minds were still clean.'

His voice had grown almost dreamy. The exaltation, the lunatic enthusiasm, was still in his face. He is not pretending, thought Winston, he is not a hypocrite, he believes every word he says. What most oppressed him was the consciousness of his own intellectual inferiority. He watched the heavy yet graceful form strolling to and fro, in and out of the range of his vision. O'Brien was a being in all ways larger than himself. There was no idea that he had ever had, or could have, that O'Brien had not long ago known, examined, and rejected. His mind *contained* Winston's mind. But in that case how could it be true that O'Brien was mad? It must be he, Winston, who was mad. O'Brien halted and looked down at him. His voice had grown stern again.

'Do not imagine that you will save yourself, Winston, however completely you surrender to us. No one who has once gone astray is ever spared. And even if we chose to let you live out the natural term of your life, still you would never escape from us. What happens to you here is for ever. Understand that in advance. We shall crush you down to the point from which there is no coming back. Things will happen to you from which you could not recover, if you lived a thousand years. Never again will you be capable of ordinary human feeling. Everything will be dead inside you. Never again will you be capable of love, or friendship, or joy of living, or laughter, or curiosity, or courage, or integrity. You will be hollow. We shall squeeze you empty, and then we shall fill you with ourselves.'

He paused and signed to the man in the white coat. Winston was aware of some heavy piece of apparatus being pushed into place behind his head. O'Brien had sat down beside the bed, so that his face was almost on a level with Winston's.

'Three thousand,' he said, speaking over Winston's head to the man in the white coat.

Two soft pads, which felt slightly moist, clamped themselves against Winston's temples. He quailed. There was pain coming, a new kind of pain. O'Brien laid a hand reassuringly, almost kindly, on his.

'This time it will not hurt,' he said. 'Keep your eyes fixed on mine.'

At this moment there was a devastating explosion, or what seemed like an explosion, though it was not certain whether there was any noise. There was undoubtedly a blinding flash of light. Winston was not hurt, only prostrated. Although he had already been lying on his back when the thing happened, he had a curious feeling that he had been knocked into that position. A terrific painless blow had flattened him out. Also something had happened inside his head. As his eyes regained their focus he remembered who he was, and where he was, and recognized the face that was gazing into his own; but somewhere or other there was a large patch of emptiness, as though a piece had been taken out of his brain.

'It will not last,' said O'Brien. 'Look me in the eyes. What country is Oceania at war with?'

Winston thought. He knew what was meant by Oceania and that he himself was a citizen of Oceania. He also remembered Eurasia and Eastasia; but who was at war with whom he did not know. In fact he had not been aware that there was any war.

'I don't remember.'

'Oceania is at war with Eastasia. Do you remember that now?'

'Yes.'

'Oceania has always been at war with Eastasia. Since the beginning of your life, since the beginning of the Party, since the beginning of history, the war has continued without a break, always the same war. Do you remember that?'

'Yes.'

'Eleven years ago you created a legend about three men who had been condemned to death for treachery. You pretended that you had seen a piece of paper which proved them innocent. No such piece of paper ever existed. You invented it, and later you grew to believe in it. You remember now the very moment at which you first invented it. Do you remember that?'

'Yes.'

'Just now I held up the fingers of my hand to you. You saw five fingers. Do you remember that?'

'Yes.'

O'Brien held up the fingers of his left hand, with the thumb concealed.

'There are five fingers there. Do you see five fingers?'

'Yes.'

And he did see them, for a fleeting instant, before the scenery of his mind changed. He saw five fingers, and there was no deformity. Then everything was normal again, and the old fear, the hatred, and the bewilderment came crowding back again. But there had been a moment—he did not know how long, thirty seconds, perhaps—of luminous certainty, when each new suggestion of O'Brien's had filled up a patch of emptiness and become absolute truth, and when two and two could have been three as easily as five, if that were what was needed. It had faded but before O'Brien had dropped his hand; but though he could not recapture it, he could remember it, as one remembers a vivid experience at some period of one's life when one was in effect a different person.

'You see now,' said O'Brien, 'that it is at any rate possible.'

'Yes,' said Winston.

O'Brien stood up with a satisfied air. Over to his left Winston saw the man in the white coat break an ampoule and draw back the plunger of a syringe. O'Brien turned to Winston with a smile. In almost the old manner he resettled his spectacles on his nose.

'Do you remember writing in your diary,' he said, 'that it did not matter whether I was a friend or an enemy, since I was at least a person who understood you and could be talked to? You were right. I enjoy talking to you. Your mind appeals to me. It resembles my own mind except that you happen to be insane. Before we bring the session to an end you can ask me a few questions, if you choose.'

'Any question I like?'

'Anything.' He saw that Winston's eyes were upon the dial. 'It is switched off. What is your first question?'

'What have you done with Julia?' said Winston.

O'Brien smiled again. 'She betrayed you, Winston. Immediately—unreservedly. I have seldom seen anyone come over to us so promptly. You would hardly recognize her if you saw her. All her rebelliousness, her deceit, her folly, her dirty-mindedness—everything has been burned out of her. It was a perfect conversion, a textbook case.'

'You tortured her?'

O'Brien left this unanswered. 'Next question,' he said.

'Does Big Brother exist?'

'Of course he exists. The Party exists. Big Brother is the embodiment of the Party.'

'Does he exist in the same way as I exist?'

'You do not exist,' said O'Brien.

Once again the sense of helplessness assailed him. He knew, or he could imagine, the arguments which proved his own nonexistence; but they were nonsense, they were only a play on words. Did not the statement, 'You do not exist', contain a logical absurdity? But what use was it to say so? His mind shrivelled as he thought of the unanswerable, mad arguments with which O'Brien would demolish him.

'I think I exist,' he said wearily. 'I am conscious of my own identity. I was born and I shall die. I have arms and legs. I occupy a particular point in space. No other solid object can occupy the same point simultaneously. In that sense, does Big Brother exist?'

'It is of no importance. He exists.'

'Will Big Brother ever die?'

'Of course not. How could he die? Next question.'

'Does the Brotherhood exist?'

'That, Winston, you will never know. If we choose to set you free when we have finished with you, and if you live to be ninety years old, still you will never learn whether the answer to that question is Yes or No. As long as you live it will be an unsolved riddle in your mind.'

Winston lay silent. His breast rose and fell a little faster. He still had not asked the question that had come into his mind the first. He had got to ask it, and yet it was as though his tongue would not utter it. There was a trace of amusement in O'Brien's face. Even his spectacles seemed to wear an ironical gleam. He knows, thought Winston suddenly, he knows what I am going to ask! At the thought the words burst out of him:

'What is in Room 101?'

The expression on O'Brien's face did not change. He answered drily:

'You know what is in Room 101, Winston. Everyone knows what is in Room 101.'

He raised a finger to the man in the white coat. Evidently the session was at an end. A needle jerked into Winston's arm. He sank almost instantly into deep sleep.

CHAPTER THREE

'There are three stages in your reintegration,' said O'Brien. 'There is learning, there is understanding, and there is acceptance. It is time for you to enter upon the second stage.'

As always, Winston was lying flat on his back. But of late his bonds were looser. They still held him to the bed, but he could move his knees a little and could turn his head from side to side and raise his arms from the elbow. The dial, also, had grown to be less of a terror. He could evade its pangs if he was quick-witted enough: it was chiefly when he showed stupidity that O'Brien pulled the lever. Sometimes they got through a whole session without use of the dial. He could not remember how many sessions there had been. The whole process seemed to stretch out over a long, indefinite time—weeks, possibly—and the intervals between the sessions might sometimes have been days, sometimes only an hour or two.

'As you lie there,' said O'Brien, 'you have often wondered—you have even asked me—why the Ministry of Love should expend so much time and trouble on you. And when you were free you were puzzled by what was essentially the same question. You could grasp the mechanics of the society you lived in, but not its underlying motives. Do you remember writing in your diary, "I understand *how*: I do not understand *why*"? It was when you thought about "why" that you doubted your own sanity. You have read *the book*, Goldstein's book, or parts of it, at least. Did it tell you anything that you did not know already?'

'You have read it?' said Winston.

'I wrote it. That is to say, I collaborated in writing it. No book is produced individually, as you know.'

'Is it true, what it says?'

'As description, yes. The programme it sets forth is nonsense. The secret accumulation of knowledge—a gradual spread of enlightenment—ultimately a proletarian rebellion—the overthrow of the Party. You foresaw yourself that that was what it would say. It is all nonsense. The proletarians will never revolt, not in a thousand years or a million. They cannot. I do not have to tell you the reason: you know it already. If you have ever cherished any dreams of violent insurrection, you must abandon them. There is no way in which the Party can be overthrown. The rule of the Party is for ever. Make that the starting-point of your thoughts.'

He came closer to the bed. 'For ever!' he repeated. 'And now let us get back to the question of "how" and "why". You understand well enough *how* the Party maintains itself in power. Now tell me *why* we cling to power. What is our motive? Why should we want power? Go on, speak,' he added as Winston remained silent.

Nevertheless Winston did not speak for another moment or two. A feeling of weariness had overwhelmed him. The faint, mad gleam of enthusiasm had come back into O'Brien's face. He knew in advance what O'Brien would say. That the Party did not seek power for its own ends, but only for the good of the majority. That it sought power because men in the mass were frail, cowardly creatures who could not endure liberty or face the truth, and must be ruled over and systematically deceived by others who were stronger than themselves. That the choice for mankind lay between freedom and happiness, and that, for the great bulk of mankind, happiness was better. That the party was the eternal guardian of the weak, a dedicated sect doing evil that good might come, sacrificing its own happiness to that of others. The terrible thing, thought Winston, the terrible thing was that when O'Brien said this he would believe it. You could see it in his face. O'Brien knew everything. A thousand times better than Winston he knew what the world was really like, in what degradation the mass of human beings lived and by what lies and barbarities the Party kept them there. He had understood it all, weighed it all, and it made no difference: all was justified by the ultimate purpose. What can you do, thought Winston, against the lunatic who is more intelligent than yourself, who gives your arguments a fair hearing and then simply persists in his lunacy?

'You are ruling over us for our own good,' he said feebly. 'You believe that human beings are not fit to govern themselves, and therefore—'

He started and almost cried out. A pang of pain had shot through his body. O'Brien had pushed the lever of the dial up to thirty-five.

'That was stupid, Winston, stupid!' he said. 'You should know better than to say a thing like that.'

He pulled the lever back and continued:

'Now I will tell you the answer to my question. It is this. The Party seeks power entirely for its own sake. We are not interested in the good of others; we are interested solely in power. Not wealth or luxury or long life or happiness: only power, pure power. What pure power means you will understand presently. We are different from all the oligarchies of the past, in that we know what we are doing. All the others, even those who resembled ourselves, were cowards and hypocrites. The German Nazis and the Russian Communists came very close to us in their methods, but they never had the courage to recognize their own motives. They pretended, perhaps they even believed, that they had seized power unwillingly and for a limited time, and that just round the corner there lay a paradise where human beings would be free and equal. We are not like that. We know that no one ever seizes power with the intention of relinquishing it. Power is not a means, it is an end. One does not establish a dictatorship in order to safeguard a revolution; one makes the revolution in order to establish the dictatorship. The object of persecution is persecution. The object of torture is torture. The object of power is power. Now do you begin to understand me?'

Winston was struck, as he had been struck before, by the tiredness of O'Brien's face. It was strong and fleshy and brutal, it was full of intelligence and a sort of controlled passion before which he felt himself helpless; but it was tired. There were pouches under the eyes, the skin sagged from the cheekbones. O'Brien leaned over him, deliberately bringing the worn face nearer.

'You are thinking,' he said, 'that my face is old and tired. You are thinking that I talk of power, and yet I am not even able to prevent the decay of my own body. Can you not understand, Winston, that the individual is only a cell? The weariness of the cell is the vigour of the organism. Do you die when you cut your fingernails?'

He turned away from the bed and began strolling up and down again, one hand in his pocket.

'We are the priests of power,' he said. 'God is power. But at present power is only a word so far as you are concerned. It is time for you to gather some idea of what power means. The first thing you must realize is that power is collective. The individual only has power in so far as he ceases to be an individual. You know the Party slogan: "Freedom is Slavery". Has it ever occurred to you that it is reversible? Slavery is freedom. Alone—free—the human being is always defeated. It must be so, because every human being is doomed to die, which is the greatest of all failures. But if he can make complete, utter submission, if he can escape from his identity, if he can merge himself in the Party so that he *is* the Party, then he is all-powerful and immortal. The second thing for you to realize is that power is power over human beings. Over the body—but, above all, over the mind. Power over matter—external reality, as you would call it—is not important. Already our control over matter is absolute.'

For a moment Winston ignored the dial. He made a violent effort to raise himself into a sitting position, and merely succeeded in wrenching his body painfully.

'But how can you control matter?' he burst out. 'You don't even control the climate or the law of gravity. And there are disease, pain, death——'

O'Brien silenced him by a movement of his hand. 'We control matter because we control the mind. Reality is inside the skull. You will learn by degrees, Winston. There is nothing that we could not do. Invisibility, levitation—anything. I could float off this floor like a soap bubble if I wish to. I do not wish to, because the Party does not wish it. You must get rid of those nineteenth-century ideas about the laws of Nature. We make the laws of Nature.'

'But you do not! You are not even masters of this planet. What about Eurasia and Eastasia? You have not conquered them yet.'

'Unimportant. We shall conquer them when it suits us. And if we did not, what difference would it make? We can shut them out of existence. Oceania is the world.'

'But the world itself is only a speck of dust. And man is tiny—helpless! How long has he been in existence? For millions of years the earth was uninhabited.'

'Nonsense. The earth is as old as we are, no older. How could it be older? Nothing exists except through human consciousness.'

'But the rocks are full of the bones of extinct animals—mammoths and mastodons and enormous reptiles which lived here long before man was ever heard of.'

'Have you ever seen those bones, Winston? Of course not. Nineteenth-century biologists invented them. Before man there was nothing. After man, if he could come to an end, there would be nothing. Outside man there is nothing.'

'But the whole universe is outside us. Look at the stars! Some of them are a million light-years away. They are out of our reach for ever.'

'What are the stars?' said O'Brien indifferently. 'They are bits of fire a few kilometres away. We could reach them if we wanted to. Or we could blot them out. The earth is the centre of the universe. The sun and the stars go round it.'

Winston made another convulsive movement. This time he did not say anything. O'Brien continued as though answering a spoken objection:

'For certain purposes, of course, that is not true. When we navigate the ocean, or when we predict an eclipse, we often find it convenient to assume that the earth goes round the sun and that the stars are millions upon millions of kilometres away. But what of it? Do you suppose it is beyond us to produce a dual system of astronomy? The stars can be near or distant, according as we need them. Do you suppose our mathematicians are unequal to that? Have you forgotten doublethink?'

Winston shrank back upon the bed. Whatever he said, the swift answer crushed him like a bludgeon. And yet he knew, he *knew*, that he was in the right. The belief that nothing exists outside your own mind—surely there must be some way of demonstrating that it was false? Had it not been exposed long ago as a fallacy? There was even a name for it, which he had forgotten. A faint smile twitched the corners of O'Brien's mouth as he looked down at him.

'I told you, Winston,' he said, 'that metaphysics is not your strong point. The word you are trying to think of is solipsism. But you are mistaken. This is not solipsism. Collective solipsism, if you like. But that is a different thing: in fact, the opposite thing. All this is a digression,' he added in a different tone. 'The real power, the power we have to fight for night and day, is not power over things, but over men.' He paused, and for a moment assumed again his air of a schoolmaster questioning a promising pupil: 'How does one man assert his power over another, Winston?'

Winston thought. 'By making him suffer,' he said.

'Exactly. By making him suffer. Obedience is not enough. Unless he is suffering, how can you be sure that he is obeying your will and not his own? Power is in inflicting pain and humiliation. Power is in tearing human minds to pieces and putting them together again in new shapes of your own choosing. Do you begin to see, then, what kind of world we are creating? It is the exact opposite of the stupid hedonistic Utopias that the old reformers imagined. A world of fear and treachery and torment, a world of trampling and being trampled upon, a world which will grow not less but *more* merciless as it refines itself. Progress in our world will be progress towards more pain. The old civilizations claimed that they were founded on love or justice. Ours is founded upon hatred. In our world there will be no emotions except fear, rage, triumph, and self-abasement. Everything else we shall destroy—everything. Already we are breaking down the habits of thought which have survived from before the Revolution. We have cut the links between child and parent, and between man and man, and between man and woman. No one dares trust a wife or a child or a friend any longer. But in the future there will be no wives and no friends. Children will be taken from their mothers at birth, as one takes eggs from a hen. The sex instinct will be eradicated. Procreation will be an annual formality like the renewal of a ration card. We shall abolish the orgasm. Our neurologists are at work upon it now. There will be no loyalty, except loyalty towards the Party. There will be no love, except the love of Big Brother. There will be no laughter, except the laugh of triumph over a defeated enemy. There will be no art, no literature, no science. When we are omnipotent we shall have no more need of science. There will be no distinction between beauty and ugliness. There will be no curiosity, no enjoyment of the process of life. All competing pleasures will be destroyed. But always—do not forget this, Winston—always there will be the intoxication of power, constantly increasing and constantly growing subtler. Always, at every moment, there will be the thrill of victory, the sensation of trampling on an enemy who is helpless. If you want a picture of the future, imagine a boot stamping on a human face—for ever.'

He paused as though he expected Winston to speak. Winston had tried to shrink back into the surface of the bed again. He could not say anything. His heart seemed to be frozen. O'Brien went on:

'And remember that it is for ever. The face will always be there to be stamped upon. The heretic, the enemy of society, will always be there, so that he can be defeated and humiliated over again. Everything that you have undergone since you have been in our hands—all that will continue, and worse. The espionage, the betrayals, the arrests, the tortures, the executions, the disappearances will never cease. It will be a world of terror as much as a world of triumph. The more the Party is powerful, the less it will be tolerant: the weaker the opposition, the tighter the despotism. Goldstein and his heresies will live for ever. Every day, at every moment, they will be defeated, discredited, ridiculed, spat upon and yet they will always survive. This drama that I have played out with you during seven years will be played out over and over again generation after generation, always in subtler forms. Always we shall have the heretic here at our mercy, screaming with pain, broken up, contemptible—and in the end utterly penitent, saved from himself, crawling to our feet of his own accord. That is the world that we are preparing, Winston. A world of victory after victory, triumph after triumph after triumph: an endless pressing, pressing, pressing upon the nerve of power. You are beginning, I can see, to realize what that world will be like. But in the end you will do more than understand it. You will accept it, welcome it, become part of it.'

Winston had recovered himself sufficiently to speak. 'You can't!' he said weakly.

'What do you mean by that remark, Winston?'

'You could not create such a world as you have just described. It is a dream. It is impossible.'

'Why?'

'It is impossible to found a civilization on fear and hatred and cruelty. It would never endure.'

'Why not?'

'It would have no vitality. It would disintegrate. It would commit suicide.'

'Nonsense. You are under the impression that hatred is more exhausting than love. Why should it be? And if it were, what difference would that make? Suppose that we choose to wear ourselves out faster. Suppose that we quicken the tempo of human life till men are senile at thirty. Still what difference would it make? Can you not understand that the death of the individual is not death? The Party is immortal.'

As usual, the voice had battered Winston into helplessness. Moreover he was in dread that if he persisted in his disagreement O'Brien would twist the dial again. And yet he could not keep silent. Feebly, without arguments, with nothing to support him except his inarticulate horror of what O'Brien had said, he returned to the attack.

'I don't know—I don't care. Somehow you will fail. Something will defeat you. Life will defeat you.'

'We control life, Winston, at all its levels. You are imagining that there is something called human nature which will be outraged by what we do and will turn against us. But we create human nature. Men are infinitely malleable. Or perhaps you have returned to your old idea that the proletarians or the slaves will arise and overthrow us. Put it out of your mind. They are helpless, like the animals. Humanity is the Party. The others are outside—irrelevant.'

'I don't care. In the end they will beat you. Sooner or later they will see you for what you are, and then they will tear you to pieces.'

'Do you see any evidence that that is happening? Or any reason why it should?'

'No. I believe it. I *know* that you will fail. There is something in the universe—I don't know, some spirit, some principle—that you will never overcome.'

'Do you believe in God, Winston?'

'No.'

'Then what is it, this principle that will defeat us?'

'I don't know. The spirit of Man.'

'And do you consider yourself a man?'

'Yes.'

'If you are a man, Winston, you are the last man. Your kind is extinct; we are the inheritors. Do you understand that you are *alone*? You are outside history, you are non-existent.' His manner changed and he said more harshly: 'And you consider yourself morally superior to us, with our lies and our cruelty?'

'Yes, I consider myself superior.'

O'Brien did not speak. Two other voices were speaking. After a moment Winston recognized one of them as his own. It was a sound-track of the conversation he had had with O'Brien, on the night when he had enrolled himself in the Brotherhood. He heard himself promising to lie, to steal, to forge, to murder, to encourage drug-taking and prostitution, to disseminate venereal diseases, to throw vitriol in a child's face. O'Brien made a small impatient gesture, as though to say that the demonstration was hardly worth making. Then he turned a switch and the voices stopped.

'Get up from that bed,' he said.

The bonds had loosened themselves. Winston lowered himself to the floor and stood up unsteadily.

'You are the last man,' said O'Brien. 'You are the guardian of the human spirit. You shall see yourself as you are. Take off your clothes.'

Winston undid the bit of string that held his overalls together. The zip fastener had long since been wrenched out of them. He could not remember whether at any time since his arrest he had taken off all his clothes at one time. Beneath the overalls his body was looped with filthy yellowish rags, just recognizable as the remnants of underclothes. As he slid them to the ground he saw that there was a three-sided mirror at the far end of the room. He approached it, then stopped short. An involuntary cry had broken out of him.

'Go on,' said O'Brien. 'Stand between the wings of the mirror. You shall see the side view as well.'

He had stopped because he was frightened. A bowed, grey-coloured, skeleton-like thing was coming towards him. Its actual appearance was frightening, and not merely the fact that he knew it to be himself. He moved closer to the glass. The creature's face seemed to be protruded, because of its bent carriage. A forlorn, jailbird's face with a nobby forehead running back into a bald scalp, a crooked nose, and battered-looking cheekbones above which his eyes were fierce and watchful. The cheeks were seamed, the mouth had a drawn-in look. Certainly it was his own face, but it seemed to him that it had changed more than he had changed inside. The emotions it registered would be different from the ones he felt. He had gone partially bald. For the first moment he had thought that he had gone grey as well, but it was only the scalp that was grey. Except for his hands and a circle of his face, his body was grey all over with ancient, ingrained dirt. Here and there under the dirt there were the red scars of wounds, and near the ankle the varicose ulcer was an inflamed mass with flakes of skin peeling off it. But the truly frightening thing was the emaciation of his body. The barrel of the ribs was as narrow as that of a skeleton: the legs had shrunk so that the knees were thicker than the thighs. He saw now what O'Brien had meant about seeing the side view. The curvature of the spine was astonishing. The thin shoulders were hunched forward so as to make a cavity of the chest, the scraggy neck seemed to be bending double under the weight of the skull. At a guess he would have said that it was the body of a man of sixty, suffering from some malignant disease.

'You have thought sometimes,' said O'Brien, 'that my face—the face of a member of the Inner Party—looks old and worn. What do you think of your own face?'

He seized Winston's shoulder and spun him round so that he was facing him.

'Look at the condition you are in!' he said. 'Look at this filthy grime all over your body. Look at the dirt between your toes. Look at that disgusting running sore on your leg. Do you know that you stink like a goat? Probably you have ceased to notice it. Look at your emaciation. Do you see? I can make my thumb and forefinger meet round your bicep. I could snap your neck like a carrot. Do you know that you have lost twenty-five kilograms since you have been in our hands? Even your hair is coming out in handfuls. Look!' He plucked at Winston's head and brought away a tuft of hair. 'Open your mouth. Nine, ten, eleven teeth left. How many had you when you came to us? And the few you have left are dropping out of your head. Look here!'

He seized one of Winston's remaining front teeth between his powerful thumb and forefinger. A twinge of pain shot through Winston's jaw. O'Brien had wrenched the loose tooth out by the roots. He tossed it across the cell.

'You are rotting away,' he said; 'you are falling to pieces. What are you? A bag of filth. Now turn around and look into that mirror again. Do you see that thing facing you? That is the last man. If you are human, that is humanity. Now put your clothes on again.'

Winston began to dress himself with slow stiff movements. Until now he had not seemed to notice how thin and weak he was. Only one thought stirred in his mind: that he must have been in this place longer than he had imagined. Then suddenly as he fixed the miserable rags round himself a feeling of pity for his ruined body overcame him. Before he knew what he was doing he had collapsed on to a small stool that stood beside the bed and burst into tears. He was aware of his ugliness, his gracelessness, a bundle of bones in filthy underclothes sitting weeping in the harsh white light: but he could not stop himself. O'Brien laid a hand on his shoulder, almost kindly.

'It will not last for ever,' he said. 'You can escape from it whenever you choose. Everything depends on yourself.'

'You did it!' sobbed Winston. 'You reduced me to this state.'

'No, Winston, you reduced yourself to it. This is what you accepted when you set yourself up against the Party. It was all contained in that first act. Nothing has happened that you did not foresee.'

He paused, and then went on:

'We have beaten you, Winston. We have broken you up. You have seen what your body is like. Your mind is in the same state. I do not think there can be much pride left in you. You have been kicked and flogged and insulted, you have screamed with pain, you have rolled on the floor in your own blood and vomit. You have whimpered for mercy, you have betrayed everybody and everything. Can you think of a single degradation that has not happened to you?'

Winston had stopped weeping, though the tears were still oozing out of his eyes. He looked up at O'Brien.

'I have not betrayed Julia,' he said.

O'Brien looked down at him thoughtfully. 'No,' he said; 'no; that is perfectly true. You have not betrayed Julia.'

The peculiar reverence for O'Brien, which nothing seemed able to destroy, flooded Winston's heart again. How intelligent, he thought, how intelligent! Never did O'Brien fail to understand what was said to him. Anyone else on earth would have answered promptly that he *had* betrayed Julia. For what was there that they had not screwed out of him under the torture? He had told them everything he knew about her, her habits, her character, her past life; he had confessed in the most trivial detail everything that had happened at their meetings, all that he had said to her and she to him, their black-market meals, their adulteries, their vague plottings against the Party—everything. And yet, in the sense in which he intended the word, he had not betrayed her. He had not stopped loving her; his feelings towards her had remained the same. O'Brien had seen what he meant without the need for explanation.

'Tell me,' he said, 'how soon will they shoot me?'

'It might be a long time,' said O'Brien. 'You are a difficult case. But don't give up hope. Everyone is cured sooner or later. In the end we shall shoot you.'

CHAPTER FOUR

He was much better. He was growing fatter and stronger every day, if it was proper to speak of days.

The white light and the humming sound were the same as ever, but the cell was a little more comfortable than the others he had been in. There was a pillow and a mattress on the plank bed, and a stool to sit on. They had given him a bath, and they allowed him to wash himself fairly frequently in a tin basin. They even gave him warm water to wash with. They had given him new underclothes and a clean suit of overalls. They had dressed his varicose ulcer with soothing ointment. They had pulled out the remnants of his teeth and given him a new set of dentures.

Weeks or months must have passed. It would have been possible now to keep count of the passage of time, if he had felt any interest in doing so, since he was being fed at what appeared to be regular intervals. He was getting, he judged, three meals in the twenty-four hours; sometimes he wondered dimly whether he was getting them by night or by day. The food was surprisingly good, with meat at every third meal. Once there was even a packet of cigarettes. He had no matches, but the never-speaking guard who brought his food would give him a light. The first time he tried to smoke it made him sick, but he persevered, and spun the packet out for a long time, smoking half a cigarette after each meal.

They had given him a white slate with a stump of pencil tied to the corner. At first he made no use of it. Even when he was awake he was completely torpid. Often he would lie from one meal to the next almost without stirring, sometimes asleep, sometimes waking into vague reveries in which it was too much trouble to open his eyes. He had long grown used to sleeping with a strong light on his face. It seemed to make no difference, except that one's dreams were more coherent. He dreamed a great deal all through this time, and they were always happy dreams. He was in the Golden Country, or he was sitting among enormous glorious, sunlit ruins, with his mother, with Julia, with O'Brien—not doing anything, merely sitting in the sun, talking of peaceful things. Such thoughts as he had when he was awake were mostly about his dreams. He seemed to have lost the power of intellectual effort, now that the stimulus of pain had been removed. He was not bored, he had no desire for conversation or distraction. Merely to be alone, not to be beaten or questioned, to have enough to eat, and to be clean all over, was completely satisfying.

By degrees he came to spend less time in sleep, but he still felt no impulse to get off the bed. All he cared for was to lie quiet and feel the strength gathering in his body. He would finger himself here and there, trying to make sure that it was not an illusion that his muscles were growing rounder and his skin tauter. Finally it was established beyond a doubt that he was growing fatter; his thighs were now definitely thicker than his knees. After that, reluctantly at first, he began exercising himself regularly. In a little while he could walk three kilometres, measured by pacing the cell, and his bowed shoulders were growing straighter. He attempted more elaborate exercises, and was astonished and humiliated to find what things he could not do. He could not move out of a walk, he could not hold his stool out at arm's length, he could not stand on one leg without falling over. He squatted down on his heels, and found that with agonizing pains in thigh and calf he could just lift himself to a standing position. He lay flat on his belly and tried to lift his weight by his hands. It was hopeless, he could not raise himself a centimetre. But after a few more days—a few more mealtimes—even that feat was accomplished. A time came when he could do it six times running. He began to grow actually proud of his body, and to cherish an intermittent belief that his face also was growing back to normal. Only when he chanced to put his hand on his bald scalp did he remember the seamed, ruined face that had looked back at him out of the mirror.

His mind grew more active. He sat down on the plank bed, his back against the wall and the slate on his knees, and set to work deliberately at the task of re-educating himself.

He had capitulated, that was agreed. In reality, as he saw now, he had been ready to capitulate long before he had taken the decision. From the moment when he was inside the Ministry of Love—and yes, even during those minutes when he and Julia had stood helpless while the iron voice from the telescreen told them what to do—he had grasped the frivolity, the shallowness of his attempt to set himself up against the power of the Party. He knew now that for seven years the Thought Police had watched him like a beetle under a magnifying glass. There was no physical act, no word spoken aloud, that they had not noticed, no train of thought that they had not been able to infer. Even the speck of whitish dust on the cover of his diary they had carefully replaced. They had played sound-tracks to him, shown him photographs. Some of them were photographs of Julia and himself. Yes, even....He could not fight against the Party any longer. Besides, the Party was in the right. It must be so; how could the immortal, collective brain be mistaken? By what external standard could you check its judgements? Sanity was statistical. It was merely a question of learning to think as they thought. Only...!

The pencil felt thick and awkward in his fingers. He began to write down the thoughts that came into his head. He wrote first in large clumsy capitals:

FREEDOM IS SLAVERY

Then almost without a pause he wrote beneath it:

TWO AND TWO MAKE FIVE

But then there came a sort of check. His mind, as though shying away from something, seemed unable to concentrate. He knew that he knew what came next, but for the moment he could not recall it. When he did recall it, it was only by consciously reasoning out what it must be: it did not come of its own accord. He wrote:

GOD IS POWER

He accepted everything. The past was alterable. The past never had been altered. Oceania was at war with Eastasia. Oceania had always been at war with Eastasia. Jones,

Aaronson, and Rutherford were guilty of the crimes they were charged with. He had never seen the photograph that disproved their guilt. It had never existed, he had invented it. He remembered remembering contrary things, but those were false memories, products of self-deception. How easy it all was! Only surrender, and everything else followed. It was like swimming against a current that swept you backwards however hard you struggled, and then suddenly deciding to turn round and go with the current instead of opposing it. Nothing had changed except your own attitude: the predestined thing happened in any case. He hardly knew why he had ever rebelled. Everything was easy, except...!

Anything could be true. The so-called laws of Nature were nonsense. The law of gravity was nonsense. 'If I wished,' O'Brien had said, 'I could float off this floor like a soap bubble.' Winston worked it out. 'If he *thinks* he floats off the floor, and if I simultaneously *think* I see him do it, then the thing happens.' Suddenly, like a lump of submerged wreckage breaking the surface of water, the thought burst into his mind: 'It doesn't really happen. We imagine it. It is hallucination.' He pushed the thought under instantly. The fallacy was obvious. It presupposed that somewhere or other, outside oneself, there was a 'real' world where 'real' things happened. But how could there be such a world? What knowledge have we of anything, save through our own minds? All happenings are in the mind. Whatever happens in all minds, truly happens.

He had no difficulty in disposing of the fallacy, and he was in no danger of succumbing to it. He realized, nevertheless, that it ought never to have occurred to him. The mind should develop a blind spot whenever a dangerous thought presented itself. The process should be automatic, instinctive. *Crimestop*, they called it in Newspeak.

He set to work to exercise himself in crimestop. He presented himself with propositions—'the Party says the earth is flat', 'the Party says that ice is heavier than water'—and trained himself in not seeing or not understanding the arguments that contradicted them. It was not easy. It needed great powers of reasoning and improvisation. The arithmetical problems raised, for instance, by such a statement as 'two and two make five' were beyond his intellectual grasp. It needed also a sort of athleticism of mind, an ability at one moment to make the most delicate use of logic and at the next to be unconscious of the crudest logical errors. Stupidity was as necessary as intelligence, and as difficult to attain.

All the while, with one part of his mind, he wondered how soon they would shoot him. 'Everything depends on yourself,' O'Brien had said; but he knew that there was no conscious act by which he could bring it nearer. It might be ten minutes hence, or ten years. They might keep him for years in solitary confinement, they might send him to a labour-camp, they might release him for a while, as they sometimes did. It was perfectly possible that before he was shot the whole drama of his arrest and interrogation would be enacted all over again. The one certain thing was that death never came at an expected moment. The tradition—the unspoken tradition: somehow you knew it, though you never heard it said—was that they shot you from behind; always in the back of the head, without warning, as you walked down a corridor from cell to cell.

One day—but 'one day' was not the right expression; just as probably it was in the middle of the night: once—he fell into a strange, blissful reverie. He was walking down the corridor, waiting for the bullet. He knew that it was coming in another moment. Everything was settled, smoothed out, reconciled. There were no more doubts, no more arguments, no more pain, no more fear. His body was healthy and strong. He walked easily, with a joy of movement and with a feeling of walking in sunlight. He was not any longer in the narrow white corridors in the Ministry of Love, he was in the enormous sunlit passage, a kilometre wide, down which he had seemed to walk in the delirium induced by drugs. He was in the Golden Country, following the foot-track across the old rabbit-cropped pasture. He could feel the short springy turf under his feet and the gentle sunshine on his face. At the edge of the field were the elm trees, faintly stirring, and somewhere beyond that was the stream where the dace lay in the green pools under the willows.

Suddenly he started up with a shock of horror. The sweat broke out on his backbone. He had heard himself cry aloud:

'Julia! Julia! Julia, my love! Julia!'

For a moment he had had an overwhelming hallucination of her presence. She had seemed to be not merely with him, but inside him. It was as though she had got into the texture of his skin. In that moment he had loved her far more than he had ever done when they were together and free. Also he knew that somewhere or other she was still alive and needed his help.

He lay back on the bed and tried to compose himself. What had he done? How many years had he added to his servitude by that moment of weakness?

In another moment he would hear the tramp of boots outside. They could not let such an outburst go unpunished. They would know now, if they had not known before, that he was breaking the agreement he had made with them. He obeyed the Party, but he still hated the Party. In the old days he had hidden a heretical mind beneath an appearance of conformity. Now he had retreated a step further: in the mind he had surrendered, but he had hoped to keep the inner heart inviolate. He knew that he was in the wrong, but he preferred to be in the wrong. They would understand that—O'Brien would understand it. It was all confessed in that single foolish cry.

He would have to start all over again. It might take years. He ran a hand over his face, trying to familiarize himself with the new shape. There were deep furrows in the cheeks, the cheekbones felt sharp, the nose flattened. Besides, since last seeing himself in the glass he had been given a complete new set of teeth. It was not easy to preserve inscrutability when you did not know what your face looked like. In any case, mere control of the features was not enough. For the first time he perceived that if you want to keep a secret you must also hide it from yourself. You must know all the while that it is there, but until it is needed you must never let it emerge into your consciousness in any shape that could be given a name. From now onwards he must not only think right; he must feel right, dream right. And all the while he must keep his hatred locked up inside him like a ball of matter which was part of himself and yet unconnected with the rest of him, a kind of cyst.

One day they would decide to shoot him. You could not tell when it would happen, but a few seconds beforehand it should be possible to guess. It was always from behind, walking down a corridor. Ten seconds would be enough. In that time the world inside him could turn over. And then suddenly, without a word uttered, without a check in his step, without the changing of a line in his face—suddenly the camouflage would be down and bang! would go the batteries of his hatred. Hatred would fill him like an enormous roaring flame. And almost in the same instant bang! would go the bullet, too late, or too early. They would have blown his brain to pieces before they could reclaim it. The heretical thought would be unpunished, unrepented, out of their reach for ever. They would have blown a hole in their own perfection. To die hating them, that was freedom.

He shut his eyes. It was more difficult than accepting an intellectual discipline. It was a question of degrading himself, mutilating himself. He had got to plunge into the filthiest of filth. What was the most horrible, sickening thing of all? He thought of Big Brother. The enormous face (because of constantly seeing it on posters he always thought of it as being a metre wide), with its heavy black moustache and the eyes that followed you to and fro, seemed to float into his mind of its own accord. What were his true feelings towards Big Brother?

There was a heavy tramp of boots in the passage. The steel door swung open with a clang. O'Brien walked into the cell. Behind him were the waxen-faced officer and the black-uniformed guards.

'Get up,' said O'Brien. 'Come here.'

Winston stood opposite him. O'Brien took Winston's shoulders between his strong hands and looked at him closely.

'You have had thoughts of deceiving me,' he said. 'That was stupid. Stand up straighter. Look me in the face.'

He paused, and went on in a gentler tone:

'You are improving. Intellectually there is very little wrong with you. It is only emotionally that you have failed to make progress. Tell me, Winston—and remember, no lies: you know that I am always able to detect a lie—tell me, what are your true feelings towards Big Brother?'

'I hate him.'

'You hate him. Good. Then the time has come for you to take the last step. You must love Big Brother. It is not enough to obey him: you must love him.'

He released Winston with a little push towards the guards.

'Room 101,' he said.

CHAPTER FIVE

At each stage of his imprisonment he had known, or seemed to know, whereabouts he was in the windowless building. Possibly there were slight differences in the air pressure. The cells where the guards had beaten him were below ground level. The room where he had been interrogated by O'Brien was high up near the roof. This place was many metres underground, as deep down as it was possible to go.

It was bigger than most of the cells he had been in. But he hardly noticed his surroundings. All he noticed was that there were two small tables straight in front of him, each covered with green baize. One was only a metre or two from him, the other was further away, near the door. He was strapped upright in a chair, so tightly that he could move nothing, not even his head. A sort of pad gripped his head from behind, forcing him to look straight in front of him.

For a moment he was alone, then the door opened and O'Brien came in.

'You asked me once,' said O'Brien, 'what was in Room 101. I told you that you knew the answer already. Everyone knows it. The thing that is in Room 101 is the worst thing in the world.'

The door opened again. A guard came in, carrying something made of wire, a box or basket of some kind. He set it down on the further table. Because of the position in which O'Brien was standing. Winston could not see what the thing was.

'The worst thing in the world,' said O'Brien, 'varies from individual to individual. It may be burial alive, or death by fire, or by drowning, or by impalement, or fifty other deaths. There are cases where it is some quite trivial thing, not even fatal.'

He had moved a little to one side, so that Winston had a better view of the thing on the table. It was an oblong wire cage with a handle on top for carrying it by. Fixed to the front of it was something that looked like a fencing mask, with the concave side outwards. Although it was three or four metres away from him, he could see that the cage was divided lengthways into two compartments, and that there was some kind of creature in each. They were rats.

'In your case,' said O'Brien, 'the worst thing in the world happens to be rats.'

A sort of premonitory tremor, a fear of he was not certain what, had passed through Winston as soon as he caught his first glimpse of the cage. But at this moment the meaning of the mask-like attachment in front of it suddenly sank into him. His bowels seemed to turn to water.

'You can't do that!' he cried out in a high cracked voice. 'You couldn't, you couldn't! It's impossible.'

'Do you remember,' said O'Brien, 'the moment of panic that used to occur in your dreams? There was a wall of blackness in front of you, and a roaring sound in your ears. There was something terrible on the other side of the wall. You knew that you knew what it was, but you dared not drag it into the open. It was the rats that were on the other side of the wall.'

'O'Brien!' said Winston, making an effort to control his voice. 'You know this is not necessary. What is it that you want me to do?'

O'Brien made no direct answer. When he spoke it was in the schoolmasterish manner that he sometimes affected. He looked thoughtfully into the distance, as though he were addressing an audience somewhere behind Winston's back.

'By itself,' he said, 'pain is not always enough. There are occasions when a human being will stand out against pain, even to the point of death. But for everyone there is something unendurable—something that cannot be contemplated. Courage and cowardice are not involved. If you are falling from a height it is not cowardly to clutch at a rope. If you have come up from deep water it is not cowardly to fill your lungs with air. It is merely an instinct which cannot be destroyed. It is the same with the rats. For you, they are unendurable. They are a form of pressure that you cannot withstand, even if you wished to. You will do what is required of you.'

'But what is it, what is it? How can I do it if I don't know what it is?'

O'Brien picked up the cage and brought it across to the nearer table. He set it down carefully on the baize cloth. Winston could hear the blood singing in his ears. He had the feeling of sitting in utter loneliness. He was in the middle of a great empty plain, a flat desert drenched with sunlight, across which all sounds came to him out of immense distances. Yet the cage with the rats was not two metres away from him. They were enormous rats. They were at the age when a rat's muzzle grows blunt and fierce and his fur brown instead of grey.

'The rat,' said O'Brien, still addressing his invisible audience, 'although a rodent, is carnivorous. You are aware of that. You will have heard of the things that happen in the poor quarters of this town. In some streets a woman dare not leave her baby alone in the house, even for five minutes. The rats are certain to attack it. Within quite a small time they will strip it to the bones. They also attack sick or dying people. They show astonishing intelligence in knowing when a human being is helpless.'

There was an outburst of squeals from the cage. It seemed to reach Winston from far away. The rats were fighting; they were trying to get at each other through the partition. He heard also a deep groan of despair. That, too, seemed to come from outside himself.

O'Brien picked up the cage, and, as he did so, pressed something in it. There was a sharp click. Winston made a frantic effort to tear himself loose from the chair. It was hopeless; every part of him, even his head, was held immovably. O'Brien moved the cage nearer. It was less than a metre from Winston's face.

'I have pressed the first lever,' said O'Brien. 'You understand the construction of this cage. The mask will fit over your head, leaving no exit. When I press this other lever, the door of the cage will slide up. These starving brutes will shoot out of it like bullets. Have you ever seen a rat leap through the air? They will leap on to your face and bore straight into it. Sometimes they attack the eyes first. Sometimes they burrow through the cheeks and devour the tongue.'

The cage was nearer; it was closing in. Winston heard a succession of shrill cries which appeared to be occurring in the air above his head. But he fought furiously against his panic. To think, to think, even with a split second left—to think was the only hope. Suddenly the foul musty odour of the brutes struck his nostrils. There was a violent convulsion of nausea inside him, and he almost lost consciousness. Everything had gone black. For an instant he was insane, a screaming animal. Yet he came out of the blackness clutching an idea. There was one and only one way to save himself. He must interpose another human being, the *body* of another human being, between himself and the rats.

The circle of the mask was large enough now to shut out the vision of anything else. The wire door was a couple of hand-spans from his face. The rats knew what was coming now. One of them was leaping up and down, the other, an old scaly grandfather of the sewers, stood up, with his pink hands against the bars, and fiercely sniffed the air. Winston could see the whiskers and the yellow teeth. Again the black panic took hold of him. He was blind, helpless, mindless.

'It was a common punishment in Imperial China,' said O'Brien as didactically as ever.

The mask was closing on his face. The wire brushed his cheek. And then—no, it was not relief, only hope, a tiny fragment of hope. Too late, perhaps too late. But he had suddenly understood that in the whole world there was just *one* person to whom he could transfer his punishment—*one* body that he could thrust between himself and the rats. And he was shouting frantically, over and over.

'Do it to Julia! Do it to Julia! Not me! Julia! I don't care what you do to her. Tear her face off, strip her to the bones. Not me! Julia! Not me!'

He was falling backwards, into enormous depths, away from the rats. He was still strapped in the chair, but he had fallen through the floor, through the walls of the building, through the earth, through the oceans, through the atmosphere, into outer space, into the gulfs between the stars—always away, away, away from the rats. He was light years distant, but O'Brien was still standing at his side. There was still the cold touch of wire against his cheek. But through the darkness that enveloped him he heard another metallic click, and knew that the cage door had clicked shut and not open.

CHAPTER SIX

The Chestnut Tree was almost empty. A ray of sunlight slanting through a window fell on dusty table-tops. It was the lonely hour of fifteen. A tinny music trickled from the telescreens.

Winston sat in his usual corner, gazing into an empty glass. Now and again he glanced up at a vast face which eyed him from the opposite wall. BIG BROTHER IS WATCHING YOU, the caption said. Unbidden, a waiter came and filled his glass up with Victory Gin, shaking into it a few drops from another bottle with a quill through the cork. It was saccharine flavoured with cloves, the speciality of the cafe.

Winston was listening to the telescreen. At present only music was coming out of it, but there was a possibility that at any moment there might be a special bulletin from the Ministry of Peace. The news from the African front was disquieting in the extreme. On and off he had been worrying about it all day. A Eurasian army (Oceania was at war with Eurasia: Oceania had always been at war with Eurasia) was moving southward at terrifying speed. The mid-day bulletin had not mentioned any definite area, but it was probable that already the mouth of the Congo was a battlefield. Brazzaville and Leopoldville were in danger. One did not have to look at the map to see what it meant. It was not merely a question of losing Central Africa: for the first time in the whole war, the territory of Oceania itself was menaced.

A violent emotion, not fear exactly but a sort of undifferentiated excitement, flared up in him, then faded again. He stopped thinking about the war. In these days he could never fix his mind on any one subject for more than a few moments at a time. He picked up his glass and drained it at a gulp. As always, the gin made him shudder and even retch slightly. The stuff was horrible. The cloves and saccharine, themselves disgusting enough in their sickly way, could not disguise the flat oily smell; and what was worst of all was that the smell of gin, which dwelt with him night and day, was inextricably mixed up in his mind with the smell of those....

He never named them, even in his thoughts, and so far as it was possible he never visualized them. They were something that he was half-aware of, hovering close to his face, a smell that clung to his nostrils. As the gin rose in him he belched through purple lips. He had grown fatter since they released him, and had regained his old colour—indeed, more than regained it. His features had thickened, the skin on nose and cheekbones was coarsely red, even the bald scalp was too deep a pink. A waiter, again unbidden, brought the chessboard and the current issue of the *Times*, with the page turned down at the chess problem. Then, seeing that Winston's glass was empty, he brought the gin bottle and filled it. There was no need to give orders. They knew his habits. The chessboard was always waiting for him, his corner table was always reserved; even when the place was full he had it to himself, since nobody cared to be seen sitting too close to him. He never even bothered to count his drinks. At irregular intervals they presented him with a dirty slip of paper which they said was the bill, but he had the impression that they always undercharged him. It would have made no difference if it had been the other way about. He had always plenty of money nowadays. He even had a job, a sinecure, more highly-paid than his old job had been.

The music from the telescreen stopped and a voice took over. Winston raised his head to listen. No bulletins from the front, however. It was merely a brief announcement from the Ministry of Plenty. In the preceding quarter, it appeared, the Tenth Three-Year Plan's quota for bootlaces had been overfulfilled by 98 per cent.

He examined the chess problem and set out the pieces. It was a tricky ending, involving a couple of knights. 'White to play and mate in two moves.' Winston looked up at the portrait of Big Brother. White always mates, he thought with a sort of cloudy mysticism. Always, without exception, it is so arranged. In no chess problem since the beginning of the world has black ever won. Did it not symbolize the eternal, unvarying triumph of Good over Evil? The huge face gazed back at him, full of calm power. White always mates.

The voice from the telescreen paused and added in a different and much graver tone: 'You are warned to stand by for an important announcement at fifteen-thirty. Fifteen-thirty! This is news of the highest importance. Take care not to miss it. Fifteen-thirty!' The tinkling music struck up again.

Winston's heart stirred. That was the bulletin from the front; instinct told him that it was bad news that was coming. All day, with little spurts of excitement, the thought of a smashing defeat in Africa had been in and out of his mind. He seemed actually to see the Eurasian army swarming across the never-broken frontier and pouring down into the tip of Africa like a column of ants. Why had it not been possible to outflank them in some way? The outline of the West African coast stood out vividly in his mind. He picked up the white knight and moved it across the board. *There* was the proper spot. Even while he saw the black horde racing southward he saw another force, mysteriously assembled, suddenly planted in their rear, cutting their communications by land and sea. He felt that by willing it he was bringing that other force into existence. But it was necessary to act quickly. If they could get control of the whole of Africa, if they had airfields and submarine bases at the Cape, it would cut Oceania in two. It might mean anything: defeat, breakdown, the redivision of the world, the destruction of the Party! He drew a deep breath. An extraordinary medley of feeling—but it was not a medley, exactly; rather it was successive layers of feeling, in which one could not say which layer was undermost—struggled inside him.

The spasm passed. He put the white knight back in its place, but for the moment he could not settle down to serious study of the chess problem. His thoughts wandered again. Almost unconsciously he traced with his finger in the dust on the table:

$$2 + 2 = 5$$

'They can't get inside you,' she had said. But they could get inside you. 'What happens to you here is *for ever*,' O'Brien had said. That was a true word. There were things, your own acts, from which you could never recover. Something was killed in your breast: burnt out, cauterized out.

He had seen her; he had even spoken to her. There was no danger in it. He knew as though instinctively that they now took almost no interest in his doings. He could have arranged to meet her a second time if either of them had wanted to. Actually it was by chance that they had met. It was in the Park, on a vile, biting day in March, when the earth was like iron and all the grass seemed dead and there was not a bud anywhere except a few crocuses which had pushed themselves up to be dismembered by the wind. He was hurrying along with frozen hands and watering eyes when he saw her not ten metres away from him. It struck him at once that she had changed in some ill-defined way. They almost passed one another without a sign, then he turned and followed her, not very eagerly. He knew that there was no danger, nobody would take any interest in him. She did not speak. She walked obliquely away across the grass as though trying to get rid of him, then seemed to resign herself to having him at her side. Presently they were in among a clump of ragged leafless shrubs, useless either for concealment or as protection from the wind. They halted. It was vilely cold. The wind whistled through the twigs and fretted the occasional, dirty-looking crocuses. He put his arm round her waist.

There was no telescreen, but there must be hidden microphones: besides, they could be seen. It did not matter, nothing mattered. They could have lain down on the ground and done *that* if they had wanted to. His flesh froze with horror at the thought of it. She made no response whatever to the clasp of his arm; she did not even try to disengage herself. He knew now what had changed in her. Her face was sallower, and there was a long scar, partly hidden by the hair, across her forehead and temple; but that was not the change. It was that her waist had grown thicker, and, in a surprising way, had stiffened. He remembered how once, after the explosion of a rocket bomb, he had helped to drag a corpse out of some ruins, and had been astonished not only by the incredible weight of the thing, but by its rigidity and awkwardness to handle, which made it seem more like stone than flesh. Her body felt like that. It occurred to him that the texture of her skin would be quite different from what it had once been.

He did not attempt to kiss her, nor did they speak. As they walked back across the grass, she looked directly at him for the first time. It was only a momentary glance, full of contempt and dislike. He wondered whether it was a dislike that came purely out of the past or whether it was inspired also by his bloated face and the water that the wind kept squeezing from his eyes. They sat down on two iron chairs, side by side but not too close together. He saw that she was about to speak. She moved her clumsy shoe a few centimetres and deliberately crushed a twig. Her feet seemed to have grown broader, he noticed.

'I betrayed you,' she said baldly.

'I betrayed you,' he said.

She gave him another quick look of dislike.

'Sometimes,' she said, 'they threaten you with something something you can't stand up to, can't even think about. And then you say, "Don't do it to me, do it to somebody else, do it to so-and-so." And perhaps you might pretend, afterwards, that it was only a trick and that you just said it to make them stop and didn't really mean it. But that isn't true. At the time when it happens you do mean it. You think there's no other way of saving yourself, and you're quite ready to save yourself that way. You *want* it to happen to the other person. You don't give a damn what they suffer. All you care about is yourself.'

'All you care about is yourself,' he echoed.

'And after that, you don't feel the same towards the other person any longer.'

'No,' he said, 'you don't feel the same.'

There did not seem to be anything more to say. The wind plastered their thin overalls against their bodies. Almost at once it became embarrassing to sit there in silence: besides, it was too cold to keep still. She said something about catching her Tube and stood up to go.

'We must meet again,' he said.

'Yes,' she said, 'we must meet again.'

He followed irresolutely for a little distance, half a pace behind her. They did not speak again. She did not actually try to shake him off, but walked at just such a speed as to prevent his keeping abreast of her. He had made up his mind that he would accompany her as far as the Tube station, but suddenly this process of trailing along in the cold seemed pointless and unbearable. He was overwhelmed by a desire not so much to get away from Julia as to get back to the Chestnut Tree Cafe, which had never seemed so attractive as at this moment. He had a nostalgic vision of his corner table, with the newspaper and the chessboard and the ever-flowing gin. Above all, it would be warm in there. The next moment, not altogether by accident, he allowed himself to become separated from her by a small knot of people. He made a half-hearted attempt to catch up, then slowed down, turned, and made off in the opposite direction. When he had gone fifty metres he looked back. The street was not crowded, but already he could not distinguish her. Any one of a dozen hurrying figures might have been hers. Perhaps her thickened, stiffened body was no longer recognizable from behind.

'At the time when it happens,' she had said, 'you do mean it.' He had meant it. He had not merely said it, he had wished it. He had wished that she and not he should be delivered over to the....

Something changed in the music that trickled from the telescreen. A cracked and jeering note, a yellow note, came into it. And then—perhaps it was not happening, perhaps it was only a memory taking on the semblance of sound—a voice was singing:

Under the spreading chestnut tree
I sold you and you sold me....

The tears welled up in his eyes. A passing waiter noticed that his glass was empty and came back with the gin bottle.

He took up his glass and sniffed at it. The stuff grew not less but more horrible with every mouthful he drank. But it had become the element he swam in. It was his life, his death, and his resurrection. It was gin that sank him into stupor every night, and gin that revived him every morning. When he woke, seldom before eleven hundred, with gummed-up eyelids and fiery mouth and a back that seemed to be broken, it would have been impossible even to rise from the horizontal if it had not been for the bottle and teacup placed beside the bed overnight. Through the midday hours he sat with glazed face, the bottle handy, listening to the telescreen. From fifteen to closing-time he was a fixture in the Chestnut Tree. No one cared what he did any longer, no whistle woke him, no telescreen admonished him. Occasionally, perhaps twice a week, he went to a dusty, forgotten-looking office in the Ministry of Truth and did a little work, or what was called work. He had been appointed to a sub-committee of a sub-committee which had sprouted from one of the innumerable committees dealing with minor difficulties that arose in the compilation of the Eleventh Edition of the Newspeak Dictionary. They were engaged in producing something called an Interim Report, but what it was that they were reporting on he had never definitely found out. It was something to do with the question of whether commas should be placed inside brackets, or outside. There were four others on the committee, all of them persons similar to himself. There were days when they assembled and then promptly dispersed again, frankly admitting to one another that there was not really anything to be done. But there were other days when they settled down to their work almost eagerly, making a tremendous show of entering up their minutes and drafting long memoranda which were never finished—when the argument as to what they were supposedly arguing about grew extraordinarily involved and abstruse, with subtle haggling over definitions, enormous digressions, quarrels—threats, even, to appeal to higher authority. And then suddenly the life would go out of them and they would sit round the table looking at one another with extinct eyes, like ghosts fading at cock-crow.

The telescreen was silent for a moment. Winston raised his head again. The bulletin! But no, they were merely changing the music. He had the map of Africa behind his eyelids. The movement of the armies was a diagram: a black arrow tearing vertically southward, and a white arrow horizontally eastward, across the tail of the first. As though for reassurance he looked up at the imperturbable face in the portrait. Was it conceivable that the second arrow did not even exist?

His interest flagged again. He drank another mouthful of gin, picked up the white knight and made a tentative move. Check. But it was evidently not the right move, because....

Uncalled, a memory floated into his mind. He saw a candle-lit room with a vast white-counterpaned bed, and himself, a boy of nine or ten, sitting on the floor, shaking a dice-box, and laughing excitedly. His mother was sitting opposite him and also laughing.

It must have been about a month before she disappeared. It was a moment of reconciliation, when the nagging hunger in his belly was forgotten and his earlier affection for her had temporarily revived. He remembered the day well, a pelting, drenching day when the water streamed down the window-pane and the light indoors was too dull to read by. The boredom of the two children in the dark, cramped bedroom became unbearable. Winston whined and grizzled, made futile demands for food, fretted about the room pulling everything out of place and kicking the wainscoting until the neighbours banged on the wall, while the younger child wailed intermittently. In the end his mother said, 'Now be good, and I'll buy you a toy. A lovely toy—you'll love it'; and then she had gone out in the rain, to a little general shop which was still sporadically open nearby, and came back with a cardboard box containing an outfit of Snakes and Ladders. He could still remember the smell of the damp cardboard. It was a miserable outfit. The board was cracked and the tiny wooden dice were so ill-cut that they would hardly lie on their sides. Winston looked at the thing sulkily and without interest. But then his mother lit a piece of candle and they sat down on the floor to play. Soon he was wildly excited and shouting with laughter as the tiddly-winks climbed hopefully up the ladders and then came slithering down the snakes again, almost to the starting-point. They played eight games, winning four each. His tiny sister, too young to understand what the game was about, had sat propped up against a bolster, laughing because the others were laughing. For a whole afternoon they had all been happy together, as in his earlier childhood.

He pushed the picture out of his mind. It was a false memory. He was troubled by false memories occasionally. They did not matter so long as one knew them for what they were. Some things had happened, others had not happened. He turned back to the chessboard and picked up the white knight again. Almost in the same instant it dropped on to the board with a clatter. He had started as though a pin had run into him.

A shrill trumpet-call had pierced the air. It was the bulletin! Victory! It always meant victory when a trumpet-call preceded the news. A sort of electric drill ran through the cafe. Even the waiters had started and pricked up their ears.

The trumpet-call had let loose an enormous volume of noise. Already an excited voice was gabbling from the telescreen, but even as it started it was almost drowned by a roar of cheering from outside. The news had run round the streets like magic. He could hear just enough of what was issuing from the telescreen to realize that it had all happened, as he had foreseen; a vast seaborne armada had secretly assembled a sudden blow in the enemy's rear, the white arrow tearing across the tail of the black. Fragments of triumphant phrases pushed themselves through the din: 'Vast strategic manoeuvre—perfect co-ordination—utter rout—half a million prisoners—complete demoralization—control of the whole of Africa—bring the war within measurable distance of its end—victory—greatest victory in human history—victory, victory, victory!'

Under the table Winston's feet made convulsive movements. He had not stirred from his seat, but in his mind he was running, swiftly running, he was with the crowds outside, cheering himself deaf. He looked up again at the portrait of Big Brother. The colossus that bestrode the world! The rock against which the hordes of Asia dashed themselves in vain! He thought how ten minutes ago—yes, only ten minutes—there had still been equivocation in his heart as he wondered whether the news from the front would be of victory or defeat. Ah, it was more than a Eurasian army that had perished! Much had changed in him since that first day in the Ministry of Love, but the final, indispensable, healing change had never happened, until this moment.

The voice from the telescreen was still pouring forth its tale of prisoners and booty and slaughter, but the shouting outside had died down a little. The waiters were turning back to their work. One of them approached with the gin bottle. Winston, sitting in a blissful dream, paid no attention as his glass was filled up. He was not running or cheering any longer. He was back in the Ministry of Love, with everything forgiven, his soul white as snow. He was in the public dock, confessing everything, implicating everybody. He was walking down the white-tiled corridor, with the feeling of walking in sunlight, and an armed guard at his back. The long-hoped-for bullet was entering his brain.

He gazed up at the enormous face. Forty years it had taken him to learn what kind of smile was hidden beneath the dark moustache. O cruel, needless misunderstanding! O stubborn, self-willed exile from the loving breast! Two gin-scented tears trickled down the sides of his nose. But it was all right, everything was all right, the struggle was finished. He had won the victory over himself. He loved Big Brother.